Return OF THE Jerk

Andrea Simonne

Sweet Life in Seattle - Book 2

Return of the Jerk
By Andrea Simonne

First Print Edition, September 2015

Published by Liebe Publishing

Edited by
Hot Tree Editing
www.hottreeediting.com

Interior Design and Formatting by
Christine Borgford, Perfectly Publishable
www.perfectlypublishable.com

Publisher's Note: This is a work of fiction. Names, characters, places, and incidents either are the product of the author's imagination or are used fictitiously. Any resemblance to actual persons, living or dead, business establishments, events, or locales is entirely coincidental.

Liebe Publishing
liebepublishing@gmail.com

Chapter One

Reasons You Don't Miss Sex

1. Being on top is fun, but too much work.

2. Deep, erotic kisses are overrated.

3. Some men need GPS tracking and a miner's hat to find their way downtown.

BLAIR MOANS SOFTLY.

Desire spirals through her as his hand glides slowly over her breast and down her stomach, caressing, moving lower until his fingers are brushing between her thighs. She knows what he wants. He loves to tease, loves to watch her arch into him, and she loves to give him what he wants as her thighs fall open for him, granting access.

"Perfect," he says, his voice rumbling with approval. "So perfect."

His body is warm and powerful at her side where she's tucked into him, his cock hard against her hip.

Blair gasps when his fingers slide home. So good. Passion takes hold, gripping her, turning her inside out.

"Please," she whispers, trying to reach for him. "Just this once."

His muscular arms keep her still.

"But why?"

There's no reply.

He's breathing hard, though. Unsteady. Blair can hear it and knows he's excited, too. It's the same every time. He drives her crazy, drives her to the edge until she's begging him to take her, but still he won't.

She turns her head to see his face in the moonlight. The room is dark, but she can see him clearly. His familiar features. The ones she fell in love with the first time she saw him. That knowing smile. But it's his eyes that grab her attention and always have, like the sun shining through stained glass. Golden-green.

"You want me," he whispers. His fingers tease again, bringing her pleasure as they deny her everything. "And you always will."

"Fuck." Blair opens her eyes as morning light streams through her bedroom window, her body still humming with arousal. She rarely swears, but she's had enough.

Five years.

That's how long it's been since she's seen Road. Five long years. And yet these dreams are plaguing her like a song stuck on repeat.

I should divorce him.

Any sane woman would have divorced him right after he left their four-month marriage. Abandoned her. Just packed his stuff and left one day. No goodbye. Just a short note left on her pillow with a simple 'this isn't working for me.' And he's never looked back. She always tells people they were together a year because the truth is too embarrassing.

Nathan 'Road' Church didn't want her. Not at all.

But whatever. She's over him. Water under the bridge, as they say. It's not like she hasn't had her share of boyfriends since then because she's dated plenty, though none of them have been serious. If someone serious *did* come along, she'd divorce Road in a second. Of course, she'd have to find him first. Last she heard, he was in Budapest doing God knows what, and before that it was Thailand, and before that, India. Her best friend, Tori, is his sister and despite Blair's standing order that they never discuss Road, occasionally information on his whereabouts slips through.

Not that I care. I've definitely moved on.

She pretends he doesn't exist and, for the most part, is successful. If it weren't for these tormenting dreams!

Blair shoves the covers back, checks her phone and sees it's almost seven. Normally, she'd be at La Dolce Vita, the bakery she co-owns with her business partner, Natalie, but it's her day off. They moved to a new location recently, had a write-up in *Seattle Magazine*, and as a result, business is booming. Blair's wedding cakes are more in demand than ever.

I'm going to call Mia today and tell her to put the paperwork through.

Mia is her divorce lawyer, the one she hired right after Road left. She had Mia draw up divorce papers, but then Blair changed her mind and told Mia to forget it. The month after that, she called Mia and told her to go through with the divorce, but then Blair changed her mind again. She usually calls once or twice a year, changing her mind every time.

I've been too busy, that's all.

Blair goes over to her closet, where her clothes are neatly organized by type and color. She grabs a pair of black track pants and a white University of

Washington T-shirt to slip on, pulling her auburn hair back into a high ponytail so she can go for a run.

Her condo is on Eastlake in Seattle, and she loves the eclectic neighborhood. There are shops, cafés, and historic buildings. She bought it three years ago when the market was low, and as a result was able to afford a corner unit with a view of Lake Union. Her run takes her all the way down to the water near the colorful houseboats and by the time she makes it there, she's breathless and dripping with sweat.

Her iPod blasts "You Keep Me Hangin' On" by The Supremes as she walks back up the sidewalk to cool down.

Near the front of her building, she notices a strange guy sitting by the entrance—some kind of bum wearing disheveled clothes. He's sporting chin-length blond hair, his head bent as he studies his phone. This is generally a safe neighborhood, but Blair is still cautious living in the city.

Is he waiting for somebody?

She wonders if she should say something to him. The front entrance is always kept locked, but what if he tries to slip in behind her? As she moves closer, she notices his jeans and shirt are wrinkled, but even sitting down, she can tell he's tall and broad-shouldered. *Maybe he's not a bum. In truth, he's kind of hot.*

When she's a few feet away, he suddenly looks up and Blair's heart stops. The Supremes are still playing. Diane Ross's sweet voice soars as all the blood rushes to Blair's head and her stomach drops.

His eyes are golden-green.

STARING IN SHOCK, Blair rips her earbuds out.

"Road?" she breathes.

"Princess." He grins at her.

She can't speak. Adrenaline rockets through her as she watches him get up from where he's sitting. There's a beat-up leather backpack next to him which he swings onto his shoulder.

"What are you doing here?" she finally manages to say.

"Just flew in this morning."

Blair's eyes roam over him, taking in his gray T-shirt and faded jeans before settling on his face again. He looks different, but weirdly the same, too.

"Why?" she asks, dumbfounded.

And suddenly it's like the first time she ever saw him. Back when she was a quiet thirteen-year-old, the new kid who kind-hearted Tori befriended and invited over one afternoon. Tori lived in a small rambler on a run-down street. The garage door was open and motorcycles were parked in the driveway. Older teenagers were playing Frisbee in the front yard while Van Halen's "Running with the Devil" blasted from the stereo. The Frisbee landed at Blair's feet and when she picked it up, the most breathtaking guy she'd ever seen in her life loped over to pluck it from her hand. "That's my brother, Road," Tori said dismissively. "He's a tenth-grader." Road grinned at her, those golden-green eyes flashing, his long blond hair pulled back into a ponytail, and Blair's entire world shifted on its axis.

It's never shifted back.

"Let's talk inside," Road says.

"I haven't seen you in five years."

He reaches down and takes the keys from her hands, somehow figuring out which one opens the main entrance. "Come on." Road holds the door open for her, and Blair has no choice but to go over. He hands her keys back and follows her inside.

When they're in the elevator, Blair tries to pull herself together. *I can't believe this is happening*. She takes a deep breath, trying to recover from the shock. Her eyes find Road. He isn't looking at her, but watching the floors light up.

"How did you know where I live?" she asks, just before the elevator arrives at her floor.

"Tori gave me your address."

Blair decides she's going to murder Tori. Right after she finds a new home for all Tori's animals.

Once they're inside Blair's condo, Road tosses his backpack down like he owns the place and turns toward her. "Need to take a shower and crash. Want to show me the way, babe?"

"Look, you can't stay here!" Blair tries to quell her rising panic. "You need to find someplace else. Just call Tori, or Kiki, or even your mom."

The kitchen and living area in her condo are all one open space. Her living room is tidy and comfortable with a white couch and wingback chair, a flat-screen television on one wall above a gas fireplace. She loves her condo, loves the perfection of it. It's small, but always clean, with everything where it's supposed to be. Her peaceful sanctuary. On the wall opposite the television are floor-to-ceiling shelves filled with books flawlessly organized by the Dewey Decimal System, which Blair prefers over the Library of Congress Classification. She's heard all the arguments and still considers LOC inferior to the purity of Dewey.

Books and baking. The two loves of Blair's life. There used to be three, but she's over Road.

So over him.

Standing there, he takes this all in before walking over to her kitchen's island, pulling out a white wooden chair to sit down. His intelligent green eyes take her in next, traveling the length of her body. She'd forgotten what it felt like to be under Road's laser focus and she squirms a little. His eyes go back to her face.

"You look good, princess."

Blair knows she doesn't. She's sweaty from her run. It figures the first time she sees Road again she's wearing track pants and no makeup.

"Can't stay with Tori and her menagerie," Road tells her, yawning. "I'll never get any sleep. Kiki's all frantic planning her wedding. And my mom . . ." Road just shakes his head. He doesn't have to say anything more. Blair already knows his mom's house is full of people partying around the clock.

"What about all your cousins or friends? There must be *someone*."

He closes his eyes for a long moment. She studies his face and notices the dark shadows under his eyes, the strain around his mouth. Road does look tired. Despite that, he's as appealing as ever. What's more, she recognizes that quivery sensation in her stomach he's always evoked.

"Babe," he says, opening his eyes. "I'm too exhausted to have this conversation right now. Shower. Sleep. Then we'll talk." He unfolds himself from the chair, grabs his backpack and heads down the hall without another word.

A few moments later, Blair hears the shower running. *The nerve of him!* She immediately grabs her phone and texts Tori.

Road is here. You are a dead woman.

Blair is pacing her small kitchen, trying to calm herself, when her phone chirps.

He's there?! Tori texts back.

Yes. Why did you give him my address?

He asked. How is he?

Blair grits her teeth. *Did you hear me? You. Are. Dead.* And then adds, *He's fine. Tired.*

Don't be angry. I didn't know he was coming to you.

I don't want him to stay here. He has to go!

I'm sure it's only temporary.

It better be.

Come on, you owe him this much.

And there it is.

Blair stares at that text for a long moment. Bites her lip. Tori is the only person in the world who knows the truth about her marriage to Road. Even Road doesn't know the whole truth.

A couple days. She texts Tori. *That's all he can stay.*

Tell him to call me!

Blair puts her phone down, taking a deep breath as she tries to figure out how she's going to handle this. She's surprised he doesn't have a woman lined up somewhere, some girlfriend to take him in. In truth, Road could walk into any bar in the city and women would be tripping over themselves to take him home.

She hears the shower go off. He was never one for long showers. All the details about him are coming back now, the running list she always kept of his likes and dislikes. His favorite food is Mexican, his favorite dessert carrot cake. Road is one of the few people she's met who doesn't like chocolate. She studied him for years, greedily cataloging every habit and nuance, hoping for the day when he'd finally notice her.

That day never came.

Blair snorts softly. *I probably know him better than he knows himself.*

By the time he comes out of the bathroom, Blair is in the kitchen making herself a latte. She turns but freezes when she sees him.

Road is standing by the island, naked except for the white towel wrapped around his waist. His blond hair is wet and parted down the center. He's studying his phone again, and Blair can't pull her eyes away from all that lean, hard muscle. Road looks like a surfer taking a break from the waves, except he isn't tan. Whatever he's been doing these past five years, it hasn't been sitting around eating candy. He's in phenomenal shape.

"Babe."

Blair's eyes flash to his face. Embarrassed to have been caught staring at his body, she gives him a haughty look. "My name is Blair. Not 'babe,' not 'princess.' Blair. Got it?"

A smile plays around his mouth. "Was just going to ask if you have a washer and dryer I could use for my clothes."

She sniffs haughtily. "There's a washer and dryer in the closet next to my bedroom."

"Thanks."

Blair goes back to making coffee, grinding the beans then loading the espresso machine. After making a few shots, she looks up and startles. Road is standing right behind her.

He's leaning against the counter, still wearing the towel.

"I assume you want coffee?" she asks, not looking at him.

"Sure."

"Do you want it iced or hot?"

"Whatever you're having is good."

She reaches into the cabinet next to him to get a couple of glasses down. His freshly showered skin smells like the citrus body wash she keeps in her bath. There's something else, though, the delicious scent that's all his own. She'd recognize it anywhere—the smoky hint of autumn leaves burning.

Ohmigod.

That smell. It goes straight to her head like a drug. Like crack cocaine. She's dizzy as all the emotions she once felt for Road come crashing over her.

Blair's hands shake and she tries to hide it, quickly turning away from him.

She grits her teeth. *I've moved on. I'm not a lovesick idiot anymore. I haven't been for a long time.*

Luckily, his eyes aren't on her, but studying his phone as he thumbs in something. She makes an iced latte for each of them and nearly adds sugar to his because she remembers that's how he takes it, but stops herself.

"Here," she says, shoving his coffee toward him on the counter.

"Thanks." He puts his phone down and picks up his latte.

She watches him take a drink. "There's a sugar bowl next to the espresso machine."

"Don't need it."

She almost corrects him. Since when doesn't Road take sugar in his coffee? But she realizes in time how stupid she'd sound.

"Thank you, Blair."

She turns her head to look out the kitchen window at the apartment building across the street. "It's just a latte."

"No, I mean thank you for letting me invade your space like this."

Blair struggles not to be rude. "Tori wants you to call her."

"Will do."

Neither of them speaks for a few seconds and finally Blair can't resist. "Why did you come here?"

He watches her, but doesn't reply.

"I'm sure there are plenty of women you could stay with in Seattle."

"Maybe." He shrugs. "Don't need that kind of complication right now."

Blair stares down into her milky drink. *Because, of course, I'm not a complication.* Suddenly, she's pissed. Seriously pissed. *How dare he show up here after all this time! What gall!*

"And besides," he puts his glass on the counter, a grin tugging at the corners of his mouth, "I'm still your husband."

She scoffs. "No, you're not." *And you never really were.*

"The law says otherwise."

Blair glares at him.

"Why is it you never filed for divorce?" He studies her curiously. "All these years, I kept waiting for papers to arrive, but they never did."

"How could I? I had no idea where you were! One day, you were gone, and all I knew was you were somewhere in Asia."

Road looks over her shoulder, taking in her condo again, and it's like he's not even listening.

She tries hard not to stare at his body, though it's difficult when he's standing in front of her in nothing but a towel. Without thinking, she starts cataloging his tattoos. The ship in a bottle on his upper right arm. The black tribal arm band on his left bicep. He has some new ones, she notices. There's some kind of writing—Sanskrit, she guesses—above his heart. Some Chinese characters running down his side. She imagines running her fingers over them, touching his smooth skin.

Blair closes her eyes.

"Why don't you put some clothes on?" she says, annoyed that she still feels any desire for him.

His green eyes flash back to her. "What's the problem? There's nothing here you haven't seen before."

Guilt washes over her, but she pushes it aside. *We should be even. He left me without a backward glance, so we're even.* But she knows that isn't true.

"Humor me and put some clothes on."

"Can't. They're all in the wash."

She lets out her breath.

One night. That's all they ever had together. The only time she ever saw Road without the towel, without anything. For one night, he was finally hers, and she took it greedily.

But that one night ruined everything.

Chapter Two

Daily List

1. DON'T PANIC.

2. Stop smelling Road like you're a crack whore and he's the pipe.

3. Remember nobody has ever actually died from embarrassment.

"YOU'D MAKE A great Buddhist." Road is drinking his iced coffee as he studies all the lists she has neatly stuck to her refrigerator.

"Why is that?"

"All your lists." He leans closer to read some of them, and she can hear him chuckling. "You really made a list of the top five things you'd save if your condo catches fire?"

"I like to be prepared," Blair mutters.

"Who's Mr. Maurice?"

"My cat."

Road turns to her and is looking around. "You have a cat?"

"Yes, I do. He's not friendly with strangers, though."

"What the hell kind of name is Mr. Maurice?"

"A perfectly good name."

Road shakes his head and goes back to reading the list. "Jimmy Choos? What's that? Another cat?"

"Shoes."

"Seriously? The second thing you'd save in a fire is a pair of shoes?"

"They're champagne crystal, peep-toe platform pumps."

"Ah, course. That explains everything."

What she doesn't mention is that they cost a fortune—more than her monthly mortgage. She bought them as a gift to herself after their bakery, La Dolce Vita, had its one year anniversary. She works hard and those shoes were a reward. A symbol.

As he's grinning at her list, she studies Road's profile. There's a small bump on the bridge of his nose from where he broke it as a kid, falling off his bike, and it gives him a slightly hawkish appearance from the side. It doesn't detract from his good looks, though. In a way, it adds to them, since he'd be almost too pretty otherwise. Her eyes drift lower to the towel then up again. His back has more new ink, but she can't tell what it is.

"Hermes scarves?" Road looks over at her. "Scarves?"

Blair shrugs. She wears scarves a lot, both in her hair and around her neck, even using them as a belt occasionally. She likes her scarves, what can she say?

"I like my scarves."

He nods slowly. "I remember them now. Always thought they were sexy. Especially the ones in your hair."

Blair's eyes widen. He did?

"Laptop computer—finally, something practical." He nods with approval. And then he continues to the last item on the list, "*The Razor's Edge*."

Road's face grows thoughtful. She wonders if he's going to comment on it. *The Razor's Edge* by Somerset Maugham was a book they both liked in high school. Blair owns a first edition. He doesn't say anything, though, and she's almost disappointed.

Instead, he moves over to the next list. "Ways I Need to Improve My Life."

"Are you really going to read all those lists? I already know what they say. I wrote them, remember?"

"Number one, lose weight." Road frowns and shakes his head. "Don't need to lose weight, princess."

Blair doesn't respond to that. She's not terribly overweight, but it wouldn't hurt to lose five pounds—ten if she wanted to be as skinny as the women Road used to date. She thinks about all his former girlfriends. The way she used to study them, trying to figure out what they had that she didn't. They were all skinny and pretty. Some had big boobs, some small ones. Some were tall, some short. They all had one thing in common, though—something she and Tori used to call Skank Factor X. All of Road's girlfriends wore tight clothes, heels, and lots of makeup, but the biggest thing that made them Skank Factor X was that every single one of them was a bitch.

Blair wonders if Road's tastes have changed much in the past five years.

I doubt it.

"Eat healthier. Learn a second language." Road looks at her with interest. "What language?"

"I haven't decided yet."

He takes this in and goes back to her list. "Number four, 'Be less obsessive,'" and she can see him grinning. "Fewer lists might help with that one, babe."

"I work a lot of hours. Plus, I like to stay organized," she says defensively. Granted, her OCD can get out of hand sometimes, and she knows she's too much of a perfectionist.

He gets to the last item and reads aloud, "Have more great sex."

Blair is drinking her latte and nearly chokes. She'd forgotten that was on there! Instantly, her face warms, and she knows she's red as a tomato.

"You want to have more great sex?" Road's eyebrows shoot up as he turns to her.

"I didn't mean that the way it sounds."

"What way *did* you mean it?"

"That's an old list. I just meant relax more, you know? Have more fun."

Road's eyes flash on the list then back to her. "It says have *more* great sex. That implies you're already having great sex."

"I'm not. Not right now, anyway. I mean, I've had great sex, of course. I just want to . . . I don't know . . ." Blair lets out her breath, groaning inwardly at how stupid she sounds.

"Have more?" Road offers.

"Something like that," she mumbles.

Road chuckles and Blair tries to act indifferent. These lists were meant for her to stay on track. She didn't have many visitors to her condo, and none of them were reading the lists stuck to her fridge.

Road quiets as he appears to be considering things. "So, who you been having great sex with, princess?"

"None of your business."

"You have a boyfriend?"

She does have a sort-of boyfriend. He's a lawyer named Graham who works for their bakery's new landlord. He works for their former landlord too, an astronomer her business partner, Natalie, recently married. Blair has been seeing Graham off and on for a while. They get along and are similar in a lot of ways, but no real sparks are flying. They've never even slept together. It's been almost a year since she's had sex and as she recalls, it wasn't great.

"Like I said, none of your business."

"Have a right to know these things, seeing as I'm your husband and all."

"Really? Are you going to tell me you've been faithful to this marriage for the past five years?"

Road smirks. "Let's not get crazy."

"Our marriage isn't real, and you know it."

He meets her eyes and is no longer smiling. "Started out real enough, though."

Blair turns her head to the side. *No, it didn't. It started on a lie. And I paid for it in every way.*

"I thought you were going to sleep now. That you were tired," she says, changing the subject.

He shrugs. "Guess not."

"Well, I have things to do today, so I need to take a shower." She goes over to the sink, rinses her glass out, and puts it in the dishwasher. Before she leaves the kitchen, she turns to him. "Look, you can stay here a couple days, but that's it, understand? After that, you'll have to find someplace else. I'm sure that won't be difficult for you."

He doesn't reply.

"And obviously, you'll sleep on the couch."

"You wound me, Blair." But there's a smile in his eyes.

Road's phone suddenly starts playing some kind of Reggae music. He picks it up off the counter. "This is Nathan."

Blair's eyes widen. Since when did Road start going by his real name? 'Road' was a nickname, but she's never heard anyone refer to him as anything else.

He leaves the kitchen and heads toward the sliding glass door, opening it to go out onto the back terrace. "Thanks for calling," she hears him say. "I'm in Seattle now."

Blair sighs then goes in to grab her robe and take a shower. Road left a small toiletry bag in the bathroom, and she's almost tempted to look through it. Surprisingly, he didn't leave the bathroom a mess, though when she gets in the shower, she notices he moved her shampoo and soap around. She stares at them with annoyance before putting them in their proper place again.

As she soaps herself under the water, the scent of her citrus body wash brings up the image of Road standing half-naked in her kitchen. His delicious smell. His too-perfect body. Even the sound of his voice brings back memories. She realizes the ache is there, the one she hasn't had for years. All the wanting she felt for Road bottled up inside of her was ready to spill out again. She'd forgotten what it felt like.

Doesn't matter. I'm over him.

Blair shoves those feelings down as hard as she can and reminds herself of the way he left her without a word.

Totally over him. He's a jerk.

AFTER HER SHOWER, Blair gets dressed in a blue and white striped shirt, a pair of navy capris, and black ballet flats.

No Skank Factor X here.

Blair remembers trying out Skank Factor X once for Road. She wore a micro-mini, a push-up bra with a low-cut shirt, and a pair of snakeskin heels to one of his mom, Lori's, BBQ parties. Tori helped her put the whole outfit together. They did her hair big, lots of glittery eyeshadow.

Tori was the only one who knew Blair had a thing for Road. She figured it out when they were still in high school. It had embarrassed Blair at first, but Tori was totally enthusiastic and desperately wanted Blair to be her sister-in-law. "It has to be you! You're like my sister already!"

Predictably, Road wasn't swayed by Blair's slutty outfit in the least. She knew why, too—there was no cherry on top. *I'm not a bitch.* He barely even looked at her, though a lot of the other guys there did, and Blair discovered wearing slutty clothes to a biker party wasn't the brightest idea.

After that, she decided to stick with being herself.

Blair grabs one of her multicolored scarves, folds it over, and ties it into her dark red hair. She remembers Road's comment from earlier and wonders if he really did think her scarves were sexy.

Whatever.

When she goes out into her living room, she finds Road sitting on the couch, still wearing a towel, with a notebook computer on his lap.

"These are for you." She places a neat pile of bedding from her linen closet beside him. "The couch turns into a bed. I understand it's quite comfortable."

His green eyes take her in from head to toe, lingering on the scarf in her hair. "Where are you going?"

"Out."

A smile tugs on his mouth. "Where?"

"I have errands to run.

"Can you get some food?"

She sniffs. "This isn't a hotel."

"Yeah, I get that, but there's no food in your house."

One of Blair's errands is to go grocery shopping, so she knows there isn't any food in the house, but she sighs as if he's asking for the moon. "Fine."

"Get some veggies and chicken. I'll make a stir fry tonight."

"You're going to cook?"

"Some beer wouldn't be out of place."

Blair crosses her arms. "Anything else?"

"Don't think so. My wallet's in the front of my bag over there. Grab some money."

Blair glances over at his beat-up travel bag. She's tempted to get his wallet out so she can see what else is in that bag, but decides against it. That's the sort of thing she would have done years ago. The old Blair.

"Don't worry about it. I need groceries anyway."

Road frowns.

Blair ignores him and goes over to freshen Mr. Maurice's water and food. She gets him new water then bends down to fill his bowl with cat food. She still hasn't seen Mr. Maurice, but knows he's just hiding. He doesn't warm up to new people easily. Even Tori, who has a way with animals, had a hard time getting Mr. Maurice to come around.

When she stands up, Road is directly beside her. "Here," he says, reaching down to take her hand.

"What are you doing?" Her pulse jumps at his touch. His hand wraps around hers as he puts something into her palm.

"I'm paying for the groceries."

He takes his hand away, and she discovers she's holding a hundred dollar bill.

"I don't need a hundred bucks to buy veggies, chicken, and beer!"

The dryer's buzzer goes off and Road heads down the hall to check on his clothes. "Buy whatever else you want then."

IT'S SUNNY OUTSIDE, so Blair takes Isadora. Isadora was the one good thing that came out of her marriage to Road. She's a beautiful 1965 convertible Ford Mustang that Blair brought up to mint condition. Isadora once belonged to Road, but when he left their marriage, he also left Isadora sitting in the driveway of the house they were renting, so Blair kept her. She started taking her to Brody, Road's cousin. He owns a garage and has done an amazing job helping Blair restore the car to her original glory.

Cruising around with the top down, Blair feels like an old-time movie star. Not the shy awkward girl she used to be, unwanted by Road, but confident and beautiful.

She obsessed over every detail restoring Isadora, and it was worth it.

Blair grabs her phone and brings up her list of errands. The hardware store, the cleaners, the library, and then lastly the grocery store.

As she drives toward Home Depot, she thinks about the hundred dollar bill tucked in her purse. After high school, Road worked as a mechanic and took classes at the community college, but she doubts he's been working as a mechanic all this time.

So, where does he get his money?

She noticed he has some nice gadgets, too. Both his computer and phone look brand new. His mom has a few shady friends, but as far as Blair knew, Road was never involved with anything illegal.

Hopefully, that hasn't changed and he's not doing something he shouldn't be, something stupid. Road has always been smart, but sometimes smart people do dumb things. She thinks about how much time he's spent in Asia. She knows people sometimes smuggle drugs from there.

For the first time, Blair wishes she'd let Tori tell her a little more about Road's life.

Since it's sunny out and seeing as she's in no hurry to get back, she takes her time at Home Depot, browsing paint colors for her second bedroom, which she's planning to turn into a home office.

Her second stop is the dry cleaners. After she pays for her clothes, her phone starts playing Eileen Barton's "If I Knew You Were Coming I'd've Baked a Cake", and she can see it's Tori.

"I'm doing my errands," Blair tells her, loading her clothes into the trunk of her car. "After that, I'll be stopping by your house to murder you. It would be helpful if you left your front door unlocked for me."

Tori laughs. "Very funny. I just talked to Road. I want you guys to come over tomorrow."

"Why?"

"Because I haven't seen my brother in ages, and I want to see you, too. Oh, and my mom's throwing a 'welcome home' party for him this weekend, and you have to come to that."

Blair gets into Isadora's driver's seat. "*Me*, why?"

"Because you're invited, that's why."

"I can't believe you gave Road my address. You could have at least warned me."

"Look, I didn't know he was planning to stay with you. I gave him that address months ago."

Blair wonders if that's the truth, or if Tori thought she was being helpful in some misguided way. They talk some more and Tori still tries to convince her to come to the party, with Blair finally agreeing to think about it.

After they hang up, she heads over to the library. She remembers how Road used to occasionally hang out at the library downtown back when they were in high school. She'd noticed him there one afternoon, sitting in a remote corner with a book. It had surprised her. As far she could tell, Road's life centered around football, partying, and girls, with the priorities changing weekly. His whole family used to show up for his games, all of them drunk and rowdy, hollering over every play. Luckily, he was good, so they were usually hollering with approval.

When Blair mentioned seeing Road at the library, Tori told her how Road also kept a secret journal. "I found it under his mattress next to a couple of *Penthouse* magazines."

"Did you read it?"

"No," Tori admitted. "That didn't seem right."

Blair agreed it wasn't right, though she wished she could read it anyway. What did he write about? Did he ever mention her? She doubted it. He barely knew she was alive.

The next time Blair saw Road at the library, she decided to push through her normal shyness and say hello to him.

"Hey." He glanced up at her then looked back down. She noticed he didn't use her name. She'd bet money he didn't know what it was, even though she hung out with Tori and was at his house all the time.

"What are you reading?"

He glanced up again. "Nothing much, just doing homework."

Blair knew he was lying. He did homework at his girlfriend's house after football practice. She knew his schedule inside and out, the secretary he didn't know he had.

"Can I see?" she asked.

"It's just homework."

"What kind?"

"Nothing."

"That book looks familiar. What is it?" She knew she was being bizarre, but couldn't help herself. Her curiosity was overwhelming.

Finally, he showed her the cover. It was *The Razor's Edge*, and she sucked in her breath. "I love that book!" It was one of her all-time favorites.

"You've read it?" Road's eyes widened.

"I've read it like three times."

"So have I," he admitted.

"Larry is an interesting character, don't you think? And Isabel, wow, she made some awful choices."

Road laughed. "Yeah, I agree."

He reached over to take his backpack from the chair next to him so she could have a seat. She discovered that Road was surprisingly well-read, though he played it down. Blair got the sense few people, if any, knew he liked to read. She tried to imagine the kind of grief his friends would have given him. Apparently, there was more to his life than partying, girls, and football after all. They talked for a while, and though Road didn't exactly fall in love with her that day, one thing did change for the better.

Every time he saw her after that, he knew her name.

BLAIR MANAGES TO stretch her errands out all day by going over to see her parents, who live in an upper-middle-class Seattle neighborhood near Lake Washington. On the way over, she replays her conversation with Tori and decides there's little chance she'll want to go to a homecoming party for

Road.

When she arrives at her parents' house, she sees her dad's at work, but finds her mom in her studio—an extension they built on the back of the house. Her mom took early retirement a couple years ago from a successful corporate career to become a painter.

"Hey, Mom." Blair cringes a little as she always does when she's surrounded by her mother's paintings. The canvases are huge and they're all various sizes, shapes, and colors of cacti.

Cacti that happen to look like penises.

Blair walks over to where her mom is mixing some cerulean paint. Her mom's red hair, the same cinnamon shade as her own, is pulled back into a high, messy knot. Her shirt is covered with paint splashes. "What do you think?" Her mom motions at her current work in progress.

Blair's eyes roam over the cacti penises. There's a group of them in this painting, all lined up like little soldiers—a smorgasbord of prickled dicks. "Looks good."

Her mom has pursued her painting with the same single-minded determination she does everything in her life and as a result, she's quite successful. A few galleries in town carry her work, and she also sells her paintings on the Internet. Blair knows her mom manages her art with a keen eye for business and keeps close track of all expenses and inventory. Unlike the usual messy artist's studio, her mom's is organized down to the last paintbrush and tube of paint.

"I've already sold this one," she tells Blair proudly. "Just putting on the finishing touches."

Blair nods. "That's fantastic."

"So, what's up?"

"Road showed up at my condo this morning."

Her mother's eyes widen. "Well, that's good, right? You can finally file for divorce."

"That's true." Her parents were never crazy about her city hall marriage to Road, and of course, hated him after he left.

"I'm having a gallery event in a couple weeks. I hope you can make it," her mom tells her. She's cleaning some paint brushes with a terry cloth rag. "Why don't you bring Graham?"

"Sure, I'll ask him."

"Ian can't make it, but Scott and Ashley already said they're coming. Apparently, they have an announcement. I have a feeling they might be getting engaged."

"Really?" Blair wasn't sure what to say to this. Ian and Scott are her two younger brothers. Ian is a civil engineer who travels a lot for work, while Scott works at Microsoft. Unfortunately, Scott's girlfriend is something of a twit. Yes, Ashley is skinny and pretty, but she's shopping-obsessed and lives at the mall. She also squeals a lot. Blair has tried to befriend her, but it's impossible.

"Though I could be wrong." Her mom shrugs.

Blair imagines Ashley as her sister-in-law. She isn't crazy about the idea, but figures as long as Scott's happy, that's what matters.

WHEN SHE ARRIVES back at her condo, Road isn't there. The bedding is still in a neat pile on the couch where she left it, and his leather bag is gone. It's late, just past nightfall. There's a pizza box on the kitchen counter with half of it missing, so obviously he ate dinner before leaving. She stayed and had dinner with her parents and was feeling guilty for ditching Road, but not anymore. Now, she's glad.

He left without a word!

She shouldn't care, should be relieved, but instead she's pissed. She lets out one frustrated breath after another as she starts putting all the groceries away. The veggies and chicken for his stir fry. The beer.

Rude jerk!

She still doesn't see Mr. Maurice anywhere, and when she's done with the groceries starts searching for him. She checks on her deck. The sliding glass door has a pet door built in and he likes to sit outside, but she doesn't see him and finally goes to check under her bed.

When she enters her bedroom, though, she stops. There's someone lying in her bed.

It's Road.

She glances down and sees his bag next to her dresser, his computer on her nightstand. The window blinds are closed.

He didn't leave after all.

A strange mix of emotions runs through her, relief followed by irritation. Blair moves forward slowly, trying to be quiet. Road is asleep on his stomach—head to the side, hands tucked under the pillow. He's not wearing a shirt, and her eyes drift down his muscular back. The room is dark, but with the light from the hall, she can see the new ink is a mandala. And as she moves closer to get a better look, she finally finds Mr. Maurice.

"There you are!" she whispers.

Mr. Maurice, her large gray tabby, is sitting beside Road. His tail flickers as his golden eyes take her in. He gets up and comes to her, so she sits down on the edge of the bed to pet him.

"I thought you were still hiding."

Mr. Maurice purrs, rubbing against her hand.

Road shifts position. One of his legs escapes from under the sheet, dusted with dark blond hair.

When she glances up to his face, she's surprised to discover his eyes are open, watching her. He doesn't say anything and for some reason, it reminds her of her erotic dream, the one where he torments her in a shadow-filled room.

Their eyes meet and stay on each other. Seconds go by. Neither of them speaks, and Blair gets the peculiar sense that Road is finally seeing her. That he's noticed her at long last.

But then she remembers all the other times she got her hopes up over the years, and how they were always crushed.

She turns away and concentrates on petting Mr. Maurice. "You're supposed to be sleeping on the couch," she finally says.

"Couldn't. It was too bright."

Blair sighs to herself. Seattle is gray and rainy most of the time, but of course, today was sunny.

"How did your errands go?" he asks, his voice husky with sleep. "Did you buy groceries?"

"Yes, I got everything you wanted."

"Why were you gone so long?"

Blair sniffs. "I was avoiding you, if you must know."

He grumbles at that. "Had to order pizza. Didn't want pizza."

"Why didn't you just go out to eat? There's plenty of restaurants nearby."

"You didn't give me a key."

He's right. She didn't give him a key, and she doesn't intend to, either.

"You're going to have to move to the couch now," Blair says firmly. "You can't sleep in here anymore."

He doesn't move.

"Look, you have to leave."

"Too tired, babe." His eyes close.

"I need to go to bed, though."

Road shrugs. "So? Get in bed. Nobody's stopping you."

"I can't sleep with you in here!"

"What do you think is going to happen, princess?"

"*Nothing* is going to happen."

His eyes open at that. "Then what are you afraid of?"

"I'm not afraid of anything."

He smirks. "You *did* say you needed more sex. Maybe I'm the one who should be afraid here."

"That's not what my list said!"

He closes his eyes again, still smiling. "Unfortunately, I'm too beat with jet lag to help you out tonight. Maybe tomorrow, but only if you ask me nicely."

She scoffs. "You're so full of yourself."

He chuckles softly.

Blair studies him in the darkened room. His back is exposed, the white sheet draped across his middle. "You're not naked under there, are you?"

"Come find out."

She tugs on the sheet a little, pulls it lower on his hip until she sees it. The band that shows he's wearing underwear.

Mr. Maurice, who has gone back to his spot beside Road, is watching her. She's surprised he's being friendly. His tail twitches and his eyes narrow, as if he's waiting to see what Blair is made of. Despite his shyness, Mr. Maurice loves to throw attitude.

Blair sighs and gets up, going into the bathroom to change into her pajamas—a white T-shirt from La Dolce Vita and a pair of loose men's boxer shorts. Then brushes her teeth.

She checks to make sure the front door is locked and all the kitchen appliances are unplugged.

When she heads back into the bedroom, Road is already asleep, so she slips into bed beside him. She lies still for a moment, but then starts to wonder about the door.

Did I turn the deadbolt? She resists the urge to check it again, but the familiar anxiety sets in and she knows she won't be able to sleep unless she gets up. She goes out to check the door again, along with the kitchen appliances.

When she's done, Blair walks into the bedroom and then stops. *One more time.* Three is usually her ritual's magic number. Mr. Maurice follows her out this time and eats some food from his bowl.

The deadbolt is locked, the espresso machine and toaster unplugged.

Blair sighs. She can hear Mr. Maurice crunching as she heads back into the bedroom.

This time, she slips into bed beside Road and doesn't get up. She doesn't sleep, either. Road's breathing is steady and deep. She wonders what he's dreaming and then the memory of her own dream comes to her again, the erotic torment of him, but she pushes that from her thoughts.

That's the last thing I need to be thinking about right now.

Chapter Three

Things You Don't Miss About Road

1. He's a selfish slob.
2. He pretends to be humble when he's really not.
3. He makes you want him.

BLAIR WAKES UP to an empty bed in the morning. Road didn't touch her at all, and she knows this because she was awake all night trying not to think about him lying beside her.

She takes a deep breath, his scent in her bedroom. On her sheets. Everywhere. Blair closes her eyes and forces her desire aside. It's just lust. Road is hot and she hasn't had sex in almost a year, so that's why she's feeling this way. So what if she's carried a torch for him since eighth grade?

I'm not in love with him anymore. That would make me an idiot, and I'm not an idiot.

After her shower, she finds Road in the living room, relaxing on the couch with his computer. A mug of coffee rests at his side. To her relief, he's dressed—jeans and a blue Henley.

Blair is surprised he's awake before her. Being a baker, she's up early even on her days off, but then remembers Road has jet lag.

"Made coffee for you," he tells her as she wanders into the kitchen. "It's in the fridge."

Her eyes widen. She opens the refrigerator and, sure enough, there's a cold latte. She reaches for it and, after adding ice, takes it into the living room and sits in the chair opposite him. She brings her pen and notebook to start her daily list. She puts them on her phone, too, but likes to start on paper.

"Thanks, that was nice of you."

"No problem." He's typing into his computer. Surprisingly, Mr. Maurice is sitting on the end of the couch near Road's bare feet. "So, I noticed you like beige and white a lot, huh?" he asks, still typing.

Blair glances around her condo. There isn't much color, as she tends to be conservative with her decorating choices. "Yes, I do."

"You know, white is a funeral color in most parts of Asia."

She frowns. "What are you implying?"

"Nothing." He grins and glances over at her. "What time do you want to head over to Tori's today?"

Blair leans back into the chair, tapping her pen against her notebook. "I need to go into work for a few hours." She's meeting with Road and Tori's younger half-sister, Kiki, who's getting married in a few months. Blair is making the cake for her as a wedding present.

Road seems distracted on his computer, but then looks up. "Can you give me a house key, so I'm not stuck here?"

"No."

"Why not?"

"Because you don't need one. Today is your last day staying with me. I expect you to be gone by tomorrow."

He lets out a frustrated breath. "Look, I need to go out for a few hours, and I won't be able to get back in without a key."

Blair picks up her latte and swirls the ice. She knows she's being kind of a bitch. She thinks about how she ditched him for dinner last night and feels a slight pang of guilt.

"Fine. I'll give you my spare key, but I want it back when you leave."

"Need my car keys, too."

Blair stops swirling the ice in her glass and stares at him. "What are you talking about?"

"Keys for Isadora, babe."

She blinks. "I'm not giving you her keys."

"Why's that?"

"Because she's mine."

Road chuckles. "Don't think so. And I need a car to get around."

"I still have dry cleaning in the back of Isadora," she lies. "You can take my Honda instead."

Road's eyes narrow at this, but then his phone starts playing Reggae music. When he sees who's calling, he sighs and answers it. "Hey, what's up?" Road closes his computer and rises from the couch. "Let me find someplace private I can talk."

Blair watches as he opens her sliding glass door to her deck. She wonders who he's speaking with that he needs privacy. He seems to have a lot of phone calls. She can see that Road has a serious expression on his face as he talks. She glances over at his ultra-slick computer and gets a prickle of unease at what he might be involved in.

He'll be gone tomorrow anyway.

But then she thinks about how he was asking for the keys to Isadora.

He can't take her back. I won't let him.

There's no way she's giving him that car. Never mind she's put thousands of dollars into her. *Isadora belongs to me now. It's as simple as that.*

She chews her thumbnail. The problem is Road has her title and is still her legal owner.

But we're still married, so I'm her legal owner, too.

BY THE TIME Blair is ready to leave, she discovers Road is still on his phone outside. She puts a spare house key and the keys to her Honda on the kitchen counter for him, along with a note telling him her parking space number in the garage. Luckily, her condo came with two parking spaces so she has one for each car.

Blair drives Isadora to work and parks behind La Dolve Vita in her usual spot. She and Natalie, moved the bakery to a larger location recently, and they both love it. Besides having more space, it's an old brick building that's quite picturesque.

The familiar smell of fresh pastries and espresso surround her as she enters through the back door, and as always, it gives her a lift. She was into baking as a hobby when she was younger, and graduated from college with a degree in English intending to teach, but after some friends asked her to make a cake for their small wedding, Blair discovered she was hooked.

Ginger, one of the part-time bakers they'd recently switched to full-time and who Blair is mentoring, let's her know Kiki has arrived and is already waiting.

"Thanks, tell her I'll be right out."

Blair quickly checks her messages and makes note of a few. There's one from the director of a women's shelter with a list of the kids' names who have birthdays coming up soon. Blair donated some cakes a few months ago, and when she heard the plights of some of these women and their children, decided to make it a regular thing.

Afterward, Blair finds Natalie in their bakery's back office, doing payroll on the computer. Her blonde hair is pulled back into a ponytail, and she's wearing jeans and a purple shirt on her curvy body. Natalie recently married the most beautiful man on Earth and has a constant glow of happiness.

Blair comes inside and closes the door, leaning against it. "You'll never believe who showed up yesterday."

Natalie concentrates on the computer, typing something with the number pad. “Who?”

When Blair doesn’t respond, Natalie looks over at her. “Everything okay?”

“*Road* showed up at my front door yesterday.”

Natalie stops what she’s doing and stares at Blair with her mouth open. “Are you kidding?”

“I wish I were.”

“What does he want?”

Blair doesn’t reply right away. What exactly *does* Road want? She’s not really sure. He hasn’t asked for anything, except Isadora. “I don’t know want he wants. It sounds like he’s moving back to Seattle.”

Natalie is studying her. “Maybe it’s a good thing. Now you can finally put all this behind you.”

“Maybe.”

“Who’s he’s staying with? Tori?”

“With me, for now.”

Natalie’s eyes widen. “Is that smart?”

“It’s only for a couple of nights. I told him he has to leave by tomorrow.”

“I see.” Natalie studies Blair. “Do you still have feelings for him? You did love him once, so it’s understandable if you do.”

Blair sighs. Natalie doesn’t know how she wound up married to Road. The only person who knows the whole story is Tori, and she suspects their mom has her suspicions. Everyone else assumes it was a normal marriage. Well, normal until Road jumped ship like a fleeing rat.

“No. I just want him out of my life. He had the nerve to ask for Isadora’s keys this morning. Can you believe that?”

“And?”

“And I gave him the keys to my Honda instead.” Blair thinks about the way Road’s eyes narrowed, his laser focus turned on. He knew she was lying. *He’s not going to give up easily.* For all his faults, she wouldn’t call Road a quitter. She takes a deep breath and lets it out, trying to calm her growing panic. “I’m worried. I think I might have a custody battle on my hands here.”

Natalie grins. “It’s just a car, Blair.”

She shoots Natalie a look. “*Just* a car?”

“All right, she’s an incredible car, I’ll give you that.”

Blair gets up. “If he thinks he can just show up and take Isadora from me, he’s in for a big surprise. I’m not giving her up without a fight.”

She leaves the office and grabs her white jacket, along with a pencil and the sketch pad she uses to design her wedding cakes, before heading out front.

“Hey, Blair!”

Blair smiles and takes the seat across from Kiki at the corner table. Kiki, short for Katherine, is Tori and Road's younger half-sister. Of the three siblings, Kiki looks the least like any of them. Blair has always thought Kiki was stunning, though. With her dark hair and tilted brown eyes, she's something of an exotic beauty.

"How is Road?" Kiki asks. "Tori said he's just arrived yesterday and is staying with you. I haven't seen him yet."

"He's fine, I suppose."

"You must be glad to see him."

Blair doesn't know what to say. "I guess."

They go over the details of the type of cake Kiki has in mind. She's already picked out chocolate coconut for the flavor.

"You might want to consider a smaller second cake or some cupcakes," Blair says. "Not everyone likes chocolate."

Kiki laughs. "Don't be silly, who doesn't like chocolate?"

"Well, your brother, for one." But then Blair wishes she could take it back, hating she still knows that about him.

"Oh, yeah." Kiki nods. "I forgot. What does Road like?"

Road's favorite cake is carrot, of course, but Blair pretends not to know. "I'm not sure. You'll have to ask him."

"YOUR CAR NEEDS a tune-up," Road tells her when Blair gets back to her condo. "It's running rough."

Blair nods, surprised to see him back before her. Apparently, he was already done with his errands. "The Honda?"

"Yeah, the Honda."

Blair heaped so much attention on Isadora that her poor Honda has turned into an unloved stepchild.

Road is sitting on the living room couch, pulling stuff from his leather backpack. There are packages and a couple of plastic shopping bags that have strange logos on them, and she realizes they're foreign.

"What is all this stuff?" she asks.

"Gifts for people. Figured I'd give Tori what I got her today."

"That was nice of you." She watches his hands as they fold over the edges of a shopping bag, the hair on his knuckles golden-blond. He's wearing a couple of braided leather bands on his wrist. His chin-length hair is cut into shaggy layers, parted in the center and tucked behind his ears. Road has what Blair always thinks of as 'guy glamour.' Without trying, he attracts attention.

"Got something for you, too, princess."

She blinks in surprise. "You brought me a gift?"

"Saw it and couldn't resist."

He grabs one of the packages wrapped in plain, brown paper and hands it to her.

Blair is speechless. Road's never given her a gift in his life. She takes it from him, and by the shape and weight it's definitely a book. She tears the wrapper off, delighted by what she finds. A hardback of Anne Rice's *Interview with the Vampire.*

"It's a first edition. I found it in a London bookstore."

"Really?" Blair runs her hand over the gold dust jacket. When she opens the cover, it releases a musty old-book smell. She notices that it's been signed by Anne Rice herself. "This is incredible. I love it," she murmurs.

She and Tori used to obsess over Anne Rice's books. Tori's birthday was on Halloween, and every year they dressed up as Anne Rice vampires. One year, they asked Road to go out with them as Lestat. His plans had fallen through because he was fighting with his girlfriend—predictably, there was a lot of drama in Road's relationships—and surprisingly, he agreed to go. With his height and long, blond hair, Road made a fantastic Lestat. They had a lot of fun dressing him up, too. He totally got into the part, quoting from the books and calling himself Wolf Killer.

"Tori would also love this," she tells him.

"I know, but somehow I thought you would appreciate it more."

Blair nods. Tori likes to read, but she wasn't quite as book-obsessed as Blair. "Thank you. This is an amazing gift. I'm not even sure what to say."

"'Thank you' is good enough."

Their eyes meet, and Blair's stomach takes a dip. She recognizes all the signs of falling into the abyss.

Road looks at her hair. "No scarf today, huh?"

"I don't wear them to work."

"What do you do for work again?"

Blair's mouth opens in surprise. *Seriously? He doesn't even know what I do?* Surely someone would have at least mentioned the wedding cake she's baking Kiki. Maybe not. But then she realizes he doesn't care. He's taken zero interest in her activities all these years. Nothing. In a perverse way, she's glad for it, though, because it helps pull her out of the abyss and back to reality.

"I make wedding cakes." She tries to hide her annoyed tone—after all, he did just give her a fantastic gift. "In fact, I'm making the cake for Kiki's wedding. I can't believe you didn't know that."

"Oh, yeah, I knew that." There's a grin tugging at his mouth. "Just forgot."

She studies him. "What exactly do *you* do for a living?"

Road eyebrows rise. "You don't know?"

"I have no idea."

"Tori's never told you?"

"It's never come up." She doesn't want to tell Road how she asked Tori not to talk about him.

He grows quiet. "I do a little of this and a little of that."

Blair watches him closely. *Is he hiding something?* "I hope it isn't illegal."

"Why would you think it was illegal?"

She points to his computer and phone. "You have a lot of nice things and you also have a lot of cash." She's still holding the book he gave her and knows a signed first edition of *Interview with the Vampire* couldn't have been cheap. She motions toward his hands, which are clean and grease-free. "Obviously, you're not a mechanic anymore."

"Not exactly."

"You can't make a living doing 'a little of this and a little of that.' What do you do for real?"

He rubs his jaw. "It's hard to put into words."

"Try."

He hesitates.

His evasiveness is starting to give her a bad feeling. "Please, tell me you aren't smuggling drugs."

Road's eyes widen. He looks shocked. Suddenly, his phone starts playing Reggae music and he glances down at it. "Got to take this, babe."

Grabbing the phone, he heads back outside onto her deck for privacy.

Her bad feeling gets worse.

BLAIR CHANGES INTO a pair of shorts, a white blouse, and ties another multicolored scarf in her hair.

As she puts on a pair of turquoise Keds that match her scarf, she mulls over Road's gift. For having never given her a gift before, he sure hit it out of the park with the first one. It was amazing and thoughtful.

But why did he get me a gift at all?

She checks her appearance in the full-length mirror in her bedroom.

I'm, like, the opposite of Skank Factor X.

She already knows Tori is going to give her grief over the Keds. She's always telling her they look like mom shoes, but Blair likes them.

"I thought you said your cat wasn't friendly?" Road asks as Blair walks back out into the living room. He's sitting on the couch petting Mr. Maurice, who is draped across Road's lap.

Blair goes over to them. Mr. Maurice is purring loudly. She watches in amazement as her cat rolls around, clearly smitten. "I don't know what's gotten into him. I think he's in love with you."

"You think so?" Road points his finger at Mr. Maurice, who tries to grab it. "Hey, pal. Don't get any funny ideas."

Blair laughs. She watches the top of Road's blond head as he scratches Mr. Maurice's chin. *At least I'm not in love with him anymore. Thank God.*

"You look pretty, princess." He glances up, quickly surveying her outfit.

"Thank you." Her face grows warm. The curse of being a redhead is that she always blushes too easily. She turns away. "Are you ready to go?"

"Sure."

On the elevator ride down to the parking garage, Road asks for Isadora's keys.

"Don't worry, I'll drive," Blair tells him.

"No, I'll drive. Give me the keys."

"They're in my purse. I'll get them out in a minute."

"You'll get them out right now."

"What's the rush?"

The elevator doors open into the garage and Road frowns. "Why do I get the sense you're fucking with me?"

"I'm not."

"I think you are. Now, hand me those keys."

They're still arguing as they make their way over to where Isadora is parked. When they get close to her, Road freezes.

"What the hell?" He turns toward Blair, his eyes wide with disbelief. "What did you do to my car?"

"What do you mean? Your car is in mint condition. She's worth triple what she was before you left."

"Babe." Road is shaking his head. "She's *green*."

"Oh, that."

"Yes, *that*! What the fuck did you do to her?"

Blair shrugs. "Well, I painted her green, obviously."

"Isadora's not supposed to be green. She's supposed to be *red*." His eyes flash to her hair. "Red, got it?"

Road walks around Isadora, inspecting her. He's still shaking his head, running his hands over the body as if a great travesty has been committed. "Don't fucking believe this," she hears him muttering.

"I've been taking her to Brody and he helped me restore her," Blair says.

"Yeah, I know. He told me."

"He did?"

"Didn't tell me she was green, though," he grumbles. Road goes to the front of the car. "Pop the hood so I can take a look."

Blair gets her keys out, opens the driver's side door, and climbs inside to release the latch.

She sits and watches Road as he leans in on his forearms, examining

Isadora's engine. Her eyes trail down his long, jeans-clad legs and back to his ass.

Road has always had a fantastic ass, ever since she's known him. It's one of those asses that looks perfect in a pair of jeans or cargo pants or, best of all, naked. She tries to look away from that ass, but can't.

I'm being held hostage.

She chuckles to herself. Eventually, the show is over, though. He stands up and moves over to the front of the car to close Isadora's hood, wiping his hands on his pants. When he sees her through the front windshield, he motions for her to get out.

She shakes her head.

He comes over and opens the driver's side door. "I'm driving, princess."

Blair looks up at him. "I'm already sitting here, so I might as well drive."

"Don't think so. Now, get out of the car."

She doesn't move.

Road bends down, his large body close to hers. "What's your problem?"

"I prefer to drive."

"Is that right?" His voice is dangerously soft as he studies her. Just her face at first, but then his eyes slowly travel downward. It's almost like he's touching her.

Blair's breath hitches.

His smoky scent drifts toward her, and it's doing funny things to her insides. Her nipples tingle when his eyes linger on her breasts. They travel lower and when they encounter her bare legs, they stay there for a while. Eventually, they go back to her face, and Blair is surprised by what she sees in them.

Those golden-green eyes are heated. She's seen that look in them once before and liked it.

Turns out, she still likes it.

Standing so close, framed by Isadora, Blair notices something else, too, something she can't believe has never occurred to her before, and she's thunderstruck.

That green she painted Isadora. The one she painstakingly picked out herself. The one that took her months to decide on.

It matches the color of Road's eyes.

My God, what a fool I've been.

All this time, she thought she was over him. That she didn't love him anymore. Only an idiot would love someone for so long who doesn't love them back.

Apparently, I'm an idiot.

"What's wrong, babe?" Road is looking at her with concern now.

"Don't call me babe."

"You look upset. Tell me why?"
She shakes her head and closes her eyes. "I can't."
"You really want to drive Isadora that bad?"
Blair nods. "Yes, I do."

Chapter Four

Daily List

1. Somehow face the fact that you're an idiot.

2. Figure out what Road is hiding.

3. Scrub the shower and sink to remove all traces of dark blond stubble.

CAN'T BELIEVE I'M letting a woman drive me around in my own damn car.

Nathan watches Blair behind the wheel. He gave in when he saw that bleak expression on her face, wondering what was really going on in her head. It felt like a kick in the chest, seeing her so forlorn.

He shifts position, trying to get comfortable. It's awkward sitting in the passenger seat. He runs a hand over the red pony leather, admires the shiny new dash, and has to hand it to Blair and Brody. They did an incredible job with Isadora. The ride is really smooth—and Blair is right, she's easily worth triple her value.

Not that I have any plans to sell her.

Still can't get over the color though. Green?

"Seriously, Blair, I have to ask what you were thinking painting my car green."

She glances over at him with those pretty hazel eyes. "It's not your car anymore."

"Yes, it is."

"Isadora is mine now. You can see how much money I've put into her."

"I'll write you a check to cover your loss."

He watches her hands grip the steering wheel. "I don't want your money!"

Nathan smiles at her tenacity. He likes that she's fighting for what she wants. She's fighting a losing battle, though. "Maybe you've forgotten, but I own the title to this car. She's legally mine."

"And I'm still legally your wife. So, I guess that makes her half-mine, too."

He shakes his head. "Nice try, but I owned this car before we got married. She doesn't come under community property."

His Uncle Lance gave him Isadora as a gift for his sixteenth birthday. She needed a lot of work. Didn't have the money back then to really fix her up, but he got her running well, at least.

Blair goes silent, plotting her next move no doubt. He's sure she'll come up with something.

He thinks back to her accusation earlier about him smuggling drugs. *Like I'd do something that nuts.* It had shocked him. Where the hell did she come up with something so crazy? It's true his family can get rowdy, and some of them are tap dancing around the law regularly, but muling drugs?

He chuckles to himself then leans back.

There's a nice breeze blowing, and they have Isadora's top down. The radio's playing the Beach Boys's "Wouldn't It Be Nice" and Nathan relaxes, takes in the sense of peace.

Forgot how much I enjoyed this car.

He notices the wind is blowing Blair's scarf around, and it makes him want to pull it off and grab a handful of that dark red hair. Blair's a pretty woman. He's always thought so, even when they were teenagers.

Have to admit, she knows how to handle Isadora, too. Goes easy on the clutch, doesn't hit the corners hard. She looks good sitting there with her elegant profile. A classy babe all the way. If they were living in the Middle Ages, she'd be highborn for sure. There's an understated glamour about Blair—not flashy like some of the women he's dated—but sexy all the same.

Problem was she was so quiet—even after they got married. Occasionally, she'd relax, but it was hard being around someone who was too shy to speak and, unlike some men, he preferred it when a woman didn't hold her tongue.

He had a feeling she'd changed after seeing that article Tori sent him about her wedding cake business, though. And he was right. Not shy at all. She's been giving him shit ever since he got here yesterday.

"You know I was only teasing earlier," he tells her. "Knew you baked wedding cakes."

Blair gives him a scathing look. "Right."

He chuckles. "I saw that article in *Seattle Magazine*. Tori sent me a copy."

"She did?"

"See, I'm not lying."

"You read it?"

"Yeah, I read it." It was a short article, one page, but there was something about the picture of Blair in it that he couldn't take his eyes off of. Just kept staring at it. She was wearing a white chef's coat, so you couldn't even see her body. It was shot from the side, with her grinning into the camera, and the way she looked? Damn. Sassy and hot. Just the way he liked his women.

And that's when this strange thought floated into his head.

She's your wife.

THEY ARRIVE AT Tori's house and Blair is glad Road let her drive. It helped calm her down. Maybe she is still in love with him. So what? The fact is she hasn't met anyone else and if she did, she'd probably fall out of love with Road in an instant.

Or maybe I'm destined to be in love with him forever.

She sighs.

Blair parks Isadora in the driveway right behind Tori's blue minivan. Ironically, Tori's ride looks like something a soccer mom would be driving around in, though she's the furthest thing from a soccer mom Blair can imagine.

Unless dogs and cats are going to start playing soccer.

"Thanks for letting me drive," she tells Road as they walk to the front door.

"No problem. Want to tell me what got you so down?"

Blair shakes her head. "It was nothing."

Road rings the doorbell and immediately, a choir of dogs starts barking inside.

A few moments later, Tori swings the door open with a big grin on her face. Her light brown hair is pulled into a messy ponytail, and she's wearing jean shorts and a black Def Leppard T-shirt. "My two favorite people!"

Blair grins back. Tori's enthusiasm is always contagious. She has a way of making every event feel like an occasion.

Tori hugs Road. "I'm so glad you're here! I missed you, big brother!"

"Missed you, too."

Then she grabs Blair. "Where have you been, stranger!"

"Tori, I just saw you three days ago."

By now, a trio of dogs—'the boys'—has come to the front door to investigate, sniffing and pawing at her and Road. Blair reaches down to pet each in turn—Eddie, the golden retriever, then Duff, a fat pug mix, and finally Tommy Lee, a tiny Chihuahua. Most of Tori's animals are from PAWS, a no-kill shelter in Seattle, and are mutts that nobody wants. Some have been abused. Tori, with her big heart, is a sucker for every hard-luck case.

Road and Blair follow her into the living room. Despite all the animals, her place is clean and smells like the apple-scented candles Tori likes to burn.

Music is playing on the stereo. Blair recognizes Ratt's "Round and Round." Tori has a love of all things '80s, especially '80s hair bands. There are two cats, one black and one white, named Joan and Lita. Both cats eye them from the top of a carpeted cat house.

"I made lemonade," Tori says. "And oatmeal raisin cookies."

Oatmeal raisin is Road's favorite cookie. Blair is annoyed with herself for knowing this. She wishes she didn't have all these lists in her head about Road. His favorite color (red), his favorite movie (*Terminator*), his favorite number (7)—yes, Road has a favorite number and she knows what it is. He probably doesn't even know it himself.

Someone needed to invent a Jeopardy game where all the categories were about Road. She'd break the bank. Of course, Road wouldn't watch it because he doesn't like game shows.

They sit on Tori's back deck where there's a table with four chairs and an umbrella set up. She brings out the lemonade and cookies. Eddie and Duff both flop beside them, and Blair reaches down to pet Duff. Tommy Lee trots out to sniff around Tori's yard.

The three of them chat for a while. Tori peppers Road with questions about his flight and if his jet lag is bad. They talk about their mom, their mom's awful new boyfriend, Garth, and all their endless cousins as Tori catches Road up with the latest gossip.

Road leans back in his chair, eating a cookie. "I have some stuff for you. It's on the counter at Blair's. Can't believe I forgot to bring it. I'll give it to you at Mom's on Saturday."

"You forgot! What did you get me?" Tori gets up to pour each of them some more lemonade.

"T-shirt from London and some chocolate."

"Yay! I hope it's the same kind as last time. That stuff was the bomb."

He nods. "Same stuff. Remembered you liked it."

Blair thanks Tori for refilling her glass. There's something peculiar about their conversation though and a strange realization is dawning on her. "When was the last time you guys saw each other?"

Road puts his glass down. "A little over a year ago."

"What?" Blair is confused. "But I thought you haven't been back in five years?"

"No, course not. Where did you get that idea?"

"From Tori." Blair turns to her. "You never told me Road was in Seattle before."

Tori's expression is pained as her eyes flash to Road, who's feeding one of the dogs a cookie, and back to Blair again. She looks uncomfortable. "My mom and I thought it was best not to tell you. We knew you didn't want to hear about him."

Blair blinks as she takes this in. "How long did he stay?"

"Not long," Tori says. "A couple weeks."

"Where did he stay?"

"I don't get it. Why would you not want to hear about me?" Road glances up from feeding Eddie the cookie. Duff gets up when he notices it and Tommy Lee comes racing in from the yard.

Blair and Tori's eyes meet. Then Blair turns to Road and decides to be honest. "Because I was unhappy with the way you left me years ago."

Road is quiet, watching her.

"And I never heard from you, not even a postcard," Blair adds.

"Princess . . ." He slowly shakes his head. "Figured you'd want to put it all behind you, that you were better off."

"And yet here you are, staying at my place."

A smile plays around his mouth. "Yeah, that's right. Here I am."

Blair doesn't say anything more. It's true she didn't want Tori or anyone else to talk about Road. As obsessively in love with him as she once was, her obsession to avoid anything to do with him ran just as deep. *Ironically, none of it worked. I'm still under his spell, even after all this time.*

"Are you moving back to Seattle?" Blair asks him.

"Looks that way."

"Where have you been living?"

"Various places. I've been in London the past year."

Blair blinks in surprise. "You've been living in the same location for an entire year?"

Tori is watching her, clearly unhappy with this conversation.

Blair takes a deep breath and exhales. "At least now that you're here, we can finally get divorced."

"What's the rush?" He chuckles. "Ironically, our marriage has lasted longer than a lot of people's."

Blair doesn't want to hear anymore. She stands up. "I need to use the restroom."

Tori gets up to follow her.

"Alone," Blair tells her pointedly, not that Tori listens. She follows her right into the bathroom and stands there while Blair pees.

"We were trying to protect you. That's why my mom and I never told you when he was here for a visit." Tori bites her lip. "You're not exactly reasonable when it comes to my brother."

Blair is silent for a long moment, then gets up and flushes the toilet.

"You said you didn't want to know anything about him. You insisted," Tori continues. "So, we didn't tell you."

Blair washes her hands in the sink. “It’s okay, it doesn’t matter. None of it worked anyway.”

Tori is watching her in the mirror. Her pretty face has a look of concern. She looks a bit like Road, since they both take after their mom. Lori was a beauty queen in her youth, though a life of partying has given her a hard look now that she’s older. Tori and Road’s dad left when Road was five and Tori was only three, so they didn’t see him while they were growing up.

“What do you mean?” Tori asks.

“I’m still in love with him.”

“Oh, sweetie.” Tori lets out her breath. “Are you sure? You’re probably just mixed up a little from seeing him again.”

Blair dries her hands on a towel, thinks about the color green she painted Isadora. She had that done well over a year ago. “Yes,” she says. “You’re probably right.” In her heart, though, she knows the truth. *I’m as crazy in love with him as ever.*

Tori shakes her head in annoyance. “My brother is so dumb. All those Skank Factor X bitches combined aren’t worth one of you!”

“Does he still date them?”

“Probably. I can’t say for sure since I haven’t met any of his foreign girlfriends. He dated someone from Spain for a while, but I couldn’t tell if she was nice or not.”

“So, you really didn’t send Road to stay with me?”

“No, of course not! He asked for your address, but I didn’t know he was planning to show up at your door yesterday. That was all his idea.”

“Why?”

“I don’t know. I’m sure it’s only for a day or two, though.”

Blair meets Tori’s eyes, and she knows what’s being left unsaid. Tori was amazingly understanding when Blair confessed the truth about what she did to her brother, and why he had to marry her. But at the same time, Tori believed it was wrong, so she never entirely blamed Road when he left.

They head out to the backyard where Road is throwing a tennis ball as the dogs all frantically chase it. Surprisingly, little Tommy Lee gets it the most.

“Oh, God, I didn’t tell you. Chase called and asked me out again,” Tori tells her.

“What did you say?” Chase was this guy Tori met at a flea market and went on a date with recently.

“I told him no. He’s nice-looking, but he’s kind of young for me.”

“How old is he?”

“Twenty-four.”

“That *is* kind of young.” Both she and Tori were turning thirty-one this year.

"Plus, he's a total player. After one date, I could already tell he'd never pass the Bandito Test."

Blair nods. The Bandito Test was something Blair and Tori gave all the men they dated. It was based on a movie they watched years ago where this woman was kidnapped by a group of banditos and her fiancé refused to rescue her because of the danger. Instead, his second in command, a man who'd also wanted to marry the woman but had been turned down, rescued her instead. He didn't care about the danger, he simply wouldn't leave her behind.

The question they always asked themselves about a guy was this: What kind of man is he? Is he a first or second man? Would he leave you behind or rescue you?

Tori sighs. "I don't know why all the wrong guys keep asking me out."

Blair's luck with men hasn't been too great, either. Of course, she wonders now if her feelings for Road have been getting in the way this whole time without her knowing it.

"Are you coming to my mom's party on Saturday?" Tori asks. "Please, say yes."

"I'll come on one condition."

"What's that?"

"You have to come to one of my mom's gallery events in a couple of weeks."

Tori gets a stricken look on her face. "The cacti penises again?"

"Yes, she has a whole new series." Blair can't help smiling at Tori's expression.

"I don't know." Tori bites her lip. "I haven't quite recovered from last time."

Blair invited Tori to one of her mom's gallery events about six months ago. She'd never seen her mom's paintings before and could barely look her mother in the eye afterward.

"Come on. I'm going to ask Graham to come, too. My mom always wants plenty of bodies at these events. And I haven't told you the latest. Scott and Ashley are most likely getting engaged."

Tori's eyes go wide. "The Shopping Queen is going to be your sister-in-law?"

"Looks that way."

Road comes over and tells her they should head out. Apparently, he has places to go and things to do, but she notices he doesn't give any specifics.

"Need the keys to Isadora," he tells her.

"I'd like to drive again."

"Not this time."

"I know the way back to my condo better than you do."

Road puts his hand out. "Give me the car keys."

"I'll feel better driving. I really will."

"Keys. *Now.*"

Blair sighs. She reaches for her purse, finds the keys and hands them to Road.

Tori is watching the two of them with amusement. "You two sound just like an old married couple."

Blair rolls her eyes. "Very funny."

"NOW, IS THIS so bad?" Road asks her after they leave Tori's and are headed back toward her condo. "You look good sitting there, princess."

Blair is quiet. She's still processing the fact that Road was here only a year ago and no one told her. *Who did he stay with then?*

Unfortunately, she can guess at the answer. There's never any shortage of women who want Road.

He pulls into a gas station, right up to one of the pumps. She gets out and tells him she's going inside the mini-market to grab a bottle of water.

"Would you mind paying for the gas while you're in there?" He pulls a bill from his wallet and hands it to her.

She gets a sinking feeling when she sees that it's another hundred dollars. "I don't know what gas prices are like in London, but it doesn't cost a hundred bucks to fill Isadora's tank. Not yet, anyway."

"That's the smallest I got."

She takes the bill and heads into the store, grabs some water, and pays for the gas.

Road is cleaning Isadora's windshield when Blair comes back out.

"Here's your change."

"Keep it."

She shrugs, sticks it in her wallet, and then leans against Isadora as she drinks her water. "So, you're throwing hundred dollar bills around like confetti these days?"

He does a final sweep of the windshield before tossing the squeegee back into the bucket near the gas pump. "Wouldn't say that. I have a few large bills in my wallet from traveling, is all."

They both get back in the car, and Blair decides she's going to get to the bottom of this right here and now.

"What do you for a living?" she asks when they pull out from the gas station.

"Thought I told you."

"No, you didn't."

"Why do you want to know so badly?"

Blair puts her bottle into the cup holder console she added to Isadora. It took her two months to pick out the exact one she wanted. Brody had to special-order it.

She crosses her legs and notices the way Road's eyes glance over at them, can't help feeling a tiny bit pleased. She already knows he's a leg and ass man.

"Cut the crap, Road. Are you doing something illegal?"

His eyes are on her legs again, but then flicker to her face before looking out the windshield.

He smirks. "You're probably better off not knowing what I do."

Blair goes still. "Why?"

"If I tell you, I might have to kill you." He grins.

She doesn't say anything the rest of the ride home and is torn about what to do. Despite everything that happened between them, she's still concerned for Road.

Okay, I'm in love with him and have been most of my life.

But this is insane.

After they get back to her condo, Road takes off with Isadora and is gone the rest of the afternoon. She wonders what he's up to, but then figures he's probably setting up his next place to stay—most likely with a woman.

Not that I care.

Blair tries to ignore her jealousy. He's free to do whatever he wants, and she can't have someone around who's involved with drugs. She's surprised Tori hasn't tried to help him with this, or maybe Tori doesn't know.

After making salad and spaghetti for dinner, Blair sets her computer on the kitchen counter and brings up the new website for La Dolce Vita. They recently had Tori update it so their customers could submit cake orders online. The change, along with the move to their new location and increased hours, has improved business so much they've been able to switch their two part-time bakers to full-time.

She's eating spaghetti and working on a new list she titled "How to Help Road Get Back on Track with His Life." When she hears the key in the front door, her pulse jumps with the familiar anticipation of seeing him.

"Hey, babe." He comes over, carrying his backpack and puts it on the chair in the kitchen next to where she's sitting.

"There's spaghetti if you're hungry."

"Nah, I'm good. Already ate."

"Where were you?"

He gets a glass down from the cabinet and fills it with water from the fridge. "Just taking care of things."

Blair watches his throat work as he drinks.

"Have you figured out where you're going to be staying after you leave here tomorrow?"

He stops drinking and lets out a breath. "All figured out, princess. No worries."

Road puts his glass on the counter. "Would you mind putting that in the dishwasher when you're done with it?"

"Sure." A grin tugs on his mouth.

"Also, if you wash clothes again, I'd like the detergent kept right next to the fabric softener."

"I'll make sure and remember that." He gives her a full-on grin. "Anything else?"

"That's all for now."

He comes closer and tucks his phone into the front of his backpack, glancing over at her computer. "What are you doing?"

"Just stuff for work."

"Is that the site Tori designed for you guys?"

Blair nods. "She recently updated some things for us."

"Can I see it?"

"Sure."

Road leans in close behind her. Looking over her shoulder, he angles the computer a little. She hears him sniff. "You smell good."

Blair only nods her reply. He smells good, too. Crazy good. She closes her eyes and immerses herself in his smoky scent. *Thank God he's leaving tomorrow. I don't think I can take much more of this without going insane.*

"Tori did a nice job." His head is right next to hers as he's clicking through the different pages for the bakery's site.

She watches his hand on her computer's touch pad. His hands are big, but oddly graceful and well-made for someone who worked as a mechanic. His nails are clean and short. She remembers all the times she stared at Road's hands, wanting things from them.

He suddenly stops surfing the bakery's website and remains still.

"What is it?" The side of his face is so close, she could kiss him if she leaned forward.

"How to help Road get back on track with his life," he reads, staring down at her notebook. "What the hell is this?"

He turns to face her, and for some perverse reason Blair doesn't move her head back, so their faces remain close.

"It's a list I made."

"I can see that." He turns to look at the list again.

"I don't know what you're involved in," she says quickly, "but I think you're on the wrong path."

Road's eyes come back to meet hers. He's close enough she can see how some of his eyelashes are tipped blond.

"You going to save me?" he asks softly.

"If I have to."

He smiles a little as his eyes drop to her mouth. "Think I'd like that."

A yearning blooms within her, a terrible yearning. And it's bad. The worst ever. She tries to force it away, yet the yearning persists.

His gaze flickers from her mouth back to her eyes.

Blair's breath hitches. And just when she's ready to damn the consequences, Road pulls away. He turns his head and is studying her list again.

"Who's Mia?"

"What?"

"Call Mia and ask her advice about Road and trouble with the law," he reads aloud.

Blair leans away from him and lets out her breath. "She's the lawyer I hired after you left."

His brows go up. "To divorce me?"

"Yes."

"But you didn't go through with it."

"No, not yet."

He nods slowly.

"Now that you're here, though, it'll be easy," she says. "We don't have any property or *children*." She stops talking and nearly chokes on the word children.

Road is watching her. He doesn't speak for a long moment, and when he does, his voice is quiet. "It wasn't anybody's fault what happened. You know that, right?"

Blair nods. She never lets her thoughts stray there, to the reason Road agreed to marry her in the first place. She swallows, trying to push back the sadness which, on a bad day, still haunts her. "I know that."

"It just wasn't meant to be, is all."

"I know that, too." She looks up at him and when their eyes meet, Blair is surprised by what she sees in his. She always thought Road didn't care when she lost the baby, that he was relieved and that's why he fled so quickly, but for the first time, she isn't sure.

He takes a deep breath and exhales. "Need to hit the sack, princess. Got a million things to do tomorrow, and I still have jet lag."

Blair turns away, staring at her computer, trying to recover from their conversation. "You have to sleep on the couch tonight," she tells him."

"Can't. Too bright out here, remember?"

"I have to be up early for work tomorrow, so I need my sleep tonight."

His eyes cut to hers. "You have a problem last night?"

Obviously, she can't admit how she was so affected by him that she barely slept at all. Especially when—annoyingly—she could hear his deep, even breathing and it was clear he wasn't having the same issue.

"No, no problem at all," she says, trying to make her voice haughty.

There's a mewing sound and Road glances down. Mr. Maurice is twining around his legs. "Hey, pal." Road bends down to pet him for a few seconds then stands. "Okay, going to crash then."

Blair watches him head down the hall to the bedroom with Mr. Maurice trailing behind. She closes her eyes. *Thank God he's leaving.*

Chapter Five

Reasons You Love Isadora

1. She's more than a car, she's a lifestyle.
2. You restored her when no one else cared.
3. Road may have abandoned Isadora, but now she's better than ever.

"HAS ROAD LEFT yet?" Natalie asks, sipping her latte.

Both Blair and Natalie are in the kitchen at La Dolce Vita. Natalie is watching Blair roll out peach fondant for a two-tiered, lace wedding cake.

Blair spreads the fondant over the table. The wedding colors are peaches and cream with a sky blue accent. The bride brought in fabric samples to show Blair, along with pictures of the flowers and venue. She's seen so many weddings that she's become almost immune to them, but sometimes there's still one that takes her breath away.

If she ever gets married again, it won't be at city hall, that's for sure. *Of course, if I ever get married again, it will be to a man who loves me, not one who's marrying me out of obligation.*

"He was still asleep when I left this morning, but he's leaving today."

"What happened with Isadora?"

Blair grabs a palette knife to cut the gum paste mixture from a lace mold. "I still have her keys."

What she doesn't mention is that she had to search through Road's stuff to find Isadora's keys. He didn't give them back to her last night. Luckily, he left his backpack on the chair. She's surprised he was so trusting, but then he had no reason to distrust her.

It was an underhanded thing to do, but there's no way she's letting him take Isadora. *Road may have her title, but I've put a lot of money into her. I think that gives me some sort of claim.*

And luckily, she didn't see anything suspicious in his bag, either. Though he probably would have gotten rid of anything illegal by now.

"Do you think that will be the end of it with Road?" Natalie asks.

"I hope so."

I mean what's he going to do? Besides, possession is nine-tenths of the law, right?

A COUPLE HOURS later, as Blair is bent over putting the finishing touches on a birthday cake, Carlos, one of their baristas, comes back looking for her.

"There's someone here to see you."

"Who?"

"A guy. Tall, blond, and straight-up hot."

Blair sighs. She only knows one guy who fits that description. "Tell him I'll be out in a minute."

She stores the birthday cake in their large back fridge then goes over to check herself in the employee bathroom mirror. Dabs on lip gloss. She suspects she knows why he's here.

"Is that Road?" Natalie and Ginger both ask when they see her headed toward the front. The bakery is worse than a sorority house sometimes, everybody knowing everybody else's business.

Blair sighs. "Tall, blond, and straight-up hot?"

They both nod. "*Very* hot," Natalie says with a grin.

"Yes, that's him."

Ginger gives her a look. "If that was my husband, I'm pretty sure I'd never divorce him. Maybe you guys should try and work it out."

"Not this situation." Blair doesn't bother taking her white chef's coat off. She wants Road to be reminded that she's at work and doesn't have time for any big discussions.

She heads out front and sees him right away, standing near their pastry case. Her insides do their usual flutter at the sight of him.

He nods. "Hey, princess."

"I'm working, so I don't have a lot of time."

"Give me your hand."

"Why?"

He reaches down and takes her hand. His hand is warm and dry, and his touch makes her breath catch. She feels him put something into hers.

"What's this?" She looks down in surprise. He's given her the Honda keys.

"Not planning to take much of your time. Just stopped by to get the keys to my car and give those back to you."

Blair shakes her head. "I'm sorry, but I'm not giving you Isadora's keys."

"Excuse me?"

"I think you heard me."

Road goes silent, stares at her with his eyes laser-focused. They narrow. "No, don't think I *did* hear you correctly. Sounded like you just told me you're keeping my car."

"I believe I have a claim to her."

"No, you don't. Now hand over the keys."

"I've spent thousands on her so, yes, I do have a claim."

"Said I'd write you a check, remember?"

Blair doesn't reply, just turns her head back toward the kitchen to indicate she needs to get back to work.

"Cut the shit, Blair. Give me the keys to my car. *Now*."

She hesitates at the demand in his voice, but then remembers how Road abandoned Isadora, just left her sitting in the driveway. He didn't care. *I care, though.*

"No," Blair tells him.

Road is studying her. "So, this is how you want to play it?"

"I'm not giving you Isadora. Like I said, she's mine."

Road lets out a frustrated breath.

"Feel free to use the Honda for as long as you need it. I think that's generous." She holds the Honda's keys out for Road, dangling them between two fingers.

He glances at them and steps closer to her, speaking in a low growl. "You don't want to tangle with me, babe. Trust me, you'll *lose*."

"We'll see."

The two of them stay that way. Blair sees the way he's assessing her. She doesn't back down, though. Instead, she meets his assessment head-on and, in fact, starts doing some assessing of her own. She already knows Road won't back down if he thinks he's right.

But I'm the one who's right this time.

He smirks then reaches over and grabs the Honda keys from her hand. Without another word, he stalks out of the bakery.

BLAIR SPENDS THE rest of the afternoon wondering what Road's next move is going to be. *Maybe this won't be so bad after all. What can he really do? Take me to court?* That will take months. And besides, he's not going to want to tangle with the authorities, not if he's involved in anything illegal.

After checking through her work calendar, she notices she'll be delivering two cakes on Friday and four on Saturday. Some brides pick up the cakes themselves, but others, especially when it's a multi-tiered cake, opt to pay extra and have Blair deliver it for them. She and Natalie bought a used refrigerated van and either Ginger or Carlos helps her with deliveries.

On the way home, she stops at Home Depot and browses through the paint section again, gathering more samples for her second bedroom/soon-to-be office. She thinks about Road's comment that white is a funeral color in Asia.

Maybe I should add some color.

She then gets annoyed with herself that anything Road said would have an influence on her. Instead, she grabs more beige and white color swatches. *There's nothing wrong with beige and white!*

When she pulls into the underground parking garage for her condo, she's surprised to see her silver Honda is in its usual parking spot. Apparently, Road decided he didn't want to use it after all.

I'm sure he knows plenty of people who would be happy to loan him a car. Plenty of women, especially.

As she heads up in the elevator, she has an uneasy feeling, like she's forgotten something. She's not quite sure what it is, but the closer she gets to her door, the feeling only gets stronger. When she finally puts the key in the lock and steps inside her flat, it all becomes clear.

The first thing she notices is the smell of food cooking, and the second thing is Road in front of the stove cooking it.

For a moment, she remains still. A swirl of emotions flood through her—joy and longing, but they only last a split-second before it all turns to anger. She walks over to the island and puts her purse down on the chair. "Just what do you think you're doing here?"

"Cooking dinner." He reaches over for the pepper mill and grinds some into the pan of food.

"No," she says icily. "What are you doing *here*?" She'd left a detailed note for Road this morning instructing him to lock her door then stick the key in her mailbox downstairs afterward. Clearly, he didn't follow instructions.

"Like I said, babe. Cooking dinner."

"You were supposed to put my key in the mailbox this morning."

"Guess not."

"You kept my house key?"

"Looks that way." His eyes slide to hers, and there's a lazy expression on his face she recognizes. It's the one he always wore when he was scheming something and wanted to appear innocent. It was usually directed at Tori or one of his friends when he was pulling a prank. She's never seen it directed at her before.

"I want it back. And then I want you to leave."

Road smirks, doesn't reply and instead keeps stirring the pan of what she now recognizes is chicken stir fry.

"And don't start with me on the irony of all this, either. Keeping my house key is not the same as me keeping Isadora!"

"Whatever you say." Road brings the spoon to his lips to taste the dish. Blair's mouth waters. She hasn't eaten since noon, and though she's loathe to admit it, the food smells delicious. *Since when can Road cook?* As she recalls, the most complicated thing he knew how to make was a peanut butter and jelly sandwich.

"Do you want a taste?" he asks.

She glares at him. "I want my key back."

"Guess we both want something then."

Blair tries to see a way out of this. There's no way she's going to give him Isadora. Not in a million years. Unfortunately, that leaves only one other option. She doesn't want to do it, but Road isn't giving her a choice. She takes a deep breath. "If you don't give me my house key and leave, I'm calling the police."

Road turns toward her, his expression stunned.

She crosses her arms. "I'm completely serious."

His brows go up as he stares at her in amazement.

"I'll do it, and I know you don't want that."

But then his expression changes again. This time, it's humor. White teeth flash at her, eyes full of mirth. She hasn't seen Road laugh in a long time and forgot how much she liked it. He has a great laugh.

Unfortunately, this is not the response she was expecting. Far from it, actually.

He's laughing so hard now that he actually has to put the wooden spoon down and rest his hands on the counter.

"I fail to see what's so amusing," she says.

"Damn, princess." He shakes his head, chuckling. "The police?" And then he starts laughing all over again.

But Blair has had enough. "Stop laughing! This isn't funny. You kept my house key, and now you won't leave. That's practically breaking and entering!"

This only makes him laugh harder.

"You think I won't do it? That I won't call? I will. I'll call them right now!"

Finally, Road takes a deep breath and seems to gain control over himself. "Go ahead, call the cops. I don't have a problem with it."

"You don't?"

"Course not. I'm not the one *stealing* something." He gives her a look.

"I'm not stealing Isadora!"

"That's not how it looks from over here. And that's not how the law is going to see it, either. All I have to do is show them the title to my car."

Blair is quiet.

"Hell, maybe I should call them myself, now that I think about it."

She shoots him a dark look.

He picks up the spoon and gets back to his chicken stir fry. "Told you not to tangle with me, babe." But then he grins. "Besides, what would you tell them anyway? That your husband refuses to leave home?"

"This isn't your home."

He looks around her condo. "I like it here."

"No, you don't. You told me it looks like an Asian funeral parlor."

"Not exactly what I said."

"Close enough," she grumbles.

Road lets out what sounds like a weary sigh. "Do you want a beer?" He goes over to the fridge and opens the door. "Think we could both use one."

"No."

He reaches in and comes out with two bottles. She watches him search through her kitchen drawers until he finds the opener. When he's done, he hands one over.

"I said I didn't want it."

Road puts her beer on the counter next to her and goes back to cooking. She watches him take a long draw from his bottle as he continues with the stir fry.

Studying him from the side, she has to admit he looks sexy standing there making dinner. He's wearing the same faded jeans and T-shirt from earlier. His blond hair tucked behind his ears.

A shudder of wanting runs through her. Her desire for Road is so deep and familiar, it's like an old friend returning, her shadow companion for years.

She picks up her beer and takes a sip. "So, when did you learn how to cook?"

"Couple years ago. Friends taught me."

Blair is silent. *Women friends, no doubt.*

"Do you want to grab some plates, babe?"

She opens the cabinet and gets them down, then pulls out silverware for both of them. Despite her anger, she figures they might as well eat. Road takes each plate and dishes out rice from another pot she hadn't even noticed he was using. He loads up both plates with the stir fry.

They take their food and beer bottles over to her small dining room table, where they sit in silence for a while as they devour the meal.

"This is good," Blair admits. She's hungry, but it's still probably the best stir fry she's ever had. "Did you put curry in it?"

"Thanks. And yeah, I did."

"I take it one of your girlfriends taught you how to cook."

He shakes his head. "Shared a flat with a husband and wife in Budapest and they taught me."

Blair raises her eyebrows in surprise.

"We took turns cooking," Road explains. "Only, I burned everything. Finally, they got so tired of my charcoal dinners they took it upon themselves to teach me how to cook."

Blair can't help her laughter. "They did a good job. From what I remember, all you could make were peanut butter sandwiches."

"Yeah, that was my repertoire, all right." Road grins. "Only, you can't find peanut butter in Hungary or if you do, it's too expensive."

"How long did you live there?"

"About six months. Right before I moved to London."

"You've been leading an adventurous life."

Road shrugs. "Some might say that."

Blair thinks about how Lori once told her how he got his nickname—why they started calling him Road instead of Nathan. She said he kept trying to run away when he was a toddler, that even then he had a hankering for the open road.

There's a mewing sound and Blair looks down to see Mr. Maurice twining around her ankles. He lets her pet him a little, but then quickly goes over to Road and jumps on his lap.

"Hey, buddy."

"I swear you've hypnotized my cat."

Road scratches under Mr. Maurice's chin. "He's got good taste, is all."

Blair is watching the two of them when she hears her phone playing "If I Knew You Were Coming I'd've Baked a Cake" from inside her purse. She gets up to answer it and sees on the display it's Graham.

"Hi." Her eyes flash over to Road, who is still petting Mr. Maurice but watching her with interest. "Let me go find someplace private to talk," she says pointedly.

Road raises an eyebrow.

"I haven't heard from you in a while," Graham says in a friendly voice. "Just thought I'd check and see if you want to get together for a movie or something?"

"Uh, sure." She heads toward the deck, but then suddenly remembers her purse. Isadora's keys are inside. She makes her way back over. Road is still watching her as she grabs her purse off the chair, his eyes calculating. "A movie sounds great," she tells Graham.

Blair goes out onto her deck and closes the sliding glass door. She can still see Road inside. He's petting Mr. Maurice, but then he gets up and starts clearing the table.

Graham is telling her a funny story about someone he works with and she laughs at all the appropriate places, but she can't take her eyes off Road. He's putting the food away now. It surprises her. She can't remember him ever clearing a dish in his life. He's always been a terrible slob. And even though she wants Road to leave, there's this odd pang of longing in her chest as she sees him standing in her kitchen. Ironically, despite their 'marriage,' this is the most domestic they've ever been with each other.

When Graham is done with his funny story, Blair invites him to her mom's gallery event. He tells her he might be in Bellingham for work, but he'll try to make it.

They hang up and when Blair goes back inside, she doesn't see Road anywhere.

Unfortunately, she already knows where he is.

Sure enough, she finds him in her bedroom, though unlike the last two nights, he isn't asleep but sitting in bed reading from a Kindle.

"Who was that you were talking to?" he asks when she comes into the room.

"You're not seriously staying the night here again."

"Answer my question."

Blair goes over to stand by the end of the bed. Road is wearing a white T-shirt, but the rest of his body is under the duvet. He definitely looks like he's planning to stay. "This is crazy. You can't just move in here."

"Was that your boyfriend?"

"Would you at least sleep on the couch? Could you do that much for me?"

Road goes back to his Kindle. She notices Mr. Maurice curled up beside him, her traitorous cat. Quite the cozy pair. "Can't sleep on the couch, babe. It'll kill my back."

Blair scoffs. "Since when do you have a back problem?"

"It's a recent thing."

"I don't believe that. You're making it up."

"Believe whatever you like." He's still looking at his Kindle, but she can see the little smirk on his face.

Blair gives up and goes into the bathroom to change into the oversized shirt and boxer shorts she wears to bed. She brushes her teeth. When that's done, she checks to make sure her front door is locked and everything is turned off. She tries to do it consciously, so she can visit the memory, instead of checking the door over and over. It's a trick she learned in counseling to help with her compulsions, though it doesn't always work.

Finally, she heads into the bedroom again. *Another sleepless night next to Road. Great.*

Road is still reading, and he watches her when she comes into the room. His eyes roam over her, and she tries not to show her discomfort at his perusal. She senses his laser focus is on.

"Is that what you always sleep in?" he asks, still studying her boxer shorts as she climbs into bed.

"Yes."

She tries to imagine what all his Skank Factor X girlfriends wear to bed. Garter belts and push-up bras, no doubt.

"Don't you have a little nightie or something?"

Blare rolls her eyes.

He grins. "A classy babe like you? I'll bet you got a whole drawer full of them."

In truth, she does have a few nighties, though they're not in a drawer but hanging in her closet. "I'm not wearing them for *you.*"

Road chuckles at that, but then his laughter quiets. "Who are you wearing them for—your boyfriend?"

Blair gives a haughty sniff as she pulls the covers over herself. She makes a point not to check and see what Road has on, though she's pretty sure it's a pair of boxer briefs. "That's right, I wear my nighties for him all the time."

Road takes this in then shakes his head. "Don't think so."

"It's true."

"That dude who called you earlier?"

"Yes, as a matter of fact, that dude who called is my boyfriend."

"No way he's your boyfriend."

"You're wrong. He *is* my boyfriend."

"Nope. And I can you tell this much, too. You're definitely not sleeping with him."

"What makes you so sure of that?"

He puts his Kindle down and rolls over so he's on his side, facing her. "Because if you were, princess, you'd be in bed with him right now instead of me."

Blair goes still at this. She's lying on her back, while Road is propped up on one elbow, the room bathed in a soft glow from her lamp.

She meets his eyes. Swallows. Remembers how it felt like he was going to kiss her last night. It feels that way again, but this time, she knows it's all in her mind. He's already slept in the same bed with her two nights in a row, and it's clear he doesn't want her. Because if he *did* want her, by now he would have done something about it.

"You're only here because I'm stuck with you," she tells him.

"We can end this anytime."

She closes her eyes. "Just turn the light off. I need to get some sleep."

He rolls away from her and reaches for the bedside lamp. But then he stops. "Tell me something first. The truth. Are you sleeping with that guy?"

"That's none of your business."

"Tell me."

"Why do you care, Road?"

"Tell me," he insists.

Blair blows out a sigh. "No. You're right. We're not sleeping together."

The light goes out and she can feel Road lie down, settling in. She rolls on her side, facing away from him. As always, his scent is everywhere. The smoky hint of autumn. She wishes he was one of those guys who wore cologne or something. Smelling him is like taking a hit off an opium pipe.

He's right about Graham, too. They keep trying to date, but there aren't many sparks flying. The few times they kissed, it felt more like she was kissing her brother.

Blair's eyes close as she waits for the sound of Road's deep, even breathing. The torment of it every night. She doesn't understand why he's being so stubborn about Isadora, either. Why does he suddenly want that car so bad? Maybe he plans to sell her. The thought makes Blair grit her teeth. *After all the energy I've poured into her?*

She lies there, trying to let her mind drift off to sleep, and starts to wonder if maybe she should just move to the couch herself. At least she'd finally get some rest. *No way is he chasing me out of my own bed, though.*

"Blair, you awake?" Road asks softly.

It actually startles her, Road's voice. She freezes, and for a second can't decide whether she should answer or not. After all, she's been fake-sleeping the past two nights, but then realizes he doesn't know that.

"Yes," she says. "I'm awake."

She feels him shift in bed. "What you said at Tori's yesterday surprised me. I never knew you were bothered about me leaving."

Blair is silent, taking this in.

"Always figured you'd want to make a clean start of it. That's why I never contacted you."

"You put a note on my pillow that said 'see you later.' How could that not bother me?"

"I know that was shitty, but I didn't have a lot of options."

"You could have told me to my face that you were leaving."

"You wouldn't let me."

Blair sighs. "Give me a break, that's the best you can do?"

"I tried to talk to you, but every time, you shut me down. Went all weepy."

Blair closes her eyes and thinks back to that unhappy time, the most unhappy time of her life. She was weepy a lot. "I don't want to talk about this."

Road exhales. She thinks he's going to say more, and she waits for it. But he doesn't and is quiet instead. And eventually, she hears it.

The deep, even breathing of Road's sleep.

Chapter Six

Reasons Tori Is Your Best Friend

1. She's the kindest and kookiest person you've ever met.
2. She's loyal to a fault.
3. She never judges your obsession with her brother.

"YOU HAVE TO talk some sense into him," Blair tells Tori. "He's your brother. I think he'll listen to you."

Tori shakes her head. "No way, José. I love you both, and I'm not getting in the middle of this. I'm Switzerland."

Blair is at Tori's house. She came over during her lunch break, hoping maybe Tori could figure out a way to convince Road to leave. "I don't want him staying with me, but he kept my house key and it's like he's moved in or something."

She thinks back to how she left Road sleeping in her bed this morning with Mr. Maurice. She was tempted to wake him, force him to keep baker's hours. But as she watched Road's face so peaceful in sleep, she didn't have the heart.

Instead, she stood there, gazing her fill. It was a rare opportunity to be allowed to look at Road as much as she wanted, and she's embarrassed to admit she took it. Even when they were living together years ago, she didn't have the chance because they slept in separate bedrooms. Watching him this morning, she was tempted to pull the duvet down a little, see even more of him, but that might have woken him up. Plus, she worried she was crossing a line already and getting all stalkerish.

If only he would leave and end this torment! *Then I can have my life back. The one that doesn't include Road.*

"Why don't you just give him Isadora? That's all he wants, and then he'll go." Tori is shaking out some treats for her cats. They're mewing and rubbing against her. The boys are waiting patiently, too, since they know they're next.

"You're seriously going to ask me that? You know what I've put into her. I love that car."

Tori sighs. "I know. And she's amazing, but Uncle Lance gave Isadora to Road for his sixteenth birthday."

"So what?"

"Uncle Lance was the closest to a dad either of us ever had. Road is never going to give up that car."

Blair goes silent at this. Uncle Lance was their mom's brother, and it's true he was a good guy. Rough around the edges, but still all right from everything she remembers. Unfortunately, he died about ten years ago. She knows Road always looked up to him as a kid. "You think Road has an emotional attachment to Isadora?"

"Of course he does."

"I don't believe it. Why did he abandon her then?" Blair shakes her head. "No, I think he wants to sell her."

Tori laughs. "That's silly."

"It's not. He probably needs the money."

"He doesn't need the money."

Blair is watching Tori as she finishes giving all the animals their snacks and goes over to wash her hands in the sink. Warrant's "Cherry Pie" is playing on the stereo from one of Tori's endless hair band playlists.

Blair waits for her to come back over and figures it's probably time to enlighten Tori about some things. "Do you know what Road does for a living?"

Tori dries her hands with a paper towel. "Of course."

Blair's eyebrows shoot up, and she has to admit she's surprised. "And it doesn't bother you?"

"Not at all. I'm proud of him."

"Proud?" Blair nearly chokes. "How can you be proud of something like that?"

Tori flops down next to her on the couch and puts her feet on the coffee table. Her toenails are painted red with a white daisy on each big toe. "We're all proud of Road. The whole family."

Blair takes this in. She's starting to get an uneasy feeling. Road's family is kind of crazy, but she never thought they were *this* crazy. "Tori, he could get into a lot of trouble for what he's doing."

"Why?"

"Because," Blair lowers her voice, "it's illegal."

This gives Tori pause. "What exactly did Road tell you he does for a living?"

"He hasn't told me in so many words, but I figured it out. And he didn't deny it when I asked." She lowers her voice again. "I know he's smuggling drugs."

Tori studies her for a second and then bursts out laughing. "Blair! How could you of all people fall for that?" She's still laughing and shaking her head. "My brother is such a goof."

"It's true."

"No, it isn't."

"He didn't deny it."

"Road is not a drug smuggler! He's a writer and a travel blogger."

Blair blinks. "What are you talking about?"

Tori sighs. "I never told you because you didn't want to hear about him, but Road wrote a book that's become a bestseller on Amazon."

"He did? Road writes?"

"It came out about six months ago. It's based on some of the stuff he wrote for his travel blog."

Blair's head is spinning as she tries to take this in. "Are you serious?"

"Totally serious. His blog gets like a zillion hits a day. Plus, he's working on a second book."

"How is this possible? I'm completely stunned!"

Tori laughs. "I know it's a lot to take in, but that's why we're so proud of him."

"I can't believe you never told me any of this."

"I wanted to, but you were so adamant about not discussing him, and I didn't want to upset you."

Blair lets out her breath. "I feel seriously stupid."

Tori smiles sheepishly. "He's a really good writer." She pats Blair's leg. "You should read some of his stuff, especially his book. It's called *Edge of Zen*, the same as his blog. I bet you'd like it."

Blair shakes her head in disbelief. All this time, Road let her think he was doing something illegal.

That jerk!

BACK AT THE bakery, Blair still tries to recover from her shock. Road is a successful writer and blogger? Once again, she feels like an idiot. He must have been laughing behind her back this whole time. She was tempted to download his book, but decides not to. Forget it. *Who cares if it's any good? He can burn in hell!*

No wonder he didn't worry about her calling the police last night. Why should he?

What's ironic is that she should be relieved. Relieved about all of it. Relieved that he's not smuggling drugs or doing something illegal.

Blair brushes a stray hair off her face with the back of her hand as she adds the final Swiss dots to the cake she's working on. Finally, she steps back to inspect it for symmetry. Looking at it from all sides, she's satisfied enough to take her gloves off. Most people would say her cakes look perfect, and her brides are typically thrilled, but most of the time all she can see are the flaws. So instead, she imagines the couple who'll be eating this cake on Saturday. All the joy and happiness they'll be sharing with their families. It's a good feeling to be a part of that.

When she gets home late that afternoon, her silver Honda is in its usual parking spot and for once, she's glad to see it. She figures Road must be upstairs.

Blair slams the front door shut behind her when she arrives and throws her purse on the couch. He's not sitting in the living area, but it doesn't take her long to find him in her second bedroom, the one she's been planning to convert into an office, only it looks like he's already done the job for her.

"What's all this?" Her mouth drops open. There's a brand new desk and office chair where Road is currently sitting.

He glances up at her. "I'm turning this into my office."

"*What?*" Her eyes bug out. "Who gave you permission to do *that?*"

"You already had a filing cabinet and a bookcase in here. Figured this was your plan all along."

Blair walks closer and puts her hand on the wooden desk. *It's a nice one, but this is crazy.* "I can't believe you bought furniture!"

"Needed a desk, babe."

There are two computers open in front of him and he's fiddling with some wires and a box that looks like a router. She also spots a new printer/fax machine in the corner. She's so stunned, she can't even speak, just watches the top of his blond head.

Finally, she finds her voice. "You're a real jerk, you know that?"

"Look, it's just some furniture. Easy enough to take with me when I leave."

"This is quite the drug smuggling operation you've got here."

Road chuckles, still fiddling with the wires. "Yeah, I know. Tori called me."

"How could you let me think that?"

"The better question is how could you think it to begin with?" He gives her a look. "Seriously, Blair."

"Don't turn this around!"

"You had me convicted and sentenced without a single shred of evidence. Quite the hanging judge, aren't you?" He chuckles some more.

"That's not true. I'll bet you had a great time laughing behind my back, didn't you?"

"Wasn't like that."

"Yes, it was."

He shakes his head. "Shouldn't you be relieved? Or are you pissed that I'm not smuggling drugs?"

"I'm pissed because you lied to me!"

"No, never lied. You made assumptions, and I admit I had a little fun with it."

"And what about that list I created?" She's mortified thinking about her 'How to help Road get back on track with his life' list. "That must have been really fun for you. I look like a total idiot!"

"I thought that list was real sweet."

"You should have told me the truth right away. You're a liar!"

"Hey, lighten up, all right?"

"Lighten up? That's all you have to say?"

He looks as if he's pretending to think it over. "In fact, wasn't that already on one of your lists somewhere?"

She grits her teeth. "I know what my next list is going to be. All the reasons why I'm never reading your stupid book. Ever! And I don't care about your blog, either!"

Blair spins on her heel and marches out of the room. She can hear Road behind her saying, "Babe."

"And stop calling me babe!" she yells, halfway down the hall. "I am *not* your babe!"

Blair goes into the kitchen and starts slamming things around as she makes herself a tomato sandwich. Right away, she notices he's bought more groceries. There's fruit in the fridge and three boxes of cereal on the counter—healthy brands that she surprisingly approves of. She moves them to the cabinet where they belong and lines the boxes up evenly.

She takes her sandwich over to the couch and eats, still fuming. It's all been too much for her. Road showing up after all this time. The ways he's stirred up all these old feelings, feelings she thought she'd conquered. Memories of things she'd rather forget. *I thought I was over him. Over all of that.* Not to mention the way he's trying to take Isadora away from her. *Jerk!* She should have known that when he left her, he'd land on his feet.

He always does.

After she eats, Blair soaks in the tub for a while and decides she's sleeping on the couch tonight. Three nights without sleep is too much, and her thinking is muddled from exhaustion.

When she gets down all the sheets and pulls the hideaway bed out from the couch, Road wanders into the living room, eating a bowl of cereal.

“What are you doing? Told you my back can’t take sleeping on that couch.”

She gives a haughty sniff. “Don’t worry, it’s for *me*.”

His brows go up and he seems at a loss for words. Apparently, this was a maneuver on her part he hadn’t predicted. “You are *not* sleeping on this couch, princess.”

“Yes, I am.”

“No. You are not.”

She turns toward him and smiles without humor. “Watch me.”

He remains silent, brooding, as she continues to make the bed. She’s wearing her oversized T-shirt and shorts again and can feel his eyes on her, but ignores him.

Eventually, he disappears into the bathroom, and Blair grabs something to read and settles into the sofa bed. She’s never slept out here before, but decides it’s quite comfortable.

NATHAN TAKES A long hot shower. Usually, he takes short ones, but tonight he wants to escape, wants to let his frustration run down the drain.

Swear to God, in some ways, I’ll never understand women.

Blair steals his car and accuses him of smuggling drugs, yet sees herself as the one being wronged here.

What the hell is she so pissed about?

He can’t believe how stubborn she’s being about Isadora, and he’ll be damned if he can figure out why. He was sure she would have given in by now, as soon as she saw he wasn’t leaving without his car, but her tenacity has surprised him. In a weird way, he even likes it. Likes seeing her stand up for herself, even if it is misguided. Somewhere over the last five years, the little mouse he left behind has turned into a lioness.

He puts his hands on the wall and lets hot water run down his back.

And then there are those little shorts she wears to bed. *Christ.* He was too out of it the first couple of nights to pay much attention, but he’s paying attention now.

Too much attention.

He had trouble falling asleep last night thinking about those pale, smooth legs. She has a redhead’s coloring, and he’s always found himself partial to it.

He wonders if she’s telling the truth about not sleeping with that guy who called. No way is that dude her boyfriend, unless he’s an idiot. No guy is going to let a woman like that out of his sight for long.

She’s not for me, though.

Blair deserves better than him and always has. Even with everything he has going on now, she deserves some guy in a suit who's going to buy her a big house and let her fill it with kids. She's not meant to be with the likes of him and all of his crazy family, who, if he's honest, are nothing but a bunch of rowdy assholes.

Nathan eventually turns the water off and towel dries himself, throwing on a shirt and a pair of sweat pants. He doesn't own any pajamas, since he usually sleeps naked.

He goes out to find Blair on the couch reading a magazine.

Those pretty hazel eyes flash up at him. She's wearing that haughty expression again. Princess Blair. He started calling her that in high school because even though she was mostly shy, she always had that royal look about her. Plus, she came from the right side of the tracks and was definitely off-limits.

He sits next to her on the sofa bed.

"Go away, Road."

"Looks like we're having our first marital tiff."

She stares at her magazine, but he can see the smile tugging on her mouth. "Did you really just use the word 'tiff'?"

"Sadly, I did. See what you've brought me to?"

She smiles, but keeps reading her magazine.

He sighs. "Can't let you sleep out here, Blair."

"It's not up to you."

"Guess I'll be staying out here, too, then."

She puts the magazine down. "What is it with you? Can't you just leave me alone? I'm exhausted, and I'd like to get some sleep finally."

"What kind of asshole would I be if I let you sleep out here while I take your bed?"

"Since when do you care about being an asshole?"

"I care. Believe it or not."

"Yeah, right."

She picks up her magazine again and he's quiet, reflecting on her words. "What do you mean 'get some sleep finally'? Aren't you sleeping?"

"If you must know, I'm not."

Nathan takes this in. He's prone to insomnia himself, but has to admit he's slept like a baby since he's been here, despite all the static she's given him. With surprise, he realizes there's something about Blair he finds relaxing.

"How can I help?" He shifts position on the bed so his arm is stretched out and he's more comfortable.

Her eyes widen at his question. "You want to help me sleep?"

"Sure. I have some melatonin in my bag. Do you want to try that? "

She seems embarrassed, and her cheeks are suddenly turning pink. He's momentarily confused by her reaction, but then understanding dawns on him and he grins. "Got to say, princess, that dude you've been claiming is your boyfriend needs lessons or something."

That pretty blush on her cheeks only deepens. He reflects back to how that list of hers said she wanted more sex.

"How long has it been for you, anyway?" he asks, curious.

She blinks at him, but doesn't look away. "You can't ask me that."

"Why not?"

"Because it's personal."

"Tell me anyway."

"I don't think so."

He softens his voice. "Come on, it's just the two of us here." Nathan doesn't know why he's pushing it. Knows he shouldn't. He needs to keep his hands off Blair. *I mean, shit, look at what happened the last time I couldn't keep my hands off her.*

She licks her lips, looking nervous, and it's turning him on. Way too much. "Almost a year," she whispers. "Eleven months."

He nods. "That's a long time."

"How long has it been for you?"

"Less than eleven months."

Blair laughs and it goes straight to his dick. That laugh of hers. He wishes he could pull the covers off her, run his hand over those pale, smooth legs. They only slept together that one time, and he doesn't remember it well, but what he does remember was good.

"You've probably never gone that long, have you?" she asks.

"No."

She smiles. "You don't even have to think about it?"

He consider her words. For some reason, women have always liked him. He's not even sure why. Figures it's mostly his size. He's tall and most women seem to like that, though a few women have told him it was his face. They said he had a pretty face, but he didn't know what to make of that.

"Nope, don't even have to think about it," he admits.

"What's the longest you've ever gone without it?"

"I don't know. Probably six months."

She looks annoyed suddenly.

"What?"

"Six months? That's it?"

Ironically, he's talking about when they got married. They never had sex even once during their short time as a married couple. Too many complications interfering. He never cheated on her, though. "It's different for me. I'm a guy."

"You think women don't want sex?"

"Course they do. I'm not saying that. Just not sure if they need it like men do."

Blair gives him a scornful look. "Give me a break. Guys are always saying that."

"Because there's truth in it."

She bites her lip and looks down. He studies her hair, the rich color. Imagines his hands in it, how it would feel brushing against his body. Her shoulders are slender. She's finely made. Elegant. He remembers that much from the one night they were together.

He takes a deep breath and exhales. His erection isn't going anywhere, and he knows what he has to do. "I'll take the couch, Blair. You go on and sleep in the bed."

She looks up at him surprise. "Really? What about your back?"

"I'll live."

Chapter Seven

Stages of Your Unrequited Love for Road

1. You're in love with him, but he doesn't know you're alive.
2. You're in love with him, he knows you're alive, but he doesn't care.
3. You're in love with him, he knows you're alive, he cares sort of, but he doesn't love you back. (And let's face it, he never will.)

BY SATURDAY MORNING, Blair wakes up feeling human enough to go for a run. She slips into a pair of track shorts and a sweatshirt, pulling her hair back into a ponytail.

It's early morning and few people are out this time of day, but she enjoys the fresh air and the low hum of the city waking up. She follows her usual route down by the water. This part of town is generally safe, though she still carries a small can of pepper spray in her pocket. She took boxing classes long enough to learn some defensive moves, and figures she could fight off an assailant if she had to. Not that she's ever had to. *Thank God*. It's good to be prepared, though.

When she gets back from her run, she heads into the kitchen to start coffee, since Saturday is her biggest delivery day and she has five cakes to get out.

Road is still asleep on the sofa bed, and she can't resist walking quietly over to look at him.

Lying on his back, he has one hand on his chest while the other drifts off to his side. He looks younger when he's asleep and reminds her of when they were in high school. He usually wears a T-shirt to bed but is currently shirtless, so he must have pulled it off during the night.

Blair knows she should walk away, should force herself to go back into the kitchen, but somehow can't stop her eyes from drifting over his naked torso. His body is beautiful. She's always thought so. Broad-shouldered with hard muscle beneath all that smooth skin, Road is healthy and strong and he looks it.

Studying the new ink on his chest, she wonders what the swirling letters say. Her eyes roam lower to his flat stomach. There's a happy trail with light brown hair running from his belly button into the top of his shorts.

She wants to touch him. Wants to run her hands everywhere. And for a moment, the desire is so intense she considers it, seriously wonders what he'd do. Would he push her away or welcome her into his bed?

But then she stops that line of thought. She already knows what he'd do. He's made it clear.

He doesn't want me.

"What are you doing?"

Blair sucks in her breath as her eyes flash to Road's face, mortified to discover he's awake. "Nothing!"

"Were you watching me sleep?"

"Of course not!"

"Because that's what it looked like."

"I wasn't."

Road nods slowly then chuckles. "Okay, good. 'Cause that would be kind of creepy."

"I wasn't watching you sleep. I was checking to see if you were up, that's all . . . and then I noticed your tattoos. You didn't have that one before," she motions, "above your heart. I don't remember it."

"No, got it in India."

"What does it say?"

He doesn't answer her, though, and instead takes in her shorts, his eyes drifting lower to her legs.

"What are you doing up early on a Saturday?" he asks.

"I work. It's my biggest delivery day."

"Yeah? Didn't know that."

"Are you planning to go anywhere today?"

"Might hit the gym later, plus we got that thing at my mom's tonight."

"I'm not going to your mom's party." She knows Tori won't be happy about this, but at least she'll get out of going to the gallery event.

Road's expression goes flat and she senses he's bothered, though she can't imagine why. "Suit yourself."

"I need to take the Honda into work, that's why I'm asking if you're going anywhere."

Their delivery van is parked behind the bakery and she usually parks right next to it, except she doesn't like to leave Isadora there all day on a

Saturday. There are fewer people around, and she worries someone might break into her or even steal her.

There's a crafty expression on Road's face. "Just leave Isadora's keys with me and I'll drive her instead."

"You know I'm not doing that."

Road shakes his head and lets out an annoyed breath. "This situation is unbelievable."

"I could drop you off somewhere," she offers.

"Forget it. I'll figure something out."

Blair nods and goes back into the kitchen to start on coffee. When her cell phone rings, she snatches it off the counter. Phone calls this early are never good news. She sees that it's Ginger.

"What's wrong?"

"I fell down the stairs this morning and sprained my ankle."

"Are you okay?"

Ginger sighs. "I'm okay, but I can't do deliveries today. I'm so sorry."

Blair lets out a breath. "Of course not, I understand. I'll try Carlos, hopefully he can help."

"Carlos is in Portland," Ginger reminds her.

That's right. *Darn it.* He went down there on vacation for a few days with his boyfriend. "Let me call Natalie," Blair tells her. "I'm sure we'll figure something out. Don't worry about it. Just go ice your foot."

They hang up and Blair calls Natalie. She's at the bakery working a half day, since they've started keeping La Dolce Vita open on weekends. Blair explains the situation, but unfortunately Natalie can't leave since she's the only baker there.

"What about Lindsay? Should I try her?" Lindsay is Natalie's younger sister. She's an artist, but occasionally helps out when they need someone. Blair has become pretty good friends with her.

"She's already coming in today to fill in for that new barista who quit. Try Zoe," Natalie suggests. "See if she can do it." Zoe is the other baker they hired full-time.

Blair calls Zoe's phone, but there's no answer. Unfortunately, Zoe is kind of a space cadet and probably doesn't even have her phone with her or turned on.

It figures.

Blair tries to think. She's getting a little panicky, since she can't exactly deliver wedding cakes all by herself. She's on the verge of calling Tori or even her parents to see if they can help when Road wanders into the kitchen.

He takes in her panicked expression. "What's wrong?"

She looks at him. He put his shirt back on, she notices. And then it hits her. The perfect solution. *Although it means I'll be stuck with Road all day.*

Maybe it's not such a good idea, but then it's not like she has much choice.

Blair explains to him what's happening.

"All you need is someone to help you deliver wedding cakes?"

She nods. "Some of them are big and heavy. That's why I can't do it alone."

"So, I'll be the muscle?"

"Basically."

He grins. "No problem."

"Really?"

"Course, just tell me what you want me to do."

"Okay, great." She takes a deep breath and lets it out. She has to admit she's relieved. "Do you have anything nice to wear, by chance?"

He shakes his head. "Sorry, all I have with me are jeans. Is that going to matter?"

"It's just that these are weddings, so everyone is dressed up. But don't worry about it." She usually likes to dress up a little for deliveries, but knows it's not necessary.

Blair takes a quick shower and makes coffee for both of them while Road gets ready. She brings her coffee with her into the bedroom to sip. After staring at her color-coordinated closet, she pulls out a teal green dress. It's classy, but with a sweetheart neckline that shows a hint of cleavage. She's not dressing for Road, but has to admit she chose it because she knows it's flattering. She'll have to wear her white chef's coat over it for her deliveries anyway. Standing in front of the mirror, she pulls her hair back into a chignon, to keep it out of the way, but leaves a few tendrils out in front. She's careful with her makeup, finishes it with peach lip gloss then slips into her crystal Jimmy Choo platform pumps. She doesn't usually wear them for deliveries, but she can't resist today. The shoes are so wonderful, she sits on her bed and takes a couple of selfies of her feet in them from different angles.

"What are you doing?" Road asks, standing in her bedroom doorway, watching her.

Blair glances over at him, embarrassed to be caught. "Nothing."

"Taking pictures of your feet?"

"Sort of. It's just that I love these shoes."

He chuckles. "Let me guess, these are the ones you'd save along with Mr. Maurice in a fire."

"Yes, but if you'll remember, Mr. Maurice came first."

When she gets up from the bed and walks toward him, his eyes travel the length of her with approval. "Damn, babe, this what you always wear to deliver cakes?"

"Of course."

"Nice."

She tries to hide her smile. *So what if I'm not Skank Factor X?*

"Thanks, you look nice, too." Road is wearing jeans and a white button-down shirt. In truth, he looks mouth-wateringly hot. She can barely pull her eyes away. His shirt cuffs are rolled up to reveal his muscular forearms, and the white shirt looks sexy. As usual, his thick, blond hair is parted in the center, tucked behind his ears.

They head out to the Honda where Road insists on driving, not that she cares. It gives her a chance to call Natalie and update her on the situation.

When they arrive at La Dolce Vita, Blair instructs Road on where to park and they go in through the back entrance, where the scent of fresh pastries surrounds them. Natalie has just pulled out black-bottom cupcakes. They have a smaller menu on the weekends and offer sweet breads and muffins, along with these crazy-delicious cupcakes Natalie came up with recently.

"I'm glad to see you found someone who can help." Natalie comes over, wiping her hands on her apron. "It's nice to meet you, Road."

"Same here." Road shakes her hand.

"Grab a cupcake if you like."

Blair can see him looking around the bakery, taking everything in. And for a moment, she's filled with pride. She and Natalie have created a solid business, and she enjoys showing it off to him.

Lindsay, Natalie's gorgeous younger sister, comes in from the front carrying an empty baking tray. When she notices them standing together, she walks over and puts the tray down by the sink.

Blair introduces her and can see Road looking at Lindsay. It occurs to Blair that Lindsay is sort of Road's type. She's not Skank Factor X exactly, but Lindsay is sexy with an edge.

"So, you're the infamous Road," Lindsay says, tossing her wavy brown curls over her shoulder.

He chuckles. "Didn't realize I was 'infamous.'"

"Oh, you are, trust me."

And that's when Blair realizes Lindsay isn't joking.

"Anyone who abandons my girl Blair is infamous and a whole lot of other choice words I'm too polite to use at the moment."

"Huh?" Road is taken aback.

"Uh, Lindsay, Road is here helping me deliver wedding cakes," Blair says quickly. "I was desperate, and he offered to pitch in."

"Sound like it's the least he could do."

Blair doesn't know what to say. In truth, she's touched that Lindsay wants to defend her. She glances over at Natalie for help, but she just sips her latte and watches Road with interest.

It figures.

There's something unusual about the two sisters, and the way they grew up, that Blair doesn't entirely understand. They're fierce and loyal, though, and once they accept you into their circle, that's it. They have your back. It was a quality Blair admired, and it made Natalie a business partner she trusted.

"Look, I don't even know you," Road tells Lindsay, still confused by her hostility.

"Doesn't matter. I know what you did to Blair, and that tells me all I need to know about *you*."

Road glances at Blair with surprise.

Blair is tempted to fill the awkward silence that has developed, but the sisters have influenced her, and she's curious to see Road's reaction now, too.

He studies the women, his laser focus turned on as all three of them take each other's measure.

Finally, Road nods slowly. "Not much I can say to that charge, since that's between Blair and me." His eyes flash over to Blair. "But I'm glad to see she has friends who care about her so much."

The sisters glance at each other. She gets the feeling Road has passed their little test, but that he still has a long way to go to win their approval. Not that it matters. She plans to divorce him as soon as possible, and then he'll be out of her life forever. She'll finally be free. Or so she hopes.

Blair glances at her phone and sees the time. They should start loading up the van. "Come on, the fridge is over this way," she tells Road. "We should get going."

He follows her to their big, walk-in refrigerator while she grabs her notebook with all the paperwork for each cake. Their first wedding is over in Ballard, and the cake is a brown and white stacked hatbox covered with edible ribbons and bows.

She points it out to him and shows him the large board they'll use to carry it on.

"You made this cake?"

She nods, flipping through her notebook. "I made all the wedding cakes in here."

"Seriously? You're an artist."

"I guess so."

He gives her a strange look as his eyes wander the fridge. "Have to admit, I don't know much about wedding cakes, but anyone can see these are amazing."

After loading the cake into the refrigerated van, Road wants to drive, but she's nervous. "You have to drive slow and easy. I can't have my cake getting knocked around in the back."

"You think I can't handle it?"

"I don't know, can you?" Road wasn't exactly a slow grandma kind of driver, though that's what she needs right now.

He takes the keys from her hand. "I got this, princess."

She gives in and goes to sit in the back so she can spot the cake.

They spend the next few hours picking up each cake from the bakery and delivering it to its final destination. Turns out, his driving is perfect. And she has to admit, Road is a huge help. She would never have been able to do this without him.

"Thank you so much," she tells him as they're driving to their last wedding. She's sitting in front with him, since the last cake is boxed and will be set on stands instead of being tiered. "I really appreciate it."

"No problem."

She glances down at her gorgeous shoes and since she's already holding her phone, decides to take a few more selfies of them. Road chuckles, watching her.

"Can tell you this much, you'd never catch a guy taking pictures of his feet, no matter what kind of shoes he's wearing."

When they drop the cake off, the bride, Rachel, comes over and gives Blair a hug. "Everything looks beautiful. I love it. You have to stay and join us. Come celebrate!"

It's always fun to be around people after they've just gotten married, with all the excitement in the air, but she rarely stays at any reception for long. "I wish I could," Blair tells her. "But it's been a busy day, and we should be heading back."

Rachel nods, but her eyes aren't on Blair anymore. Instead, they're following Road as he carries stuff out to the van. "Who's that? Did you guys hire a new baker?"

"No, that's my husband." *My God!* Blair stops breathing. *Where did that come from?* She's shocked herself and can't believe she said those words, much less the easy way they rolled off her tongue.

Rachel grins. "He's cute! I didn't even know you were married."

Blair tries to smile. "He's just helping out for today."

AS THEY DRIVE back to the condo, Road keeps glancing over at her.

"What?" she finally says. "Why do you keep looking at me?"

"Did you a big favor today, right?"

"Yes, I already told you that."

"A *very* big favor?"

And then Blair sees where he's going with this. "Forget it, I am not handing over Isadora's keys. Don't get me wrong, I appreciate your help, but I'm not giving you my car."

"*Your* car?" He gives her an incredulous look.

"Okay, our car. How's that?"

"Sounds like you have pronoun confusion, babe. Isadora belongs to the person with his name on her title."

Blair doesn't respond. She should probably feel guilty, but doesn't. He abandoned Isadora.

Road is drumming his fingers on the steering wheel. "Okay, how about this? Come with me to my mom's party tonight."

She frowns. "Why?"

"Because I just did you a big favor, and it's the least you could do."

"No, I mean why do you want me to come at all?"

"You're my wife, and I want you there."

She squirms uncomfortably, thinking about how she just told someone Road was her husband. Only she did it for real. "We both know that isn't true. What's the actual reason?"

Road pulls up to the gate in front of her parking garage and presses the button so it will lift. "A lot of women show up at these parties."

"And?"

"And I'd rather not deal with them."

"Since when don't you like women?"

He grins. "Babe, I *love* women, but ever since word got out that I'm doing all right, they've been coming out of the woodwork at me. You get my meaning?"

"I guess. Are you saying women are throwing themselves at you?"

"Basically, yeah."

"Some men would like that."

"I know, but I just don't need that kind of hassle right now."

Blair chews on this. He doesn't want that kind of hassle? Is he talking about Skank Factor X? She doubts it. Doubts it very much. On the other hand, he *did* do her a big favor today. "All right, fine. I'll come to the party tonight."

Once inside, Blair slips into a pair of jeans and a green striped shirt. She wears her hair down, but straightens it with the blow dryer, trying to tame her curls.

When she goes to find Road, he's on his computer in her second bedroom that he's turned into an office. He looks annoyingly at home sitting at his desk with the two laptops open in front of him. It's like he owns the place. "I wouldn't get too comfortable in here if I were you."

He doesn't even bother looking up. "What's your damage?"

"My damage?" Blair scoffs. "You've moved in and taken over half of my home! I mean, just look at all this stuff." She waves her hand at his desk, the computers, the tangle of wires, the fax machine in the corner. Suddenly, she notices the wall behind him. "My *God*, you've even hung pictures on the wall!" She stares in amazement at the framed photos. They're mostly city shots, *quite nice actually*, but still. "This is unbelievable."

"Told you I'd take it all with me when I leave."

She studies his blond head, the intent expression on his face, and the fast click of his fingers on the keyboard. In some ways, none of this should surprise her. Road has always been bold.

"You better," she mutters. "Or you might find I've sold all of it out from under your smug butt."

He glances up at her, a grin pulling on his mouth.

"I'm going to the store," she says. "That's what I came in here to tell you. We should bring something to your mom's.

"Let's just grab something on the way." He focuses on his computer. "You don't need to make a separate trip."

"I need to pick up a few things anyway."

He stops typing and gives her his full attention. "Which car are you taking?"

"Isadora, why?"

"Nothing." His expression goes lazy, and she can tell he's trying to look innocent. "Just curious."

Blair goes silent. She doesn't like that expression, knows he's scheming something.

She drives to the store and picks up a few groceries along with a bottle of white wine—remembering how Lori prefers white—and some chips and salsa for the party.

When she gets back to her condo, Road is still on his computer, but comes out as she's putting the groceries away.

"Look, Blair, this is enough. You need to give me the keys to my car. I'm driving Isadora to my mom's tonight."

She ignores him, continuing with the groceries.

"You hear me?"

"Yes, but you already know what I'm going to say."

Road watches her. Blair senses his frustration building, how he's wrestling with something, but she doesn't know what it could be. She folds the shopping bags up to put them in the recycle bin.

Finally, he lets his breath out. "Sorry, babe, but this ends now."

"What do you mean?"

And then, before she can stop him, he grabs her purse off the kitchen chair and strides into the living room with it.

"Hey! What do you think you're doing?"

"Taking back my property, that's what."

"You can't just go through my purse!"

She goes after him, but he's already dumped the entire contents out on the couch.

"Stop it!"

When he finds her key ring with a big cursive 'B' on it, there's a triumphant grin on his face.

"Give those back to me!"

"Sorry, princess. You played a good game. Even admire your tenacity, but this game is officially over." He sifts through her key ring then frowns. "What the hell?"

Blair tries to hide the smile on her face. Thank God she took precautions. She knew he was up to something.

Road's turns on her. "Where are they?"

"I'm sorry, but that's privileged information."

He tosses her keys on the couch and strides back over to the kitchen.

Blair shoves everything back into her purse, ignoring the impulse to organize it, figuring she'll do it later. She puts her purse back onto the chair and watches as Road methodically searches each kitchen drawer.

"You just drove her, so the keys have to be here somewhere," he mutters.

Blair stands, leaning against the chair. She doesn't say anything as he continues his search. After prowling through the final cabinet, his eyes flash back to her. They narrow.

"Empty your pockets."

Blair lets go of the chair. "I'm not emptying my pockets."

"You have something to hide?"

"No."

He starts coming toward her and Blair backs away. Road is big and formidable when he wants to be. She scoots to the other side of the couch.

He grins. "The keys are in your pocket. I know they are."

"No, they aren't."

"Don't believe you. Come over here and show me."

"I don't think so."

Road moves toward her again and Blair circles back around to the kitchen. She laughs. "The keys are not in my pants pockets. I swear!"

He doesn't appear to be listening anymore, though, and is intent on reaching her instead.

And that's when Blair decides to run.

She's not even sure what possesses her to do it. Her only plan is to get to the bathroom at the end of the hall, and she almost makes it, too, but Road is fast. He's right on her heels and before she can even reach the bathroom door, his muscular arm swoops around her waist.

"Let go!" she squeals with laughter.

"Don't worry, princess. This won't hurt a bit." He struggles with her as she pushes at his arm. "Just give me what's mine and we're good." Road holds Blair tight against him, trying to reach into her jeans pocket.

"I told you, I don't have . . . them." She manages to push his hand away and nearly manages to squirm out of the arm that has her captured.

"Hold still," he says, laughing as he tries to maintain his grip on her and search her pockets at the same time. "Christ, you're stronger than you look."

Blair smiles to herself. She's tempted to use some of the defensive moves she's learned from her boxing class on him, but those involve foot-stomping and ball-kneeing, and despite everything, she doesn't actually want to injure Road.

He's still trying to stick his fingers in her pockets without much success, when abruptly he changes tactics. Instead of holding her from behind, he spins her around. Before she knows it, Blair's back is pressed against the wall, while her front is pressed against Road as he holds her captive with his large body.

His fingers snake into both her front pockets at the same time now. "Thought you could mess with me, but you're playing in the big leagues now."

Blair can't help her scoff of laughter as his hands continue their exploration. She feels them slide to her rear, checking the pockets in back.

Her eyes fall shut. She's not sure when she decides to give in and stop fighting him.

His hands are on her ass, his smoky scent surrounds her and for a long moment, she lets herself enjoy it. The solid feel of him pressed against her.

Blair tilts her head to look up at him. The hall is dim, but she can see the exact moment when he realizes all her pockets are empty. The perplexed expression on his handsome face.

"I'll be damned," he mutters.

"I told you I don't have the keys," she says, breathless. "You should have believed me."

His eyes cut down to hers. "Why did you run?"

"Because you were chasing me."

"No." He shakes his head. "You ran first."

Blair doesn't say anything to this. Why did she run? Why didn't she just show him her pockets were empty?

Maybe it's because she wanted Road to chase her, to make the effort.

For once.

Her breath catches. When she meets his gaze this time, she's aware of his hands still on her ass as she grips his muscular forearms. Road shifts position, pulls back, but not all the way. His body still touching hers, his hands slide up her sides so they're resting on her hips.

Excitement skitters through her.

"Why did you run?" he asks again, but this time his voice is soft, and there's a note in it she recognizes. A seductive note.

And that's when it all comes back to her, like a song she once knew. The melody of Road. She remembers being with him, remembers *it*. Not the tormenting dreams, but the actual night they spent together five years ago.

She hasn't thought of it in years, wouldn't allow herself to think of it.

The memory washes over her like warm rain. The feel of his skin under her hands and the taste of his mouth on hers. It was indescribable at first, the heady thrill of touching Road. So powerful, the way he filled her senses. She'd wanted him so much it made her reckless and blind.

But she wasn't blind for long.

He was a surprise to her, but unfortunately, not in a good way. Because as it turned out, Road was not that great in bed.

In truth, he was terrible.

Granted, he'd been drinking whiskey all night, so she had to take that into consideration, but he was still a letdown. It was the only time she'd ever seen him drunk, though his drunken state was the reason they'd done it at all. Blair knew sleeping with her wasn't a choice he would have made if he were sober.

This was back when she was still roommates with Tori. Road showed up late one night, hammered. Drinking straight from a bottle of Jack Daniels.

"Princess," he said, standing on the front porch, grinning like a pirate.

"Road?" Blair was surprised to see him. "Is everything okay?"

"Guess you haven't heard."

"Heard what?"

He snorted. "Nothing. My sister around?"

"No, it's just me here."

He turned to go, but Blair stopped him. "Do you want to come inside for a little while?" He was obviously drunk, and she decided it was safer than sending him away.

He studied her for a few seconds then shrugged.

Blair figured he was probably looking for a place to crash-land anyway.

"Tell you one thing, they deserve each other," Road muttered as he made his way into the living room and flopped down on Tori's couch. "What do I care, right?"

"Who?"

"Gwen and Logan. Caught 'em in my bed together. Can you believe it? Screwing each other in my own damn bed!"

Logan was one of Road's best friends, and Gwen was Road's live-in girlfriend. Blair listened in silence as he ranted on about the two of them, too stunned to even speak. How could any woman be so dumb as to cheat on Road? It boggled her mind.

"Christ, why do I keep ending up with all these bitches?" Road muttered,

then took a swig from his bottle. "Need to change, need to find something better." His eyes flashed over to where she was sitting on the end of the couch. "Someone more like you. A good girl."

Blair studied his handsome face, his long, muscular body splayed out before her. Even drunk Road was incredibly hot.

He took another sip of whiskey, licked his lips, then put his head back and closed his eyes.

That's when her heart began to hammer, her breath unsteady because she knew what she was going to do. Saw opportunity where previously there was none. Saw how a path once dark and closed to her had lit up and was flashing a neon 'open' sign. Blair knew this was her chance to finally be with Road. Her one and only chance.

And she was going to take it.

Chapter Eight

Reasons You Hate Parties At The Church House

1. The people are loud and crazy.

2. It's like a Skank Factor X convention.

3. The women are all in lust with Road.

NATHAN GRIPS THE steering wheel and listens with annoyance as the Honda's engine struggles with sixty-five on the interstate. *This car sounds like shit.* He decides he's taking it into Brody's and giving it a tune-up and oil change himself. *Hell, if things continue on the way they are, who knows how long I'll be driving this damn car.*

He glances over at Blair. She hasn't said much since the incident in the hall, and he can guess why. Wonders where she really hid Isadora's keys, if they were even in her condo at all. She could have put them anywhere. She's smart, smart enough that he never should have underestimated her.

Going to have to start bringing my A game to this situation.

Blair fiddles with the radio, and a whiff of perfume from her hair drifts his way. It smells clean and elegant, just like Blair herself. He likes it. Too much.

Nathan lets his breath out and thinks back to what happened upstairs. The feel of her soft curves pressed against him. Another thing he liked too much. He wonders how this is going to work with him staying there, if his willpower can possibly hold out.

He knows he should feel guilty invading Blair's space, and he does, but he also knows she's keeping something of his. That car is important to him, means something, and he's not leaving without it.

"Just pick one," he says in irritation as she keeps flipping from station to station on the radio. "Any station will do."

She shoots him a haughty look then continues changing stations. "I'll stop when I find something I enjoy, and not before then."

He chuckles to himself, amazed at how much she's changed from the shy Blair he used to know. Even back then, he'd suspected there was more to her than meets the eye. It was one of the reasons he'd offered to marry her.

Should have known it would end in disaster.

They'd only had the one night together, though that's all it took. In truth, he was so drunk he barely remembers it. He rarely drank like that, but it had been tough finding out two people he trusted were sticking a knife in his back.

He thinks about Blair in the hallway upstairs again, their bodies touching just right, until he'd finally come to his senses and pulled away. And then he thinks back to the night they had together years ago. Good girl Blair. He remembers wondering if she'd be shy in bed, but she wasn't at all. She took what she wanted from him, and seeing that side of her had made him think later how a marriage between them might work.

Not that they ever had a chance to find out.

A messy business. That's what it was, and he was sorry it went down the way it did. *Never wanted that.* He was ready to make a go of it, but it went bad right from the start, with Blair bleeding almost immediately after they took their vows at the courthouse. They spent their wedding night in the ER and their three-day honeymoon in the hospital before being sent home on bedrest.

He moved into the second bedroom of the house they'd just rented, while her family moved in to help care for Blair. He'd go to work at the garage early every morning and come home late every night feeling like a stranger, like he didn't belong.

But that wasn't the worst part.

And then there was the way they all looked at him—her whole tidy, upper-crust family, but especially her mom—like he was nothing but a piece of trash. Some lowlife scumbag. The scumbag who'd gotten their perfect good girl daughter pregnant. Didn't matter that he'd agreed to marry her. And what sucked was he knew they were right. He never should have slept with Blair. It was selfish and he wasn't thinking clearly, but deep down, he hoped some of it would rub off on him, too.

Some of that good girl magic.

They stuck it out for as long they could, but things never improved. Blair kept bleeding. Finally, she lost the baby. His child.

That was the worst part.

Nathan takes a deep breath and exhales.

It was a long time ago, and you can't hold onto those things. You have to let them go or they'll chew you up. He knows that better than anyone.

He didn't leave her right away and stuck it out for another month, but the writing was already on the wall. Scribbled there in ugly black marker. Blair barely said two words to him in a day, and her family glared at him with open hostility whenever he was around, so finally he stopped being around. Bought a plane ticket to a place that was as far away as he could go. India. And he'd always figured everyone was happier that way.

AS SOON AS they turn onto the street where Road and Tori grew up, Blair hears music. Loud music. It isn't until they're closer she recognizes AC/DC's "Highway to Hell."

For someone who was never into heavy metal, she knows every single song. Of course, Tori loves heavy metal, but that's not why Blair knows them all.

There are cars parked all along the street and the driveway is lined with motorcycles. It looks like the party's been going for hours already. Of course, at the Church house, the party never really stops.

Road pulls the Honda beside the open garage onto a grassy area. Blair sees people standing out front on the porch with bottles in their hands, talking.

The house is a worn-down rambler, the last one on a dead-end street, surrounded by woods on two sides. Tori once told her how one of her mom's boyfriends had set up a still out there, making illegal moonshine. Compared to her own family, the Church's house seemed wildly exotic, and Blair sometimes felt like a foreign exchange student visiting Tori.

Blair always tells herself she would have been best friends with Tori no matter what, even if Road hadn't been her brother, even if he hadn't rocked her world that first day, because Tori was an amazing friend. But deep down, she can never be one hundred percent sure. Road's allure was too powerful. She knows it's one of the reasons she kept going back, lying to her parents, playing down the amount of partying that went on at that house, because if they'd known the truth, they never would have let her spend time there at all.

"Ready?"

Blair turns to find Road watching her. "I don't see Tori's van here. I hope she's coming."

He reaches for his door handle. "Wouldn't worry about that. She'll be here." He swings the door open.

They both get out and walk toward the house together. It's early evening, and the sun is starting to sink in the sky. Heads are turning their way.

Blair hears a loud shout then another as someone yells Road's name. Suddenly, Kiki is running toward them.

Kiki throws herself onto Road as she squeals with delight. "You're here!"

Blair smiles, watching the two of them. Kiki used to be pretty wild, but has toned it down quite a bit the past few years. Getting engaged seems to have helped calm her.

"Hey, freak!" Road laughs, hugging her back.

"Everybody's been waiting for you!" Kiki tells him after she untangles herself.

"That right?" he asks with a grin.

"Yes!" She grabs his arm and pulls him toward the house. Kiki turns and waves enthusiastically at Blair. "Hey, Blair! I'm glad you came!"

More people are coming toward them and before she knows it, they're surrounded by a crowd as they head toward the front door. People are shouting "Dude!" and "Roadster!" Some muscular guy with long, dark hair is hugging Road, and she sees it's his cousin, Brody, who helped her with Isadora.

"'Bout time you came back home, jackass!"

Road laughs. "Guess I missed being around a bunch of assholes!"

Everyone's laughing and talking at once, and then Lori is there. People step aside to let her through.

Lori grins at Road. Her blonde hair is pulled up at the sides, teased into a frizzy halo around her aging beauty-queen face. "Waited long enough to come see me, didn't you now?"

"Saving the best for last, is all."

She laughs. "Come here, you!" The two of them hug each other as people around them whoop and holler.

Blair forces a smile, but already feels uncomfortable and wishes Road hadn't talked her into coming. She isn't good at parties, and these are the worst kind. Without Tori at her side, she's just some weird, preppy chick who looks and feels like a square peg.

Mother and son pull apart. Standing next to each other, it's easy to see their resemblance. Lori's eyes are blue, though, not green. No one in Road's family seemed to share his remarkable eye color, and she'd once asked Tori if her dad had green eyes, but Tori said she didn't know.

"Blair!" Lori turns to her, smiling. "It's so good to see you, honey. How have you been?" They hug each other and when they pull apart, Blair smells the alcohol on Lori's breath. Lori's eyes are bloodshot and, if Blair had to guess, she'd say Lori's probably been drinking since this morning.

Garth, another worthless loser in a long line of the loser men Lori dated, is trying to talk to Road. Blair could never understand why Lori dated nothing but losers. Pictures of her pageant days proved she'd been a fresh-faced beauty, and even now she was still attractive. Although, all the partying had taken its toll, and there were deep lines etched around her eyes and mouth.

"I'm well, thank you," Blair says politely. Despite everything, Blair likes Lori. Lori has always been kind to her and had shared in her sadness about what happened years ago.

"Tori should be back soon," Lori tells her. "She had to leave and check in on one of her animals."

Blair nods in relief then holds up the grocery bag. "I brought some food and wine. Should I put it in the kitchen?"

"That'd be wonderful, hon."

Blair heads through the crowd of people. The house was built in the seventies and very little has been updated since then, so the kitchen still has avocado counters and chipped, white cabinets. Blair spent so much time here as a teenager it's almost endearingly familiar. There's already plenty of food laid out. She has to say one thing for Lori's friends. They can cook. The food is always rich, with plenty of heavy pasta salads and fried or barbecued chicken, but it's always delicious.

Blair dumps the chips in a big wooden bowl she finds in one of the cabinets and the salsa into a small soup bowl. She tries to arrange everything neatly on the table, cleaning up some of the mess people made, resisting the impulse to line things up perfectly.

She sticks the bottle of wine into a fridge that's already stuffed with more food and bottles. Then she goes through it and throws out stuff that's clearly gone bad.

Shifting things around, Blair notices a glass bowl of vodka gummy bears. She figures Tori brought them, since Tori likes whimsical stuff like this. She made vodka gummy worms for one of their girls' nights a few months back. Blair picks out a gummy from the bowl and puts it into her mouth, rewarded with a burst of sweet alcohol.

"What's that?"

Blair turns and is surprised to see Road standing behind her. She figured he'd still be out in the living room, hugging people and being affectionately called jackass by all his cousins.

"Vodka gummy bears. Tori's doing, I'm sure."

"Let me try one."

Blair reaches into the bowl and picks out a green gummy bear to hand to Road. He ignores her hand, though.

"Pop it in my mouth."

Blair hesitates. He leans in closer, opening his mouth for her, and she brings the gummy close to his lips and pushes it inside, her fingers brushing against him.

Road watches her with a mischievous grin, but when he starts to chew the gummy bear, his grin changes.

"Yuck!" He looks as offended as a kid who's been fed a piece of broccoli by mistake. "Gross!"

Blair laughs, watching with amusement as he goes to the sink and spits out the vodka gummy bear. He keeps spitting a few times, trying to get the taste out of his mouth.

"Damn, that's foul."

She laughs some more. "I like them. I think they're good."

"You can't be serious. Tastes like a piece of rubber soaked in alcohol." He comes back to the fridge and searches inside, reaching for a bottle of pale ale. "Want a beer?"

"Sure, why not."

He pulls two bottles out, twisting the cap off one before handing it over to her.

"There you are! I've been looking for you everywhere, handsome." A woman about the same age as Blair is suddenly sliding up next to Road, hugging him. Her perfume's so strong, it's like standing in a cloud of gardenia scented bug spray.

"Hey there, Marla," Road says, hugging her in return, and when Marla finally pulls away, Blair recognizes her. Marla was one of Road's old Skank Factor X girlfriends. They'd dated for a little while after high school.

"What are you doing over here?" Marla asks, still staying close to Road. She puts a hand up and runs it possessively through his blond hair. "Lori told me you went out to your car to get something."

"Yeah, had a few gifts for people."

Marla smiles, and Blair notices with annoyance that she's still gorgeous.

"I hope you got *me* something," Marla says with a wicked grin. "Because I might have something for *you*, too."

Road takes a swig from his beer. "I'm just over here seeing what my wife is up to in the kitchen."

"Your *wife*?" Marla's scowls.

"Yeah, you remember Blair, don't you?"

Marla turns toward her. Blair can see Marla's light brown hair is tipped blonde on the ends. She's wearing a lot of dark eye shadow with a line of shiny blue on the inside corners. It should look weird, but instead it looks great. Her white Harley Davidson tank top is tight and low-cut, with plenty of smooth, tan cleavage on display. She's studying Blair with confusion, but then her confusion clears. "Oh, that," is all she says before turning back to Road. Not even a hello to Blair.

Typical Skank Factor X behavior.

Marla stares down at Blair's navy Keds with a superior smirk on her face. "You guys are still married?" she asks Road. "I thought that wasn't for real."

"Oh, it's for real, all right," he says.

Blair glares at him, but can see him pretending not to notice.

"Huh." Marla takes this in. And then she smiles, puts her hand up to

Road's cheek and leans in, starts whispering something in his ear.

Blair watches the two of them, watches Road's face as he chuckles over whatever Marla is telling him, and wishes she could strangle them both.

This was once her life. She remembers it so clearly now, remembers the constant acidic taste in her mouth as she watched Road with all these horrible women.

Not anymore, though. That's over.

She turns to leave the kitchen, to escape, when suddenly she sees Tori headed her way.

Thank God.

"Blair!" Tori waves. She's carrying a plastic container of food and comes over to put it on the counter.

By now, Marla has stopped whispering in Road's ear and gives Tori a fake smile.

"Is that your black Escalade parked outside?" Tori asks her. "Because I think the headlights are on."

"They are?" Marla's face changes. "I'd better go check." She turns to Road and tries to pull him along with her, but Lori has come into the kitchen telling Road he needs to go see the 'Welcome Home' cake they got him.

Once Marla's gone, Tori lowers her voice, "God, she's such a bitch. I hate her."

"Were her car lights really on?"

"I don't know."

Blair laughs, and then wonders what happened to make Tori hate Marla so much. Tori can usually find the good in everyone.

"She's been trying to take over Kiki's entire wedding, constantly offering all this unsolicited advice. It's driving everybody crazy."

"Why would Marla be involved in the wedding?"

"She's Austin's older sister, and Kiki made her a bridesmaid."

"I didn't know that." Austin is Kiki's fiancé.

"Plus, I think she wants to get her hooks into Road."

"What makes you say that?" Though, judging by the little show she just watched, Blair isn't exactly surprised.

"Because she's called me twice since she heard he was back in town, asking all sorts of questions about him. She's going through an ugly divorce and is obviously looking for her next victim."

"You don't think Road would be interested in her again, do you?"

"I hope not." But then Tori shakes her head. "No, he's isn't that dumb. Oh, that reminds me, I want to show you something."

Blair follows Tori into the living room. There are people everywhere and the party appears to be in full swing. Without trying, she spots Road standing over by the large front window, her radar for him as highly tuned as ever.

He's surrounded by a group of guys, most of them muscular and covered with tattoos. They're drinking beer and laughing with each other. She recognizes a few of them as his cousins. Brody sees her and waves. Blair waves back. A couple of women are there—including Marla, who's eyeing Road like a spider lining up its next meal.

"Here it is," Tori says. After searching through a pile of magazines on the coffee table, she finally finds what she's looking for. Tori holds up a copy of *The Literary Voice*. "You have to read this."

"Why?" Blair takes the magazine from her. She puts the beer to her lips for another sip.

"There's an excerpt from Road's book in it."

"What?" Blair almost chokes on her beer. She stares at the magazine Tori just handed her.

Tori nods. "It's really good. I want you to read it."

Blair's mind turns to chaos. She's still staring at the magazine cover. "How did he manage this?"

"I don't know. I think it was his media rep's idea to submit it."

"What?" Blair holds the magazine as if it contains a venomous snake. "Road has a media rep?"

Tori laughs at Blair's reaction. "She approached him after his book started selling so well."

Blair's eyes flash over to Road, who's nodding, engrossed in some conversation.

A beeping noise starts coming from Tori's purse and she reaches inside to grab her phone, turning the beeping off. "I have to go check on a cat I'm watching tonight."

"Do you want me to come with you?" Tori works at a vet's office part-time.

"No, that's okay. She had surgery on her paw, and I'm just keeping an eye on her dressing. I'll be right back. Read that article. Seriously."

Blair looks down at the magazine in her hand.

"Oh, and I made vodka gummy bears! They're in the fridge."

After Tori leaves, Blair takes the magazine and her beer over to a corner chair. Judas Priest's album *British Steel* is blasting on the stereo, and if it's weird that she's sitting in the corner reading a magazine at a crowded biker party, nobody seems to notice or care.

She takes another swig from her bottle then puts it down on the small side table. She opens the magazine and flips through the pages. It doesn't take long to find the book excerpt.

Edge of Zen by Road Church.

Blair studies his byline. Despite what she'd said a few days ago about never wanting to read anything from him, she's curious. An excitement hums through her, the excitement she always feels when she makes a new discovery about him. Her thirst for Road is unquenchable, the answer to the riddle of him always just out of reach.

She starts to read and discovers it's a book excerpt about his time in India, right after he left her. It describes him trying to find his way in a foreign culture. *Didn't know I was a pilgrim until I turned toward the dawn . . .*

Blair sits in the chair and reads non-stop for the next twenty minutes. She ignores her beer, ignores the people around her. The excerpt is ten pages long with an author bio and picture of him at the bottom of the last page. He looks meditative in the photo, his hair longer than it is now and pulled back into a shaggy ponytail. There's some kind of Asian temple behind him. She stares at it for a long time.

When she's finished, Blair shuts the magazine and takes a deep, cleansing breath, lets it out. She closes her eyes, and her head spins with amazement.

Holy shit. Road can write.

Chapter Nine

Daily List

1. Google 'Road Church' until your fingers cramp.

2. Obsess over the realization that Road has become successful.

3. Set yourself up for a day of the sweetest torture.

BLAIR STARTLES AT the metallic sound of a key sliding into her front door. Her eyes flash to the time on her computer screen. It's almost noon.

Road didn't come back from the party last night. She drove the Honda home alone because he said he'd catch a ride later, but he never showed.

Not that I care.

Quickly, she exits the browser where she was looking at Road's blog. She was up most of the night reading *Edge of Zen*, which she downloaded onto her Kindle as soon as she came home. It's a bestseller on Amazon with hundreds of rave reviews, and after reading it, she understands why. It's a great book and hard to put down. His writing style is clean and eloquent, with just the right amount of self-deprecating humor. Spare, like his speech, not a lot of window dressing, but the people and places he described are as fresh and vivid on the page as if they were standing right in front of you. His laser focus is clearly turned on full-blast when he writes.

The first thing she did this morning was Google everything about him she could find. She'd never allowed herself to look him up on the web in all this time. Not even once. Her willpower was ironclad, so she had no idea of everything he's been up to. It was quite a shock to discover how many items appeared when she Googled Road Church.

She found his blog right away, and it's far more polished than what she'd imagined when Tori mentioned it to her. It's way beyond some simple blog, but a huge website geared toward travelers and ex-patriots. There are tons of articles and photos about various places with links to information. There's even a store attached. Quite an enterprise. And when she finds the 'About Us,' it says—

Nathan 'Road' Church: Founder, Managing Editor, and Contributor.

There were other people listed as well, and it dawns on Blair that Road has employees, that he's a business owner just like herself. She stared at that page for a full five minutes, barely breathing.

Unbelievable.

The front door opens, and Blair pretends to be working on the computer as Road strolls over, his smoky scent wafting around her. She's sitting on one of the tall kitchen chairs.

"Hey, princess." He's carrying a couple of Tupperware containers.

Blair glances up at him. "Hey." She goes back to her computer, but can't resist watching his backside as he takes the containers over to the fridge. That perfect ass. He's wearing the same jeans from last night, but has a different shirt on today. A dark blue one that advertises Brody's garage.

"What's in those?" she asks.

He shoves both plastic containers onto the top shelf and Blair cringes. The top shelf is for bread items only.

"Leftovers from my mom's. She insisted."

"That was nice. Do you think you could move them to the bottom shelf?"

"Why?"

"That's where leftovers go."

He takes the containers from the top, squeezes them onto the bottom shelf, and closes the refrigerator.

She cringes again because he didn't line them up right, but figures she'll fix it later. "Thank you."

Road turns back toward her. The front of his T-shirt is tucked in and she can see his brown leather belt with the brass buckle, along with the bulge of what's below it.

She quickly looks away.

"You make it back okay last night?" he asks.

"Yes, obviously."

He stands there, leaning against the counter, watching her as she pretends to work on her computer. He doesn't say anything, and Blair finally looks up at him. His hair is damp and there's blond stubble on his face. She wonders if he's hungover, but then immediately rejects the notion. For all the partying that goes on at his mom's house, Road's never been much of a drinker. Except for that one night they were together, a few beers is the most she's ever seen him down.

His sea-green gaze takes her in. He definitely doesn't look hungover. The whites of his eyes are clear and bright, his skin unmarred. He looks relaxed standing there, too relaxed. And that's when it hits her.

Road must have gotten laid last night.

Welcome home!

She hopes to God it wasn't Marla. *Please, don't let it be Marla.* But then, who *would* be acceptable? Who could Road sleep with where it wouldn't bother her?

No one.

Blair grits her teeth and turns back to her computer. She hates this, hates this obsession. Wanting someone she can never have. The sick irony of being married to him. *Married!*

Road is still watching her. His laser focus hums like an electric power line. "Are you pissed about something?"

"No."

"What have you been up to all morning?"

"Nothing."

"You look seriously pissed, babe."

"Don't call me that."

He chuckles. "Now I *know* you're pissed. Is it because I didn't come back last night?"

"I don't care what you do." She moves her mouse around the computer screen aimlessly, pretending to be busy. "I don't want you here in the first place."

Reggae music blares from his phone and Road pulls it out of his front pocket but doesn't answer it, just turns the music off.

"What are you doing today? Do you have plans?" he asks.

She doesn't reply right away and wonders why he's asking. "Not really."

He gets a mischievous smile. "What do you say we take Isadora for a spin?"

Blair looks up. "What do you mean?"

"Just what I said. Let's go for a drive."

"And who's going to drive?"

"Me."

"You're going to drive Isadora?"

"Yeah."

She shakes her head in amazement. "How stupid do you think I am? If I give you her keys, you'll never give them back."

"Don't you trust me?"

"Of course not."

Road chuckles. "I see. What can I do to earn your trust?"

"I don't know. Sign her title over to me."

There's a flash of white as Road laughs with what sounds like approval. "Damn. You've grown a pair, that's for sure." His laughter quiets down. "Not going to happen, though. What else can I do?"

She throws him her haughtiest look. "Nothing."

He mulls this over and after a long moment appears to come to a decision. "How about this—what if I *promise* to give the keys back to you?"

"And why would you do that?"

"Because I want to take my car out for a drive. Check out Seattle. I haven't been back in over a year."

Blair picks up her coffee and swirls the ice around with her straw.

"Look, I know how much time and money you've put into Isadora," he says. "Brody told me all about it last night at the party, so let me experience her."

Her eyes roam over him. She wonders who got to experience him last night, but decides not to go there. "You've already 'experienced her.' You drove her that day back from Tori's house."

"That was nothing. Just that one time doesn't count."

They're still eyeing each other and Road's expression is so earnest that, against her better judgment, she softens a little.

"Come on," he says, lowering his voice, coaxing her. "It's sunny outside. We'll put the top down. It'll be fun."

Blair is tempted, and a part of her wants to go with Road, but then she comes to her senses. "No. You'll never give the keys back." The problem is she knows him, knows him better than he could ever imagine, and she knows if he gets those keys, it's all over. "You're trying to manipulate me."

"I'm not." His eyebrows go up and he looks genuinely surprised by her accusation. "Let me convince you. What can I offer you in exchange?"

Your body? It's the first thing that comes to mind and it almost makes her smile. She wonders what he'd say if she put that on the table. Imagines his astonished face. *He'd say no anyway.*

"How about my wallet? It's got my driver's license, credit cards, everything. You can keep it in your purse while I drive."

Blair imagines them spending the whole day together. The sweet torture of being with Road. And the selfish part of her, the part that's always hungry for him, the part that's wanted him her whole life is telling her to say yes, because this is it. This is all she's going to get, and it's better than nothing.

"All right," she says, before the sensible part of her kicks in again. "Let's go for a drive, but I want your wallet *and* your phone before I give you the keys."

I HOPE I haven't made a stupid mistake. They're driving toward downtown Seattle. She's worried because Road looks too happy. Too relaxed, cruising with the top down and the radio blasting.

His wallet and phone are both safely inside her purse and if he tries to keep Isadora's keys, she's not giving either of them back.

"So, where should we head to first, princess?" he asks, raising his voice above the music and the wind noise.

"That depends. What did you miss the most?"

He's wearing black Ray-Bans, and his hands manage to look both strong and graceful on the steering wheel. He grins. "Everything."

The radio is playing Pearl Jam's "Alive", and Blair thinks about Road's book. All the people he's met and the places he's traveled. He's become worldly these past five years, and she feels a peculiar envy.

"Why did you come back to Seattle?" she asks, curious. "Why now?"

Road's eyes are steady in front of him as he drives. "It was just time to come home, is all. Take a breather."

She thinks about how he's like the character Larry from *The Razor's Edge*. A traveler who's come home wiser than he left. She almost tells him this, but then realizes he doesn't know she's been reading his book and his blog. Perversely, she doesn't want him to know, either.

I'm not Isabel, though. The woman who loved Larry, but wouldn't travel with him when he asked her, who refused to give up her cushy life. *If Road had asked me, I would have gone with him anywhere.*

Road drives around lower and upper Queen Anne a bit then heads over to Fremont. He compliments her on the car a few times, but doesn't talk much beyond that.

Blair wishes she could think of something witty or insightful to say. In truth, she's nervous. It annoys her, but she can't help it. This whole thing almost feels like a date. She even indulges in a fantasy, pretends they're a real married couple out for a Sunday drive. Afterward, to be nice, she'd agree to go to a hardware store or an auto supply store. Then they'd go home and have the hottest sex ever. Nothing like that one horrible time. In her fantasies, Road is always hot and sensual in bed, and she's never left dissatisfied.

"You hungry?"

Blair startles. "What?" She was imagining them back in the hallway again, except this time Road's hands weren't on the outside of her clothes, but the inside. His mouth was at her ear, his voice low and seductive, telling her all the naughty things he had planned for her.

"Do you want to grab a Dick's burger?"

Blair looks around. They've already made their way up to Wallingford without her noticing. She sees Dick's Drive-In up ahead. Road doesn't wait for an answer, but turns off NE 45th Street and pulls Isadora right up to Dick's, parking the car.

She tells him to get her a burger and fries and waits for him in Isadora, figuring they'll take everything to a park or back to her condo to eat. When Road comes back and sits in the driver's seat, though, he starts taking food out right away.

"What are you *doing*?" Her eyes widen in horror.

He digs around in the bag then hands her a burger. "I'm getting the grub out so we can eat."

"We can't eat in the car!" She tries to hand the burger back.

"Why not?"

"Because . . . ," she sputters. "We just can't!"

Road gives her a strange look. "We're at Dick's." He ignores the burger she's trying to hand back and starts handing her french fries now, too.

As if he were a small child, Blair patiently explains to Road how nobody is allowed to eat in Isadora. Ever. It's an ironclad rule. No exceptions.

Road puts her fries on the armrest between them and Blair immediately snatches them up.

"Isadora is not just any car," she explains. "I don't want crumbs everywhere or," *God forbid*, "grease stains. Plus, I don't want her to smell bad and stink like food."

By now, Road has his burger out and has opened his ketchup cup, dipping french fries into it.

"Are you even listening to me? Have you heard a single word I said?"

"Sure." He eats the fries then picks up his burger. Blair watches him push the paper down around it and take a huge bite.

"Then why are you still eating?"

Road closes his eyes for a long moment as he chews. "God, that's good. A year is too long." He takes another bite and moans in appreciation.

Blair sneaks one of the french fries from the bag she's still holding on her lap. She's not sure what to do. She looks around at all the other ordinary cars where people are eating their food. Isadora isn't an ordinary car, though. Clearly, he doesn't care. *Typical Road.*

"Aren't you going to eat?" he asks.

She shoots him a daggered look.

Road chuckles.

Jerk!

He eats more of his fries, but she can see now that he's studying her. Laser focus on. "You're kind of tightly wound, aren't you?"

"I don't know what you mean."

He continues with his laser beams. "Yeah, you do."

She grits her teeth.

"You need to unwind more. Live a little."

"Be more like you, huh?"

He doesn't say anything for a few seconds, just keeps eating. "All I'm saying is you should try to relax."

"I don't need to relax."

But Road starts talking. "I mean, damn, all those lists you've got posted everywhere, and then you're making more lists every day." He takes another bite and chews, considering her. "And why do you check your front door so many times at night?"

Blair's face grows warm. She thought she was being more discreet about her OCD behavior. "I'm just checking to make sure it's locked."

"Ten times?"

"Three times."

"Why not check it once?"

She squirms in her seat, looks back down at her food, finally gives in and eats another fry. "I just want to be safe."

"Are you worried someone is going to break into your place? Because I'm there, and I'll kick anybody's ass." He grins. "Me and Mr. Maurice."

Blair smiles a little. "The action duo."

"Hell, I'll just throw Mr. Maurice at them. He can use his ninja claws."

She laughs. "That would be something."

Their eyes meet and Blair doesn't look away, let's herself fall into the kaleidoscope of green. "You have an amazing eye color." The words slip out before she can stop them.

"Think so?" He continues to meet her gaze.

"I'm sure you've heard that a lot."

"I've heard it."

Blair can only imagine how many times he's heard it. *I'm sure every girlfriend he's ever had has gushed about his eyes.*

"I think you have pretty amazing hair."

She blinks. "You do?"

He nods. "Always liked it. I'm partial to redheads."

This is news. *Since when?* She wants to ask, but then she'd have to explain how she's cataloged every single woman he's ever dated and that would sound freaky. Even she can see how it *is* freaky.

His green eyes are drifting over her as he murmurs, "All that smooth, pale skin."

Blair's breath catches at his tone. She shifts in her seat as pleasure glides through her. Desire. Her endless desire for him. *It's just meaningless flirtation. I've seen him do it with lots of women.*

His eyes have moved lower, taking in her sundress. They linger and she wonders why as a small thrill races through her. *Is he checking out my legs?*

"Are you going to eat that burger?" he asks.

Blair sighs. "Do you want it?"

"Only if you're not going to eat it."

She hands her burger over to him, and he pushes the paper down so he can eat this one, too. Despite his hearty appetite, Road has never been fat. She watches him enjoy the burger. He takes his time, doesn't wolf it down like the first one, relishing it instead. He's not a messy eater and is surprisingly fastidious, like a cat.

"I take it there were no Dick's burgers in all the places you've traveled to?"

"I've had some great food, but this tastes like home, you know?"

Blair nods.

When he's finally finished eating, he stuffs all the garbage in the large paper sack. Blair finally broke down and finished her french fries while Road ate the second burger, so she hands him her trash, too.

He gets out of the car to throw it away. On the way back, a couple of guys comment to him, pointing at Isadora, and Road stops to talk to them.

Blair takes the opportunity to indulge in what was once her favorite pastime—Road watching. If there was ever a sport she'd win an Olympic gold medal in, this was it. She was a champion at spying on Road.

She slouches a little in her seat, to make herself less obvious. Road is still standing there talking to the two guys. Between the sunglasses on top of his head and his long, blond hair, he looks like he's giving an interview to *Rolling Stone* magazine. He's using his hands as he talks, those well-made hands, and the two guys are nodding, listening.

After a few minutes, he heads back toward the car, so Blair pulls the sun visor down and pretends to look at herself in the mirror. This is why she'd take home the gold every time. Her ingenuity. Blair's eyes stay on Road. He's tall and carries himself well. It's something she's certain he inherited from Lori, who has a similar kind of fluid grace. Blair's always imagined it served her well in her pageant days.

Road's jeans are butter soft and hug his muscular thighs. His shoes—red and black striped sneakers—are the only real giveaway that he's been out of the country for a while, since they don't look in the least bit American.

He slips into the driver's seat.

"Fans of Isadora?" Blair asks, flipping up the visor.

"Yeah, apparently one of the guys' dad has a '65 Mustang that needs some work, so I was telling them about what you and Brody did." He turns to looks at her. "Do you get that a lot? People asking about Isadora?"

"I do." She nods. "I've gotten used to it." Oddly, Blair knows it's been good for her. Owning Isadora has helped her to be less shy.

"You've done a beautiful job with her," he says, but then amends it. "Except the color, of course."

Blair rolls her eyes.

Road starts up the engine and they head back toward downtown Seattle, though he doesn't tell her where he's going. Eventually, he pulls into a parking garage near Pike Place Market and searches for a spot.

"Are we going to the Market?" she asks after he parks and closes Isadora's convertible top.

"Yeah." He reaches up in the corner to latch the top in place, and Blair does the same with the one on her side. "Figure we'd grab a couple of cold ones and sit outside."

They get out of the car and Blair follows Road down the parking garage's urine-scented stairwell.

It's a sunny Sunday and there are people everywhere. She can hear guitar music from a busker drifting their way. Road is walking with purpose, and Blair asks him if he has someplace specific in mind.

"Heard there was a good Mexican place down in Post Alley."

The place he's talking about is kind of hidden, but eventually they find it. They're seated outside on the restaurant's terrace with a fantastic view of the water. Blair looks around in amazement. She's never heard of this place, but Road is back in town less than a week and already knows the coolest spots. *It figures.*

Their waiter comes over with menus, along with chips and salsa, asking them in a heavy Spanish accent if they'd like water, to which they both say yes.

Road studies the menu while Blair studies Road. She can't pull her eyes away. He's in a spotlight from the sun, and it's making the stubble on his face shine golden-blond. He's so dazzling, she could sit here all day and admire him.

She thinks back to how relaxed he's been, and how she's sure he got laid last night. She can't help wondering again who it was.

Probably that bitch, Marla.

A fierce jealousy takes hold. Twists in her gut like a knife. All the years of being in love with Road, all the wishing and wanting. She turns her head away, gazes out at the water and tries to crush these terrible feelings to dust.

When their waiter comes back with the water and asks to take their order, Road surprises her by speaking in Spanish. The waiter seems surprised, too, but then smiles as the two of them converse for a few minutes.

Finding out Road speaks Spanish isn't helping her mood. Blair decides she needs a drink. A real one.

"Cadillac Margarita."

The waiter leaves and Road raises an eyebrow. "Didn't know you were a margarita fan."

She shrugs. *I am today.* "Since when do you speak Spanish?" she asks.

"Spent some time with a friend in Madrid."

Blair can tell by the inflection in his voice the friend is a woman. And then she remembers how Tori told her he had a Spanish girlfriend. The jealousy knife twists deeper, even though she knows it's irrational. She and Road were never a real couple, despite being married. And she's certainly had boyfriends, though none of them could evoke even a tenth of what she feels for Road.

He's eating chips and salsa, relaxed and happy, admiring the view of the water, while Blair is struggling with a hurricane of emotion.

What would he do if I just flat-out told him the truth?

If she admitted her feelings to him, had the guts to do it, cleansed her soul, would it change anything? Would he even care?

Road, I've been in love with you since the day we met. Crazy madly in love.

Really, babe? That's great.

Did you hear what I said? I am out of my mind in love with you and have been for years.

That's real nice, princess.

I know it was horrible what happened between us, but I have to confess, a tiny part of me was glad I carried your child inside of me, however briefly, because it was yours. I'd do anything for you, and I wanted our marriage to be real, but then you left me the first chance you got. Escaped was more like it!

Look, I only slept with you because I was drunk, and I only married you because you were pregnant.

Yes, and that's how pathetic I am! Despite everything, I'm still madly in love with you. Don't you see? The truth is I haven't divorced you because I don't want to. I'll never get over you, and I'll probably love you till the day I die.

Babe, that's sweet.

Sweet? There's nothing sweet about it! I'm so crazy in love with you I'd open a vein if you told me to. I'd jump off the roof of this building if you said it'd make you happy!

Really? Maybe you could give me back my car.

I don't think so.

"So, what are we going to do about this, princess?"

"Huh?" Blair's eyes flash to Road's. "What did you say?" She realizes Road has been talking to her, but she hasn't heard a word.

"About all your list making and checking the front door. Maybe I can help?"

The waiter brings them their food and drinks. It turns out Road ordered a beer and nachos, and he immediately digs into them.

"I can't believe you're still hungry after eating two burgers."

"I'm always hungry." Road leans back for a moment and pats his hard, flat stomach. "Got to feed the monster."

Yeah, right. Blair continues to watch him eat. She has a few bites herself, but is more interested in her drink.

"Why does everything have to be so perfect for you all the time?" he asks. "The lists, the car, worrying over where every fork or spoon goes."

"I don't know. I've always been this way. Everyone in my family is a perfectionist." Granted, she's the worst of the bunch.

"Life's not perfect."

"I know that."

"Maybe it's time to get over it."

Blair was stirring her margarita, using the fat straw it came with, but now she looks up at him. "Get over it? That's your great advice?"

"Yeah." He chuckles. "I know that sounds simplistic, but sometimes you have to let things go."

"That's easy for you to say."

"Why's that?"

"Because you don't have any weaknesses."

"I have weaknesses."

"Like what?

He thinks about it. "I'm too impulsive. Don't always look before I leap."

Blair rolls her eyes. She knows him so well that she already knows he doesn't believe this is a weakness. He'd see this as being bold, and being bold is a strength.

"I'm also too blunt," he continues. "Don't mean to hurt anyone's feelings, but sometimes I do."

"Give me a break. You're naming all these weaknesses that you secretly think are strengths."

"No, I'm not."

"Yes, you are."

He gets an annoyed expression. "What makes you think you know me so well?"

And there it is. Blair almost tells him how he was under her microscope for years, but she doesn't. Instead, she sucks greedily on her margarita while Road sips his beer, watching her.

"Maybe you should slow down a little, have some more food."

"No, I'm not hungry." Happily, the margarita is starting to kick in and she feels better, like she's floating in a hazy cloud. "I'll tell you one thing," she says, the tequila making her brazen. "You'd never pass the Bandito Test."

"What's that?"

Blair explains the whole thing to him, and thinks of the irony. She gives this test to every guy she dates, while the guy she's been in love with her whole life wouldn't even pass it. Road would never risk his life to save her from the banditos.

When she's done explaining it, Road shakes his head. "I swear, chicks come up with the weirdest shit."

"It's not weird."

"Yes, it is."

Their waiter comes over and says something to him in Spanish, and Road turns to her. "We're finished, right?" He starts speaking Spanish again, but Blair interrupts.

"I'd like another margarita, please."

Road looks at her in surprise.

The waiter nods and looks at Road, who says something about *cerveza*, so Blair figures he's getting another beer.

"Why are you drinking so much?" he asks once they're alone again.

"What are you? My mother?"

"Just curious, is all."

When their drinks finally arrive, Blair immediately goes to town with hers. She knows Road is right and she should slow down, but she's feeling reckless for a change.

Road leans back in his chair, his golden-green eyes watching her. "You really think I wouldn't pass that test of yours?"

"That's right."

"Why? You think I'm a coward?"

"No." She takes another long pull on her straw. The margarita is bright, sour-sweet, and very strong. "I don't think you're a coward."

"Then what?"

She knows Road isn't a coward, and if it was any other woman, someone he cared about, was in love with, she knows he'd pass that test with flying colors. He wouldn't hesitate to put his life on the line for her.

It's me he'd never rescue.

Road is waiting for her to answer, but she ignores him. He takes a swallow from his beer, still considering her.

If only I could fall out of love with him.

That would solve all her problems. She thinks about how she'll be thirty-one on her next birthday, but it's like part of her life is standing still. And now that Road is here for good, there's no escape.

I'm like a junkie.

Blair flashes back to that one night they had together and how Road was a terrible lover. She even wonders if that's why his girlfriend cheated on him. At the time, she thought it was mind-boggling that any woman would cheat on Road, but now she sort of gets it. Of course, not all of his ex-girlfriends cheated—some of them lost their minds when he broke up with them. She remembers one Skank Factor X who smashed every window on Isadora with a tire iron. Most of his girlfriends were so self-involved they probably didn't even notice he was a bad lover. Occasionally, one of them would break up with *him*, though, and she imagines they were fed up, because how long could you put up with someone who was never willing to satisfy you?

Not long.

If only she had the same access to him as all his bitchy girlfriends.

It might actually cure me of this addiction.

And that's when it comes to her. The craziest idea ever. Her breath catches at the audacity of it. Even in her tequila-induced haze, she knows it's beyond nuts.

What if I could have sex with Road again? She knows he'd refuse if she asked him, that even if she threw herself at him, he'd refuse. *So how could I entice him?*

Isadora.

But I love Isadora! I could never give her up. Never!

But then she imagines herself free of Road, free of the tormenting dreams, free of this obsessive love, which—let's face it—isn't exactly healthy.

She tries to imagine the freedom. And it's wonderful, so wonderful it might actually be worth the price.

How long would it take, though? It would have to be more than one night, she decides, because one night didn't work last time. How long then? A week? Would a week of underwhelming, unsatisfying sex with Road be enough to cure her once and for all? It would be like an inoculation. She already knows he's a selfish asshole in bed. She tries to imagine it, how badly she wants him, and then discovering that every time they were together he was a jerk.

And then she smiles, because the crazy thing is, it just might work.

Chapter Ten

How to Use Adult Beverages Wisely

1. Beer ~ Drink occasionally at parties to be social.

2. Wine ~ Drink occasionally at home to relax.

3. Tequila ~ Drink rarely because all your stupid ideas sound brilliant.

"*WHAT?"* ROAD'S MOUTH is open, his expression incredulous.

"You heard me." Blair leans in closer, hoping her voice didn't carry. The restaurant has grown more crowded since they first sat down.

He glances at her drink. "Damn, babe, you must be hammered."

"I'm . . . not. I know what I'm doing." She gives him her best haughty expression. In truth, she *is* getting kind of drunk, and can't help wondering if she's going to be happy or horrified by this conversation tomorrow. On the other hand, if she hadn't been drinking, she'd never have thought of this great idea, much less had the nerve to ask him.

A grin tugs at Road's mouth. "What a crazy day this is turning out to be. Let me get this straight. You want to have sex with me in exchange for Isadora?"

"That's right."

Road chuckles. "Look, Blair, I think you're a pretty woman and all, but I'm not giving you my car in exchange for sex."

She stares at him in confusion. *His* car*? What's he talking about?* Blair realizes he's misunderstood what she's saying. *He thinks I'm offering myself to him so he'll give me Isadora, but Isadora is already mine!* She knows she needs to set him straight, make it clear it's *his* body that's up for auction, but all she can seem to focus on is the fact that he said she was pretty. "Do you really think I'm pretty?"

He nods. "Course."

"I don't believe you. And I don't believe you have a thing for redheads, either. You're lying."

"Why would I lie?"

She leans back and tries to pull it together but can't because her head is spinning. "Where's my drink?"

"It's gone. You finished it."

"I did? Well, I want another one."

"Babe, you've had enough."

Blair licks her lips in frustration. Her tongue feels too big for her mouth, and then she notices the sun is getting low in the sky. They've been out together all day.

"Come on, I should probably take you home before you come up with any more crazy ideas."

"I don't wanna go home!" Blair knows she sounds drunk. "God." She burps. "Those garder . . . marder . . . mardergarders really snuck up on me."

Road's hand is on her arm as he leads her to the front of the restaurant. She can hear him chuckling. "Didn't think it was possible margaritas that big could sneak up on anyone."

SOMEHOW NATHAN MANAGES to extricate his wallet from Blair long enough to pay the bill. She immediately demands its return.

"Don't trust you," she tells him, fumbling and shoving it back into her purse. "Even though you're like Larry."

"Who's Larry?"

"You *know.*"

"No, I don't know."

"*Larry!*"

"Sorry, princess, don't know anybody named Larry." *Christ, I've never seen Blair this shit-faced.* He manages to get her out of the restaurant. She's still ranting about some dude named Larry but he tunes her out, trying to get her back to the car in one piece.

Once they're finally driving to her condo, she's singing to the radio—loudly, and mostly off-key, but at least it's keeping her occupied.

When they're almost there, Blair starts to wind down and by the time he gets her upstairs, she's more docile. He figures she's probably getting sleepy, though she starts talking about Larry again.

"Maybe you are Larry," she says, pointing at him. "But I am *not* Isabel!"

And that's when it hits him. "You're talking about *The Razor's Edge*?"

"Of course!"

Nathan chuckles to himself. *Now it makes sense.* He uses his key to open her condo and when they're inside, he immediately goes to the kitchen to get her some water. He's tempted to make coffee, though he's dealt with enough drunks to know coffee doesn't sober anybody up.

She's leaning against the counter, rambling on about Larry and Isabel again. "I'm not Isabel . . . because I would go with you."

"Go with me where?" he asks, getting down a glass.

"Anywhere. I'd go anywhere . . . but you didn't ask. Never asked!"

Nathan fills the glass with cold water from the fridge then hands it to her, telling her to drink. "We should get you to bed. Let you sleep it off."

And that's when Blair gets that same half-crazed expression she had on her face earlier at the restaurant. "Yes! Take me to bed!"

"No, babe, you need sleep."

She starts mumbling, "The cure . . . the cure . . . need the cure!"

"Drink some water," he encourages her. "You'll thank me tomorrow."

Blair takes a swallow from the glass then another. "Want to end this addiction . . . end it . . ."

He's been around people who drank too much his whole life, so he knows the shit that comes out of their mouths.

"What kind of addiction?" he asks, placating her, figuring she's talking about her perfectionism, all her lists.

"You!"

"Me?" Nathan is taken aback. "What do you mean?"

But Blair just shakes her head, drinks more water, then puts the glass down. "And do you know what's the real . . . pisser? You'd fail the Bandito Test!"

He rolls his eyes. "Not that stupid test again."

"It's not stupid! You're only saying that 'cause you'd fail." She hiccups. "Can't believe you're the worst I ever had."

Nathan watches her, still trying to figure out why she's going on about that test so much, and how could he be an addiction? Blair's eyes are bloodshot, and that amazing hair is a mess of cinnamon curls. She usually tames it, but he has to admit he likes it this way. Sexy. He's surprised to see her so hammered and knows it's not normal for her. Even after five years, he can tell she's still a good girl. She's always been the same as him about alcohol and seldom drinks to excess, though he's sure her reasons are different than his. Not sure what got into her tonight, though.

"Wait, what did you just say?" Her last words suddenly sink in.

"What I said was," she waves her arms in an elaborate drunken gesture, "you *suck* in bed."

He opens his mouth. "I . . . uh . . . what?"

"You're the worst lover I ever had!"

"Babe . . ."

"Don't 'babe' me." She closes her eyes, swaying a little. "God, I was so disappointed."

Nathan stills for a long moment, stunned. He leans back against the counter and thinks back to the one time they were together. Granted, he was plastered, but he doesn't remember it being *that* bad.

To be honest, he barely remembers it at all.

He thinks harder. His impression has always been that it was good. Real good. Blair, so sweet and pretty. She had an elegant body with nice legs and a great ass, and she'd turned out to be eager in bed. Unfortunately, his overriding memory of the incident is tainted by how he felt afterward.

Guilty as hell.

That's what he remembers the most.

He'd been selfish, taking advantage of the situation. He'd wanted her that night, though, remembers that clear enough, wanted her badly. She hadn't been a disappointment in any way.

But I was?

He looks over at Blair, who's watching him, bleary-eyed. Her pink tongue darts out, licks her lips, and he feels his groin tighten at the sight of it. There's a flash of memory. Blair going down on him, using that pink tongue. She'd been surprisingly uninhibited.

Definitely not a disappointment.

"I was drunk that night," he says. Might be an excuse, but it was the truth.

"So? So what?"

"So, that's why it was . . . you know . . . ," he feels his face warm, and can barely believe he's having this conversation, "not that great."

"Uh-huh, of course." She nods, but it's obvious she doesn't believe him.

Is this what she's always thought of me?

A part of him is tempted to take her to bed again when she's sober, just to prove he's not a bad lover, but he knows that's stupid. *Pride is all. Ego.* And there's no way he's making the same mistake twice. Though he finds himself staring down at her legs anyway. She has great legs. Shapely and elegant.

Bet they'd feel fantastic wrapped around my back.

Christ. He wishes he could remember more about that night.

Blair is studying him with an expression that looks like pity, and even though she's drunk, it grates on him.

"Look, I was seriously wasted that night, all right? Don't usually drink like that, but I was feeling like shit about what happened."

"Your girlfriend cheating on you?"

"Yeah, that's right."

Blair stares at him with raised eyebrows. He's confused by her expression for a second but then he gets it, gets what she's implying.

I don't fucking believe this.

"Hey, Gwen didn't cheat on me because I was a bad lover! She cheated on me because she wanted to hurt me."

This much he knows is true. Hard to believe he could ever have thought himself in love with someone so heartless. Afterward, she came crying to him, begging him to take her back. She spit fire when she heard he was marrying Blair.

"Of course." Blair nods slowly. "Sure."

"No woman has ever left my bed complaining, I can tell you that."

Their eyes meet and he realizes he's looking at a woman right now who's complaining.

"Whatever." Blair puts her water down. "Whatever you say."

She sways a little, walking off down the hall toward her bedroom. Doesn't even bother saying good night.

There's a mewling sound and he sees Mr. Maurice twining around his legs. Nathan squats down to pet him. "You believe me, don't you, buddy?"

Mr. Maurice purrs.

"Yeah, we guys got to stick together."

As he's petting the cat, he notices Blair's purse sitting on the floor right where she dropped it. He stares at it, realizes this is his chance. He can grab his wallet and phone, and since he still has Isadora's keys, he'll be home free.

I can finally take my damn car back.

"CAN I HAVE a sip from that bottle?"

Road's long body was sprawled on Tori's couch with the bottle of Jack Daniels held loosely at his side. His brows went up. "You want some whiskey?"

She moved closer so she was sitting right next to him, her heart still hammering at the decision she'd made. "Just a taste."

He passed the half-empty bottle over to her. She brought it to her mouth. The smell was strong, nearly overpowering. Blair realized she'd never drunk straight whiskey before. It burned going down, and she tried to hide her grimace when she handed the bottle back.

"Have more if you want."

"No, that's okay." She didn't want to risk getting intoxicated, didn't want anything to dilute this experience.

He shrugged, took another swig, and closed his eyes again.

Blair watched him with an indecent pleasure. Slowly took in his handsome face then traveled lower, enjoying the look of him, the ridges and planes of his muscular body. He was wearing a black Metallica T-shirt, and she knew she'd never hear Metallica again without thinking of this night.

"I'm sorry about what happened with your girlfriend," Blair said, knowing she wasn't sorry in the least bit.

"Thanks."

"You deserve better." In this, she was sincere. It was the truth. Road wasn't perfect, but he was decent and kind, and it was rare to hear him speak ill of anyone. He deserved better than all the Skank Factor X women he kept choosing.

He must have heard the sincerity, too, because he opened his eyes and looked at her.

"You're better than all of them," she whispered. More truth. "I only wish you could see that."

He blinked.

She put her hand on his arm. His skin was warm, and Blair let her fingers trail lightly over the smoothness of his inner forearm. She nearly closed her eyes, stunned by how erotic it was to touch him.

Road was watching her and she could tell he was trying to turn on his laser focus, but he'd had too much whiskey and couldn't quite manage it.

Her pulse raced and her breath grew unsteady. Nothing was going to stop her now.

I'm going to remember this night for the rest of my life.

BLAIR WAKES UP with a splitting headache, her mouth as dry as kindling. She groans, rolls over in bed, and closes her eyes again.

Last night comes back to her like images from a flickering movie screen. Road. Tequila. Jealousy. More tequila. Barter for sex.

My God!

Her eyes fly open. *Did I really offer up Isadora in exchange for sex?* But then she remembers it didn't quite go as planned. There was some misunderstanding involved. More parts of the evening continue to play back to her. She remembers Road paying the bill. Road driving them home in Isadora. The weight of his wallet and phone inside her bag.

Ohmigod.

Where's my purse?

She scrambles out of bed, barely noticing that she slept in the sundress she wore yesterday. Her head is killing her, but she manages to stumble out of her bedroom and down the hall.

What time is it?

Her brown leather Coach bag is sitting on one of the tall kitchen chairs and she rushes over, shoves her hand inside and starts rummaging through it.

Shit, shit, shit.

Blair grabs the purse off the chair and hurries over to the couch, dumping the entire contents out, searching frantically, but she already knows the miserable truth.

They're both gone.

It's over.

Road took his wallet and phone back, and now he has Isadora's keys, too.

She falls back onto the couch.

Her stomach churns and tears burn her eyes. Hard to accept, but she'd actually believed Road's promise that he'd give her Isadora's keys back.

I am such an idiot.

She should have known better. He was just manipulating her, though she can't believe he'd stoop to outright lying.

Jerk!

What am I going to do?

Blair shoves everything back into her purse, doesn't even care that it's not organized, that her lip gloss is floating freely and mixing with her wallet and tissue pack. *Who cares? I've lost Isadora!*

She gets up and pours herself some water from the fridge, gulps down half of it, and finds the Tylenol.

This is like a nightmare I wish I could wake up from.

Road's backpack isn't anywhere, and she notices the couch bedding he used to sleep with is stacked and folded. It's sloppy and the corners don't match. She wants to refold it, but instead heads purposefully toward her second bedroom he's been using as an office.

All his stuff is still there. *It's not like he could move out that quickly.* There's only one computer on his desk instead of two, but as far as she can tell, nothing else is missing. She thinks about losing Isadora and her heart hurts. *How could he do this to me?*

Blair marches over and unplugs his laptop, rips the cord out of the wall in frustration. Tears blur her vision but she ignores them, quickly wiping her eyes.

Glancing around, she checks to see if there's anything else she could take. She starts going through the desk drawers, but they're mostly empty. Road hasn't been here long enough to fill them with stuff.

What's this?

In the last drawer, she finds a large, beat-up mailing envelope. She pulls it out and stares at it. It's covered in foreign stamps on the outside and says 'Nathan Church' on the front, with an address in the UK. In a normal situation, Blair would never consider going through someone's stuff like this. It's too dishonorable.

But this is not a normal situation.

She immediately dumps the contents out. There's a bunch of papers and some colorful foreign money—Euros, Pound Sterling, and Forint. She sifts through the papers and discovers they're official documents from various countries, work-related as far as she can tell. As she's shuffling through the pile, she suddenly notices a few letters tucked in. They're written on blue-striped stationary.

Blair pulls one out and opens it. Right away, she can see it's a personal letter. She hesitates. *Should I read it?* But her eyes have already started. It's addressed *Querido Nathan* and is written in a foreign handwriting, but she can tell right away it's a woman's hand.

The body of the letter is in English and from what she can gather, it's from a woman Road was involved with. It talks about school and her family, and then goes on about how much she misses him and wants him to come back to Madrid.

The Spanish girlfriend. Blair feels ill. Ill from her tequila hangover and ill from reading some letter from a woman he had a love affair with.

She wishes now she hadn't read it. Hadn't touched it.

She puts it back in the pile then notices a page torn from a magazine that looks familiar. Blair unfolds it and is surprised to discover a picture of herself. It's from the write-up *Seattle Magazine* did on La Dolce Vita a few months ago. She remembers Road mentioning how Tori sent him a copy of the article, but is surprised to see he kept it.

He's been traveling around with a picture of me?

Blair studies it, tries to see herself objectively. It's a good photo. She had her hair and makeup professionally done, and the photographer was a cute guy who kept flirting with both her and Natalie. As a result, he managed to capture Blair with a playful expression on her face.

Why would Road keep this?

She can't think of a single reason. And then she notices a green slip of paper sticking out from the pile and her breath stops. It's worn and folded, but right away she knows what it is.

Isadora's title.

Yes!

Immediately, she shoves everything back in the envelope, except for the title. Puts it all back in the bottom drawer, grabs the computer, and heads to her bedroom. Once there, she tucks everything into her underwear drawer, figuring it's safe there. The odds are slim to none that Road will ever be looking at her panties.

Not in this universe.

Obviously, he can order another title, but that takes time. In truth, she's not even sure how to use this to her advantage, but figures it's worth keeping just in case.

You never know.

Chapter Eleven

How Not To Have Fun On A Date

1. Glare at your date, especially if he's being nice.

2. Check the time on your phone every five minutes as you consider whether to create a fake dying relative.

3. Give a loud, spastic laugh during conversations for no apparent reason.

THANKS TO HER tequila hangover, her misery over Isadora, and her fury at Road, Blair nearly forgets she has a movie date with Graham that night. She almost cancels, but decides to grit it out instead. She's not letting Road ruin her social life the same way he's ruined everything else.

I'm going on this date, even if it kills me.

Graham shows up on time, dressed in his usual preppy style—light khakis and a blue button-down shirt—bearing a small box of chocolates.

"Thanks, that's sweet of you," Blair says, tossing them on the counter as she stares at the clock.

Where is Road, anyway?

It's seven at night and he still hasn't come back yet. *He's probably out celebrating. Celebrating my misery!*

"It's great to finally see you," Graham is saying. "It sounds like your work schedule has been as crazy as mine lately."

Blair nods and tries to focus on him, determined to have a good time.

I'm going to have fun, even if that kills me, too.

They drive to the movie theater in his BMW, and Blair can't help but notice for the hundredth time that Graham is exactly the kind of man she should be with. He's smart, successful, and handsome. He's a classy dresser with good taste. His car is spotlessly clean, and she'd bet money his refrigerator is organized down to the last piece of lettuce. *He even smells nice.* She breathes in his subtle, pine-scented cologne. In truth, he's perfect in every way, and she knows they look great together. Like a matched set of luggage. Barbie and Ken.

So, why can't I fall in love with him then? Why? Instead of some long-haired, tattooed asshole?

"Is everything okay?" Graham asks as they stand in line to get popcorn.

"Of course."

"Are you sure?"

"Yes, I'm sure."

"Because you seem kind of upset about something."

"I'm *fine*!" she snarls.

Graham's brows shoot up. "Whoa."

Blair sighs. "Sorry, it's been kind of a stressful day."

"I see." He nods, though he looks a little nervous.

The movie, some kind of highbrow drama she'd normally enjoy, might as well be about Smurfs for all she cares. Her mind keeps going back to Road, wondering what he's doing. Cruising around in Isadora, no doubt, with some horrible Skank Factor X at his side. Probably Marla, though the image makes Blair want to scratch her own eyes out.

How dare he lower Isadora's standards like that!

Blair squirms in her seat. *This movie is lasting forever.* She wonders what time it is, but resists the impulse to check her phone again. Road probably isn't coming back tonight anyway. Why should he? She's sure he has other plans. He's probably lining up his next place to live and Marla's already slipped him her key. The whole thing makes her sick to her stomach. A couple of his cousins will likely show up tomorrow to help him move the furniture out of her office.

Good riddance!

Then she'll finally have her peaceful sanctuary back. No interloper there to leave crumbs on the counter and toothpaste globs in the sink, to torture her with his long, muscular body and delicious scent. No one there to remind her of all the things her heart wants, but can never have. And Mr. Maurice will have to get over his boy crush, too. Both of them caught under Road's spell.

She sighs.

When the movie is over, Graham drives her back to her condo.

"Why don't you come up?" she says, still trying to put a good spin on this somewhat disastrous date.

He looks at her with surprise. "Are you sure? You seem like maybe you want to be alone."

"No, I apologize. I've been a bit preoccupied. Come up and have a glass of wine."

"Really?" He hesitates, but then finally shrugs. "All right, if you really want me to."

Graham parallel-parks his car on the street in front of her building, and they both take the elevator upstairs.

I'm going to have a glass of wine and relax. Maybe even try to get excited about Graham.

Those plans go out the window as soon as she unlocks her door. First thing she sees is Road's beat-up leather backpack along with his red and black sneakers dumped on the floor by the entryway.

Adrenaline spikes through her. Her eyes flash over and sure enough, there he is, standing in the kitchen, leaning against the counter casually eating one of his endless bowls of cereal. As always, the sight of him causes her stomach to flutter, and for a split-second she feels joy, but then she lets her breath out in anger.

Road looks over and she can tell the exact moment he sees Graham walking in behind her, the way he stops chewing, his spoon hovering in midair.

She marches over to the kitchen and throws her purse down on one of the tall chairs. "I'm surprised to see you here."

Road's eyes are still on Graham, but now they cut to her. "Why's that?"

She glares at him, her voice icy. "You know why."

"No, I don't." He resumes eating his cereal, but she gets the sense he's on high-alert, his laser focus vibrating like a tuning fork.

Graham is standing awkwardly beside her, and Blair realizes she's being rude. "Graham, this is Road." She motions. "Road meet Graham."

The two men eye each other and Graham puts his hand out first. Road reaches over to shake it.

"Are you a friend of Blair's?" Graham asks, obviously bewildered to come upstairs and find a man in her apartment.

"He's no one," Blair says quickly. "Just an old acquaintance."

Road's expression goes flat, and she can tell he doesn't like that. He puts his bowl of cereal down. "I'm Blair's husband."

Graham stiffens beside her. "Excuse me?"

"Road, stop it!" Blair hisses.

"You're her *what*?" Graham's brows draw together.

Road's expression is still flat as he looks straight at Graham and says, "Husband."

"That's enough." Blair glares at Road. She turns to Graham. "It's not what it sounds like."

"You're married?" Graham's mouth is open as he stares at her in shock.

"I am, but it's not a real marriage," Blair tries to explain. "He just showed up here unannounced last week."

Graham is shaking his head, trying to process everything. "How long have you been married?"

"Five years, but like I said, it's not a real marriage. I haven't seen—"

"*Five years*?"

"Let me pour you a glass of wine and I'll explain the whole thing to you. It's not as bizarre as it sounds."

But Graham's face is red, and he's clearly disturbed. "I think I'd better go." He turns, heads back toward the door, and Blair follows him.

"I'll call you tomorrow, okay?" she says. "Just give me a chance to explain all this."

Graham doesn't respond and before she knows it, her door has slammed shut and he's gone.

She whirls around. Road is still standing there, leaning against the counter, a little smirk on his face. Blair marches over, her vision so clouded with rage that before she can stop herself, she shoves him in the chest as hard as she can.

He barely budges.

"What the hell is wrong with you?" she yells. She goes to shove him again, but this time his hands fly out and grab her wrists.

"Let go of me!"

"Calm the fuck down then."

She tries to extricate her wrists, but he's still holding them tight. "Let go!"

He doesn't reply, just continues with his iron grip. Their eyes meet, and his are searching hers. "Does that guy mean this much to you?"

Blair is breathing hard, trying to gain control of herself. "Why did you tell him we're married? You chased him away!"

Road smirks, and even has the gall to chuckle. "He ran out of here pretty fast." He's still watching her. "Guess he'd fail your little test, too, huh?"

Blair blinks. "You don't know anything about it."

"Maybe not."

They're standing close to each other with Road still holding her wrists. As always, his burnt autumn smell surrounds her, permeating her senses. And in that moment, she wants so badly to be done with him, to exorcise every part of herself that he's somehow laid claim to.

"How could you do it?" she whispers meeting his gaze.

"I was just seeing what he's made of, is all. Besides," he snorts, "somebody had to set him straight."

"No." She shakes her head and takes a deep shaky breath. "Isadora."

Road's expression changes to confusion.

"I know you tricked me," she says. "You lied."

"What the hell are you talking about?"

"I'm surprised you came back. Are you here just to gloat?"

"What?" Road stills, his eyes roam her face. Then suddenly, he drops her wrists. "I don't believe this. You think I kept Isadora's keys?"

"Didn't you? Your wallet and phone were gone when I woke up, and you already had her keys."

"No."

"No, what?"

"Took my wallet and phone out of your purse because I *need* them. Left her keys here."

"You did? Where?" Blair glances around.

But Road is shaking his head. "You really think I'd go back on my word? Jesus, it's some high opinion you have of me."

"Where are they?"

"Did you even bother looking?"

Blair shifts uncomfortably. In truth, she didn't look for them at all, just assumed he had them—that he'd betrayed her. She lets her eyes roam around the kitchen then the dining room, but she doesn't see them. Blair turns her head toward the mirror she has hanging near her front door and that's when her eyes widen. She sees them right away, hanging on one of the hooks. It's the place she always kept them herself before she had to start hiding them.

At the sight of those keys, she feels queasy. She knows Road is telling the truth—they've been there all day. Between her hangover and crazed state of mind, she didn't even notice.

"I don't know what to say." She tries to smile, but it's obvious he's pissed.

"Let me tell you something, Blair. You're not going to like hearing this, but you *need* to hear it." He's watching her intently. "That is *my* fucking car. Got it? No more games. My uncle gave me that car, and seeing as he's one of the few people in this world who ever gave a damn about me, it's not something I'm willing to part with."

Blair is silent. *Tori was right.*

"Why did you abandon her then?" Blair thinks about the way he left Isadora sitting in the driveway of the house they'd rented. "If she means so much to you?"

"Didn't abandon her, babe. I left Isadora in your *care*."

"Give me a break."

"It's the truth."

"How do you figure that?"

"I said so in that shitty note I wrote you before I left."

"No, you didn't." Blair thinks back to the note Road left her. It's burned in her brain even after all this time. He wrote that he couldn't stay with her anymore, that it wasn't working for him. He signed it, 'See you later, Road.' The p.s. mentioned Isadora, but only asked if she could take care of Isadora and check whether Brody had a place to store her.

Blair's eyes flash to his face.

Road is nodding at her. "Remember it now, don't you?"

"Well, I did take care of her."

"Yeah," he agrees. "That you did, princess."

Blair's throat goes tight and her heart hurts as the reality of what he's saying sinks in. *It's all over. I've lost her anyway. Despite everything.* Tears burn her eyes and she turns her head, trying to hide them.

"Why does Isadora mean so much to you? I don't get it," he asks. "It's obviously not the money."

She tries to answer, but the words won't come. It's all too overwhelming. How does she explain that fixing Isadora was like fixing herself? It helped her move past what happened, but also helped her in other ways, too. The confidence she gained driving her. Somehow, she and Isadora became strong and whole together.

"Talk to me, babe."

Blair shakes her head. "I . . . can't." The tears and hurt that have built up inside her burst free. She tries to get away from Road, to go cry in private, but he doesn't let her, and instead pulls her in.

Before she knows it, Road's strong arms are wrapped around her, and she's completely enclosed. Her head is pressed against his shoulder as she continues to cry.

He's murmuring something, but Blair is too miserable to pay attention. One of his hands strokes her back, and all she can think is, *I've lost her.*

After a little while, she starts to quiet down, though she stays in his arms, her own wrapped around his waist. She pulls back and looks up at him.

"Guess that car means something to both of us," he says softly.

Blair nods, sniffing, still trying to pull herself together. "Yes," she whispers.

He tilts his head to the side a little, considering her. His hand comes up to her cheek, and she feels him gently wipe away some of her tears with his thumb. It's a sweet gesture, but then he does something surprising.

Road puts his thumb to his lips, tasting her tears.

Blair's breath stops at the sight. Stunned. She stares at his mouth, the same mouth she's stared at a million times with wanting.

His expression is intent, laser focus turned on. He pulls the thumb away from his lips and brings it back to her face, slides his fingers into her hair, holding her head still.

Road's eyes drop to her mouth, and she knows exactly what he's going to do. Blair is almost dizzy. She's imagined this moment so many times that it's like it isn't even real. A hazy mirage. An unattainable place she's always dreamed of traveling to, but never thought she would.

He bends toward her and the mirage becomes solid at long last as Road leans in and kisses her.

She's too stunned to respond, to even breathe. His mouth is so tender on hers.

The kiss stays soft at first, but then his lips move and Blair opens her mouth to his with a breathy whimper. He seems to like this because his kiss grows stronger, deeper. Their tongues explore each other as his hand continues to hold her head still for him.

Without thinking, Blair's arms move up and slide around his neck, pulling him closer. A storm of desire crashes through her and she knows she should pull back, shouldn't let herself go all in, but the rest of the world has ceased to exist. The taste of Road, so exquisite. Clean and unvarnished. This kiss is the most erotic experience of her life.

Until she remembers why he's kissing her. Why she's crying to begin with.

Isadora.

In a daze, Blair draws away from him.

Road's mouth is open slightly and she can still taste his breath, so close, intoxicating, like every lovesick dream she's ever had. Road's hand moves deeper into her hair, his other hand on her ass. He's resisting her attempts to pull away.

It occurs to her that he doesn't want to stop. He wants to keep going, and why shouldn't she, too? She's finally getting what she wants—Road. Her desire for him knows no bottom. But then something else occurs to her and her heart sinks because she realizes they don't want the same thing. Not at all. He can't give her what she really wants, and being with him will only hurt her more.

Blair sighs in disbelief at the crazy decision she's about to make, but like a junkie finally facing her addiction head-on, she knows what she has to do.

If I'm ever going to get over him, I have to have the strength to start somewhere.

NATHAN SENSES IT. The moment Blair stops responding to him, her body stiffening.

He's confused by it because a moment ago, he could tell she was one hundred percent into it. She wanted him. So, why the sudden change?

At first, he doesn't want to let her pull away, wants to keep tasting her because she tastes good. So sweet. Her elegant curves fit into him just right. Once again, he wishes he remembered more from that night they had. He's been thinking about it all day, trying to remember. *Can't even remember what her breasts look like.* He imagines they're as pretty as the rest of her, though.

Blair breaks their kiss. His hand is on her ass and he's wondering if there's some way to convince her this is a good idea. Part of him knows it's a bad idea, but the part of him touching her ass isn't agreeing.

"I'm sorry," she says, not looking at his face. She lets out her breath. "I can't be with you. Not like this."

Nathan thinks back to last night and how she was so drunk she'd actually offered herself in exchange for Isadora. Crazy. But then he remembers all the rest of it, too. Her telling him he was the worst lover she ever had.

"Why?" he asks, curious.

Blair doesn't give anything away, though. It occurs to him that, in some ways, she's as taciturn as he is, and maybe he's misinterpreted some of her shyness in the past.

He wonders if it's because she thinks he'll be a disappointment in the sack again.

Christ, it's hard to believe that's what she thinks of me.

Those pretty hazel eyes are looking at him now. Even her brows have an elegant arch to them and he moves his hand up, running his thumb over the left one.

Her eyes drift shut at his touch. He wants to kiss her again, and so he does. He runs his tongue along the seam of her mouth, hearing her intake of breath. But she opens to him, letting him inside. They kiss some more, and Nathan wants her. Wishes he didn't, but he does. He feels himself go even harder, trying to forget why this is a bad idea, and trying instead to figure out the logistics on how to make it work.

Blair breaks the kiss this time, too. Turns her head to the side and appears to be struggling with something.

"You okay?"

She doesn't reply, and he wishes he knew what was going through her head.

There's something about Blair that keeps pulling at him, despite everything. She's uptight, but he's beginning to see there's more to it. All her lists and tidy ways, always trying to smooth out the rough corners of life, trying to make things better. He saw her doing it at his mom's house the other night. Rearranging all the food so it was easier for people to get at, cleaning up the selfish mess others had made.

She's thoughtful in a way few people notice. Not just a good girl, he realizes, but a good woman.

He thinks about that dude who came here earlier. Right away, Nathan saw he was exactly the type Blair should be with. Clean-cut. Straight as an arrow. The kind who wears a suit to work every day and doesn't have a single relative who's ever been in rehab or prison.

Shouldn't have chased him off.

Nathan knew it was a dick move. He was being an asshole, but couldn't stop himself. He has no claim to Blair, none at all, but for some reason, it bothered him seeing her with that guy. Though he has to say, the dude split way too fast. *Must be dumb as a stump.* If that guy was into Blair, he should have listened to her, given her a chance to explain things. *So, maybe I did her a favor.*

He knows that's bullshit, though. *Shouldn't have done it.*

He felt bad laying down the law about his car with her, too. Hated the hurt expression on her face, those tears. Blair crying like a tragic beauty over Isadora. What a terrible sight.

It had to be done, though.

Uncle Lance is the closest thing to a father he's ever had, and Isadora was an extraordinary gift. No one's ever given him a gift like that. Not ever. That car is not something he can sell or part with and unfortunately, no amount of tears can change it.

Blair slips her arms out from around his neck. "I need to go to sleep," she says. "I keep baker's hours."

Nathan nods, part of him wishing there was something he could say to change her mind, though he knows he shouldn't want it to begin with. "Guess I'll get some work done." He needs to check his site stats, make sure everything is running smoothly, and sort through the email from James, his assistant. Needs to get some work done on his book, too.

And then she turns away and leaves. He's standing in the kitchen alone.

He sighs to himself, reaches for the laptop on the counter, and heads into the office he set up. Right away, he sees something missing. *What the hell?*

"WHERE THE HELL is my computer?" Road is standing in her bedroom doorway, frowning.

"Uh . . ." Blair's hands fidget with the night clothes she was ready to change into.

He watches her, looking more mystified than angry, though she suspects this might change.

"I have it."

"Where?"

Blair gives him a sheepish smile, puts her pajamas down and goes over to her underwear drawer. She can feel Road's eyes on her as she shifts stuff aside. She pulls out his computer, notices Isadora's title in there, too, but realizes she can't let him see that.

He'll know I went through his stuff. I'll have to sneak in there and put the title back when he's not around.

"Here you go," she says, handing him the computer.

He takes it from her, then motions with his head over to where she'd hidden it. "What's in that drawer?"

Blair pauses. "My underwear."

Road's brows go up and he grins. "You hid my computer with your panties?"

Her face grows warm.

He chuckles, but doesn't seem bothered. "Damn, babe," is all he says.

It occurs to her that he's probably dealt with plenty of over-the-top Skank Factor X antics over the years, and this is tame by comparison.

"I'm sorry," she says. "I was angry."

He nods, a grin still tugging at his mouth. "Guess I know where to look next time you get angry."

BLAIR RAN HER fingers across Road's chest, over his Metallica T-shirt. His body was solid, but she already knew that from all the times she'd observed him shirtless. As a teenager, it was after football games or in his yard at home, and as an adult, it was when he occasionally helped his mom by mowing her lawn. Twice, she'd been lucky enough to be there when he was out front, cursing and fighting with their worn-out lawn mower. She'd spied on him discreetly through the living room window, though it had never fooled Tori. "Stop ogling my brother. It's grossing me out." Understandably, Tori never wanted to know too many details about Blair's passion.

"What are you doing?" Road asked in a lazy drawl, as Blair's fingers continued to trail over the letters for Metallica.

Her eyes flashed to his face and she could see he was watching her, but in a mellow drunken sort of way.

"I'm touching you," she said softly.

He nodded slowly and closed his eyes. "Feels nice."

She smiled to herself and continued stroking, wondered who was getting more out of this, certain it was her.

Eventually, she changed position. Road's eyes opened and he took another swallow from the bottle, offering it to her. She took it from him, but instead of drinking, she placed it on the coffee table.

Road watched her in silence.

And when she leaned over and whispered, "I want to kiss you," he stayed silent then, too. His eyes drifted down to her mouth and lower to her body, but that was all.

Excitement drummed through her. Working her nerve up, Blair moved closer. He was still watching her, and she assumed this meant he was willing.

Finally, she made her move and leaning in close, she put her mouth to his.

I'm kissing Road!

At long last . . .

Right away, there was a problem, though. He wasn't kissing her back. She waited a few seconds, but nothing happened. Blair pulled away, wondering if she'd made a fool of herself. Road's eyes were closed. Was he asleep? Or maybe he didn't want this.

But then his eyes opened. He shifted position as his hands reached for her hips, dragging her closer. Clearly, he'd moved past any conflict he might've had.

"Come here," he growled.

And then they were kissing again, only this time he opened his mouth to her, their tongues mingling. Exploring. He tasted like whiskey, but she didn't mind, even liked it, because the dam had burst and desire was flooding through her.

So many years of fantasizing about Road, watching and wanting him. Hard to believe it was finally happening. Admittedly, it wasn't ideal, since she'd prefer he were sober and not in misery over another woman. But Blair was pragmatic, and determined to ignore it and make the most of this.

His kiss was passionate, if not a little sloppy, but Blair ignored that, too, figured it was just from drinking. She stretched out over him while his hands roamed her body, squeezing her ass.

Blair kissed him with abandon as she tried to remember everything. Every detail of having her dream come true.

Chapter Twelve

How to Get Over Road

1. Pretend he really is a jerk.
2. Focus on his flaws. (Which, let's face it, are numerous. See previous lists.)
3. Whatever you do, don't think about that kiss.

BLAIR AND ROAD fall into an uneasy truce during the next week. There are no more disputes involving Isadora. He leaves the car keys hanging right by the front door and lets Blair drive Isadora as often as she wants. Of course, what's left unspoken is that Isadora belongs to him and only him.

"I don't know what to do," she bemoans her situation to Natalie. "I feel like I've lost her, even though I'm driving her every day!"

"Maybe you should talk to a lawyer," Natalie says, finishing up the butter cream rosettes on a lemon drop cake. "It sounds like it's time to take it to the next level."

That's the problem. Blair did talk to a lawyer. She called Mia, and Mia didn't have good news. Mia pointed out something Blair hadn't even considered. Blair's condo, all her assets, even her share in La Dolce Vita, all came *after* her marriage to Road. If Road wanted to, he could ask for half of everything. Of course, there are extenuating circumstances since they were only physically together a few months before he left, plus Road clearly has assets of his own. But the long and short of it is, if she chooses to fight him over Isadora, they could wind up in a long, drawn-out and expensive court battle.

And then there's the simple fact that she understands why Road doesn't want to let go of Isadora.

Ironically, he wants her for the same reason I do. She means something to him.

Blair sighs.

Of course, there's the other thing which has started to eclipse even her panic about losing Isadora.

That kiss.

Ohmigod.

She can't stop thinking about that crazy kiss.

Especially the expression on Road's face, right before he kissed her. It was different than the other time they were together years ago. No drunken lust in his gaze. It was soft, something real. Certainly an expression she'd never seen him wear before, and now it's seared into her brain forever. Hard to ignore when one of your lovesick dreams finally comes true.

If only Road were actually in love with me.

But she knows she needs to stop thinking like that. It's time to end her obsession. Crush it to dust.

That kiss is making it hard, though.

So, the uneasy truce between them persists. He hasn't said anything about moving out, and she hasn't asked him to, because she doesn't want him to take Isadora with him.

She's been trying to call Graham all week, has left one voice message after another, but he's ignoring her calls. Her mom's gallery event is this Saturday, so she has to assume he's no longer going with her.

Unfortunately, Tori has been trying to wiggle out of it, too, but Blair keeps reminding her, "I went to *your* mom's party."

"I know, but that was totally different. There were no," Tori lowers her voice, "*penises* involved."

Blair laughs. Tori was surprisingly demure sometimes. "They're cacti."

"Please. I think I know a penis when I see one."

"I will *expect* you at my place no later than seven o'clock," Blair informs her. "We can drive there together."

Tori sighs. "Fine. Is Road going?"

"No, I haven't invited him."

"You should."

"Why?"

"Because Marla keeps sniffing around my mom's, asking about him. I don't want him tempted by that bloodsucker."

But I don't want to be tempted by Road. "We'll see."

By Saturday afternoon, Blair is done with her deliveries for the day. She's changed clothes and has just finished tying a white scarf in her hair when there's a buzz that someone is at her building's front door.

"Yes?" she asks, pushing the intercom button.

"I'm looking for Nathan Church?" A female voice comes through the speaker.

Blair pauses. *Who the heck is this? Marla? It doesn't sound like Marla, though. And why would she call him Nathan?*

"I'm sorry, but he's not here right now." Road has been out since she got home earlier.

"So, he lives here?"

"Yes, he's staying here, but like I said, he's not here right now."

"I just flew in from New York, and this is the address he gave me. I'm a friend of his."

Blair frowns. "Why don't you try calling him?"

"I *have.* Don't you think I would have thought of that? He's expecting me. Is this Blair?"

"Yes, it is." Blair considers this. *Is Road expecting someone?* "He hasn't mentioned any friend visiting."

"He must have forgotten. May I please come upstairs?"

"I have no idea who you are."

"You can't just leave me out here on the street like this! Please!"

Whoever she is, she sounds desperate. Blair wonders if maybe she's a traveler friend of Road's who has run out of money and is maybe even destitute. *It would be hard being alone like that in a strange city.* Blair hesitates, but then decides to help her and buzzes her inside. She figures they'll call Road again together. Hopefully, he'll be back soon anyway. Blair goes into the kitchen to start making herself an iced latte when there's a knock on her door. Going over, she opens it, completely unprepared for what she sees on the other side.

It's Road's friend.

And she is *gorgeous.*

So gorgeous, Blair is momentarily stunned into silence.

This woman isn't having the same reaction to Blair, though. In fact, she barely even glances at her as she turns to some man beside her, instructing him to bring all her luggage inside.

"Um, what . . . ?" Blair says as they both push past her, the guy dumping a large travel bag and two Louis Vuitton suitcases in the middle of Blair's entryway. Blair watches in stunned disbelief as this woman pays the man before he leaves, realizing he must be a cab driver.

Blair's mouth is open as she stares bug-eyed at all the luggage. She turns to the woman, who is raking her brilliant blue eyes over Blair, an assessing gaze on her astonishingly beautiful face.

"Who are you again?" Blair asks. It's obvious this woman is not a poor traveler in need of assistance—far from it. Blair realizes too late it was stupid to let a stranger up here, even one who claims to know Road.

"*You're* Blair?" the woman asks accusingly.

"Yes, and who are you?"

She tosses her long, black hair over her shoulder. "Fiona."

And then Fiona marches straight into Blair's condo as Blair watches, stunned. Fiona is wearing a belted leopard-print raincoat with a black skirt beneath it. Her legs are long and shapely, covered in pale, almost white stockings, a pair of black Christian Louboutin's stiletto pumps on her feet. (Blair recognizes the red soles.) She'd guess her age to be early thirties.

"This is where you *live*?"

"Yes, it is." Blair isn't enjoying this woman's tone at all. "Maybe you can explain who you are and what you're doing here."

Fiona ignores Blair, walks over to the front window, and looks out at the partial water view. "Pitiful. Though I guess it's better than *nothing*."

Blair studies Fiona's lithe form from behind, her fall of shiny dark hair, and then it hits her. When Road told her he didn't want the women at his mom's party hassling him, Blair thought maybe he wasn't into Skank Factor X anymore. But now she sees that isn't it at all. Apparently, Road has moved up in the world.

Fiona isn't just Skank Factor X.

Fiona is Skank Factor X times a million.

It's clear all his bitchy girlfriends were pitiful amateurs compared to this.

Normally, Blair would offer a guest something to eat or drink, but this woman isn't a guest. Fiona is walking around the living room. She seems inordinately interested in Blair's bookcase for some reason and starts carefully scanning the titles. She shoots Blair a look. "You're Nathan's wife?"

Blair isn't sure how to respond to this, so she simply says, "Yes."

Fiona's eyes rake over her again. "Where is your restroom?"

"Look, I think it would be best all-around if you just called another cab, removed your luggage, and used the restroom at the nearest hotel."

The woman gapes at her.

"I'll call one for you," Blair says with a polite smile. "It's no trouble."

"May I at least use your restroom first?"

Blair wants to tell her no, but then sighs. "It's straight down at the end of the hall."

"Thank you." Fiona marches off, her heels clicking on the hardwood floor, a cloud of expensive perfume trailing behind her. As soon as Blair hears the bathroom door shut, she finds her phone. She doesn't call a cab yet, but tries to reach Road instead.

"What's up, princess?"

Blair pauses. She hates to admit it, but she loves his voice on the phone. It's smooth with just the slightest hint of a low growl. "Someone named Fiona just showed up here for you."

"Come again?"

Blair explains how Fiona has apparently arrived from the airport and that a cab driver dumped all her luggage in the entryway. "Who is she?"

"I don't believe this," Road groans. "Unbelievable."

"Why is she here?" Blair asks.

"Look, I'm just around the corner. I'll be there in a few minutes to take care of this."

Blair puts the phone down. She figures Road can sort Fiona out when he gets back here. *Maybe they can both go stay at a hotel together.*

"I CALLED ROAD," Blair informs Fiona when she emerges from the bathroom. "He'll be here shortly."

"Perfect." Fiona walks over to the couch, pushes the bedding Road folded aside and sits down. She pulls her phone out. "I'd like a coffee. I'm on East Coast time."

"There's a Starbucks about a block away from here."

Fiona stares up at her with those bright blue eyes. "Is this how you treat all your guests? You're very rude."

"*I'm* rude?"

Fiona nods. "Yes, you are. Of course, I understand why now."

"You do?"

"Yes, I've already figured it out."

Blair is about to ask her what exactly she's figured out, but then sees how Fiona is pointing down at the bedding Road folded and stacked. Of course, Blair had to refold it. *Not a single corner matched. He may as well just have wadded it into a ball, which is probably what he did.*

"Marital problems?" Fiona smiles with perfect white teeth, though they're obviously as sharp as knives.

Blair doesn't get a chance to respond because there's the sound of a key in the door. *Thank God.*

Road enters and stops for a second when he sees all the luggage piled in the entryway. His expression hardens. "Jesus Christ, Fiona!" He steps around the suitcases, comes toward them and drops his backpack on a kitchen chair. "I told you not to come."

Fiona only smiles. She gets up from the couch and saunters over. "Nathan, I'm here because you need me."

"No, I don't."

"Yes, you do." Fiona stands next to him, and she's almost as tall as he is in her heels. Her voice softens. "I'm here for you."

Road's face is still hard, but Blair is mostly staring at Fiona. Her skin is pale and luminous, her tawny eyes have a slight tilt at the corners, and her full lips are a perfect cherry red. As much as Blair hates to admit it, Fiona is one of the most beautiful women she's ever seen.

But this is good. Very good. See? Because now I know what I'm up against and how hopeless anything with Road really is.

In truth, Blair is mystified why Road isn't more pleased to see her. Fiona is seriously gorgeous, and she's high-class Skank Factor X.

They broke the mold when they made this one.

"Let's go speak in private," Fiona purrs, shooting Blair a bitchy look.

Road rolls his eyes, grabs his backpack, and stalks off toward the office with Fiona happily trailing behind him, heels clicking away.

And that's that.

Blair goes ahead and finishes the iced latte she started for herself earlier, wishing she could put her ear to the door to hear what they're saying. Though it turns out she doesn't have to, because Fiona starts yelling almost right away.

"I'm not *leaving!* I traveled three thousand miles!"

She hears Road's low rumble, but can't tell what he's saying. *Probably telling her to stop yelling.* Ironically, for all the shrill women he's dated, Road is surprisingly cool-headed and rarely loses his temper.

"My *God*, don't tell me you're on track. You need my help! Why do you think I'm *here?!*"

More low rumbling.

"That's got nothing to do with it!" Fiona shrieks.

Blair can't help but laugh a little. *He's got his hands full with this one, that's for sure.*

But then Blair thinks about that kiss she and Road shared a few days ago, and her laughter dies. Imagines him kissing Fiona like that, looking at Fiona the same way he looked at her. The thought makes her stomach hurt, and she puts her iced coffee down.

Her building intercom buzzes and when Blair goes to answer it, she discovers Tori is downstairs. Blair presses the button to let her in, surprised by how late it's gotten.

By now, Road and Fiona have come out of his office. Neither of them look very happy. When Fiona sees the coffee Blair is drinking, she gawks at her.

"I hope you made one for me!"

"Um . . ."

"You *didn't*, did you?"

There's a knock at the door and Blair goes to let Tori inside, happy to escape Fiona's withering glare.

"What's all this?" Tori asks when she sees Fiona, who's still pouting about the coffee.

"This is Fiona," Blair tells Tori pointedly. "She's here for Road."

Tori's brows shoot up. "Fiona? Oh, hi, we've spoken on the phone a couple times. I do some work for the website." She puts her hand out.

Fiona's bitchy expression clears. "Tori? Oh, yes, the sister, right? Hello, it's nice to meet you in person," she says politely, shaking hands.

Tori smiles, and Blair is mystified why these two would have spoken on the phone and why they're shaking hands.

"*Who* are you exactly?" Blair asks Fiona, trying to figure this out.

"Road hired her," Tori says, answering for Fiona. "What's your job title again?"

"I'm a media and marketing specialist," Fiona says in an officious voice.

"Really?" Blair asks.

Fiona nods as she shoots Road an exasperated look. "I'm here to help with the new book. Clearly, he's stalled."

"I don't need your help with the goddamn book," Road says, his jaw tight. "And as I keep telling you, I'm not stalled."

Fiona rolls her eyes. "Artists. You think I'd be more used to them by now."

"Are you two going out somewhere?" Road asks, looking over at Tori and Blair.

"We're going to a gallery event for Blair's mom tonight," Tori tells Road. "In fact, why don't you guys come with us? The more the merrier, right, Blair?"

"Uh, Tori, I don't know if that's a good idea." But nobody seems to be paying attention to Blair, because Fiona is clapping her hands.

"A gallery event? Fantastic! I *live* for gallery events! Is this a painter?"

"Yes, it is." Tori nods.

"Perfect!"

Road seems to have his doubts, too, but between Tori's prodding and Fiona's harassment, he's convinced to go, as well.

Blair doesn't know how it happens, but somehow the four of them wind up in Isadora, heading toward downtown Seattle to attend her mom's event. Naturally, Road is driving. She reached for the keys, but the expression on his face made her back off. It's clear he isn't putting up with any nonsense tonight. Blair takes the passenger seat, while Tori and Fiona sit in back.

Fiona makes them stop at a Starbucks drive-thru on the way there and takes ten years to order the most complicated drink Blair has ever heard, yelling it over Road's shoulder at least three times. And then, when she finally gets her coffee, she complains they got it wrong.

"Baristas are *all* idiots," Fiona tells them in her accusing voice.

Only when you order something impossible.

Fiona may be working for Road and not be his girlfriend, but Blair is convinced Fiona has a romantic interest in him. *I mean, why would she travel all this way? To help with his book? I'll bet there's more to it than that.*

Once they get downtown and head toward Pioneer Square, Blair instructs Road on where her mom's gallery is, so he parks in a garage about a block up the street.

"How quaint," Fiona says, as they all get out and walk through one of the oldest parts of the city past a group of derelict winos. "Seattle is very quaint, isn't it? Even these bums are quaint."

Nobody responds, not even Tori, who strangely seems to like Fiona. Not that this stops Fiona from chattering endlessly. She comments on every single thing, flitting back and forth between utter inanity and breathtaking bitchiness.

Blair can honestly say she's never met anyone as bizarre as Fiona. She even criticized Isadora, calling her a 'jalopy' and refusing to get inside her until it was made clear this was the only ride.

She'd better not say anything mean about my mom's cacti.

Blair knows her mom's paintings are odd, what with the whole penis thing, but if Fiona makes one rude comment, Blair is going to let her have it.

Once they arrive at the gallery—which is very crowded, so her mom must be thrilled—Blair discovers she needn't have worried. Fiona takes one look at the paintings and declares them brilliant.

"Oh, my fucking *God*!" Fiona's eyes sweep around the room, taking in as much as she can. "These are genius! Your mother is the artist? Seriously? Amazing!"

Fiona raves about them so much, Blair watches her closely, trying to decide if she's being sarcastic. Strangely, she appears sincere.

Blair glances over at Tori who's already cringing with embarrassment. "I hope there's wine," Tori says. "There's wine, isn't there? Please?"

Blair laughs and directs her toward the far wall. "There's usually lots of wine. Go help yourself."

Road is checking out all the paintings with raised brows and a stunned expression. When his eyes meet hers, he grins. "Damn, babe."

"They're cacti."

"Sure they are."

Their eyes linger on each other, and Blair's stomach takes a dip. It hadn't occurred to her how she might feel being with Road in a room full of paintings like this.

Her face warms. Despite everything, she and Road did once share something intimate between them.

"Which one is your mother?" Fiona wants to know. "*Who?*"

Blair looks around, then finally points through the crowd, when she sees her mom. "Over there, with the dark green dress. Her hair is the same color as mine."

"I see her!" And then Fiona rushes off, leaving her and Road alone.

"Where did Tori go?" he asks.

"To get wine and hide in the bathroom until it's time to leave."

Road nods, his eyes still on hers, and he doesn't seem to want to look away. "You look pretty tonight. I like the scarf."

Blair's blushes at the compliment. *Am I going to spend the whole night in a constant blush? Maybe I should go join Tori in the bathroom.*

"Thank you," she says, trying not to let his compliment go to her head. After all, she could never compete with someone like Fiona.

"I didn't know your mom painted."

"Yes, she started after she took early retirement," Blair says. "So, I take it Fiona showing up here was a surprise?"

His expression changes. "Yeah, you could say that."

"And she works for you?"

"She sought me out at a blogger's conference in London last year."

"Is this typical for her to fly three thousand miles wanting to help?"

He shrugs. "Who can tell with Fiona? Knows her stuff, though—she's good. Really helped get my book noticed."

Blair nods and takes a deep breath. "I finally read *Edge of Zen*," she admits. "I checked out your blog, too." She tries to keep it light, not admitting the actual truth which is that she scoured the web and read everything by and about him she could find.

His eyes were on a painting in the corner, a large purple cactus with three small red ones beside it, but they cut to her now.

"You're a very good writer," she tells him.

He doesn't reply right away. "Think so?"

"Yes, I do. I was stunned." Blair decides to be completely honest. "Your book was an absolute pleasure to read. You have a unique style. I never knew you wrote at all."

Road shrugs. "It's nothing much."

Blair watches him and is surprised by his humility. It occurs to her that he's not as arrogant as he used to be. "You're an artist," she says, realizing it's the same thing he said to her about her cakes.

"Thanks." He motions behind her. "Think Fiona has your mother trapped."

Blair turns to see Fiona talking animatedly with her mom, while her mom watches in a daze. "I should probably go over and rescue her." Not that her mom can't take care of herself, because she certainly can. "I need to say hello. Do you want to come with me?"

Road shifts uncomfortably. "You go on ahead."

She studies him. "Is everything okay?"

He tries to smile, but then lowers his voice. "Look, Blair, I know your parents hate me."

She blinks.

"It's okay." He lets out his breath. "Can't say I blame them."

Blair opens her mouth but doesn't know what to say, because he's right. *My parents do hate him.*

"Probably shouldn't have come tonight, though there's nothing to be done about it now." He gives her an embarrassed grin. "Except maybe avoid them."

She reflects on the situation and finds herself wishing she could make this right somehow, not even sure why she feels this way. The facts haven't changed, after all. Road left her after barely four months together, and now he's taking Isadora.

It's because I'm so in love with him. It clouds everything.

But somehow, Blair isn't convinced that's the whole reason. Strangely, a part of her is starting to see how things with Road are not as simple as they appear.

"All right, I'm going to say hello. There's wine on the back table, and beer, too," she says, remembering how he isn't much of a wine drinker.

"Okay, good to know."

Blair heads over to her mom, though she doesn't see any sign of Fiona anymore. She spots Tori, a glass in her hand, talking to a guy. A cute one, from what Blair can tell.

"Blair," her mom says, putting her arm out to hug her. "Honey, I'm so glad you could make it."

"This is quite a turn-out." Blair takes in the rich scent of Coco Chanel, her mom's favorite fragrance.

"Isn't it wonderful?"

"The gallery must have done a great job getting the word out."

Blair's dad comes over with a small plate of food and she hugs him, too. "Are Scott and Ian here? I haven't seen them."

"Ian couldn't make it, but Scott's here. He brought Ashley and they're around somewhere," her father says, popping an hors d'oeuvre into his mouth. These gallery events weren't really her dad's thing, and he typically ate non-stop the whole time.

She talks to her parents for a little while as people occasionally interrupt to congratulate her mom on the show.

Blair is always amazed how well people respond to her mom's paintings. With the exception of Tori and herself, nobody else seems embarrassed by them.

"Did you really come here with Road?" her mom asks, taking a sip from her wine. Her dad just left to get more food.

Blair tries to act casual. Her parents don't know he's staying with her, and probably won't be too pleased when they find out. "Tori invited him at the last minute."

"Because the strangest woman approached me a little while ago. She said she arrived here with you and Road and claims she's some kind of marketing specialist who works with him. Is that right?"

"Fiona," Blair groans. "I'm sorry about that."

Her mom is nodding, but also seems puzzled. "Why does Road need a marketing specialist?"

Blair explains everything she can about his book and travel blog.

"I see." Her mom takes all this in. She looks like she wants to ask more questions, but some people interrupt, so their conversation ends.

Blair decides to grab a glass of wine. She sees a few more people she knows and stops to chat with them. As usual, her Road radar is highly sensitive, and she spots him without trying. He's standing with a beer in his hand, talking to one of her mom's guests. She wants to go over, but every time she tries, another person is pulling her into a conversation. Blair has known many of her mom's friends since she was a teenager, and doesn't want to be rude to anyone.

Eventually, she manages to excuse herself but doesn't see Road anywhere, so she heads toward the restroom.

"Hey, there you are." Someone touches her arm and Blair turns, surprised to see Graham.

Her eyes widen. "Wow, you made it."

He smiles, embarrassed. "I'm sorry I didn't return your calls. I finally listened to them, and I realize now how stupid I acted. I should have let you explain things on Monday."

"It's okay, I understand. The whole thing is obviously kind of strange."

"I should have listened, though, and not run out of there."

Blair nods. "I agree."

"I hope it's all right I came here tonight," Graham says. "I just wanted to apologize in person."

"No, I'm glad you came."

"Are we still friends?"

"Of course."

Graham is quiet, studying her. "I think it's time one of us asked this—are we *more* than friends?"

Blair takes him in. His handsome face, preppy blue bowtie, and friendly expression. *I wish I felt something. Anything.* She shakes her head slowly. "I really like you a lot, but I think we're meant to be just friends."

He nods. "Okay, I had a feeling you were going to say that." Graham lets out his breath.

"It's not because of what happened. I'm not holding a grudge or anything."

"No, I understand. I feel like we keep trying to move from the friendship zone, but we're sort of stuck there, aren't we?" He grins helplessly.

"We are. And it's a shame, because we look so perfect together."

Graham chuckles. "Yes, we do. And I think I'd still enjoy being your friend."

Blair puts her hand on his arm, and pretty soon, they're giving each other a hug.

When they pull apart, something catches her attention. It's her Road radar going off. It picks him out across the room where he's watching her and Graham together, and even from this distance she can see his laser focus is turned on, though she can't place his expression. He's standing alone, but then Fiona walks over to him and says something, and he nods. Blair watches as Fiona moves closer and rests her head on Road's shoulder. He puts his arm around her. Blair's stomach sinks and there's a bitter taste in her mouth, all of which she tries to ignore.

It figures.

Graham is commenting on her mom's paintings, telling her how he used to paint in college. Blair is mildly surprised, since she wouldn't have pictured Graham being an artist. She tries to pay attention to what he's saying, but her eyes keep straying toward Road and Fiona.

I was right all along. She wants him.

Chapter Thirteen

Daily List

1. Figure out what Fiona is scheming.
2. Try harder (no pun intended!) to understand your mom's art.
3. Take pleasure in being rude for once in your life.

"DO YOU WANT me to stay and help clean up?" Blair asks her mom as the gallery starts to empty out, though there are still plenty of stragglers.

"No, don't worry. A few friends are staying to help, and then we're going out for a late dinner." Her mom pulls her aside. "Do you by chance have Road's phone number? I'd like to call him and ask about Fiona."

Blair tries to hide her surprise. "Sure, I have it." She gets her phone out and dictates the number to her mom, who puts it in her own phone.

"Thanks, sweetheart, and thanks for offering to stay and help clean up. Scott and Ashley have already left."

Blair sighs. She didn't even get a chance to talk to her brother. Unfortunately, Ashley seems to be leading him around by the nose, or more likely another body part.

After hugging her parents goodbye, she heads over to where Road, Fiona, and Tori are all waiting. Road is wearing a sullen expression on his handsome face. All three of them look ready to call it a night, except maybe Tori, who still has some of her usual sprightly energy. They head out together. Graham already left a while ago. The two of them hugged goodbye and agreed to meet soon for lunch.

It's a cool spring night, and the city air smells like damp cement from when it rained earlier. Road and Fiona are walking ahead, and Tori is telling her about the guy she met tonight.

"I saw you talking to someone," Blair says, stepping over a cigarette butt on the ground. "He was cute."

"He's hot, isn't he? And he's super nice, too. We talked for like an hour non-stop."

"Really?" Blair grins. "Is he single?"

"Yes, and he asked me out, but I said no."

"Why?"

Tori lowers her voice. "He's a cop."

"So what?"

"Come on, you know how my family is. Can you imagine what they'd all say if I started dating a cop?"

"That's silly." Blair thinks it over. While most people trust the police, it's true, Tori's family is sort of the opposite. "Do you really think they'd give you a hard time?"

"Trust me, nobody would like it. I'd never be able to bring him anywhere."

"That doesn't seem fair. If you like him, that's what matters."

But Tori just shakes her head.

When they finally arrive at the car, Fiona, who's been uncharacteristically quiet on the walk over, suddenly balks at sitting in the backseat.

"If I'm forced to ride in this death trap again, I'm sitting in the front this time!"

Blair, who's already climbed into the front seat, decides not to budge an inch. "I'm already here," she says sweetly.

"I don't care. Get out!"

"Sorry." Blair puts her seatbelt on. She's curious to see how Road is going to handle this. *If he tells me to move, I'll be throwing a temper tantrum of my own.*

"I need more room," Fiona says. "There's no room in back. I can barely breathe!"

Road sighs heavily, his hand gripping the open car door. "Cut the shit, Fiona. Just get in back."

"Why are you letting *her* sit in front again? I'm the guest here."

"Because it's my car and my decision."

"That's not an answer!"

Blair turns to look at Tori, who's watching the whole spectacle with a big, amused grin. She's like a kid at Disneyland.

"Listen to me carefully, Fiona," Road says, his voice low and dangerous. "You can get in the backseat of this car and shut the fuck up, or we can *leave* you here. What's it going to be?"

Fiona rolls her eyes. "My *God*, what's eating you?"

Road's doesn't respond, just glares at her.

"Whatever. *Fine.*" Fiona climbs in back, making a production out of squeezing past the tilted driver's seat, going on about how there isn't any air. "I'll probably suffocate back here. Poor Tori and me, hope you'll be happy then."

In truth, Road does seem in a black mood, though Blair isn't sure why. She's also surprised at the way he's treating Fiona. They seemed so close earlier.

Blair braces herself to listen to Fiona complain the whole way home, but amazingly that doesn't happen. Instead, when they arrive back at her garage and park the car, it turns out Fiona has fallen asleep.

"She sure is pretty, isn't she?" Tori says softly, as they all watch Fiona sleeping.

"She is," Blair agrees. It pains her to say it, but it's true. Between Fiona's dark hair, porcelain skin, and perfect features, she looks like Snow White waiting for the prince's kiss.

Road doesn't say anything, only watches Fiona sleep.

And I guess we all know who the prince is.

"It's almost a shame to wake her," Tori breathes.

"It's a shame, all right," Road says, his voice dry.

"She looks like an angel," Blair admits.

"An angel with a forked tongue and a pointy tail," he says.

"I heard that," Fiona mutters, her eyes still closed.

Road smirks. "Good."

TORI LEAVES TO go home, while Blair, Road, and Fiona all head upstairs. Road immediately disappears into his office, and Fiona snatches one of her travel bags and disappears into the bathroom.

Blair grabs a bottle of water and sits in the living room, going over her daily list for tomorrow. She figures Fiona is planning to stay at a hotel and that Road will drive her, but is quickly dissuaded of this notion when Fiona emerges from the bathroom wearing a long, silky black nightgown.

"What are you doing?" Blair stares at her in shock.

Fiona's hair is pulled back in a high ponytail and her face is scrubbed clean. Without makeup, she looks like a teenager. "I'm going to sleep. What does it look like?"

"You're not going to a hotel?"

"Of course not."

"I really think you should go to a hotel."

Fiona ignores Blair, though, and lugs one of her big suitcases over to the living room, opens it, and starts rifling through the contents.

By now, Road wanders into the room. He's staring at his phone, but freezes when he glances over and notices Fiona's nightgown.

"I'll take the couch." Fiona stands up, holding a large pillow she apparently travels with. "Even though I'm your *guest*. I'll make that concession."

"I told her she can't stay here," Blair says quickly. "That you'll take her to a hotel, right?"

Road nods. "Yeah, Fiona. You can't stay here."

"Why not?"

"Because there's no room," Blair says.

"What are you *talking* about?"

"Road will drive you." Blair doesn't understand why this isn't Fiona's plan to begin with. Shouldn't she be trying to seduce Road? Get him alone in a hotel room?

"You're being seriously rude again!" Fiona shrieks. "I'm not going anywhere. I'm sleeping right here on this couch."

Blair and Road's eyes meet from across the room.

Fiona is watching both of them. "God, you two are so *stupid!* Obviously, one of you has been sleeping on the couch, but get over it. You're married."

And with that, Fiona starts pulling off cushions and turning the couch into a bed. Both Blair and Road watch her, but neither of them say a word. Blair is trying to understand this situation. *There's something going on here. Something I'm missing.*

"I guess I should get ready for bed, too," Blair says to no one in particular, though she glances at Road.

"Sure." He nods.

Blair isn't certain what they're going to do about the sleeping arrangements, but since Fiona is mostly Road's problem, she decides to just put her pajamas on.

By now, Fiona is all settled in for the night and has already pulled a black sleep mask over her eyes.

After changing into her T-shirt and shorts, Blair does her nightly ritual with the front door and the appliances. Checks them each three times.

Road is standing in the kitchen eating a bowl of cereal. She can feel his eyes on her, but he doesn't say anything, just watches her routine. Mr. Maurice trails behind her until she gets him his nightly snack.

Finally, Blair tells him goodnight.

"Night, princess."

She goes back to her room and turns the light off. Settles into bed, still wondering what Road is planning to do. She hears him go into the bathroom and tries to ignore him and go to sleep, but of course she can't.

Eventually, she hears him leave the bathroom and walk back down the hall.

Is he going to join Fiona on the couch? Maybe this is their weird thing? Fight with each then sleep together.

I hope not. Ugh.

Blair's whole body is tense as she tries to hear what's happening in the other room.

She doesn't hear anything, though.

Her mouth opens and she keeps completely still, straining to listen.

Suddenly, her doorknob turns and the sound startles her so much, she nearly hits the ceiling. Adrenaline rockets through her

Oh, my God! He's coming in here*?*

Sure enough, Road comes inside, quietly closing the door behind him. The room is dark, but there's plenty of ambient light as she watches him move toward her.

Blair is light-headed—dizzy, actually—and realizes she's been holding her breath this whole time.

"What are you doing?" she asks, gulping for air, trying to keep the hysteria out of her voice.

The mattress dips when he sits down. "I'm coming to bed."

She knows they slept together in the same bed the first couple of nights he stayed here, but that feels like a million years ago.

"Scoot over." He motions to her since she's in the middle.

"Um, maybe you could sleep on the floor? I think I have a sleeping bag somewhere."

Road stills. "Babe, did you seriously just ask me to sleep on the *floor?*"

"I have a sleeping bag. It wouldn't be so terrible."

"My back would kill me after that."

"Please. Not this back thing again. I already know you're making that up." She remembers the day he helped her deliver cakes. His back seemed fine, *more* than fine. At one point, he even helped some of the caterers move a heavy banquet table. Road's back is as strong as the rest of him.

"Look, I'm not sleeping on the floor, so move over."

Blair bites her lip with embarrassment. Maybe that wasn't a nice thing to ask, but she knows she won't be able to sleep if he's in bed with her. Come to think of it, she doubts she'd be able to sleep if he were on the floor next to her, either.

She sighs and moves over to the left side to give him space.

Road pushes the duvet away, and the whole bed shifts as he lies down and tries to get comfortable. His presence beside her is large and male, and the whole feminine vibe of her room is completely changed.

Eventually, he settles in.

Blair glances over. He's lying on his back with his right arm tucked under his head. She can just make out his profile in the dark.

She wonders if it's going to be like before, where he falls asleep almost instantly while she listens to his every breath. His smoky scent is already drifting her way.

She closes her eyes and lets herself enjoy it for a moment. An addict getting her fix.

If I'm going to be lying here awake, I might as well stop fighting it.

"What did you really think of my book?"

Blair opens her eyes. "Pardon?"

"You said you read it," Road continues in a low voice. "I want to hear your thoughts."

"I told you I liked it."

"Why?"

"I think you're a good writer."

"Be more specific."

Blair can't help her laughter. "Are you fishing for compliments?"

"Basically." He laughs now, too. "I want to know why you liked it. Tell me."

"No, I should let you suffer. Maybe it'll drive you to greater artistic heights."

He chuckles then rolls onto his side so he's facing her. "Tell me," he says, his voice low and intimate in the dark.

So she does. Tells him how his writing is clean, eloquent, and a pleasure to read. Then tells him which parts of his book she liked the best. When he was in India, of course, but also the part where he described a family he stayed with in Vietnam. The way the kids kept touching his face with their small hands, his blond beard and hair a curiosity. Another part where he described watching his first pink and gold sunrise on a beach in Thailand.

"I envy you," she says quietly. "You've seen so much and been to so many places." She hadn't realized it until this moment just how much she envied the adventure in his life.

I need more of that in mine.

"You could travel, babe" he says softly. "I know you have the bakery, but you could still go places."

She thinks of Larry and Isabel from *The Razor's Edge* again. *If only I was Road's Isabel. If only he had wanted me at his side.*

Blair draws in a shaky breath and lets it out. Tries to ignore the ache as strong and familiar as ever, the wanting that never goes away.

"You okay?" he asks.

"I'm fine."

Road is quiet for a long moment. "So, you and that dude are back together again, huh?"

It takes Blair a second to follow the shift in conversation. "Graham?"

"Yeah, that's the one." Road turns, so he's lying on his back once more. "Saw him there tonight."

"He came by to apologize for the way he acted."

Road lets out his breath. "Not so dumb after all."

"What do you mean?"

But before Road can answer, there's some kind of sound from the other room. There's talking and then what sounds like loud crying.

Blair sits up partway. "Is that Fiona?"

"Yeah."

Blair tries to get out of bed, but Road stops her. "Just let her be. She's on the phone it sounds like."

"How do you know?"

"She has a broken heart. It's why she came here."

This gives Blair pause. *A broken heart?* Her first thought is she's surprised Fiona has a heart at all. "Is Fiona in love with you? Is it that serious?"

"What?" Road is taken aback. "Why would you say that?"

"Because she flew all the way out here for you."

He starts to chuckle. "Fiona's not in love with me. Trust me, I'm not her type."

Blair doubts this very much. She knows she's biased, but it's hard to imagine Road not being any woman's type. "How do you know?"

"Because Fiona's a lesbian. Her girlfriend broke up with her and moved to Seattle recently."

Blair's brows shoot up. "Fiona is gay? She doesn't look gay."

"Don't think looks have much to do with it."

"No, obviously not, but she's so gorgeous." Blair is quiet as she mulls this over, realizes she was wrong about everything with Fiona. *No wonder she didn't care about Road and me sleeping in the same bed together.* In truth, she feels stupid for jumping to conclusions.

"Gosh, I'm sad for her now." Blair knows a lot about loving someone who doesn't love you back. *I'm basically an expert.* "How do you know all this?"

"'Cause she told me."

"So, you two are, like, friends?"

"Unwilling on my part," he says with humor in his voice. "But yeah, we've become friends over the past year."

Blair lies down on her side. They're both quiet for a while, and she doesn't hear anything in the other room anymore. "I think Fiona's gone back to sleep."

"Yeah."

And that's when she senses it. A shift in the air, something subtle, but electric. A dance of energy.

"Blair," he says softly.

She doesn't reply, just thinks about the way he said her name. Not calling her babe or princess, but using her actual name. Road has very good instincts, she realizes.

Without her noticing it, he's shifted position, too, and he's on his side again, facing her.

Neither of them speaks, though she can hear Road's soft breathing.

And then she feels it, his hand on her arm, his fingers lightly stroking down her skin.

"Are you in love with that guy?" he asks.

She's too stunned by his touch to answer right away. It's like the Fourth of July going on inside of her. "No," she finally manages to say.

"Good." And then he's right there. Before she knows it, Road has pushed her onto her back, his mouth on hers. Kissing her.

Blair's mind turns to chaos. She knows she's supposed to be stopping him, trying to end this terrible addiction, but all she can think is how incredible he feels. Surrounded by Road. His long, muscular body. His smoky scent everywhere, so intoxicating.

This will either cure me or kill me.

Her hands reach for his head, soft hair, long enough to fall around her. She touches his face. His mouth, hot and sensual, tastes like every feverish dream she's ever had.

Road draws back for a moment. Blair can hear his labored breath, her bedroom filled with the sounds of the two of them.

Desire rolls through her. If only the lights were on. *I want to see him like this.* Not the drunken arousal she witnessed years ago, but the real thing.

Road's hand is on her ass but then it travels upward, slips beneath her shirt, stroking until he's touching her breasts. She doesn't stop him, lets him fondle and mold her, her nipples beading. Blair's eyes fall shut as a soft moan escapes her.

Road seems to like this. She hears his breath hitch as he shifts position, pressing his lower body into her, his erection large and obvious beneath his sweats.

She swallows, and it's like her most erotic fantasy coming to life. He gives a low groan when she pulls him closer to kiss him again, unable to get enough of his taste.

A tiny part of her is saying maybe this is a bad idea, maybe she should stop, but the rest of her is saying, only a little more. Just a little. Because it's so good.

These long, drugging kisses aren't in the same universe as the sloppy, drunk ones they shared years ago.

He breaks the kiss and sits up. Puts his arms behind his head to yank off his shirt.

Blair watches in a daze. The plains of his muscular body in the darkened room. The ink on his chest. She reaches out for him without thinking about it, but he's whispering something in an urgent tone.

"Take yours off."

She's too aroused to speak, but lets Road help pull her T-shirt over her head.

He tosses it aside, but when she starts to lie down again, he stops her. His hand reaches behind her hair, where it's pulled back in a low, messy bun.

"This, too."

She reaches behind, tugs at the band holding her bun together, and lets it fall loose.

His hand slides in at her scalp, bringing a handful of her long curls forward. "Love your hair," he murmurs.

Her breath catches at his words. Road's never said anything remotely like this to her before.

Instead of touching her breasts, his hand glides from her neck, over her shoulders and down her arm. He picks up her hand, turning it over. "So elegant, the way you're made."

Blair doesn't know what to say, only watches as Road kneads her fingers and then her whole hand. She's not sure why, but she finds it astonishingly arousing. He brings it to his mouth. His lips are soft when he kisses her palm, though his unshaven face is bristly.

His eyes are on her. Despite the dark room, she can tell he's focused, and she wonders if this is what he's always like when he makes love. It's something she used to wonder about a lot.

He puts her hand down and leans in, taking her mouth again. Hot and wet. Blair whimpers, her arms going around his neck.

Road picks her up, brings her over so she's on his lap, straddling him. The two of them press together, skin to skin. His hands are all over her now, roaming everywhere as they're moving against each other. She's drunk on his scent and taste, the feel of his body hard against her.

I'm spoiled for anyone else.

It's like a warning bell deep within her.

He's lifting her again, has her rise up on her knees in front of him, so he can slide his mouth down to her breasts. Lapping at her nipples, first the left, then the right, then both pushed and molded together.

God. She clutches his head, hands tangled in his hair. It's all sensation. Caught in a storm. His fingers find their way into her shorts, snaking their way inside her panties.

"Babe," Road groans when he touches her. His fingers move through where she's slick and hot and ready.

She gasps when two of them slide home, her breath thready, her body pulsing around him with want.

"Feel so nice," he murmurs, his voice low and rough. His fingers are doing all sorts of wicked things to her down there. She's not even sure what exactly, trying to pay attention because no one's ever done it quite like this.

So good.

Her eyes are falling shut, and then she stops paying attention and surrenders to it.

When her climax is close, she makes herself slow down, takes in the moment, the surreal nature of all this. Being with Road in reality when she's had so many fantasies. She holds back as long as she can, but then finally lets herself go.

She gasps as the first rush of ecstasy washes over her, then another, and another still, until she's finally lost in the storm, moaning and clutching Road, riding it out. Long and intense. Years in the making. It feels endless, and when it eventually winds down, she collapses, her face pressed into the side of his cheek.

Wow . . .

They're both still as Blair tries to recover, her body still shaking.

"Goddamn . . . you're noisy," he mutters, turning so his mouth is pressed next to hers. "Don't remember that."

"What?" Blair draws back, breathless. "Do you think Fiona heard?"

Road chuckles. "Babe, I think the whole *building* heard."

She sucks in her breath, mortified. "I didn't even think. I should have been quieter."

"Screw that, don't be embarrassed. I liked it."

"You did?"

"Hell yeah," he growls then slides his mouth over hers, the kiss deep and demanding. His hand comes up, holding her head still for him as they kiss crazily with tongues and teeth.

Eventually, they surface for air, panting.

"Come here," he says, pulling her down to lie on the bed with him. Once there, he takes her hand and puts it directly inside his sweatpants and underwear, right on his cock, and wraps her fingers tightly around him.

He's very hard. Rigid. His flesh scorching. And as soon as she touches him, Road releases a long, shuddering breath.

"That's right," he says, as she starts to jerk him off. "Do it like that."

Blair keeps at it, their faces so close, his breath mingling with hers. Despite her shattering orgasm, she's already completely turned-on again. She swallows, trying to get a hold of herself.

Road's hand moves lower between her thighs and she opens them for him, giving him better access. He slides his fingers roughly into her panties and seems desperate to touch her. She sobs with relief when he finds her center.

His breath turns ragged as he plays with her. Fingers doing that magical thing again as Blair squirms against them. His cock is as rigid as iron in her hand.

She's so aroused, she's half out of her mind and knows she's going to come again soon. There's nothing to be done about it. When she finally gives in, helpless to stop it, Road puts his mouth over hers, swallowing her moans. He gives a low groan himself, and Blair realizes he's there, too, pulsing and coming in her hand.

"Damn, that was *good,*" he breathes afterwards.

Blair closes her eyes and nods in agreement.

Neither of them says anything more as they lie on their sides, facing each other. Road pulls away and gets out of bed while she remains there, exhausted, listening to him go into the bathroom.

He isn't gone long and returns with one of her towels. They both use it to clean up. When they're done, he tosses it aside then strips out of his sweats and underwear so he's naked.

Beside her again, she feels his hands on her hips, tugging her shorts and panties off. He has her turn so he's behind her, spooning her with his warm body.

Blair lies there in a daze. His smoky scent is everywhere . . . *on me, around me, in me.* Like an imprint, a part of her now.

She thinks about how wrong she was. Road isn't a bad lover. *He's incredible. And that was just using our hands.* She flashes on that crazed ex-girlfriend from years ago, the one who smashed Isadora's windows after he broke up with her. *I think I kind of get it.*

She sighs, wonders if she'll be able to sleep with him wrapped around her like this or if she'll be awake all night. But then she realizes it isn't like before, being with him in the same bed, aroused and on edge. Instead, she's totally relaxed.

Road shifts behind her, seems to sense her active mind and kisses her shoulder. "Go to sleep, Blair," he whispers.

She lets out her breath.

Then, amazingly, she does exactly what he says and falls asleep.

Chapter Fourteen

Daily List

1. Become better acquainted with the wicked witch.
2. Obsessively relive the best night of your life until it's tattooed on your heart and soul.
3. Discover the friend zone is a vast place.

THE BED IS empty the next morning.

I'm still naked, so it couldn't have been a dream.

Blair slept hard and deep. Two of the most intense climaxes of her life probably had something to do with it. There's a hazy memory of Road's hands on her in the early morning, caressing her back.

Where did he go?

She gets up, searches around for her pink robe, and wraps it around herself. After a quick stop in the bathroom, she ventures into the other room where there are voices and the delicious aroma of coffee and breakfast.

"Look what the cat dragged in," Fiona says when she sees Blair. "Don't you look . . . *refreshed.*"

Fiona is sitting in one of the tall chairs at the kitchen counter. Her dark hair's pulled back in a ponytail, and she's wearing a sapphire blue velvet hoodie along with black-framed reading glasses.

Road turns from where he's standing in front of the stove. "Hey, princess."

"Hey," she says softly. Their eyes meet and last night passes between them, sending a shiver of delight through her. "What are you doing?"

"Making pancakes. Want some?"

Blair takes him in. He's wearing gray sweats and a white crew-neck shirt. His blond hair is disheveled and tucked behind his ears. She wishes she could go over and stand behind him, wrap her arms around his waist, hug him close, but despite what happened last night, she knows she can't.

As good as it was, that wasn't exactly romance.

To be honest, she's not entirely sure what it was, so instead she goes over and sits next to Fiona, who is studying her phone.

"I'd love some pancakes," Blair says, enjoying the fact that he's the one making them. All part of the new, improved Road, the one who knows how to cook.

"I just spoke with a humorist I know," Fiona tells Blair, not looking away from her phone. "He sounds interested."

"Interested in what?"

Fiona rolls her eyes. "Your mother, of course. *God*, keep up."

"Fiona, back off," Road growls from over by the stove. "She's just barely awake."

Fiona smirks. "My, oh, my, somebody's feeling like the big protector this morning."

Blair watches Road flip a pancake with a deft hand. The same one that brought her such pleasure last night. *Such magical fingers. I should have guessed. But why would I?* He wasn't like that before. Plus, she doesn't remember any of his girlfriends commenting on it years ago. Not that they would, necessarily, though they commented on other things. Mostly about how horny Road always was.

"Anyway," Fiona continues. "I've spoken to this humorist I know and he wants to see your mother's paintings. We're thinking at the very least a book, some posters, though a whole line of merchandise could be in the works."

"Really? Don't you think my mother's paintings sort of look like... um..."

"Cocks?" Fiona asks.

"Yes."

Fiona smiles. "They do and they don't, and that's what makes them so brilliant."

"Brilliant?"

"They're whimsical. Charming. With the right caption beneath them, I believe they could be quite witty, as well."

Blair tries to imagine it and strangely, she can sort of see what Fiona's talking about.

"You should be more supportive of your mother." Fiona shoots her a look. "What kind of daughter *are* you?"

Road places a plate in front of Blair with a few pancakes. "Here you go, babe." He turns to Fiona. "Play nice."

Fiona smirks. "I'm enjoying this new side of you, Nathan. Now, aren't you two glad I forced you together last night?"

Blair looks up from her plate and Road flashes her a quick grin. "I'm not complaining."

"Maybe that's why your book is stalled," Fiona continues. "All this marital strife. Some artists thrive on it, but others, not so much."

Road sighs with annoyance and goes back over to the stove. "I'm not stalled."

Fiona picks up her coffee cup. "It's not uncommon to struggle with the sophomore book when the first one does well."

"Not struggling," he grumbles.

Fiona raises an eyebrow at him but doesn't say anything more on the subject, just goes back to her phone.

"What exactly does a media and marketing specialist do?" Blair asks Fiona.

"I help bring visibility and success to independent writers and artists." She pauses then smirks. "Only the ones I deem *worthy*, of course."

"Like Road?"

"Yes, Nathan caught my attention right away."

Blair nods. "You're very pretty." She studies Fiona's perfect profile. "Were you ever a model?" she asks, eating her pancakes, which are buttery and delicious. "These are really good," she tells Road.

"Thanks." He pours the last of the batter into the pan.

Fiona scoffs. "Of course not."

"Really? I'm sure you could easily model."

"Why would I bother with something like that?"

Blair shrugs. "The money's probably good."

"Fiona is too *old* to be a model," Road says, and she can see him grinning. "Plus, she's richer than shit, so she doesn't need the money."

Fiona looks up from her phone, over her glasses. "Nathan is correct, I am very rich. But I'm *not* too old to model."

Road flips the pancakes. "Forty is way too old."

"You're forty?" Blair's brows go up. "You look much younger."

"That's one of the benefits to being a stone cold bitch," Road explains to Blair earnestly. "You never age. She'll look this way when she's a hundred."

Fiona laughs with delight. "If only I could bottle and sell it."

"If only," Road agrees.

Blair eats her pancakes while Road and Fiona continue bantering. Finally, Road announces he's going to go take a shower. As soon as he's gone down the hall into the bathroom, Fiona turns to her.

"Who's Marla?"

Blair freezes. "What?"

Fiona is watching her steadily. "Someone named Marla called Nathan this morning. It sounds like he's going over there today."

There's a sick feeling in Blair's stomach as she finishes chewing the pancake which now tastes like dirt. "She's an old girlfriend of his."

Fiona nods. "I knew it. There was *something* in the tone of his voice."

Blair stares at her plate, picking at her food. She feels like throwing the plate at the wall. *I guess last night really didn't mean anything.*

"You're in love with him." Fiona says it as a statement.

Blair's head jerks up. She can hear Road turn on the shower.

"Don't try and deny it. Obviously you are, but he's not in love with you."

Blair stares at Fiona.

"Was Nathan *ever* in love with you?" she demands to know.

"I . . ." Blair isn't sure whether she should be insulted or impressed by this conversation. "He married me, didn't he?"

"Yes, but something's off. *Why* did he marry you?"

"Love, of course."

Fiona rakes her brilliant blue eyes over Blair. "I doubt that." She drums her short, dark nails on the counter. "No, there had to be another reason. What is it?"

Blair gets up and takes her plate over to the sink. "As entertaining as this conversation is, I'm done talking now. I have plans today."

"*Plans?* What plans?"

"I'm meeting Tori. We're going to go shopping and have lunch."

"Perfect. What time?"

"I'm not inviting you."

Fiona's mouth falls open. "I cannot *believe* how rude you are!"

Blair doesn't reply, but instead goes into her bedroom to pick out clothes. She's still in shock about Road meeting up with Marla. All Marla did was call and he immediately goes running to her. *He didn't even ask me what my plans were today.*

Despite all this, Blair can't find it in herself to regret what happened last night. Road's scent is still on her skin, in her bed, everywhere, and being so close to him was incredible. He may have spent all these years traveling and having one adventure after another, but last night was her own adventure.

So what if that makes me pitiful?

As she's thinking this, Road comes into the bedroom. He's fully dressed in jeans and a gray hoodie. "Hey, babe, I'm headed out. Just wanted to let you know I'm taking Isadora."

Blair's stomach sinks. *He's going to drive around with Marla in Isadora?*

"You all right?" he comes over to her. His hair is damp, and he smells like the citrus body wash in her shower.

"I'm fine." She tries to give him a haughty look, but can't quite pull it off.

His hand goes to her hair, which she knows looks like a large tangled bush, then slips beneath to the back of her neck. "You're not regretting last night, are you?"

"No," she admits. His hand feels good, and she tries not to let it affect her.

His green eyes search hers. "I know we have . . . history. A shitty history." He lets out his breath. "Thought it was good last night, though." He's still studying her and seems keenly interested in her response.

"It was great."

Road nods, his laser focus apparently satisfied. He takes his hand away and seems uncomfortable all of a sudden. "Catch you later."

And then he leaves the bedroom.

He didn't even kiss me goodbye.

She sighs.

Definitely not romance.

Blair tries to go into the bathroom to get ready and discovers Fiona in there with the door locked.

When did my peaceful sanctuary get so crowded?

Fiona spends what seems like two years in the bathroom. When Blair finally enters, she discovers bottles of lotion and makeup strewn all over the counter. There are two wet towels on the floor.

Blair is tempted to dump all that makeup in the trash and see how Fiona likes it. Instead, she straightens up, organizing by group.

"This is not a hotel," Blair tells her when she finds Fiona in Road's office after getting ready.

"Don't I know it." Fiona is standing, looking out the window at the city street.

"And I am not your maid, so pick up after yourself."

Fiona doesn't say anything. There's something off about the way she's standing there, her hand touching the window frame.

"Why are you hanging out in here?" Blair asks.

"Isn't it obvious? I'd like some *privacy*, if you don't mind."

Blair turns to leave, then hesitates. "Road told me why you're really here."

"Oh? And why is that?"

"He said you have a broken heart."

Fiona whirls around. "Yes, a pitiful state I imagine *you'd* know plenty about."

Blair is taken aback. Her mouth opens. "Go to hell."

She turns to leave for real this time, but Fiona suddenly bursts into tears. Howling. Her mouth open and distorted. Fiona may be beautiful, but she doesn't cry pretty, that's for certain.

The two of them stand there while Fiona cries and carries on, her face still contorted in a mask. Blair would normally try and comfort someone crying, but senses it's the last thing Fiona wants.

"You're really ugly when you cry," Blair tells her.

"I . . . know." Fiona nods, still crying hysterically. "H . . . h . . . hideous."

"You look just like the Wicked Witch in *The Wizard of Oz*."

"It's true!"

Blair leaves and goes into the bathroom, grabs the box of tissues and comes back. She puts it on Road's desk for Fiona.

"Thank . . . you." She pulls out some tissues, wipes her eyes, and then blows her nose. Her breath is still shaky.

"Guess Road was right about why you're here." Blair starts to organize Road's desk as she stands there, stacking the envelopes and lining up all the papers so the corners match. Some of them don't fit, and she frowns with annoyance.

Fiona watches her, still sniffling. "He's only partly right. My girlfriend, Sachi, left me. Apparently, she doesn't want to be together anymore." She starts sobbing again. "I can't b . . . believe it."

"Why?" Blair gathers Road's pens, wipes out an old coffee cup with tissue and puts them all in there. She can't help peeking at some of his paperwork. It's mostly work stuff, technical data of some sort. She also sees what looks like some kind of article about Frankfurt, Germany, that's marked up and edited.

"Various reasons. Mainly, she says I won't move here for her."

"To Seattle?"

Fiona nods. "She moved to New York for me, but now says I won't move for her."

"Is that true?"

"I don't want to live in Seattle!" Fiona starts wailing again. "Can you imagine me living here?"

Blair thinks about it. "I can, actually."

Fiona swallows, wipes her face with a tissue. "Really?"

"I could see you living downtown or over on the Eastside with all the other rich bitches."

Fiona smiles a little. "Thank you for saying that, for trying to make me feel better, but we both know I'd never fit in."

"I guess you have to decide what's important to you then."

Fiona's phone starts playing some classical piano music, and she answers it. "Yes, I'm ready right now. Let me ask her." Fiona looks over at Blair. "It's Tori, are you ready to go? She's coming over to pick us up."

"What?" Blair's mouth opens. "You invited yourself?"

Fiona gives her a crafty smile. "Blair's ready, too. We'll see you soon."

Blair stares at her.

"I don't give up easily," is all Fiona says, as she brushes past her and walks out of the room.

Tori picks them up in her blue minivan, and Blair enjoys the annoyed expression on Fiona's face when she sees all the dog hair and mess.

"What's that smell?" Fiona asks, climbing into the back, brushing the seat.

"Tori has three dogs and two cats," Blair tells her without holding back the glee in her voice. "She also works part-time at a vet's office. Isn't that great?"

"Why don't any of you people have normal cars?" Fiona grumbles.

"Aren't you glad you forced yourself on us?"

Tori gives Blair a look. "Poor Fiona called me and said you and Road were both ditching her today, even though she's alone in a new city."

Blair rolls her eyes. *Poor Fiona?* Of course, Fiona would know how to manipulate someone as good-hearted as Tori.

"She said you guys tried to force her to go stay in a hotel last night," Tori continues. She glances behind her to Fiona in the backseat. "You're welcome to come stay with me. I have a second bedroom."

"Yes," Blair says, smiling at Fiona. "What a terrific idea. Why don't you go stay with Tori? You wouldn't have to sleep on the couch, and you'd have your own room where all of Tori's animals could keep you company."

Fiona opens her mouth, a horrified expression on her face. "I'd love to, but I'm allergic to cats."

"Really?" Blair says. "I have a cat. Mr. Maurice, surely you've seen him."

"I meant dogs, not cats." Fiona shakes her head in a 'silly me' gesture. "It's dogs I'm allergic to."

"Give me a break," Blair says, but can't help her laughter.

The three of them stop first at Fred Meyer, where Tori and Blair shop some of the sales. It's a crowded Sunday, and it isn't long before it becomes clear that Fiona has an ulterior motive for why she wanted to join them today as she starts quizzing Blair about her marriage again.

"I never even knew Nathan had a wife until recently."

"Hmmm," Blair responds noncommittally as she holds a striped shirt in front of herself.

"So, why did he marry you? Did you need a green card?"

Blair forces a laugh. "Yes, that's it. I'm originally from Sweden. How did you know?"

Tori looks confused. "Why are you so curious about Road and Blair's marriage?"

"Because I need them to fall in love."

This gets both Blair and Tori's attention.

"Why?" Tori asks.

"Well, I need Nathan to fall in love," Fiona amends. "Clearly *she's* already in love."

Tori's brows go up as she looks at Blair. "Did you tell her all this?"

"Of course not." Blair hangs up the striped shirt, since she already owns four of them. She turns to Fiona. "You should work for the FBI. Your talents are wasted being a marketing and media specialist."

Fiona smirks. "Believe me, I'm very good at what I do. And you forget I've read Nathan's blog detailing his life the past few years and he *never* mentions you. Not even once."

"That's nice to know," Blair mutters.

"You might as well tell me what the story is between you two. I'll figure it out anyway."

"Why don't you just mind your own business?" Blair picks up the striped shirt again. *So now I'll own five of them.*

"This *is* my business."

"How do you figure that?"

"I suspect Nathan is stalled because of you."

"Me?" Blair laughs. "I seriously doubt that."

"Maybe he's not in love with you, but there's something going on, and obviously you were together last night."

Tori's blue eyes flash up at Blair from the jeans she's holding against her hips. "You were with my brother last night?"

"Sort of."

Fiona snorts. "Sounded like a lot more than 'sort of' to me."

Tori's eyes grow wide. "You and Road are together?"

"It was lust."

Tori makes a face.

"Sorry." Blair smiles at her. "But you asked."

"Lust between you two didn't work out so great last time."

Blair sighs. "I know."

"I thought you were putting all that behind you. Moving on, that you'd *moved* on."

Fiona is watching this with interest. "So, it was lust? But why bother getting married? That doesn't make any sense. Were you pregnant or something?"

Tori and Blair's eyes meet, but then they look away from each other.

Fiona sucks in her breath. "My *God*, that's *it*." She grows still, mulling this over. "But where's the . . . ?"

Blair sighs and hangs the shirt up again. *I don't need to waste money.*

"Fiona, don't go there," Tori says, an edge to her voice. "Seriously. Do not go there."

"I understand." Fiona lets out her breath. "I'm so sorry. I really am. Believe it or not, I love children. They're so cute and grubby. And they smell like mustard. What's not to love?"

Blair glares at her.

"I mean it! I have two nephews, and I love them dearly."

"Whatever." Blair wanders down the aisle to get away from her. *This just keeps getting better and better.*

The three of them roam the store mostly in silence now, except for Fiona's occasional bitchy comment about the merchandise. "I've never been in one of these stores. Is this where everyone in Seattle shops? Aren't there any *normal* stores?"

"Sorry," Blair tells her. "This is all there is, so you'll just have to get used to it."

Fiona tosses her ponytail over her shoulder. "I *know* you're only saying that to frighten me." She glances around. "Though, I have to admit, it's working."

When they stop to look through the household goods, Fiona starts talking to her again about Road. "He's not in love with you, but there's something there."

Tori is at the end of the aisle, examining dog beds. Despite herself, Blair is listening.

"He's interested in you," Fiona continues.

I wish. "What do you mean?"

"Just what I said. He's interested. I can tell. We need to help him along and get this sorted out. Don't you want him to fall in love with you?" She pauses then speaks with relish. "It would be *perfect* for this next book. I can already see it."

Blair laughs. "You're kidding, right? That's what this is all about? Good luck."

Fiona grows serious. "Nathan doesn't understand this yet, but his life is about to seriously change. *Edge of Zen* is doing extremely well, and I suspect we can push it even higher. It's certainly putting him on the radar. This next book could put him on the map."

Blair watches how Tori checks out the softness of each cushion for the doggie beds. "How do you know?"

Fiona smiles. "Trust me, I just do. But we need to help him, because he's blocked and after reading his first draft, I know why. He's missing his theme. A love story would be perfect. You *need* to make him fall in love with you!"

"And how do you suggest I do that?"

"Seduce him with your body first and then your mind."

Blair is silent. *If only it were that simple.* She thinks about how they spent last night together. And look where he is today? With Skank Factor X Marla.

Fiona is wrong. Road isn't interested in me. Last night was just lust for him. Sure, he likes me in a friendly sort of way. And then as she's thinking all this, she sees exactly what she needs to buy.

Tori pushes the cart over as Blair shoves the long box inside of it. "You're buying an air mattress?"

"It's for Road. I'm going to put it in the office."

"I don't know if his back can handle an air mattress."

"His back?" Blair stares at Tori.

"My *God.*" Fiona is gawking at the box. "Did you even hear a single word I just said?"

Blair pointedly ignores Fiona. "I thought he made that up. Is something actually wrong with Road's back?"

Tori nods. "He was in a fender bender a few months ago in London. Although, now that I think about it, aren't air mattresses good for back pain?"

"You should be buying lingerie, not an *air mattress*!" Fiona practically shrieks. "How stupid *are* you?"

"Fiona, I know you mean well," Tori says, while Blair snorts, "but this is probably for the best."

"No, it isn't!"

"This isn't a game," Blair tells her. "It's my life, okay? I'm done with Road. I've been in love with him since eighth grade, and it's time to move on."

"*Eighth grade?* Oh, my fucking *God!* I would have had that man on his knees in less than a week!"

"What do you even know about it?" Blair says, irritated. "I thought you were gay."

Fiona rolls her eyes in exasperation. "I used to date men. I dated men for years! Until I discovered I was a big old dyke." She laughs merrily. "And then I met Sachi." Fiona's eyes suddenly fill with tears. She doesn't start in with the hysterical crying again, thank goodness, but her lips turn down and her face contorts into the evil witch from *The Wizard of Oz* again.

Tori immediately releases the shopping cart and goes over to put her arms around her. "You poor thing. It's going to be okay."

"No offense," Blair mutters, "but I don't need advice on my love life from someone who's so clearly made a mess of their own."

But neither of them are paying attention to Blair as Fiona tries to get herself under control. Eventually, they make their way up to the front and pay for everything, then load it all into the back of Tori's minivan.

Blair thinks about all the things Fiona told her about Road.

What does she know anyway?

Chapter Fifteen

Daily List

1. Set up air mattress with clean sheets.
2. Start the most dangerous adventure of your life.
3. Pretend this might not kill you.

"WHAT THE HELL is this?" Nathan mutters when he sees the air mattress sitting on the floor next to his desk, all neatly made up for bed.

Christ.

He's had a shitty day, and this is the last thing he wants to deal with. First, he gets a call from the technical consultant he hired last week, filling him in on a whole list of problems with his website's expansion. Then Marla calls him this morning, asking him if he'd come help with a surprise gift for Kiki's wedding. He said yes, because he wanted to do something nice for his little sister.

Turns out Marla's idea of a 'surprise' involved him driving her around in her black Escalade all day, going from store to store looking at furniture. He figured she wanted him to help pay for something and then help carry it, but that wasn't it at all. She was just spinning her wheels, wasting their time.

"Look, Marla, I'm done. I can't look at another couch. Just let me know the amount, and I'll give you the money."

"I thought you wanted to help me pick out something nice for the happy couple." She slid her hand down his arm. "We're going to be family soon, after all."

"Yeah," he muttered under his breath.

When they weren't looking at couches, Marla wouldn't stop talking about her divorce, telling him every intimate detail. Going on about how lonely she felt, about what a prick her ex was—not that he's ever met the guy, though apparently he was unfaithful to her.

"You and I had a real good thing once, didn't we, Road?" she asked, putting her hand on his leg. "You have to admit that."

"Sure, I guess." In truth, he remembered how she was always a little crazy, even back then.

"I hear you've become some kind of successful blogger now. Your mom was telling me all about it the other day."

He frowned, wishing his mom would quit bragging to everybody about him, not to mention learn who her real friends were.

Then there was the way Marla kept putting her hands on him as he was driving her car. Touching his arms and chest, rubbing his thigh, even trying to grab his dick. "Jesus, Marla, cut it out." But she only laughed. He kept swatting her hands away, dodging her lascivious fingers. She was aggressive as hell, and he damned near felt molested. At one point, she actually straddled him in the driver's seat after he parked the car.

"God, you were always so handsome." Marla licked her lips. "And you still are."

"Thanks." He had his hands on her waist, trying to pick her up and remove her from his lap without hurting her. "Can you get off me?"

"Do you still think I'm hot? You used to, remember?"

"Sure, course."

"Let's go back to my house and spend the afternoon in bed. What do you say?"

"Listen, Marla, I'm married," Nathan said with relief, remembering he had the perfect out.

"Oh, come on, that's bullshit. You and Little Miss Priss? I know you're not serious. There's no way that's real."

"It's real, all right." Nathan thought about last night, Blair moaning and grabbing him. *That was plenty real.* He always liked it when a woman was noisy, but with Blair, it seriously turned him on. Some women put on a little show, but that was no show. Blair's responsiveness was hot and unexpected. He can't believe he would have forgotten that about her, no matter how drunk he was. And then it hit him, the reason he didn't remember Blair being noisy all those years ago. *I didn't make her come.* He felt embarrassed all over again, but figured he at least made up for it some last night. It seemed like she had a good time.

Then why in the hell am I staring at an air mattress?

He sighs, reaches over to shut off his computer, then leans back in his office chair. Blair cleaned up his desk and organized it. Normally, he's funny about anyone messing with his stuff, but he can see she was only being helpful.

Should leave Blair alone. It's obviously what she wants.

Knows he should, but in truth, he was hoping for another night with her. Been thinking about her all day as he was fighting off Marla. Even this morning, talking to Blair alone in her bedroom, he was feeling the pull of her. Touching her neck, her skin so smooth.

Had to get out of there.

It's not like Blair's in love with that dude—she said so herself—but he knows he should let her be with that guy if it's what she wants.

Not exactly what I *want, though.*

He wants to feel her pressed against him again, listening to all those pretty sounds she makes. Selfish, but there it is. Despite their shitty history, he's attracted to her. She's sweet and classy and way too good for him.

What did Marla call her? Miss Priss. Blair did have some prissy ways, but even that turned him on. Those haughty looks. He's always liked a woman who could throw some sass.

I should let her be, should leave her alone.

He's still telling himself this as he unfolds himself from the chair, leaves the office, and walks down the hall toward her bedroom.

Not sure what he's going to find when he quietly opens the door, expecting she might be asleep, but it turns out Blair's awake, sitting in bed reading.

She looks up from her Kindle, and he can tell she's wearing her usual T-shirt and shorts. Remembers teasing her about not wearing nighties.

Not complaining about those shorts, though.

He imagines her in a sexy little nightie and figures it's just as well she's not wearing something like that.

Probably give me a heart attack.

"What are you doing here?" she asks, but he can see on her face she already knows why he's here. "I set up a place for you to sleep in the office."

"Yeah, I saw it."

The room is dark except for the lamp glowing on her nightstand, and he can see Blair's eyes on him as he makes his way over to the bed to sit down.

"Why?" is all he asks.

She bites her lip, but doesn't look away. The two of them study each other. He knows he should give her the space she wants, shouldn't push it, but the stubborn part of him, the part that wants to stay, is curious to hear her reasons.

"Is it because of that guy, Graham?"

Blair eyes widen a little. "No, that's not it."

"Then what?"

But she just shakes her head.

"Is it the past? Our history?"

Blair doesn't reply. Her hands are still gripping her Kindle, though she's not looking at it. Her head is tilted a little, and her hair is pulled back in a way so he can see the lines of her slender neck.

"Tell me," he says softly. He wants to reach out and touch her, let those red curls brush against him again. Something about Blair keeps drawing him in.

"Having you here has stirred things up for me."

"I get that."

"It's not as if I'm hanging on to it. A lot happened, and even though some of it could have been good, it wound up being all bad." Her eyes meet his. "You know?"

"Yeah." He nods. "That's the truth."

Neither of them speaks or moves after that. The room is quiet except for the noises of distant traffic outside her neighborhood.

Nathan shifts position on the bed so he's turned toward her. Without a word, he reaches over and takes the Kindle from Blair's hand, placing it on the closest nightstand. He feels like an intruder in her private space, but doesn't let it stop him. He licks his lips then motions slightly with his head. "Let your hair down for me."

She remains still for a long moment, and he wonders if she'll do it or if she'll tell him to go. But then she reaches behind her and pulls the band off so there's a riot of fiery curls falling over her shoulder.

He lets out his breath.

Blair considers him. "Take your hoodie off." A little smile plays around the corners of her mouth.

Nathan reaches for the collar around his neck and pulls the thick, cotton material over his head, tossing it on her dresser. He's still wearing a white T-shirt and jeans.

They eye each other. She leans closer and whispers, "It's your turn."

And those three words stir some kind of voodoo magic in his blood.

"Your shorts." His voice comes out hoarse as he looks down at her waist.

He can tell she's surprised he didn't ask for the shirt, but this way he gets to see those legs as she pushes the covers aside and wiggles out of the shorts. Watches her toss them over on the dresser with his hoodie.

Blair is sitting up now, knees folded beneath her, eyes roaming over him, and he wonders what her next request will be.

"Your pants."

Nathan gets off the bed, trying to hide his grin. He unzips his jeans and shoves them off, so all he's left wearing is the T-shirt and a pair of blue boxers. The T-shirt is long, but not long enough to hide the hard-on tenting his boxers.

Blair's eyes linger on it, and the way she's lingering is making him go even harder.

"See anything you like?" he asks.

"I do."

Blair is still sitting on the bed with her legs folded beneath her and gives him a coy smile. "Your turn."

Nathan takes her in, liking what he sees, too. *Can't wait to see all of her.* "The shirt."

She reaches down for the hem of her shirt and pulls it over her head, throws it over with the rest of the clothes on her dresser.

Lust hits him hard at the sight of her nearly naked body. His breath catches, and he automatically starts telling himself to relax. *We got time. No big rush.* Her breasts are nice and fit the elegant way she's made. Nipples a rosy pink. But the most amazing part is her skin, so pale and smooth it's nearly luminous. *Didn't get to see this last night.*

Blair's watching him, and he wonders if she can see his strong reaction to her. "Come here," he says, surprised at the command in his voice.

But she slowly shakes her head. "No."

He chuckles then lets out his breath, putting both his hands behind his neck and takes another breath. "All right, what's it going to be?"

"Your shirt."

Nathan reaches back and yanks his shirt overhead, tossing it aside. Her eyes are on him, roaming so intently, he's relieved to not be the only one affected.

"Now, your underwear," she says, a little catch in her voice.

He smiles to himself. He likes that little catch. "Don't think so. My turn, remember?" She's wearing pink-striped panties. His pulse kicks into overdrive. "Take 'em off, babe."

Blair's fingers slip into each side of the fabric as she slowly slides them lower, revealing what he can see even in the dim light is a red bush that's only a shade darker than the hair on her head. *That*, he does remember from years ago. *Not likely to forget it, either.* Despite an attraction to redheads, he's only been with a few women who were natural.

"Satisfied?" she asks softly.

"Very."

She looks pointedly down at the last vestige of clothing between them, so he pushes his boxers off quickly and kicks them aside. His erection bobbing free. "Now come here," he tells her.

Blair is shaking her head again, though. She lies down on her side. When she speaks, her voice is playful. "No, you have to come to me."

BLAIR WATCHES HIM get on the bed. He starts with her left foot, holding it in his hand, kissing the side then the top, playing with her toes. "What are you doing?" She giggles. "Do you have a foot fetish?"

"Looks that way."

She's lying back on her elbows, taking in the way Road's head is bent over her foot, his blond hair falling forward as one hand holds her calf and the other plays with her toes. She giggles some more. The excitement of being with him like this, the joy of it, and the complete disbelief are all exploding inside her.

So much for having him sleep on an air mattress.

But how do you resist years of erotic fantasies being offered up on a silver platter?

Suddenly, Road nips her instep, and Blair lets out a small shriek.

He chuckles. "I have a fetish for all the pretty bits I'm seeing here." He runs his hand over her calf, working his way up her leg. Touching her knee, inner thigh, stroking her hip. By now, Blair's giggles are gone, turned into something else entirely.

"Kiss me," she says, breathless, reaching for him.

But Road isn't in any hurry. Instead, he's still gazing at her under the soft bedroom light, stroking his hands over her body. "You have amazing skin," he murmurs. "Just beautiful."

This quiets her. Blair closes her eyes, and all she can think is *thank you*. Thank you, God, the universe, whatever it is that's letting her have this moment.

Road shifts position and moves up, so their faces are close. His large body presses against her. As always, she can smell him. His smoky scent drifts over her and she inhales, takes a deep hit off him which sends desire careening through her.

His hand moves up to her breasts, stroking and molding as Blair studies his face, grateful for the light so she can see him. He's watching his hand touch her, but then turns his head. Their eyes meet. Golden-green, the color she's been in love with her whole life, and she realizes it doesn't matter if she's alone in her feelings. She'll never regret being with him like this. No matter what. Not ever.

I don't care if it kills me.

"What did you say, babe?"

She licks her lips. "Kiss me, or else."

"Or else?" A smile plays on his mouth.

Blair doesn't reply, only slides her hand from his shoulder, down his muscular body, right to his cock. Wraps her fingers tight around where he's hard, hot, and clearly in need of attention.

Road's breath hitches.

"Or else I'll stop doing this."

His green eyes go half-lidded with pleasure. That little smile is still on his lips, but she sees the exact moment his arousal eclipses it.

And then he's on her, kissing her with demand. Nearly consuming her, until she's turned inside out.

God, he really knows how to kiss.

She made such a study of Road all those years. Her endless quest to understand the mystery of him. What a thrill to find territory she's never explored. A new continent. Because it's obvious now the drunken night they had years ago was a false version of reality.

Road breaks the kiss and before she knows it, he's wrapping his arms around her and rolling them both over, so she's on top. She gives a breathless laugh and brings her hands up. Her long hair falls around them, and she pushes it over to one side.

He kisses her some more then lightly slaps her on the ass.

"Hey, watch it."

"Or else?" He's breathing hard, but there's a mischievous glint in his eyes.

"Don't test me. There's still an air mattress with your name on it."

Road chuckles. "I'll keep that in mind." He grips both her ass cheeks. "Scoot up, time for me to explore Red Willow Valley."

"What?"

"You heard."

Blair rolls her eyes and laughs to herself. *Red Willow Valley?* This isn't the first time a guy has commented on her being a natural redhead, though no one's ever called it anything quite so imaginative.

"Come on." There's another light slap. "Move up and give me a taste."

Blair would be lying if she said she's never had this fantasy about Road. If she had to add up all the times she's thought of it over the years, the number was probably about . . .

Oh, one million.

Not bothering to hide her grin, she does as he asks and scoots up. Road's hands are still on her ass, and he seems eager to start his exploration as he helps negotiate her into a sitting position over him.

She reaches out to the wall in front of her, feeling shy suddenly about this kind of exposure, but when she looks down and sees the intent expression on Road's handsome face, her shyness fades.

His hands are caressing her skin, hips, thighs, and ass. One slips between her legs, gently stroking, opening her a little for him, and then he lifts his head and she feels it. His mouth, right *there*.

Blair's eyes fall shut.

Yes, Virginia, there is a Santa Claus.

She sucks in her breath.

God.

"Move a little closer," he breathes, pulling her hips down.

She lowers herself more and then he does exactly what he said. He tastes her. And then he tastes her some more, and then he keeps tasting her until it's all Blair can do to not shatter into a million pieces.

One hand is on the wall to steady herself, the other grips his head. Blair opens her eyes, determined to fully experience this. The pleasure like a flame, licking at her, ready to consume. Shadows from her lamp bounce on the wall. When she looks down at Road, his eyes are closed and she watches him.

His head nods with the movement of his mouth, his lips and tongue. Wet sounds. She swallows, and a whimper escapes.

Road's eyes open at this. He's looking up at her and when their eyes meet, a powerful emotion surges through her. Takes her breath away. Electric.

This is the only man I'll ever love.

It comes to her with absolute certainty. The truth. She doesn't understand the why. Doesn't understand the near mystical power he continues to hold over her.

Their eyes are still on each other as the flames grow hotter. His are glazed with lust, *but mine are glazed with love.*

And then the fire takes her and all she knows is mindless pleasure. Hot and indecent. Lets it consume her finally. Burn her up.

Ohmigod.

It takes her a long time to come down. She's shaking all over, still on her knees, forehead pressed against the cool wall.

Road's hands are sliding over her body, soothing her. She takes a deep breath, then another.

"I forgot to be quiet again," she mutters.

"Thank God."

She looks down at him. He's watching her with a little grin, so she changes position and lies down beside him. Kisses him. Puts her hand up to his face, damp from her, and kisses him again with everything she's got. He grabs a handful of her hair, and like last night, he takes her other hand and puts it directly on his cock. And like earlier, he's hot, hard, and definitely in need of attention.

Drawing back, she watches Road in the dim light as she works him with her hand. The grin on his face is long gone and all she can see is the need.

"Am I doing it right?" she asks softly.

"Yeah." Road licks his lips, his breath unsteady. His hands are on her body, roaming from breasts to ass, though his eyes are on her face and she's surprised to see he wants the intimacy of that. "You're doing it just right."

So she continues, his gaze half-lidded, and it doesn't take long before she's the one putting her mouth over his, swallowing his deep groans of pleasure as he gives in to it, being consumed.

IT'S THE CRYING that wakes her. Her bedroom's dark, Road's warm body still beside her. She wondered if he'd go back and sleep in the office now there's a bed in there, but he didn't.

"You awake?" he whispers over her shoulder.

"Yes."

They're both quiet, listening to Fiona's dramatic sobs. Road's arm is still around her.

"How long has she been crying?" Blair asks.

"Don't know. I just woke up."

Mr. Maurice jumps on the bed. Blair didn't even know he was in the room with them. Another loud sob drifts through the walls. "Are you sure I shouldn't go out there to her?"

"Doubt she'd want that."

Blair remembers how Fiona acted earlier today, staring out the window then lashing out when Blair tried to be sympathetic. Road is right. Fiona doesn't want to be comforted.

Mr. Maurice moves up on the bed between them, purring loudly, and Road reaches over to pet him.

They can hear Fiona's voice talking on the phone to someone.

"Have you ever met Sachi?" Blair asks, curious.

"Yeah, met her once in London."

"What's she like?" Fiona was so beautiful, but it was hard to imagine anyone willing to put up with her personality for long.

"Sachi is all right. Not what you'd expect."

"Is she beautiful like Fiona?"

"No."

"Is she a bitch like Fiona?"

Road chuckles. Mr. Maurice rubs his head against Road's hand. "Sachi seemed more the quiet type to me."

"Fiona obviously loves her, though. Do you think there's a chance they'll get back together?"

"Can't say for sure, but I'm thinking no."

"Really?" Blair looks over at him, just barely making out his features in the dark. "Why do you say that?"

"Just an impression. But I don't think she's in love like Fiona is."

"Poor Fiona." Blair lets out her breath. "There's nothing worse than loving someone who doesn't love you back."

Road continues to pet Mr. Maurice, but she senses a shift, his laser focus turned on. "Sounds like you speak from experience."

Blair is quiet, realizing she probably shouldn't have said that. She closes her eyes and thinks of the irony of having this conversation with Road. "I do," she finally admits.

Having his boy-crush satisfied, Mr. Maurice now remembers Blair is the one who feeds and houses him and perhaps deserves some attention, too, so he nudges his head against her hand.

"Did someone break your heart?" Road asks.

"Yes."

"A recent thing?"

She nods.

"Didn't know that. I'm sorry to hear it."

Blair rolls over, lies on her back and continues to pet the cat, listening to his purr. Road is propped up on his elbow beside her.

"It's not that Graham dude, is it?"

"No." She pauses. "It's someone else."

"Are you still in love with him?"

Blair feels her throat tighten. *What a question.* "Yes, I am, but he doesn't love me back. He never did."

Road is quiet, absorbing her words. He puts his hand on her hip over the covers. "That's rough, babe."

She nods. Her breath goes shaky and her eyes sting with tears as she tries to contain herself. "It is," she agrees.

Road's hand slides up from her hip, caresses her arm. He leans over and kisses her lips, soft and sweet. Tears are sliding down the sides of her face into her hair as he kisses her, but she does a good job hiding her crying from him.

"This guy must be a real dipshit," he whispers.

And Blair smiles, despite herself. "Yes, he is."

Road kisses her again, strokes her hair. She touches his face, runs her fingers over the stubble on his cheeks and chin. "Have you ever been in love?"

"Yeah."

"With who?"

He draws back and takes a breath. "Gwen."

Blair's mouth opens with surprise. Gwen was the live-in girlfriend who cheated on him years ago. "So, you were really in love with her?"

"I was, yeah."

I should have known. The way he was drinking so much that night.

"Even thought I was going to marry her."

This gives Blair great pause. "Really?"

He chuckles. "You sound shocked."

"I just didn't know your feelings for her were that strong."

He shrugs. "They were. Once."

“Is she the only woman you’ve ever been in love with?”

Road goes quiet at this, doesn’t answer right away, and Blair has a premonition she isn’t going to like his answer.

He licks his lips. “There’s someone else, too. Right before I came out here.”

Blair tries to hide the riot of emotion coursing through her. She feels queasy, thinks about those letters she saw. “And you’re in love with her?”

He rolls over onto his back. “She’s Spanish and wanted me to come to Madrid with her, but I didn’t go.”

“Why not?”

“Came back here instead. Decided to come home.”

“I see.” Blair swallows, is finding it difficult to breathe. She notices he didn’t answer her question, either. He never said whether he was in love with this woman or not.

Road snorts softly. “Guess we both have problems with our love life, huh?”

“Guess . . . so.”

He rolls toward her, his body close so he’s lying over her. As always, his smoky scent goes straight to her head. “What do you say we forget about our problems for a little while?” He puts his mouth to her ear and whispers, “Maybe that guy isn’t here for you right now, but at least I am.”

Chapter Sixteen

How To Survive An Adventure

1. Keep your wits at all times.
2. Pack light, and only bring what you can stand to lose on the journey.
3. Guard anything breakable, including your heart.

SO, THIS IS my new life.

Every night for the next week, Road is in her bed sleeping beside her, his warm body wrapped around her after bringing her indescribable pleasure.

It hasn't killed me.

Not yet anyway.

It hasn't cured me either, though.

Sometimes, they go right to sleep after, though more often they wind up talking, especially if Fiona is carrying on. He tells her stories of his travels, so many remarkable places he's been these past five years, so many people he's met. Some of them she recognizes from his book, but others, the more recent places he's traveled are going in the next book.

"Are you ever scared?" Blair asks one night, thinking she'd be scared to travel alone to some of the out-of-the-way places he's been.

"I've felt nervous," he admits. "But that's how life is. Sometimes, even if you're scared or nervous, you still have to go for it. I always try to stay safe, though."

She listens with a combination of admiration and envy as Road describes his adventures, and the more she listens, a realization comes to her.

He's changed.

Not in every way. His sense of humor hasn't changed, and he still has a mischievous streak. In a lot of ways, he's the same Road. Even-tempered—unless he's really pushed—doesn't judge, and rarely says anything bad about someone unless they deserve it.

His world view has changed, though. It's clear he sees the big picture now, and she wouldn't have said that about him before. Not to mention his self-worth has grown by leaps and bounds. Road always had an ego, but it was more bluster before. The person he is now seems confident in a way that's entirely new.

"You're different," she tells him one night as they're lying in bed together. The condo is quiet, since Fiona hasn't started crying or talking on the phone yet. "It's like you've learned who you are."

He doesn't reply, though she can tell he's listening as he caresses her back. This was another new thing—Road didn't used to be such a good listener.

"I understand why you started using your real name, instead of Road," she tells him.

"You do?"

"It was a clean break for you, wasn't it?"

His hand on her back stills. The room is dark, but she can still make out his features, the way his eyes take her in. "Yeah, that's right. When I left for India, I decided some things needed to change, and that became part of it."

"It's a good, solid name."

"It is," he agrees, still watching her.

"Nathan," she murmurs, enjoying the sound of it, letting it sink in.

"Like the way you say it, babe." He moves closer, pushing her onto her back. "Say it again," he demands, his voice low and rough.

Blair reaches out to touch his face. "Nathan . . ."

And then there are no more words. Just his mouth on hers, his soft hair falling around her face as pleasure slices through her, sharp and poignant.

Nathan.

LATER, SHE ASKS him why he decided to come back to Seattle. "You could live anywhere. Why here?"

He shrugs. "Just needed to see if this is where I belong or if it isn't."

Blair senses there's more beneath those words, wonders if the Spanish girlfriend is involved somehow. She suspects he might still be in contact with her. The other day, he was on the phone, standing out on the balcony talking, and seemed both quiet and out of sorts afterward.

"Plus, Fiona's right." Nathan lets out his breath. "As much as I hate to admit it."

"What do you mean?"

"I'm stalled."

"With your book?"

"Yeah. Don't know how to end it."

Blair turns on her side in bed, facing him. "What are you going to do?"

"Get it done somehow."

"I wonder why you're struggling."

He sighs. "Wish I knew. Maybe it's what Fiona said, how the expectation is high for this book, since my first one has been doing so well."

Blair nods, but doesn't say anything more. Instead, they both listen as Fiona starts wailing from the other room. The bitchy ghost who haunts them every night.

"Why do you think she stays here instead of a hotel?" Blair wonders aloud.

"Suspect she's lonely, that's all I can figure. Don't think she has a lot of true friends."

Blair is silent, and realizes Nathan is probably right.

"It's kind of you to keep letting her stay," he continues. "I know she's a handful."

"Maybe she really can help with your book. Though, it seems like she's mostly on her phone or computer every day."

"She claims she already is helping."

"How?"

He shrugs. "Don't know."

Blair wonders if that's true. Fiona claims she's here to help, but all Blair can see is the disarray she creates. The living room is cluttered with all Fiona's work stuff, while the kitchen is filled with empty take-out containers and coffee cups. After work, Blair usually finds her talking with a Bluetooth in her ear, pacing the living room, heels clicking on the hardwood. Nathan is holed up in his office, typing on the computer or talking on the phone, as well.

It's bizarre.

How did my life get turned upside-down?

She's not sure how her peaceful sanctuary has become this chaotic mess. Fiona with her demanding and entitled ways. Blair is constantly on the verge of throwing her out, but worries if she does, things with Nathan might change. It's gotten so Blair almost dreads coming home every day.

But then there are nights.

The incredible nights.

God.

Being in Nathan's arms every night is beyond words. The pleasure surreal. It's worth everything, even putting up with Fiona. And they're not even having actual sex with each other, instead just doing what they have been.

Using their hands, or he goes down on her. It turns out Nathan loves going downtown.

And he's crazy good at it.

"You should write a book about your technique," she jokes one night, trying to catch her breath after he brings her to a second shattering climax. Between his magic fingers and magic mouth, he's nothing short of a maestro. "I'll bet you'd make a million dollars."

He scoots up next to her on the bed, chuckling, enjoying her little joke. "At least I wouldn't have to worry about writer's block anymore."

"That's for sure. See, I'm full of good ideas."

"Think I'll call it *Journey to Red Willow Valley*."

She laughs. "I don't know about that title."

"Course, I'll need to spend a lot more time down in the valley," he pauses and grins, "for research purposes."

As much as Blair enjoys him going down on her, she never reciprocates. She feels guilty and knows she's being incredibly selfish, but something keeps holding her back, and she's not even sure what it is.

Nathan never asks her to, never says a word about it. He seems happy enough with her jerking him off or sometimes he just does it himself while he's visiting the 'valley.' *He probably thinks I don't like giving blow jobs.* Though, that isn't it. If there's anyone she'd be eager to give a blow job to it's him, and she did go down on him years ago, but still doesn't do it now.

She looks forward to their conversations, too, as much as the physical intimacy, probably even more. Nathan is intelligent and thoughtful. After five years, it's clear everything she ever loved about him has only crystallized into the man he is now.

Talking together in her dark bedroom, she doesn't feel the same shyness she once did. He seems to like talking to her, too, not just about himself, but asking questions about her life. He's figured out Graham is only a friend, and instead seems curious about the guy she told him she's in love with, the one who doesn't love her back. To her amusement, Nathan continues to call him 'dipshit.'

"Why do you keep calling him that?" Blair finally asks one night, unable to stop her laughter.

"Babe, if he can't appreciate a woman like you then he *is* a dipshit."

Blair's laughter stops at this, and her throat goes tight. She doesn't know what to say, the reality of what she's doing here breathtakingly real. The eventual agony waiting for her at the end of this journey. *I'm the one walking the razor's edge.*

"So, how long did you date the dipshit anyway?" Nathan wants to know.

"A while."

"Do you still see him?"

"Sometimes."

He's quiet, mulling this over. "Are you still romantically involved?"

"No." *We were never romantically involved, and still aren't.*

"What about your test, does he pass that?"

"The Bandito Test?"

"Yeah, that one."

"No, he doesn't pass."

He snorts softly. "Has any guy ever passed this test?"

"Of course."

"And where is he now?"

Blair thinks about some of the men she's dated the past five years. There were a couple of guys she thought would pass. Of course, she wasn't in love with either of them, despite their feelings for her.

Nathan doesn't wait for an answer and continues with his questions. "What does the dipshit do for a living?"

"He owns his own business."

He nods. "Could see you with someone like that."

"He's also an artist."

"Really?" This gives him pause, and she can tell he's surprised. "Wouldn't have pictured you going for an artist."

"Why is that?"

"I don't know. A classy babe like you? Seems like you'd be more into the business type."

"Some men are both."

Nathan is lying beside her and Blair reaches over and puts her hand on his chest, thrilled to touch his warm skin. Solid and real. *This is no fantasy.* And she loves to remind herself of it. She can just make out the Sanskrit above his heart, traces her fingers over it.

"And besides, I'm here with you, aren't I?" she says.

"Yeah, but that's different."

Blair doesn't say anything to this, doesn't bother asking why it's different. She already knows why. He's not in love with her.

Her stomach sinks because that's where the problem begins and ends. By night, Nathan is in her arms, the lover of her dreams, but by day, he treats her like a good friend. She doesn't know what to do or how to change it.

I'm like a beggar taking whatever scraps I can get.

And it's not like she can blame him, either. He's never unkind. In fact, he's generous in every way—not just in bed, but in other ways, too. He shops for groceries, fixes dinner, and tries to run interference between her and Fiona as much as he can. He lets her drive Isadora every day, while he takes the Honda. She knows the situation is not Nathan's fault. The truth is she could kick him out anytime—Fiona, too—but she doesn't. She doesn't because then these amazing nights would go away.

I walked into this with my eyes wide open.

IRONICALLY, NATHAN ALSO starts keeping the same schedule as her baker's hours. He's a morning person and decides the early hours suit him. As a result, they're both up together at the crack of dawn, taking turns in the shower, until one morning, about a week and a half into their little adventure, Nathan suggests they take one together.

"Come on, princess. It'll save time."

"I guess." She hesitates, knows she's already in neck-deep with all this, so what's one more layer of intimacy? She's just not sure how much her heart can take.

He comes over and stands in front of her, trails his fingers down her back. "You doing something private in there?"

"And what if I am?"

"Well, I need to know all about that." He grins. "So I can help."

She groans to herself. He's helped plenty. Nathan doesn't know it, but he's been helping her for years.

"All right."

They shower together and Blair has to admit it's fun soaping each other up, seeing his amazing body under some light for a change. She knows he goes to some guy gym downtown to lift weights and play basketball. *Whatever he's doing, I hope he doesn't stop.*

"You never told me what the Sanskrit here means over your heart." She runs the soap on his chest. "What does it say?"

"Tell you later."

"Is it a secret?" she teases. "The name of some lover you inked on yourself in a moment of anguish?"

His expression goes lazy. "Not at all. It's no big deal." She can see on his face he isn't telling the truth, but decides not to push it. *I probably don't want to know anyway.*

Instead, she washes her hair while Nathan takes the soap and rubs it over her, paying special attention to her breasts, ass, and between her legs.

"You know, there are other parts of my body, too."

"Don't I know it. I'll get to those soon enough."

After finally rinsing herself, he starts trying to soap her again. "Hey, stop it." She laughs, swatting his hands away. "I'm clean."

Nathan grins. "Just trying to be helpful."

"Sure you are."

She closes her eyes and smiles to herself, rinsing the conditioner out of her hair. When she opens them, Nathan is studying her, but he's not grinning anymore. There's a serious expression on his handsome face, his green eyes intense.

"What is it?" Blair asks. "What's wrong?"

He takes a deep breath and lets it out. "Nothing."

"Are you sure?"

He shakes his head. "Just had a crazy thought, is all."

"What?"

"Wondered how it would have been if things had turned out different for us years ago, you know? If they hadn't gone south the way they did."

Blair blinks, tries to hide the impact of his words. A hammer to the chest.

"You ever wonder about it?" he asks softly.

"No," she lies. "Never."

He nods, seems to accept this. "Yeah. Not good to dwell on the past anyway."

She swallows. "Best to let it go."

They finish their shower, both of them quiet. Blair wants to go back to their playful joking, but can't find it within herself. Nathan doesn't seem in a playful mood anymore, either.

After getting dressed and disappearing into his office with a bowl of cereal, he finally emerges a short while later to tell her he's taking the Honda to Brody's today.

"Is there something wrong with it?"

He snorts. "That car runs like shit, needs a tune-up."

"I see."

"If I'm going to keep driving it around, might as well take care of it."

And then he's out the door. Doesn't kiss her goodbye—not that he ever has, despite their intimacy.

He made me come three times last night, yet I'm still in the friend zone. Talk about crazy.

Taking her iced coffee with her, Blair goes over to the living room with her daily list. Fiona is still asleep on the couch, her black eye mask covering her face. There's writing on the mask Blair never noticed before, and she stops to read it. Written in fancy cursive, it says, 'The Bitch is Sleeping.'

Blair laughs to herself. Since Fiona's been staying here, Blair usually hangs out in her bedroom during the mornings, but perversely decides to sit in her comfy living room chair and experience her normal routine for a change.

Maybe I can pretend she isn't here.

After a few minutes, that proves difficult when Fiona pulls her mask up and glares at her. "*What* are you doing?"

"I'm working on my daily list in my own living room."

Fiona lies back down, sighing with annoyance. "It's bad enough I can't sleep all night with the way you two carry on, but now you're going to *sit* out here, too?"

Blair stares at her in amazement. "You're complaining about Nathan and me being noisy?"

"I'm glad you worked out your marital issues, but my *God*, do you have to be so loud? It's like listening to bad porn every night."

"You're one to talk, with all your weeping and wailing!"

Fiona sniffs and pulls her black mask back down. "I don't know what you're referring to."

"Of course you don't."

It's Monday, Blair's day off, so she goes back to writing her list until Fiona flips her eye mask up again.

"Could you just *go*?"

Blair taps her pen against her notebook. "You *do* realize this is *my* home, right? And I'm not the servant here to clean up your messes or do your bidding." She taps more rapidly. "In fact, I really wish you'd leave and go stay in a hotel." *And to think I actually felt sorry for Fiona.*

"What's eating you this morning?" But then Fiona gives a wicked laugh. "Or maybe someone's *not* eating you this morning, is that it?" She laughs some more and lies back down, covering her eyes again.

Blair pushes up from the chair, grabbing her iced coffee to take with her. She walks past Fiona then turns and, before she can stop herself, dumps the entire drink on Fiona's breasts.

"Aaaaah!"

Blair smiles as Fiona screams, rips her eye mask off, and leaps out of bed.

"Are you *crazy*?" Fiona shrieks, dancing around like an evil queen from a fairy tale as she tries to brush the freezing coffee off her silky black nightgown.

"Oops," Blair says with a smile. "Guess I spilled my coffee by accident."

"Accident!" Fiona screams. "That was no *accident*!"

"Gosh." Blair tilts her head to the side, amused to see a small ice cube stuck to the lace in front of Fiona's nightgown. "I'm not usually so clumsy."

"You did that on purpose. Admit it!" Fiona glares at her.

"Of course not. Why would I pour freezing coffee all over you?"

"Aren't you going to at least apologize?" Fiona demands.

Blair smiles sweetly. "I'm really sorry about that."

Fiona continues with her glare, though for some reason, there's the hint of a smile around her mouth. "Oh, *God*, don't bother. I already know you're not in the least bit sorry."

AFTER THE COFFEE incident, Blair goes into the bedroom to change clothes. Unfortunately, she spilled a little bit of it on her jeans, though they're dark enough she doubts it'll stain.

Fiona is in the bathroom. Blair cleans up the coffee mess in the living room, pulling the sheets off the bed and hoping the couch's mattress doesn't stain.

Even so, it was worth it.

When Fiona emerges from the bathroom, she's dressed more casually than Blair has ever seen her in ripped designer jeans and a faded black T-shirt Blair is certain cost a fortune.

"I'm taking you out for coffee," Fiona announces.

"Pardon?"

Fiona gives her a wicked smile. "Seeing as you accidentally spilled yours."

"Don't bother."

"No, I insist. I'm going out with you. I want to," Fiona pauses for dramatic effect, "*apologize* to you for my abhorrent behavior."

Blair's brows go up. "You do?"

"I do. So please, let me buy you a coffee."

"I don't know." Blair mulls this over, suspicious of Fiona's intentions. "You've been a terrible guest, and I think I've been more than generous."

"Very generous. That's why I want to apologize."

"Any sane person would have thrown you out by now."

"It's true!"

"I should probably still throw you out."

"Please, don't. Not yet. Let me try and make it up to you first." Fiona's expression is so sincere that, against her better judgement, Blair finds herself agreeing to go have coffee.

They drive Isadora to La Dolce Vita. Blair has a couple of cake sketches she wants to grab anyway, as a few new ideas have come to her about an upcoming wedding.

"This is your bakery?" Fiona questions with wide eyes.

"Yes, it is. My business partner, Natalie, and I own it." She glares at Fiona, almost daring her to say something rude, but Fiona only nods, looking around with interest.

It's early morning and busy, since they just opened. Blair tells Fiona to have a seat, and she'll be right out. In the kitchen, she says hello to everyone and grabs the sketches she needs, especially the ones for Kiki's cake. She talks to Natalie briefly, who seems amused Blair brought Fiona with her.

"The Wicked Witch is here? I may have to come out and say hello."

Blair gives a dry laugh. "You should definitely come experience her for yourself."

When Blair goes back out front, she sees Fiona has found a window seat and has already ordered a coffee for each of them.

"Did you actually pay for those?" Blair asks. She knows from Nathan that Fiona avoids paying for anything whenever possible.

Fiona picks up her drink. "Of course. I told you I wanted to buy you a coffee."

"I was really more interested in the apology."

Fiona sips her drink then appears stunned. "My *God*, this coffee is perfection."

Blair can't help her grin. "I'll tell Carlos you said so."

"No, you won't. I'll tell him myself. A talented barista is a gift." Fiona smiles, but then her eyes narrow as she considers Blair. "I must admit, you're more successful than I imagined."

Blair snorts softly. "I know that's supposed to be a compliment, but why does it feel like an insult?"

Fiona smirks.

"So, are you really going to apologize to me?" She studies Fiona. In the window's natural light, there are a few faint lines near Fiona's eyes, though she still doesn't look forty.

Fiona leans forward and lowers her voice. "Why is it you don't comprehend the huge favor I've been doing for you?"

"Favor? I don't think so."

"Nathan's in your bed, isn't he?"

Blair stops swirling the straw for her iced latte.

"Do you honestly think he'd be there if I hadn't intervened?"

Blair reflects on this and isn't entirely sure of the answer. *Would he be in my bed?* Obviously, it's one of the reasons she never kicked Fiona out.

"So, is Nathan in love with you yet?"

Blair doesn't say anything.

"What exactly *is* going on?"

"None of your business, that's what."

"Why not tell me? I'm a surprisingly good listener."

"I find that doubtful."

Fiona tilts her head a little. "Try me."

Blair looks into Fiona's blue eyes, thinks back to what happened in the shower with Nathan, and then the way he left without kissing her goodbye. The way he treats her like a friend. A strange desperation grips her.

It's not like there's anyone else I can confide in about this.

She can't tell Tori, since she's not going to want to hear about her brother's sex life—plus, understandably, her loyalties are divided. And despite her friendship with Natalie, she's not sure if she wants to tell her either, since she'd then have to explain the whole pitiful history.

And I don't want anyone to know how pitiful I am.

But after hearing Fiona cry on the phone every night, begging Sachi to take her back, one thing is abundantly clear.

Fiona knows all about pitiful.

So Blair lowers her voice and tells Fiona. Not every detail, but enough to understand the problem.

Surprisingly, Fiona leans in and listens carefully as Blair explains the situation. She doesn't respond right away, just considers things.

"So, he's still talking to Sonia." Fiona picks up her coffee.

"Who's that?"

"The Spanish girlfriend."

"Have you met her?"

"No, but from everything I've heard, you're lucky I'm here to help you with all this."

"Why?"

"Because you *need* me." Fiona speaks earnestly. "Believe it or not, I used to be a real bitch."

"*Used* to be?" Blair can't stop her laughter.

"I've mellowed considerably."

"Really?"

"Yes, I've mellowed since I fell in love." Fiona's voice quivers a little on the word *love*.

"I'm afraid to think of what you were like before."

"Quite the terror."

"How's it going, anyway?" Blair asks. "With Sachi."

Fiona doesn't say anything, just glances around then lets her breath out. "Since you've shared with me, I'll share with you. I can do that."

Blair waits, as Fiona seems to be trying to gain some composure. Oddly, for all Fiona's personality defects, Blair can't help still feeling sympathy since they're kind of in the same boat.

"It's not going well at all." Fiona grips her coffee cup. "I'm not quite sure how I got into this situation. You're lucky to be in love with a *man* who doesn't want you, instead of a woman."

Blair tries not to be insulted by Fiona's phrasing. "I don't feel lucky."

"Men are so easy. Such simpletons. They think with their dicks first." Fiona sighs. "Women are far more complex. Sachi says she doubts my sincerity, thinks I'm being," Fiona pauses, "overly dramatic. That I love the drama."

Blair nods. "You *are* kind of dramatic. Maybe you could try toning it down."

Fiona shoots her a look. "The love of my life is ditching me. What would you have me do?"

"Instead of weeping and wailing into the phone every night, maybe try talking to her."

"I *do* talk, but then I get upset!"

Blair nods. "I know, but you're trying to win her back, right? You need to show her you care about what she wants, too."

Fiona seems to mull this over. "Maybe."

They talk a little more about Sachi and just as they're leaving, Natalie comes over. Blair introduces the two of them.

"Very nice to meet you," Fiona tells her. "I was just telling Blair how impressed I am with your bakery. There's so much *more* you can do, though."

"Excuse me?" Natalie says.

And then to both Blair's and Natalie's astonishment, Fiona starts laying out a crash-course marketing plan for them. Telling them how they first need to create a cookbook with baking recipes. "That's a *must*," Fiona insists. "You should do that right away. Don't wait!" She tells them they also need to start selling merchandise with their name on it—aprons, coffee mugs, and T-shirts. They need to do everything in their power to capture their brand. She talks about the kind of ads they need to focus on, ways to get more media exposure. "Love the name, love it! But my *God*, you must *own* it."

After Fiona goes to the restroom, Natalie's eyebrows are still raised. "She's weird, but I have to admit, that was incredible. I loved every single idea."

Blair nods in amazement.

Driving home, Blair turns to Fiona. "What are you, like an idiot-savant or something?"

Fiona smirks. "Or *something*."

Chapter Seventeen

Daily List

1. Ignore Fiona and all her busybody advice about Nathan.
2. Consider some of her busybody advice about La Dolce Vita.
3. Know you'll treasure the Wicked Witch's iced coffee dance forever.

LATER THE SAME night, Blair is in bed reading, trying to pretend she isn't waiting up for Nathan. *How long does it take to tune-up a car?*

Nobody was around when she came home after her errands, so she just hung out with Mr. Maurice, enjoying the peace and quiet.

She glances down at the oversized T-shirt and shorts she wears to bed every night. Fiona was full of advice on the drive back from the bakery about how she needed to ramp up her game.

"You're not torturing him enough. *That's* the problem."

"I don't want to torture Nathan."

"Yes, you do. If you want him, that's exactly what you need to do."

Blair rolled her eyes.

"Don't worry," Fiona said. "I'm going to help."

"Please, just stay out of it. I don't want your help."

"Yes, you do. You *need* my help!"

Blair throws the covers off and goes over to her closet, stares at the few nighties she has hanging there. *Hearing Fiona's business ideas about La Dolce Vita was one thing, but am I really going to start taking advice on my love life from the Wicked Witch?*

She sighs.

And just as she's changed into a silky crimson nightie with spaghetti straps and matching panties, she hears the front door open and close.

Blair stops, listens. There are no voices, just footsteps—definitely Nathan's—heading toward the bedroom. She freezes, but he walks past and goes into the office instead.

Quickly, Blair throws her clothes in the hamper then pulls the band out of her hair and shakes it loose. She takes some perfume off her dresser and squirts a mist of it in the air before walking through it.

Then she puts on her pink robe and goes out to find him.

Nathan's sitting behind his desk wearing a dark gray Henley, his blond hair pulled back into a short ponytail. She hasn't seen it like that in years, and the sight stops her.

God, he's beautiful.

He glances up from the open computer in front of him. "What's up, princess?"

"Nothing. I heard you come in and just thought I'd say hello."

Road scrolls through his phone for something, then types into his computer.

"Did you go out somewhere with Fiona?" she asks.

"No, dropped her off at Sachi's."

"Really?"

He nods, continues typing.

"Hopefully, that's a good sign."

"Yeah, hope so." Nathan starts to chuckle. "Did you really pour iced coffee on Fiona while she was sleeping this morning?"

Blair doesn't say anything. It figures Fiona would rat her out despite their supposed bonding today.

He stops typing for a moment and glances up at her. "Take it by your silence it's true?"

"She made me mad."

Nathan chuckles some more, but doesn't seem bothered. "That's some crazy shit, babe."

"I'm not usually like that. She brings it out in me."

He smirks but seems focused on his work again.

Blair continues to stand there. She studies the air mattress he never uses and probably never will. She shifts her weight from one leg to the other, feeling awkward and stupid. *Why did I even bother with the nightie and perfume?*

"You're obviously busy," she says. "I'm going to go."

There must have been something in her voice, though, because Nathan looks up again. His laser focus is already turned on, and she can see he's directing it at her.

He takes in her face, hair, robe, legs, and then goes back to her face. A smile pulls at his mouth, his eyes interested. "Guess I'm done now."

"Are you?"

"Yeah, definitely. Don't go." She watches him close his computer down. He pushes his chair back, but doesn't get up. "Come over here."

Blair feels awkward, like it's so obvious she's trying to seduce him. "You can keep working on your computer. I don't care."

"Don't want to anymore." He's watching her. "Don't be shy. What's underneath that robe?"

"Nothing much."

"Why don't you show me?"

She sees the heat in his eyes and decides, *if I'm in, might as well be in all the way.* Blair walks over and stands in front of him, his gaze steady on her the whole time.

He motions with his head. "Let me see. Are you naked underneath?"

Blair unties the robe and slips it off so all she has on is the crimson nightie. It's silky and short, and drapes over her hips and breasts in a way she knows is flattering.

"Goddamn." Nathan's brows go up when he sees her. "Is today my birthday?"

She laughs, knowing his birthday is in December. "This old thing? All my other clothes are in the wash."

There's a flash of white from his grin. "Laundry day."

"Afraid so."

He licks his lower lip. "Lucky me. Let's make sure we have laundry day more often."

Blair smiles, though the expression on his face has her catching her breath.

"Come here." He reaches out for her. "Have a seat."

She goes to sit on his lap, but he stops her. "Not like that. Face me."

Blair does as he asks and climbs onto Nathan so she's straddling him. It's a tight fit in the office chair, but doable. She can feel the thick column of his erection beneath his jeans, pressing at her center.

He takes his hands away. Doesn't touch her, just leans back for a second, lets his eyes roam over her, clearly enjoying the view. "Damn. I don't care what you say, today is definitely my birthday."

Blair pretends indifference, though secretly she's pleased.

Nathan reaches across and brushes her hair off her shoulder, trails his fingers down her neck and arm, leaving sparks on her skin. "So elegant," he murmurs. He takes her wrist then runs his thumb down over her palm, studying her.

"You keep saying that."

"Because it's true. You're one of those girls I was always supposed to keep my hands off."

"What do you mean?"

But he just shakes his head, lets her wrist go and grips her hips instead, then slides his hands around to cup her ass. "Nothing. That shit doesn't matter anymore."

Blair isn't entirely sure what he's talking about. She brings her arms up and rests them on his solid shoulders, reaches around to tug on his ponytail. "I like this. It's cute."

"Had to keep my hair out of the way while I was working on the car."

"How did it go?"

"Good. Definitely running better."

"Thanks for doing that."

His eyes are on hers, and he doesn't seem to want to look away. They drop to her mouth. "No problem," he says. He leans in and kisses her, then kisses her some more.

She sighs with bliss because he tastes so good. Feels so good. His smoky scent drifts around her, pulling her into the undertow. He deepens the kiss and she's all-in for a while, but then pushes him away.

"What's wrong?" he breathes, trying to draw her back again.

She turns her head to the side, but doesn't say anything.

Nathan looks at her questioningly. "Something on your mind?"

Blair nods and lets out a deep sigh. "What exactly are we doing here with each other?"

He grins a little, runs his hand down her spine. "Thought we were celebrating my birthday."

Blair smiles, despite herself. "You know what I mean." She pauses. "Are we friends, lovers, what?"

He considers this. Shrugs. "Guess we're kind of exploring things."

"Are you sleeping with anybody else?"

"Babe, how could I be? I'm here with you every night."

She gives him a look. "You know what I mean."

He reaches up to tuck some hair behind her ear and speaks in an earnest voice. "This is really putting a damper on my birthday surprise."

"Nathan, I'm serious."

He meets her eyes and shakes his head. "No, I'm not with anybody else. I don't want to be."

"What about Marla? Fiona told me you were out with her a couple of weeks ago."

"Christ, no." His expression turns slightly horrified.

Blair watches him closely, but it's obvious he's telling the truth. "What about that night at your mom's party when you didn't come back."

Nathan's brows come together. "What about it?"

"Who were you with then?"

"No one."

Blair studies him.

"So, what, now you're the jealous wife all of a sudden?"

She sighs, looking down at the drape of red silk in her lap. "This just isn't the way I do things. I'm not a casual sex person. Even though I know we're not actually having 'real' sex, it's close enough." She looks back up at him.

His eyes soften. Nathan puts his hand up to her cheek, slides his fingers into her hair. "It's okay, I know what you mean. You're a good girl," but then he amends it, "a good woman. I get that."

Blair doesn't say anything to this, can't, because she knows the truth about what she did to him all those years ago. *And there was nothing good about it.*

"COME ON, LET'S take this into my bedroom," Blair said, getting up from the couch and pulling on Road's hand.

He grabbed the bottle of Jack Daniels from the coffee table and followed her out of the living room.

Blair led him straight to her room then closed the door behind him. She felt like a thief, stealing something that didn't belong to her, but then decided that was absurd. Gwen cheated on him. The truth was none of his Skank Factor X girlfriends deserved him to begin with.

Road grinned at her, tried pulling her over onto the bed, but Blair had other plans. She took the bottle and put it on her nightstand, turned back to him.

"Strip for me," she said.

Road chuckled. "Ladies first."

"Come on." Blair softened her voice. "I promise I'll go next."

Road shrugged. He reached behind to pull his T-shirt off. Blair sat on the bed, ready to enjoy the show, but to her amazement he was undressed in less than ten seconds. His black Metallica shirt, faded jeans, boxers, socks, shoes, all of it was in a pile at the foot of her bed.

She opened her mouth. Road stood before her—one long, naked, muscular man, cock semi-hard. She stared at it with raised brows.

He walked back over to the nightstand to grab the bottle, clearly comfortable with his nudity. She had to admit he looked incredible. After years of imagining him without clothes, she wasn't disappointed.

"All right, princess." He took a swig of whiskey and motioned at her. "Don't keep me in suspense."

Blair stood up and decided to be like Road, stripping her clothes off quickly. She didn't leave them in a pile on the floor, though, but put them neatly on the chair.

When she was done, Road stared at her body with a lust-filled grin. "Damn," he murmured. "Had no idea you were this good-looking."

She walked toward him, took the whiskey from him, and put it down. He was still grinning. Blair stood close, not touching him yet, letting her eyes wander over him as she took a deep breath. His smoky scent, even tinged with whiskey, was indescribably good.

Road didn't move either, though she noticed his grin was gone. Blair reached up and touched the tattoo on his upper right arm—a ship in a bottle—tracing the outline of it.

"I've always liked this one," she said softly.

Road didn't say anything and when Blair looked up to his face, she was surprised to see he was watching her intently.

There was a black tribal arm band on his left bicep and she touched this one next, slid her fingers to circle it. She could hear Road's breath now, turning ragged, see the movement of his chest. When she looked to his face again, his eyes were heated.

"Road . . ." she whispered.

But he only shook his head. "That's enough," is all he said. And then his mouth crashed onto hers, hot and needy, devouring her. There was only one thought blowing through Blair's mind, like a mantra through the cloud of desire.

Finally. Finally. Finally.

THINGS AT THE bakery are crazy all week so Blair works late every day, which is just as well, since her condo is still overrun. Despite Fiona spending time with Sachi, they're not exactly a couple again. At least, not yet. Nathan is on his computer constantly and admits to Blair one night he's making progress with his book.

"You have an ending?" she asks with surprise.

"No, but other things have started coming together for me."

"Does this mean you're not writing *Journey to Red Willow Valley*?"

He chuckles. "Oh, I'm still writing that one. Just need more research is all." And then Blair gasps as Road reaches for her, deciding he needs more research right away.

The truth is she's fallen even more deeply in love with him these past few weeks. Loving someone from a distance and loving them when they're sleeping beside you, she now realizes, are two different things.

She even accidentally tells him 'I love you' one night. Freezes as soon as the words leave her lips. In truth, it felt good to say them, makes her wish she could say them all the time, but she knows that would be the end. No more incredible nights. *Strange to think telling someone 'I love you' is a bad thing.* Luckily, it was right after he made her come with his magic fingers, so he believed her when she told him it just slipped out.

"Were you thinking about the dipshit?" Nathan asks, lying beside her.

Blair goes still, doesn't know how to answer this.

"It's okay." He strokes her back, trails his fingers down her spine. "I figure he's probably on your mind sometimes. That you probably can't help it."

"I guess." Blair doesn't like this, though, doesn't like how he accepts she might be thinking of another guy, doesn't like how he might be doing the same thing. "Do you think of anyone else when we're with each other like this?"

"No. Only thinking of you."

"What about that woman you were involved with from Spain?" she can't resist asking. "Do you still think of her?"

Road is quiet. She hates when he goes quiet because it usually means he's contemplating his answer, that he has *something* to contemplate.

"Occasionally," he admits. "But not when you and I are together."

"Gosh, how tactful you are."

"You think I'm lying?"

"Of course not."

Nathan props himself up on one elbow. "You got something to say?"

I have a million things to say, and I wish I could say them all. But she knows she can't. In her heart of hearts, one thing's for certain. *I'm not ready to give him up yet.*

"Forget it. It's nothing."

"Babe, I already told you, I'm not with anybody else. Only you."

She sighs. "I know."

THE NEXT DAY at work, while Blair is checking on some of the sugar art for Kiki's wedding cake, Natalie comes over. "Hey, I need to talk to you about a couple of things. Can we go in the office for a second?"

Blair looks up at her. "Of course."

She follows Natalie into the bakery's small back office where they sit down across from each other. First, they discuss one of the caterers who hired them to provide desserts for a private party recently, and then Blair reminds Natalie she'll be gone the weekend of Kiki's wedding, which is still a ways off.

"Carlos and Ginger will be handling the Saturday deliveries that day," Blair tells her. "Also, I think Ginger is ready to start doing wedding cakes on her own."

Natalie nods, but has a funny little grin on her face.

"Was there something else you wanted to talk to me about?" Blair asks.

"I'm pregnant."

Blair's eyes widen. "That's wonderful!"

"It is." Natalie nods, beaming.

"Congratulations! I'm so happy for you." Blair smiles and reaches over for Natalie's hand, clasping it. "Anthony must be thrilled."

"He is." Natalie laughs. "The girls, too," she says, referring to her daughter and step-daughter—Chloe and Serena.

"How far along are you?"

"Three months. We've known for a little while, but decided to keep it to ourselves for a bit until we were sure everything is okay. I just told Lindsay this morning."

"That's understandable." Blair flashes back to her own miscarriage years ago. "How do you feel? Are you throwing up?"

"A little queasy. I'm mostly tired, though."

Blair asks her when the baby is due and they talk about the logistics, working around the pregnancy and Natalie's maternity leave.

"Saturdays have been so busy, I've been thinking we should hire another baker for the weekends anyway," Natalie says. "Lindsay is still filling in as a barista, too, but I don't know how much longer she can do it."

"We'll figure it all out," Blair says with a grin. "Don't worry about anything."

Later, as Blair is finishing up for the day, she happens to see Anthony come into the kitchen. He's been picking up Natalie from work every day and now she understands why.

"Hey there, looking for your wife?" Blair asks, untying her apron.

"That I am."

She goes over to him. "I just heard the happy news. Congratulations!"

She gives him a quick hug then steps back to find him grinning. She can't help being slightly affected by it. Anthony is one of the most handsome men she's ever met.

"You two are going to be amazing parents," she tells him. "You already are!" Anthony and Natalie both brought a daughter with them to the marriage, and Blair's always thought they did an incredible job combining families.

"Thanks, we're all really excited. And the girls are both hoping for a little brother."

"Little brothers are fun. I have a couple of them myself. And just think, you'll have built-in babysitters."

Anthony chuckles. "Yeah, we'll see. At this point, all they seem interested in is how to clothe him. I keep explaining a baby isn't like a doll."

Natalie comes in from the front area carrying a couple of empty cake platters, smiling when she sees Anthony. Blair flashes back to that terrible day when Natalie came into work pale and upset, telling Blair how her husband at the time had dumped her for another woman. It was a bumpy ride, but Natalie really turned her life around.

That's what I need to do.

Though, Blair knows the journey isn't over and, unfortunately, the ride is only going to get bumpier.

BLAIR'S MOOD TURNS dark after this. It's not that she isn't happy for Natalie and her beautiful life, because she certainly is. Her mood isn't so much about Natalie at all, but more about her own life and the mess it has become lately.

"Hey, princess," Nathan says when she gets home. He's in the kitchen making dinner. Some kind of pasta dish, dirtying what looks like every single pan in the house. Blair puts the slices of carrot cake she brought home for him into the fridge.

Fiona is, as usual, blathering into her Bluetooth as she clicks around the condo in her thousand dollar shoes. Blair once asked her why she even bothered with the heels, but Fiona only looked at her like she was a moron. "Because I'm *working*!"

Blair goes straight to her bedroom and lies down on the bed, trying to push her dark mood aside, but finds it difficult.

She wants her sanctuary back. Everything clean and organized, tidy and in its proper place. So maybe there were too many hospital corners in her life before, but who cares? Since Nathan's been sleeping with her, she's actually forgotten to do her nightly routine altogether. *What if I leave the front door unlocked? Or what if the plugged-in toaster causes a fire?*

I don't even recognize myself anymore.

"You all right?" Nathan opens the bedroom door, looking in on her. "You seemed upset when you came home."

"I'm fine."

He comes over and sits down beside her on the bed. He's wearing jeans and a green T-shirt that makes his eyes look as if they're lit from within. She stares at him as hard as she can, trying to untangle this Gordian Knot, to solve the puzzle of him once and for all, but knows it's hopeless.

"Talk to me, babe. What's going on?"

She doesn't respond.

"Do you want me to leave?" he asks softly.

"*What?*" Her eyes widen as a shot of adrenaline spikes through her.

"Leave?"

He nods. "Yeah, leave you alone for a while. Call you when dinner's ready."

"Oh." Her pulse starts to calm. "Okay, that would be nice. I just need a few minutes alone."

Nathan gets up and goes. She watches him close the door.

And then she starts to cry.

By dinner, she's almost normal again, manages to eat the delicious meal he's cooked and compliments him on it. Manages to ignore Fiona's theatrics as she carries on about some imaginary problem that only a person with too much money could have.

"It's not even a first edition!" Fiona says, ranting on about some bookseller she was on the phone with earlier. Apparently, she's buying a gift for Sachi.

Later, when they're in bed, Nathan teases her about the T-shirt and shorts she's wearing.

"No more sexy nighties?"

"I'm sorry, but your birthday only comes once a year."

"What about laundry day?" he pleads. "That's more than once a year."

"Come to think of it, I should probably put my sweatpants on and wash these shorts."

"Christ," he snorts. "Next thing, you'll be wearing a flannel nightgown, granny glasses, and a cap to bed."

Blair knows he's only trying to lighten her mood. Nathan's laser focus was turned on all evening, directed at her, and it's clear he senses something is off.

"Are you describing the wolf from 'Little Red Riding Hood'?"

"Apparently, I am." He laughs. "Weird."

"Things aren't quite *that* desperate. I'm still human after all—and female."

"That you are," he murmurs, rolling toward her. "You should let me pick out your clothes sometime, though. Think I'd like that."

Blair smiles at him, plays with his hair as he draws her in closer. "What would you have me wear?"

"That's easy, a short skirt to show off your legs. You've got great legs, babe." As if to make his point, he runs his hand down her leg, squeezing along the way. "And of course, a tight shirt. Low-cut with no bra, or maybe one of those pretty ones you have with all the lace. Yeah," he's nodding slowly, "and lace panties. That sounds real good. Can wear those sexy shoes of yours, too."

"So, you'd dress me up like a call girl?"

He chuckles. "Hey, this is only for me. You're not going out in public like that."

"Why not?"

"Because I don't want a bunch of horny assholes staring at my wife."

Blair blinks, tries to hide the effect his words have on her. She knows he only means it as a joke, but his words are like a knife.

She closes her eyes for a long moment.

He doesn't even know he's being cruel.

"Do I get to dress you, too?" she asks, still trying to cover the impact of what he said.

"Course. What do you have in mind?"

Blair thinks it over. In truth, she wouldn't change a thing about Nathan's clothes. He looks hot in everything.

"A suit," she says, realizing she's never seen him in one before, knows he'd look devastating, especially with his hair long like it is.

He frowns, though. "You'd want me to wear a suit and tie?"

She nods. "I'll bet you'd look great in one."

Nathan grows quiet, and his playful mood appears to have evaporated. "I'm not that guy and never will be. You get that, right?"

"What guy?" Blair is confused. "I thought this was supposed to be for fun."

Nathan doesn't appear to be having fun anymore as he pulls away from her.

"Are you angry?" she asks. "A moment ago, you were dressing me like a hooker. If I might remind you, I'm not a hooker."

"Yeah, I know." He gets out of bed and throws his clothes back on. "I'm going to get some writing done."

He leaves, not quite slamming the door behind him. Blair wonders if she should go after him and try to resolve this, but figures maybe he just needs some time alone. She listens as Fiona starts in with her nightly weeping. *Right on schedule.* Fiona's been toning it down the past couple of days, but it sounds like she's in a fine state tonight.

How did my life get like this?

The next morning, Nathan is up with her at their usual early hour. Despite Fiona's wailing, Blair managed to fall asleep and didn't even notice when he came to bed. They take their shower together. As far as she can tell, he's not angry from last night anymore. Things feel mostly normal as he's soaping her up, being playful, sliding his hands everywhere. She grabs him, too, reaches down for his cock. Hard and ready.

"Why is it we never have sex?" she blurts out. "The real kind."

Nathan's hands slow down and she senses the way he's gone on alert. "Figured you didn't want to. You seem comfortable with this."

Blair doesn't say anything, brings her arms up and rests them on his shoulders as she looks into his face.

"Do you want to have regular sex?" he asks, studying her. His hair's wet, and there are water droplets in the blond stubble on his cheeks from the shower.

Blair tries to sort through the jumble of emotions coursing through her. *Do I want that?* She figures at this point, her heartbreak will be the same no matter what. "I think so."

"You think so?"

She licks her lips. "I do. I want that with you."

His eyes search hers. She can see he's aroused, maybe conflicted a little, but those golden-green eyes are definitely aroused. "You still on the pill?"

Blair pauses, then takes a deep breath. "No, I'm not on it anymore."

"Didn't work for us last time anyway."

"No."

"All right, I'll get some condoms at the store today."

"You don't have any?"

He shakes his head. "No, haven't needed any, obviously."

She smiles a little at that. "I guess we'll have to wait then."

"Guess so." But then he also smiles, pulling her in close. "Good thing we know plenty of other ways to keep each other satisfied."

After their shower, Nathan seems in great spirits. Blair figures knowing he's going to be getting laid for real is probably a factor, but has to admit she's enjoying his happy mood. In truth, she wants this kind of intimacy with him, too.

If it's going to kill me, I might as well make it something worth dying for.

She's standing over by her closet, still wrapped in a towel as she's trying to decide what to wear.

"Let me help dress you," he says, coming up behind her, bringing the scent of citrus body wash and a hint of smoke. His hands are on her hips as he kisses the back of her neck.

"As long as I don't look like a 'working girl.'"

She can feel his smile. "No worries, babe," his voice low in her ear. "How about I take care of the undergarments?"

"I guess that's fine."

Nathan lets go of her and walks over to her dresser. He's wearing jeans and a fitted gray T-shirt. She turns to watch him.

"This the pantie drawer?" he asks, opening the correct one. Starts looking through it, holding up various items and grinning. "You have some nice lingerie, princess." She's admiring his muscular back when suddenly her stomach drops because she remembers something in her underwear drawer. Something that shouldn't be there.

"Wait, stop!" Blair moves toward him in a panic, but sees it's too late. Nathan already has it in his hand.

"What's this?" he asks, holding up a piece of green paper.

"I can explain. It's not what you think."

He unfolds it and the grin on his handsome face disappears. "What the hell?" His brows slam together as he stares at it. "Why do you have Isadora's title?"

"It's just a silly mistake," she says quickly. "I meant to put it back, but I forgot."

Nathan stares at the paper some more, then at her. "How did you get this?"

Blair bites her lip, squirming. "I got it from your desk."

She can see the way his mind is working. "You went through my stuff?"

"I know how it looks, but it's not like that. It was the day I thought you took Isadora's keys. Remember? I was upset and took your computer, but I gave it back."

Nathan is shaking his head and doesn't appear to hear a word. "Exactly what were you planning to do with this? Steal my car?"

"No! I was angry. I saw it and grabbed it."

"This was in an envelope with a bunch of other papers. Personal papers. Letters. You look through all those, too?"

"I wouldn't normally do something like that. It's not my nature, but I was really upset."

He lets out his breath. "Jesus Christ."

"Look, I'm sorry.

"Don't give a shit that you're sorry!" He slams her underwear drawer shut. "Can't believe you'd invade my privacy like that!"

And that's when Blair loses it. All the emotion building up inside of her these past weeks erupts like a volcano.

"Really? I'm invading *your* privacy?" She steps closer and yells, "Fuck you, Nathan!"

He stares at her, eyes blazing.

"Take a look around! Who's the invader here?" She throws her hands in the air. "You and the Wicked Witch! But I'm done. Do you hear me? DONE!"

Blair strides out of the bedroom, still wearing nothing but a towel. Before she even plans it, she goes into her hall closet and yanks out her large over-night bag, brings it into the bedroom and throws it on her bed.

Nathan stands there, arms crossed, watching her as she rapidly pulls clothes from her closet and stuffs them into the bag then marches over to her drawers, pulling out more clothes. She remembers her Jimmy Choo platform pumps and grabs them, shoves those in, too.

"What are you doing?" he asks, somewhat bewildered.

Blair rips her towel off so she's naked, grabs clean panties and a bra along with jeans and a striped shirt. Nathan's eyes are still on her, taking in every movement, but she ignores him as she quickly gets dressed.

"Seriously, Blair, what the hell are you doing?"

She zips her overnight bag shut and shoots him a skewering look. "I'm leaving, that's what!"

Nathan uncrosses his arms. His mouth twitches. "Babe, you can't leave. This is *your* place."

"Really? It sure doesn't feel like it!"

"Look, I'll leave if that's what you want. Fiona, too."

"Don't bother. You've obviously made yourself quite at home!" Blair grabs her overnight bag and lugs it to the bedroom door. She turns to glare at Nathan, whose laser focus is glowing red-hot. "And you better take damned good care of my cat!"

And with that, she heads for the front door.

Chapter Eighteen

HOW TO ACT CRAZY ~ PART I

1. Move out of the beautiful condo you adore and pay a mortgage on every month.
2. Let a couple of freeloading interlopers, who are both selfish slobs, live there instead.
3. Yell, curse, and run around butt-naked.

NATHAN TRIES TO stop her, but Blair pushes right past him. "Get out of my way!"

"This is seriously whack, babe." He follows her down the hall to the entryway.

"Don't call me that!"

"Let's talk about this."

Before he knows it, though, she's gone. The front door bangs shut behind her. He's tempted to go after her, but what's he going to do, drag her back?

Nathan heads back into the bedroom and sits on the edge of the bed, trying to think. He rubs his face with both hands then pushes his hair back.

Jesus Christ.

He could tell something was bothering her last night when she came home from work. Come to think of it, she's been out of sorts the past few days.

Hell, I'm the one who should be pissed here! Can't believe she was going through my stuff. Took Isadora's title. What was she thinking?

He gets up and grabs his phone from the nightstand, but decides to wait on calling her. Give Blair some time to consider her actions. *This is her place, after all. She can't leave.*

Fiona comes into the bedroom with wide eyes, taking it all in, her black eye cover pushed to the top of her head like sunglasses.

Nathan shakes his head. "Not now, Fiona."

"Marital stress?"

"Seriously." He strides past her. "Just stay the fuck out of it."

Fiona watches him. "I don't blame her. She's probably fed up with both of us. I mean, my *God*, I'd be, wouldn't you?"

He goes into his office and slams the door shut.

Nathan takes a seat and decides this is all going to blow over.

Blair will come to her senses. Course she will.

He starts up both his computers. Tries to get some work done. The first computer runs his site while he keeps the other open to the file with his book. He skims his site first, checking the stats, glad to see everything looks in order with no obvious problems. No messages from his tech guy, either. There are some new ads running and he checks on those next. He finally hired someone before he left London to handle advertising. Nathan sorts through the email forwarded from his assistant, James. The ones from clients and other bloggers go into a top-tier folder so he can look them over later today. Other emails and more low-level stuff he tries to work through as quickly as possible.

After a short while on the blog, he turns to work on his book, but it isn't going so great. Can't stop thinking about Blair. The way she yelled 'fuck you' at him. He's never seen her that pissed before. Doesn't think he's ever even heard her swear. Watching her whip that towel off in a fury had been something else, too—nothing but ass, breasts, and creamy white skin. He'd been momentarily blinded. To be honest, the whole thing had turned him on.

Had no idea she had such a fiery temper.

Nathan stares at his book. He still doesn't have an end, but he did figure out part of the problem with it. He was missing something—a theme to tie everything together. He thought a lot about what made him leave Seattle to begin with and how he was back now. Blair had a lot to do with that. Their doomed marriage.

Eventually, he reaches for his phone and decides to call Blair, waits as it rings. She doesn't answer, though. He tries again, and there's still no answer. "Shit," he mutters, listening to her voicemail.

"Don't know what you're doing," he growls. "But we need to discuss this."

Where would Blair go?

Either Tori's or her parents, he figures. He calls Tori first, but she doesn't answer either, so he leaves a message for his sister to call him. He brings up his list of contacts, sees he still has Blair's parents' house number, and wonders if it's the same from all those years ago.

One way to find out.

He hears the phone ringing and when a woman answers, he recognizes her mom, Cherise's, voice. He takes a deep breath and politely tells her it's

Nathan, that he's trying to get a hold of Blair.

"Who is this?"

"Sorry, it's Road," he says, remembering she doesn't know him as anything else.

"That's right," Cherise says. "You go by Nathan now."

"Have you talked to Blair today by chance?"

"No, she should be at work. Have you tried her cell?"

"Yeah, no luck, though."

"You could try the number at La Dolce Vita. Otherwise, I'll tell her you called."

"Okay, thanks." He's ready to hang up when he can hear Cherise still talking.

"Actually, I'm glad you called. I was planning to phone you myself. I wanted to ask you about Fiona."

He nods. "Sure, what do you want to know?"

Cherise starts asking him ten million questions. He remembers her being tough, and it's obvious she hasn't changed.

"Do you trust her? I guess that's what I'm really asking," Cherise finally says.

"Fiona is kind of a character, but I have to say I do trust her. She knows what she's doing."

The phone is silent as Cherise seems to take this in. "All right, thank you. I'm glad to hear you're doing so well, Nathan. I know that wasn't an easy time years ago. For any of us."

You can say that again.

They hang up and Nathan turns back to his computers, but his thoughts go back to that lousy scene this morning. What sucks is he was in a great mood before it happened. Blair telling him she wanted to be more intimate while they were in the shower had both surprised and pleased him.

How did it go so wrong so fast?

When it's lunchtime, he goes to see what kind of food Fiona wants. They've gotten into a routine with each other where they either go out for lunch or, more often than not, order takeout, which he usually picks up. It turns out they're both workaholics, and except for the way Fiona balks at paying her part of the bill, have an oddly compatible daytime relationship.

Fiona is reading something on her computer and holds up her finger, so he doesn't interrupt. He checks his phone while he's waiting. Still no word from Blair. He decides to try a different tactic and sends her a text.

We need to talk.

"Let's go out for lunch today," Fiona says, closing her computer. She gets up.

He shrugs. "Sure."

Nathan goes to grab the keys to the Honda and discovers they're gone. Isadora's keys are the only ones there.

This stops him cold.

She didn't take Isadora?

He stares at the Mustang's long, silver keys and his gut goes tight. For some reason, this bothers him more than anything—more than her cursing him out, more than her packing a bag even.

There's a note of finality to it that makes him uneasy.

He and Fiona go to a nearby sushi place that, as he recalls, meets with her approval since she only complained about five things last time they were there, as opposed to the usual twenty.

After they place their food order, Fiona goes to the restroom, and he decides to try Blair's phone again. He listens to it ring, but she's still not picking up and he's annoyed when her voicemail comes on.

"This is bullshit, Blair. Call me."

"Are you kidding?" Fiona gawks as she takes the seat across from him again. "You're going to have to sweet talk her better than *that*."

"Told you to stay out of it."

"You need to tell her you're sorry. Be humble."

"Just like you and Sachi, huh?"

Fiona sweeps her long, dark hair over her shoulder, but doesn't reply, just pretends to read the drink menu.

"Hear you weeping every night, but don't hear you telling her you're sorry. Maybe you should follow your own advice."

"Probably," she admits. "But if you want Blair back, you're going to have to apologize."

Nathan sneers. "For what? Hell, I'm the injured party here." He thinks about Blair going through his stuff. She had no right to do that. "She went through my private things and took Isadora's title," he says, regretting already that he's sharing any of this with Fiona. "Stole it," he adds.

"Your private things? My *God*, listen to you. You're pathetic."

Nathan glares at Fiona. Uses his toughest meanest glare, the one he pulls out for emergencies, like trying to stop a bar fight.

Of course, it has no effect. He has to hand it to her. *She is one Teflon bitch.*

"Are you both blind *and* stupid?" Fiona continues ranting. "You come back after five years, move in then take over her entire apartment!"

Nathan is silent. "She tell you that?"

"Yes, she did."

It's true. He did do that. Admits it was kind of a dick thing to do even.

"She's my wife," he says instead.

Fiona rolls her eyes. "Do you seriously believe I'm that dumb? It's obviously not a real marriage."

"Why do you say that?"

"Because I've never even heard of her until a month ago. Not to mention neither of you wears a wedding ring."

He glances down at his bare left hand. Hasn't seen that plain gold ring in years. It's still at his mom's house, as far as he knows.

"What else she tell you?"

"She told me you're still in contact with Sonia."

He frowns. "Where did she get that idea?"

"I don't know. Is it true?"

"She calls sometimes, but it's over between us."

"Are you sure?"

"Definitely." He was conflicted about Sonia, but coming back to Seattle was the right thing to do. It helped clear his head.

Fiona softens her voice. "I think you have feelings for Blair. I can see it when you two are together."

Nathan doesn't say anything, simply turns and watches the waiter bring over their food.

"What are you going to do?"

He lets out his breath. "No fucking clue."

"WHAT DO YOU mean she won't speak to me?" Nathan is standing out on Tori's front porch. He finally tracked Blair down and discovered this is where she's staying.

"You brought this on yourself. You know that, right?" Tori says.

"What the hell are you talking about? Let me inside the house so I can see Blair."

"No, I don't think so." Tori blocks the doorway. "What exactly are your intentions toward her?"

"My intentions?"

"Yes. She's told me you've been staying at her place the past few weeks, sharing her bed. But what are your intentions?"

"I don't have any intentions!"

Apparently, this was not the right answer because Tori is now glaring at him. "I see. So you want the milk for free? Without buying the cow, is that it?"

"Jesus Christ, I bought the cow, remember? I'm married to the cow." He stops talking and takes a breath. "That didn't come out right."

"Just so you know, I've tried to be Switzerland, but that's over. I'm on Blair's side now."

Nathan is bewildered. *There are sides?* He studies his sister, knows when she gets into protective mode she's not always reasonable, also knows it goes back to when they were kids and had to deal with all their mom's shit. He tries to bring logic back to this conversation. "Look, I care about Blair and just want to talk to her a little bit, figure out what's going on." *And how to get her to come back.*

"What's going on is you need to smarten up and stop messing with her head, okay?"

"I'm not messing with anybody's head!"

Tori just frowns at him. "I can't believe my own brother would fail the Bandito Test. Blair certainly deserves better than that."

Nathan rolls his eyes. "Not this dumb test again. Swear to God, you two are like Lucy and Ethel. Where did you even come up with this crap?"

"That sort of attitude is not going to get you anywhere." Tori's golden retriever suddenly slips through the doorway past her and comes out to greet Road.

"Hey, buddy." He puts his hand out and lets the dog smell it.

"Blair is going to be staying here for a while. She'll call you when she's ready to talk."

Nathan pats the dog, but there's a sinking feeling in his gut. "Does she want me to move out?" he asks quietly, glancing up. "That what this is all about?"

Tori doesn't say anything, just hovers in the doorway.

"Guess I've overstayed my welcome."

"That's between you and Blair." She motions at her dog. "Come on, Eddie."

The golden retriever immediately goes to Tori and trots into the house as she holds the door open.

Nathan sighs to himself. As he leaves, he walks past the Honda. *So Blair won't speak to me. What the hell do I do now?*

He doesn't feel like going back to the condo and dealing with Fiona and all her busybody advice, so he calls his cousin, Brody. He and his girlfriend, Kiera, are going out to a club tonight to watch some live music, so Nathan decides to join them.

He doesn't plan it, but winds up telling Brody all about the situation with Blair.

"Dude, you chased Blair out of her own place?" Brody chuckles. "That's messed up."

When the band is between sets, Kiera goes to the restroom. The club is noisy and smells like alcohol and stale sweat.

"Can't believe she'd just leave like that." Nathan motions to the waitress for another beer. "Still not even sure what happened. Have to admit, I got pissed off when I found out she'd gone through my stuff and taken Isadora's title."

Brody leans forward. "Blair loves that car. Poured her heart and soul into it."

Nathan frowns. He fiddles with his empty bottle, but doesn't say anything. Can feel Brody studying him. Despite being cousins, they don't look much alike since Brody's dad is part Native American and those genes came out strong.

"I like Blair," Brody says. "Don't fuck with her, all right? She doesn't deserve that."

Nathan looks up. "Jesus, first Tori and now you. Why does everybody think I'm out to screw Blair over?"

"I'm not saying that. It's just that you've been gone a long time, and no one knows whether you're planning to stick around."

"I am. Think so, anyway."

Brody nods. "All right, good."

Their waitress brings over Nathan's fresh beer and lets her eyes linger on his. He turns away, uninterested. The only woman who seems to have captured his interest these days is the one who's deciding to avoid him.

It's late when he gets back to the condo. Fiona is talking on the phone as she paces the living room in her black nightgown. He has to admire Sachi's patience. Maybe he was wrong about those two and they'll get back together.

He goes into Blair's room, can still hear Fiona talking though it hasn't hit the weeping stage yet. Grabbing his Kindle, he decides to read in bed for a little while. Mr. Maurice comes over to sit at his side, watching him.

"Bet you're wondering why your mistress isn't here." He pets the cat. "I'm wondering the same thing."

Nathan tries to read, but is too distracted. He can't stop thinking about Blair. It feels strange being in her bedroom without her. Can smell her perfume faintly on the sheets and wishes he was smelling it on her instead.

This is bullshit.

So maybe I have worn out my welcome, there's still no reason for her to act this way.

He glances around her bedroom, everything done in various shades of peach and pink—so feminine. All her scarves are hung neatly on hooks by her dresser, clean and organized like everything else in her life. He finds it relaxing, especially since it's the exact opposite of what he grew up in.

He reflects back to this morning and the way he'd been sifting through all her pretty lingerie. And then to the shower where she'd told him she wanted him, wanted more of him.

Be damned if I didn't feel like a million bucks after that. None of this makes any sense. If she wanted me to leave then why did she say what she did in the shower?

Frustrated, he turns off the bedside lamp and lies on his back with his arm tucked under his head. Fiona has started weeping out in the living room, and he feels annoyed all over again about this situation.

Had every right to be pissed about Blair taking Isadora's title.

Though, in truth, he's mostly pissed now because she isn't here next to him.

Nathan closes his eyes and tries to sleep, but can already tell it's not going to happen. He's had insomnia since he was a kid and knows when sleep isn't going to come.

"Dammit." He lets out his breath, throws the covers back and sits up, eliciting an annoyed meow from Mr. Maurice. "You and me both, pal." He decides to get his computer and write for a while.

NATHAN SPENDS THE next few days away from the condo, though he goes back there to sleep at night. At first, he brought his computer with him and tried hanging out at his mom's to get some work done, but that was impossible as always. Not to mention, her boyfriend, Garth, is a serious dick who wouldn't leave him alone. Garth kept trying to borrow money from him, claiming he could double it. Apparently, Garth has a sports gambling addiction. So instead, Nathan went to Brody's garage, figured he'd sit in the office and work there, though it wasn't long before Brody was handing him a grease-stained Toyota Celica manual.

"What's this?" Nathan asked.

"My mom's car needs the head gasket and valves replaced. I don't have time, but you do."

"You're kidding."

"Nope. All you're doing is sitting here on your ass anyway."

He flipped through the manual. It's been years since he replaced a head gasket. It took hours and was labor-intensive work.

Brody grinned. "Figure you can mope over Blair and make yourself useful at the same time."

"Christ, I never should have told you anything."

"Probably not." Brody laughed. "Come on, don't be such a pouty little girl."

"Not pouting," Nathan muttered. "Plus, I'm very busy." But he turned his computer off and got up anyway.

He worked on the Celica for a couple days to trace some timing and electrical issues then started helping Brody with an engine rebuild yesterday. It's killing his back, but it's been good for readjusting his focus. After working on cars all day, he usually works on his blog all night since his insomnia has come back with a mighty roar. Clearly, he took for granted how well he slept with Blair beside him.

"Oh, my *God,* look what the cat dragged in," Fiona says the next morning when he emerges from the bedroom. He's been leaving every day before she wakes up, but didn't get to sleep until nearly dawn last night. "Where have you been? It's like you've fallen off the face of the Earth!"

"Whatever," he grumbles and goes to the cupboard to get down a box of cereal.

"Seriously, where have you been all week?"

He shrugs. "Around."

Fiona smirks. "Blair called me yesterday afternoon."

He opens the fridge to get some milk, pretending indifference. "She coming back?"

"No. Apparently, Tori is going to stop by later this morning and get some more of her things."

"What for?" Nathan turns around now with a scowl.

"I guess she needs more stuff. Blair said we could stay here, though, temporarily."

"We need to both move out."

Fiona shrugs. "I think she's being quite generous. Have you apologized to her yet? Because that's what you need to do."

He pours the milk over his bowl of cereal.

"You're not handling this the right way," she rants. "You know that, don't you? You need to apologize, and then you need to start courting her. That's what women expect, especially *her* type."

Ignoring Fiona, he takes his bowl of cereal with him back into his office. Can still hear her carrying on. "I don't know why you're not listening to me!" she shrieks. "I'm trying to help you!"

Nathan closes the door loudly.

Christ, does she ever shut up?

He eats his cereal in peace. Told Brody he'd stop by later and help work on the engine rebuild some more. He was surprised how much he enjoyed working on that first car, the Celica. It felt good to work with his hands again, though he hasn't been getting much writing done and still has no idea how he's going to end this book. He thinks about Blair calling Fiona yesterday.

Why the hell didn't she call me?

In frustration, he pulls his phone from his front pocket. He hasn't called Blair at all the past few days, hoping she'd cool down and come to her senses. Apparently, that's not the case, though. He listens to her phone ring, but she doesn't answer.

"This is ridiculous," he says to her voicemail. "I'll move out, if that's what you really want."

He hangs up.

Hits redial two seconds later to leave another message.

"Look, didn't know you were feeling crowded. You should have said something." He hesitates, almost tells her how much he misses her sleeping beside him, misses all their talks, but stops himself. He's even tempted to make up something about Mr. Maurice, since he knows that would get her attention.

But I'm not that desperate.

Or pathetic.

He goes to put his empty bowl in the kitchen sink, hoping to catch Tori before he leaves for Brody's. Fiona is working, but starts harassing him again. He ignores her, but she won't leave him alone, still giving advice about how he should handle Blair. She even tries following him into the bathroom.

"Go away. Jesus Christ, can't I take a piss in private?"

Fiona scoffs. "Like you have anything *I'm* interested in."

When Tori finally comes by to get more of Blair's things, he attempts to get a straight answer from her about what's happening, but it feels like she's speaking in riddles.

"Is she staying away because of me?" he wants to know.

"You'll have to ask her that yourself."

"But she won't speak to me."

Tori puts some of Blair's shirts into a leather bag then gets makeup from the bathroom, and finally grabs a few of her scarves.

"Exactly how long is she planning to be gone?"

Tori shrugs. "A while longer."

He doesn't like that answer. Doesn't like it at all. Once he's at the garage and working on the engine rebuild, he keeps thinking about Blair, getting more frustrated because he's starting to understand part of the problem.

The part where I'm an asshole.

He keeps telling himself he's going to start making arrangements to move out so she can move back in, but he hasn't done a damn thing. Nothing. Just can't bring himself to do it for some reason.

We need to have a conversation first.

That evening he decides enough is enough. He leaves the garage and heads straight for Tori's, determined to talk to Blair once and for all. Unfortunately, when he arrives, he discovers Blair isn't there.

"Where is she?"

Tori stands in the doorway, blowing on her freshly painted fingernails. "She's out with some guy."

This stops him cold. "What guy?"

"I forget his name. It's someone she used to date."

"Graham?"

"No, someone else. They went out for dinner, and I don't think she'll be back until late."

Nathan doesn't move. Can barely breathe. Is it possible Blair is out with that guy who broke her heart? The dipshit who was too stupid to see how incredible she is?

"Why do you think they'll be out late?"

Tori smiles. "Just a feeling. I'll tell her you stopped by, though."

Chapter Nineteen

How To Act Crazy ~ Part II

1. Move into your best friend's tiny house.
2. Sleep in her guest bedroom with a gang of smelly dogs.
3. Come to the strange realization that you prefer this over your own home.

"MY BROTHER WAS just here looking for you," Tori says.

Blair walks into the kitchen, carrying a couple of grocery bags. She's just come back from getting provisions for the girls' night they're planning tomorrow. "He was?"

"I told him you were out on a hot date with an old boyfriend." Tori laughs. "You should have seen his face."

"You shouldn't have lied. He'll figure it out anyway."

"No, he won't. Plus, it's for his own good. He needs to wake up and smell the reality."

Blair puts the veggie platter in the fridge, then starts putting away the rest of the groceries she bought. It's like entering a time warp staying with Tori again in her same old bedroom. *The scene of the crime.* Or at least that's how she occasionally thinks of it, since that's where she and Nathan had their ill-fated night.

"Did he seem bothered?" Blair can't resist asking.

Tori smiles. "Yes, he did actually." She goes over to the counter to get one of the cookies Blair brought home from work. "These are incredible." She chews for a bit. "Enough is enough, you know? I don't want to lie to my brother, but at the same time, I'm tired of watching him make stupid decisions about women. I mean, what if he actually winds up with a Skank Factor X for life? I have to protect him from that. Plus, I'm still hoping he ends up with you."

Blair doesn't say anything as she folds up a paper grocery bag for the recycle bin, can feel Tori's eyes on her.

"This whole thing with you staying here, I think I finally understand it."

"You do?" Blair looks over at her. "Because I'm starting to wonder if I understand it myself."

"This is about Road, isn't it? You're obviously still in love with him."

Blair sighs and puts the bag down. "Yes, but I don't know what to do about it anymore. I feel like a crazy person."

"So, what else is new?" Tori laughs. "I mean, let's face it, you've never been rational when it comes to my brother."

"And I'm still not. Look at me." Blair throws her hands up. "I can't believe any of this. I'm staying here with you all week while those two live in my condo. Talk about the height of irrational!"

"I don't know." Tori's expression grows thoughtful. "I think putting some distance between you and him is a good idea. Especially for Road. He doesn't always see what's right in front of him, but he might see it if it's not there anymore."

"All I know is I was feeling overwhelmed. Like I had to get out of there and try to think clearly for a change."

"Do you want Road to move out of your place?"

Blair bites her lip. "No, I don't want him to leave. That's the problem." She meets Tori's gaze. "But one of us had to."

"See, maybe this whole thing isn't so crazy."

"Maybe." Blair laughs. "Except instead of sleeping with the guy I'm in love with, I'm sleeping with a bunch of snoring dogs every night."

"Hey, the boys like you. It's a compliment."

"Lucky me."

"And what about Fiona? Are you going to let her keep staying there?"

Blair sighs and goes back to putting the groceries away. "I don't know how she does it, but she keeps making me feel sorry for her."

"Good, because I invited her to our girls' night tomorrow."

"What?" Blair turns around, annoyed. "Are you serious? Why would you do that?"

"Because she's lonely and doesn't have many friends. You told me so yourself. Plus, you said she cries half the night. That's so sad."

Blair doesn't say anything more. The mention of Fiona's weeping makes her think of all those nights with Nathan. The truth is she misses him. Too much.

She wonders if Tori is right, and maybe this distance will help him see their relationship in a different light. *I hope so*. Though it doesn't seem like it. He's left messages, but he mostly sounds grouchy and annoyed with her. *At the very least, this will help me decide what my next step should be.*

THE NEXT DAY, after delivering wedding cakes with Carlos, Blair comes back and helps set up stuff for their girls' night. By the time Natalie and Lindsay arrive, she and Tori have laid out fun snacks and the fixings for cocktails, and of course mocktails for Natalie. Tori leaves to go pick up Fiona.

"I can't believe she invited her," Blair groans, taking a seat on one of the living room chairs with her drink called a 'Pink Squirrel.' Tori loves drinks with silly names and printed up recipes for some great ones, including 'Sex with an Alligator,' 'Blue Balls,' and 'Satan's Whiskers.'

Natalie takes a sip from her virgin drink, an 'Atomic Cat.' "I thought Fiona was interesting. Plus, she sent me the outline of a great marketing plan last night. She said it was free of charge. Payment for letting her stay at your condo."

"She did?" Blair says with surprise.

"I'm curious to meet her, too." Lindsay sits on the couch next to Natalie. One of Tori's cats—Lita, a blonde tabby—comes over and rubs against her legs. "She sounds like a character."

Both sisters are dressed casual in jeans, though Lindsay's jeans are ripped and she definitely has more of a bohemian vibe. Natalie is short and curvy with long, straight blonde hair, while Lindsay is tall and slender with dark, wavy hair. They barely look like sisters, but Blair has noticed in profile they have the exact same nose.

Blair picks up her drink. "You haven't seen how she treats everyone like a servant, though."

"Why haven't you kicked her out?" Lindsay reaches down to pet Lita. "I wouldn't put up with that."

Natalie reaches over to pet the cat, too. "Kick them both out. I don't understand why you're letting them stay there while you move in here. None of this makes any sense to me."

Blair sighs. "I know it's strange, but there's more to it."

She can see the way Natalie and Lindsay are both looking at her. Blair takes a deep breath and decides to tell them the truth about her marriage.

"So, he married you out of obligation?" Natalie asks, when Blair is finished explaining.

"Basically."

The sisters are studying her. "So, where do things stand now?" Lindsay wants to know. "Are you still in love with him?"

"Yes." Blair sighs. "Pitiful, I know."

"That's not pitiful," Natalie says. "There's no shame in loving someone.

He's an idiot for not appreciating you more."

The front door suddenly opens. They all turn and watch as Tori and Fiona come inside. Tori bounces over with her usual sprightly energy, while Fiona saunters in, swinging her dark hair like she's ready for the catwalk in Milan.

Fiona gets an excited grin on her face when she sees Blair. "There you are!"

"Hi, Fiona."

Fiona comes over and positions herself so the whole room has to take notice of her. "I come with good news. Your torture is working!"

"My torture?" Blair asks.

"My *God*, I've never seen Nathan so miserable. Moving out and leaving him there was pure genius. I doubt even *I* could have thought of something so ruthless!"

Lindsay laughs with what sounds like approval.

Fiona comes over and takes a seat. She doesn't seem to know how to behave and is acting overly excited toward everyone. Blair decides maybe it was nice of Tori to invite her after all, and with annoyance finds herself feeling sorry for her again.

Drinks are poured, snacks are dished out, and while all the women chat, Blair can't stop thinking about Fiona's comment, wondering if it's really true. *Is Nathan really miserable because of me? I doubt it.*

"Hey, if that marketing plan is payment for staying with me, why didn't I get a copy?" Blair asks Fiona.

"Because I could tell Natalie is far more receptive to my ideas." Fiona takes a sip from her drink, 'Mountain Dew Me.' "*She* listens."

"Give me a break. You need to send me a copy."

Fiona only sniffs and tosses her hair over her shoulder. "I'll think about it."

Blair grips her glass tighter and resists the urge to do something satisfying, like pour the contents on Fiona.

As the women are all talking, Lindsay announces that she's been accepted into an artist residency program in Berlin, Germany.

"That's amazing, congratulations!" Tori says, and there are murmurs of agreement around the room.

"The only bad thing is I'll be leaving right after the baby is born." Lindsay looks at her sister. "I feel like the timing is all wrong."

Natalie shakes her head. "It's fine. You have to take this."

"I applied over a year ago," Lindsay admits. "I was starting to doubt I'd even get in."

The women all talk it over, and everyone agrees Lindsay should go to Berlin. That it's a once-in-a-lifetime opportunity.

A couple hours into their girls' night, Fiona tells them all about her problems with Sachi. As everyone offers advice and opinions, Blair gets up to go to the bathroom. On the way back, she checks her phone and notices a voicemail from Nathan.

"Oh, my God." Blair sucks in her breath, as she walks back into the living room. "Nathan says he's calling about Mr. Maurice!" She shoots a look in Fiona's direction. "Is there something wrong with my cat that you didn't tell me?"

Fiona, who is on her second or possibly third cocktail by now, looks up at her slightly bleary-eyed. "The *cat?* Your fucking *cat?*" She shakes her head. "That cat is in *love* with Nathan."

"Is Mr. Maurice okay?"

"Of course."

Blair bites her lip. Mr. Maurice was the one thing she's been feeling guilty about all week staying with Tori. She knew she couldn't bring him along, though. He'd be miserable around all of Tori's animals, especially her three dogs.

"I'm going to call him back."

Everyone watches as Blair puts her phone to her ear. She waits while it rings then hears Nathan's deep voice, "Blair, finally!"

"I just got your message. Is Mr. Maurice okay?"

"Didn't mean to alarm you. He's okay, except . . ." Nathan pauses and his voice goes soft. "Think he misses you."

"Mr. Maurice misses me?"

Fiona lets out a laugh as she picks up a tortilla chip. "That cat couldn't care less she's gone. Mr. Maurice clearly prefers *men*."

Lindsay and Natalie are both cracking up while Tori is watching Blair with concern. "I'm sure Mr. Maurice does miss her," she tells the others.

Blair walks into the dining room with her phone so Nathan can't hear them all talking.

"Trust me," Fiona says, dipping her chip into the homemade salsa. "It's not the *cat* who misses Blair."

"Think you need to come home," Nathan is telling her in earnest. "It'd be best all around. Especially for Mr. Maurice."

"Mr. Maurice wants me to come home?" She feels torn. "I don't know. Fiona says he's fine."

"Fiona? You going to listen to Fiona about this instead of me?"

"I guess I could come by and see him for myself."

"Good idea. Why don't you come over right now?"

"Right now? No, I can't drive. I've been drinking a little."

"That's okay," he says quickly. "I'll come get you."

"You will?"

"Yeah, definitely."

Nathan tells her he'll be over in a half hour. They hang up, and Blair doesn't know what to think. "He'll be here shortly," she tells the others, walking back over to the couch. "I'm going to go check on my cat."

Everybody is giving her a knowing look.

"He obviously wants to see you," Lindsay says. "That's what's really going on."

"I think she's right," Natalie agrees.

"Of course that's it." Fiona laughs. "That cat hasn't even noticed Blair's gone!"

"I'm sure that's not true." Tori shoots Fiona a quelling look. "But I agree with everyone. It sounds like my brother is making this whole thing up."

Blair considers this. "You really think so?"

They all nod.

Blair changes into a green sundress that comes to right above the knees and a cream-colored cardigan sweater. She's wearing her hair loose and long. Everyone agrees she should wear flip-flops and not sandals.

"You don't want to look like you're trying too hard," Lindsay says.

"But the dress is perfect." Fiona nods in agreement. "Men love skirts." Everyone looks at her, but Fiona only shrugs. "Like I said, I *used* to date men."

All the women are seated casually in a circle when Nathan arrives. He follows Tori into the living room after she answers the door.

"Hello." He nods to the group, and they all murmur their greetings in return. He looks over at Blair. "Are you ready to go?"

She's sitting on the couch, trying to appear nonchalant, though the sight of Nathan nearly makes her heart stop. He's wearing his usual jeans with a fitted T-shirt and, as always, wears them extremely well. She can see part of the brass buckle on his leather belt. Those red and black sneakers. Blond hair tucked behind his ears.

When their eyes meet, Blair can't stop the smile on her face. She just can't help it. *It's so good to see him.* He smiles when he sees her, too, his eyes roaming over her almost greedily.

Blair gets up and grabs her purse. Everyone is saying they hope Mr. Maurice is all right, though she can hear the humor in their voices. She hopes Nathan doesn't hear it. Lindsay and Natalie make no bones about thoroughly checking him out as he stands there waiting for her.

"We'll see you later," she says as everyone watches them leave. They all wave goodbye with more knowing looks.

The Mustang is parked at the end of Tori's driveway, right behind Lindsay's red Mini Cooper, and the sight of it makes her happy.

"I've really missed Isadora," Blair says, buckling herself into the passenger seat. She smiles at the car's familiar red interior. It's early evening and though it was sunny today, some clouds have moved in, and Blair wonders if she should have worn pants instead of a dress. Although, Nathan's eyes keep lingering on her legs.

"I was surprised when you didn't take her with you to Tori's," he says, climbing in beside her.

Blair doesn't reply. She's not sure why she didn't take Isadora. Probably because Isadora belongs to Nathan. *He made that quite clear.*

"So, what the hell was that back there anyway?" he asks, starting the engine. "Some kind of meeting?"

"No, we're having a girls' night."

"Really? Felt more like a witches' coven to me," he mutters, backing out of the driveway.

Blair laughs. "You were being thoroughly dissected."

"Yeah." Nathan smirks. "I noticed that."

They start driving toward Seattle, and they're being overly polite with each other. Neither of them comments about the fight they had or Blair moving out. She asks how things are going with both his book and blog. Nathan tells her how he's been helping out at Brody's during the day and working on everything else at night.

"You're at the garage all day? When do you sleep?"

He snorts. "Never. I have insomnia."

"You do?"

"Yeah, had it since I was a kid."

Blair takes this in, surprised to discover something about him she didn't know.

"It's what got me into writing in the first place," he tells her. "I kept a journal and used to write in it at night when I couldn't sleep."

They keep driving, but he's not headed toward her place and is going west instead.

"What are you doing? I thought you were taking me home to see Mr. Maurice."

"In a little while. Figured we'd go to the park and walk around first. Hang out and talk." He looks over at her. "That okay?"

"I guess. I'm worried about my cat, though. Tell me the truth, how is he?" She's watching Nathan's profile.

"Told you, Mr. Maurice misses you."

Blair wonders if everyone was right and Nathan is making this whole thing up just to see her. She wants it to be true too much to trust it, though.

"Don't worry. Other than that, he's fine," he continues talking. "Just gave him some tuna right before I left to come get you, so he's fat and happy right now."

Nathan drives them to Gasworks Park and finds a corner spot in the parking lot near the large gasworks structure. It's a little breezy outside, and Blair buttons up her sweater, grateful she wore it. They head over to one of the walking paths that leads toward the water.

"So, how's it going at Tori's?" he asks as they leave the parking lot.

"It's fine."

Neither of them says anything more as they walk, though Blair senses something is on Nathan's mind. It's nearly dark out and the city is lit up like a box of jewels. This is one of her favorite vantage points to see Seattle.

Nathan suddenly breaks the silence. "Tori said you were out with some guy last night. Was it the dipshit?"

Blair nearly chokes on her own spit. "I . . . I'd rather not talk about it." *Thanks a lot, Tori.*

"Have you started seeing him again? Is that what this is all about?"

"What do you mean?"

"You moving out. Is it because of him?"

"No, of course not." The wind is blowing her skirt around and she tries to tame it.

"Then what?" He stops walking and faces her, his expression intent. "Tell me."

"It's hard to put into words exactly."

"Tell me anyway."

Blair doesn't know what to say.

"You still pissed off at me? Is that it?" Nathan lets out his breath. "Look, I'm sorry I got so angry about Isadora's title. Just took me by surprise, is all."

"No, I'm the one who should be sorry. I shouldn't have gone through your stuff. That was wrong of me."

"So, what the hell is happening here?"

"I don't know." Blair looks out at the view of the city. "I guess I just needed a break from things."

He's still watching her, and she can sense he's bothered. When he speaks, there's an odd note in his voice. "From *me?* That what you needed a break from?"

Blair turns back to him and is surprised to see the hurt in his eyes.

"Because I thought we were exploring something here," he continues, his laser focus turned on, drilling into her. "Has that changed?"

"No, it hasn't changed. I still want that." Her breath catches. "I still want you." Blair is amazed at her own words. *I can't believe I said it!* The closest she's ever come to admitting the truth to him.

"You do?" The hurt clears, and a grin pulls on his mouth as he reaches down for her hand. "I want you, too."

His touch feels so good, Blair almost closes her eyes. Joy surges through her at his words. She hopes they mean the same thing hers do.

It's fully dark outside and starting to sprinkle rain, so they head back to the car, holding hands. Once inside, though, Nathan doesn't start the engine and instead leans back in his seat, grinning at her.

"What is it?" she asks.

"This night is going my way so far."

She laughs. "Is it?"

"Definitely." He looks around outside the window at the deserted parking lot then back at her with a sly expression, licks his bottom lip. "Come here."

"What do you mean?"

"I mean, come here and sit on my lap."

Blair is looking around outside the window now, too. It's dark and they're parked in the corner of the lot near some trees. "I don't know if that's a good idea."

"Course it's a good idea." He reaches down and adjusts his seat, so it's pushed all the way back creating more legroom. "It's a great idea." He puts his arm out for her.

She watches him steadily. "I've never made out in Isadora before."

"Glad to hear it."

"Have you ever?"

He chuckles. "Best if I don't answer that on the grounds it might incriminate me."

"Don't ask, don't tell?"

"Come on, Blair." He lowers his voice. "Just let me kiss you a little. Touch you."

God. Pleasure from his words washes through her so strong she can barely breathe.

Without thinking further, she gets off her seat and starts climbing over the cup holders to get to him. Nathan helps orient her so she can straddle his lap without the steering wheel digging into her back. "This is kind of awkward because I'm wearing a dress," she murmurs.

"Trust me babe, this is *perfect* because you're wearing a dress." His hands are already sliding up each leg as she finally sits down and brings her arms to rest on his shoulders. As always, his smoky scent surrounds her. She closes her eyes and breathes him in, listening to the patter of rain against the convertible roof. Cozy and dark. Their own little cocoon.

"So, what kind of naughty things did you used to do in my beautiful car?" she asks softly.

His hands are still sliding down her bare legs, trailing his fingers. "So she's *your* car now, huh?"

"Answer the question."

He smirks. "I was sixteen when my uncle gave me Isadora. Use your imagination."

"I don't want to use my imagination." *I'm sick of using my imagination.* Blair puts her hand on Nathan's jaw, slides it to grip the back of his neck. "I want you to show me."

His fingers stop trailing her legs. "Show you what?"

"Everything you've ever done in this car."

Nathan's body stills as his eyes go hot. She can see it even in the darkness. Hears his breath change. Both his hands slide up her dress to grip her hips, pulling her in. "Forbidden fruit," he murmurs.

"What?"

"That's what girls like you always were."

"Girls like me?" She remembers him mentioning this before, but didn't know what he meant.

"You know, good girls."

She takes a deep breath. "I'm not so good." *Trust me.*

A smile plays around his mouth. "Course you are. Don't even bother trying to deny it."

They're both quiet, the only sound the rain pattering against the top of the car.

"Even so," Blair leans in close, "I still want you to show me."

He licks his lips. "That what you really want?"

She tries to answer, but can't because his mouth has come down hard on hers. Kissing her hungrily, kissing her like he's starved, making up for not having kissed her for days.

Her heart pounds. He tastes delicious. So good, desire is careening through her, reckless and wild. She pulls him close, whimpering and grabbing him as they continue to kiss.

Nathan starts tugging at the buttons on the front of her sweater. When they finally break apart, she watches the way his hands shake a little as they work each one.

"We're fogging up the glass," Blair breathes, glancing around at the windows.

"Yeah."

He doesn't look around, though. His laser focus is turned on and completely directed at her. Once the buttons are undone, he yanks her sweater off. Immediately, he reaches around for the zipper in the back of her dress, yanking that down, too.

"Maybe I should keep it on," she whispers. "In case we need to make a quick getaway."

"No," his voice rough and desperate, "I have to touch you."

That desperation is all Blair needs to hear. She helps him pull the front of her dress lower, slipping her arms out. His hands unclasp her bra next, and then before she knows it, she's naked to the waist.

Nathan immediately presses his face to her breasts, his hands molding them together, then sliding to her back. "Goddamn," he mutters into her skin, holding her tight. "I missed you, Blair."

Her breath stops at his words. A flood of emotion rages through her as she hugs him fiercely. "I missed you, too."

His mouth comes back up to tangle with hers. More reckless kisses. Enough of them to make her crazy. One of his hands slips beneath her dress as he fingers his way into her panties. She moans when he touches her.

"I have a condom," he breathes.

"You do?" Blair pulls back, amazed. "You bought some?"

"Yeah, I did. Put one in my wallet."

She tries to catch her breath as his fingers are still working magic.

"Do you want me to use it?" he asks.

"Yes." *God.* "Of course, I do."

He grins, with what looks like relief. "Good."

Nathan pulls his hand out of her panties and shifts position, lifting his body a little. "It's in my back pocket."

She rises up, the steering wheel pushing into her bottom as she tries to give him some room to maneuver. The whole thing is an awkward struggle.

Finally, he has the wallet in hand and pulls out the condom.

Blair sits down and pushes his shirt up, then reaches to undo his belt, the column of his hard-on pressing into his jeans. She tries to unzip him, but that's awkward, too, and she can't quite manage it.

"Let me do it," he says. "Be easier."

She lifts again, laughing as Nathan now struggles to work his pants down.

"Jesus Christ." He laughs, too. "Maybe I'm getting too old for this shit."

Eventually, his erection is free. She stays lifted, though, watching him as he slips the condom on.

When he's done, he eyes her, both hands traveling beneath her skirt to grasp her hips.

Blair looks down with a wry smile. "We've been here once before, haven't we?"

Nathan takes this in and seems to reflect on her words. "No," he finally says. "Not like this. This is different."

Blair nods slowly, trying to keep her emotions in check.

"Come here." He pulls her closer. "Lower yourself onto me."

"But I'm still wearing panties."

"We'll push them aside.

Blair lowers her body. Nathan's breath is unsteady as he helps position himself, his fingers pushing her underwear over.

"That's right," he murmurs as Blair sinks down, taking him in.

She goes slowly, the sensation so exquisite, her eyes fall shut. And while

Nathan's breath is getting more erratic, Blair discovers she can barely breathe at all.

"Open your eyes."

At his voice, Blair does as he asks and discovers Nathan watching her intently. She meets his gaze, so intimate in the confines of Isadora.

His hands are on her hips and when he pushes upward, she gasps. Passion spiraling through her, Nathan grips her harder. He's still watching her as they start to move with each other. Blair is overwhelmed with sensation now, gasping and moaning, stripped down to nothing but pure pleasure and raw emotion.

It suddenly occurs to her Nathan will witness everything—her true feelings for him. She tries to hold back, but it's impossible. This had never even occurred to her before.

What am I going to do?

Her only option, she decides, is not to come.

Because otherwise, how will I hide it?

After a short while, Nathan slows things down, leans in and kisses her deeply.

"Blair," he whispers.

He tugs on her hair and his mouth goes to her throat, licking and biting. She moans. His fingers slip to where they're joined and he starts to play with her.

"Don't do that." She pushes his hand away.

"Stop holding back."

"I'm not."

"You are," he breathes. "I can tell."

She closes her eyes.

"Don't hold back from me," he whispers. "I want to see everything."

"No, you don't."

She senses his confusion. "Babe, I do. I want to watch you come like this, with me inside you."

Blair is worried, though. Worried he'll see all the love bottled up for years, spilling out.

"Come on, Blair."

She swallows, tries to catch her breath. Nathan is already moving again, and she realizes she doesn't have a choice anyway.

When her climax comes, it hits her like a tidal wave, a tsunami washing over her, through her, sucking her under. No more hiding anything. And in that instant, she doesn't care if he sees the truth because all she can think is how grateful she is. Grateful to be with him in this moment. It's love. There's no shame in that. *So, what else matters?*

Nathan's gaze is fixed on her, his laser focus bright as a diamond. He looks stunned. Eyes open wide as she takes him inside her. And Blair realizes he sees it all, but he doesn't understand it.

Then his face changes. His mouth goes into an almost grimace—not with pain, but too much pleasure. Nathan is lost in her. Grabbing her hips hard, he groans and it's like something torn from him.

Afterwards, he doesn't collapse against the seat, but is kissing her instead. Holding her head with both hands as he kisses her with a crazy passion she's never seen before. When he breaks the kiss, he wraps his arms around her, hugs her tight, still vibrating. She runs her hands down his back, damp with sweat, trying to soothe him.

It should be me who's shaking.

But it's not, and instead she feels strangely calm. At ease. Blair realizes it's because in her own way, for the first time in her life, she was finally honest with him.

AS THEY HEAD back to her condo, Nathan keeps glancing over at her, his gaze lingering. Blair suspects he's trying to make sense of what just happened between them in the car. As they take the elevator upstairs, she discovers she's glad to be home, excited even. That is until she walks through the front door.

"I don't believe this!" Blair's mouth falls open in shock as she looks around. Her condo is a *mess,* and not just because of her OCD—it's a mess by anybody's standards. "I've barely been gone a week. Can't you guys at least clean up after yourselves?"

"Babe, I've been trying. It's Fiona who's the slob."

Blair doesn't know what to say. There are takeout boxes on every surface. Clothes and papers piled in haphazard stacks. She knows he's partly telling the truth, sees that most of this mess is Fiona's, though he's not exactly innocent, either.

"This is unbelievable," Blair says. "I expect you guys to clean up this catastrophe!"

"Sure, course." Nathan is nodding.

She resists the urge to start cleaning herself, and instead searches around for Mr. Maurice, finally finds him curled up on her bed. "There you are." She sits down and the cat gets up, stretches his lithe body before finally coming over to let her pet him.

Nathan sits on the bed next to her, and as she pets the cat, Nathan pets her. Running his hand down her arm, nuzzling her neck.

"That tickles." She can't help laughing.

"Take your sweater off."

Blair ignores him, though, and strokes Mr. Maurice instead, even though he's already climbing over her lap trying to get at Nathan.

"Mr. Maurice seems perfectly fine."

"Course he is. Now that you're here."

She gives Nathan a look. "Tell me the truth. Did you make this whole thing up just so I'd come over?"

His expression goes lazy. "Don't know what you're talking about."

She raises a skeptical brow.

"Mr. Maurice was missing you," he says, trying to push the cat away, who seems desperate to get to him.

Blair watches as her cat finally makes it past Nathan's hand and onto his lap.

"He's been forlorn," Nathan insists, while Mr. Maurice purrs loudly with relief at having reached his destination.

"I can see that."

"Don't know what's gotten into him all of a sudden." Nathan tries to look earnest. "Guess he's cheerful 'cause you're here."

Blair smiles. "God, you are the worst liar ever."

"What? I'm not lying."

"You're terrible at it."

"Don't know what you're talking about." He finally gives in and pets the cat. "And for your information, I'm a great liar."

Blair only shakes her head and laughs.

They both continue to pet Mr. Maurice for a little while and even though her cat clearly prefers Nathan, she's glad to see he's okay.

Lucky for you, Mr. Maurice, I understand your obsession.

"All right," Blair sighs. "I guess you can take me back to Tori's now."

"What?" Nathan stops petting the cat and stares at her. "What are you talking about?"

"I'm going back to Tori's tonight."

"The hell you are."

"Yes, I am."

Nathan goes silent, and she can see he doesn't like this. He gently pushes the cat off his lap. "We just went over all this."

"I know and I'm still staying at Tori's."

"No, you're not."

Blair gets up off the bed. Nathan doesn't move, just sits there with a scowl.

"You have to drive me back." She wonders if she should grab more clothes, but figures she'll get them when she visits her cat next time.

He shakes his head. "Why are you doing this?"

"Because I need to." She realizes it's bizarre, but it's like she's following an instinct. All she knows is that if there's a chance for them, it has to be this way.

"Jesus Christ." Nathan lets out his breath, gets up off the bed. "This situation is ridiculous."

Chapter Twenty

How To Change The Past

1. Live with your best friend, former roommate and '80s addict.
2. Be courted by the only man you'll ever love.
3. Try to forget all those secrets you've been keeping.

"IS THAT CHASE calling again?" Blair asks. She's been staying at Tori's for a few weeks now, and this Chase guy has been calling almost every day.

Tori sighs and turns her phone off. "Yes, he's persistent."

"Too persistent. I don't like it."

"He'll get the message eventually. They always do."

Blair frowns. Tori is so sweet and pretty, but for some reason, just like her mom, she seems to attract asshole men. Unlike her mom, though, Tori wants nothing to do with them.

Tori sighs. "I wish I would meet someone nice. It's romantic the way you and my brother have been dating. I've never seen him act this way with anyone before."

Blair can't help her smile. It's true, since she's been staying here, Nathan has been quite solicitous in his pursuit of her. She's not sure what's gotten into him, either. They've been going to the movies, to dinner, for walks around Green Lake. And he keeps bringing her little gifts. Flowers or scarves for her hair. The other day, he brought her a pint of her favorite ice cream from a local shop she likes.

"Are you guys going out tonight to celebrate?" Tori asks.

They're sitting on the back deck where Tori is working on her computer. Apparently, she does a fair amount of work for Nathan's blog, something

Blair never knew until she moved in.

Nathan has been coming over directly from the garage, though Blair doesn't let him stay the night. Lately, they've been hanging out on the couch watching TV, or Blair reads while Nathan naps beside her. She's starting to suspect it's the only sleep he's getting. Apparently, Brody is paying him for the work now, since one of his mechanics quit and he's down a man. Nathan is filling in until Brody finds a replacement. It's ironic because they're basically in the same place they were years ago. He's working at the garage while she lives with Tori.

"Celebrate what?"

"You haven't seen this?" Tori turns her computer toward Blair.

"What is it?"

"Road's book has made it onto *The New York Times* best seller's list."

Blair's mouth drops open. "Oh, my God! He hasn't said a word!" She stares at the screen in amazement and sees *Edge of Zen* by Road Church at number seventeen.

"Fiona emailed me about it a little while ago. Pretty cool, huh?"

When Nathan shows up after work, he's pleased, but typically mellow and understated about the whole thing. "Yeah, Fiona called me."

"You're both a mechanic and a bestselling author," Blair jokes. "Talk about eccentric."

He chuckles. "A real renaissance man."

After Nathan uses the shower, Blair sits in her bedroom with him. He's rummaging through his leather backpack for a change of clothes as she admires his muscular back. His perfect ass is currently wearing white boxers. *Only Nathan could make a pair of white boxers look this good.*

"This is kind of a big deal," she says as he gets dressed. "I think we should go out and celebrate, don't you?"

"Sure."

"What do you want to do?"

He grins. "Rent a hotel room and have sex all night."

Blair laughs. "I'm serious."

"So am I."

"Aren't you excited about this? It's not every day your book is a *New York Times* best seller. We should have a fancy dinner or something."

"Don't get me wrong, babe. It's great news, but it's not like it's at number one."

Blair blinks. "Are you actually complaining?"

"No, just saying."

"That it's not number one?"

"Right."

She rolls her eyes. "You're never satisfied."

He chuckles and gets on the bed, playfully pushing her onto her back. “Sure could use some satisfaction,” he murmurs before kissing her.

She puts her hand up to his hair, still damp from the shower. The scent of coconut shampoo drifts toward her.

“You should move back home tonight,” he says. “Because that would be something to celebrate.”

She’s amazed at his persistence. Nathan asks her to move back every day. “I’ve already told you, not yet.”

“How much longer is this going to go on?”

“I don’t know.”

“Babe, I’m *living* with Fiona. Think about that for a second.”

Blair laughs.

“Yeah, real funny when it’s not happening to you.” He shakes his head with exaggerated anguish. “How has this strangeness come to pass?”

“Is she still weeping every night?”

“Course. Though, I think there’s progress with Sachi. She came over the other morning and visited for a while.”

“Really? Wow, I wish I could meet her.”

“She’s nice. Think you’d like her.” He rolls over onto his back and props himself up on his elbows, lets out a deep sigh as his eyes wander the bedroom. “Maybe I should just move in here.”

“You can’t.”

“Why, because you won’t let me?”

“Yes, but also because of Mr. Maurice.”

He shrugs. “I’d just bring him along.”

“He’d never be able to handle Tori’s dogs.”

Nathan nods slowly. “You’re right, those dogs would be too much for him. He’d need cat therapy after that.”

They eye each other, and Nathan’s gaze lingers like he doesn’t want to look away. Blair has noticed him doing this a lot. She used to sneak glances at him, but now finds whenever she does, he’s already looking at her.

“How about this,” he says. “Let’s go away for the weekend.”

Blair smiles. “Uh-oh. Is the travel blogger getting restless?”

“Yeah, I am. We should take a trip together. Be fun.” He rolls on his side toward her again and runs his hand down her hip. “Plus, I want to get you alone somewhere and have my way with you.”

“You already did that,” she teases.

He snorts. “One time. Two weeks ago. We need a firm mattress and a lot of hours together.” He gets a sly grin. “Plus, it’s been ages since I’ve visited Red Willow Valley.”

Blair closes her eyes for a second and lets out her breath. *He’s got me there.* “What happened to being a gentleman and giving me space?”

Nathan goes quiet as his laser focus turns on. “Aren’t I being a gentleman?” he asks softly.

And she has to admit he is in every way. She gets the feeling Nathan has been trying to woo her in the manner he thinks she’s used to or maybe expects. The whole good girl thing. They haven’t had sex at all, not since they did it in Isadora, though they’ve made out a few times. She senses Nathan is waiting for her to give the okay. Of course, it’s clear he’s hoping she gives the okay soon.

“Yes, you are being quite the gentleman.” She puts her hand up to his jaw and lets herself fall into his green eyes—warm as a summer day. She wishes she could gaze into them forever. “As a result, I’m inviting you to stay the night here on Saturday.”

“You are?” His brows go up.

“We’ll have the house to ourselves. Tori is staying at Kiki’s for some kind of bridesmaid wedding thing.” Blair was invited, too, but declined.

“This Saturday?”

She nods.

“Thank *God*.” He lets out his breath and closes his eyes. When he opens them, he’s grinning. “Hallelujah.”

BLAIR HAS FOUR cakes to deliver on Saturday, but things go smoothly so she’s back at Tori’s by one. Two of the cakes were Ginger’s, and it was fun watching her protégée step out on her own for the first time. Ginger was nervous, but handled herself well.

At the store, Blair picks up a few snacks along with some beer. Nathan already told her he planned to bring the groceries since he wanted to make Hungarian goulash, something he learned from that couple he lived with in Budapest.

“I want you to have fun while I’m gone,” Tori says as she folds up her bathrobe and tucks it into her overnight bag. “But please, don’t divulge too many details when I get back.”

Blair laughs. “All right.” She’s sitting in Tori’s bedroom keeping her company, along with the boys—Eddie, Duff, and Tommy Lee. They seem to sense their mama is going somewhere.

“Seriously, I’m glad my brother is finally seeing what was right under his nose for years.” Tori smiles. “And I like the way you call him Nathan instead of Road.”

“It’s who he is.”

Tori’s eyes soften. “I can see you’re in love with him.”

Blair, who’s petting Eddie, the golden retriever, flashes up at her. “Is it that obvious?"

"To me—yes. I doubt he knows, though. Men are so dense. But I think you should tell him how you feel."

"Really?" Blair's eyes widen. "You don't think that would freak him out?"

"Maybe." Tori thinks about it for a second. "I don't know, maybe not. It's so cute the way he acts around you."

"I doubt I have the nerve to tell him the truth." Actually, Blair feels light-headed with terror at the thought of telling Nathan her true feelings. "He'd probably run for the hills like he was being chased by wolves."

Tori laughs. "Hopefully, he's smarter than that."

Blair thinks about how she hadn't seen Nathan in five years before all this. He didn't run because she professed her love, but he sure did run from their marriage. Fast and far, too.

After Tori leaves, Blair gets ready for Nathan. She spends too much time blow-drying her hair, too much time on her makeup, and finally way too much time picking out something to wear. Basically killing herself to achieve the unattainable. Perfection. Her old enemy. Somewhere in her mind, she realizes, she's still competing with his Skank Factor X girlfriends.

Every one of them was as mean as a rattlesnake, but unfortunately, they were all knockouts.

She can't get what Tori said out of her mind—how she should tell Nathan her true feelings. *But how can I?* She's too scared. Scared of what he'll say. What if he feels sorry for her? Or even worse, pity?

I couldn't handle that.

Another part of herself, the brave part, wonders if it's a mistake not to tell him.

He's the only man I'll ever love. Shouldn't I tell him the truth at least once? What kind of ridiculous coward am I?

But then she realizes she can't tell him the truth, because then she'd have to come clean about all of it. About what she did to him, and the reason he had to marry her to begin with.

He can never find out about that.

The thought makes her blood run cold.

My God. He'd hate me.

By the time Nathan arrives at four, she's obsessed about it so much that she's worked herself into a state. In fact, the first words out of his mouth when she opens the door aren't 'hello' or 'hey, babe' but—

"What's wrong?"

"Nothing's wrong!" She tries to smile, but her compulsive thoughts are like a train run off its rails. She's already decided to wash all the towels and was starting in on scrubbing Tori's refrigerator. The dogs were following her around, though they seem mostly baffled.

"Is Tori still here?"

"No, she left."

Nathan studies her. She's wearing one of her frilly aprons over the blouse and turquoise capris she decided on. "What are you doing?"

"Scrubbing the inside of Tori's refrigerator."

"Now?"

"Yes."

"Why?"

Because I'm terrified of all these secrets I'm keeping from you.

"I don't want anyone to get food poisoning."

Nathan keeps studying her. "Did something happen?"

"No, I'm just having a little . . . fit." She shifts uncomfortably. "Sort of."

"You're having a fit?"

She nods then swallows. "Yes."

Nathan is still holding the groceries, but he puts them down right there in the entryway. "Come here, babe."

Blair goes to him and he pulls her in, hugging her tight. Her eyes sting. "God, you're so nice," she chokes out.

He chuckles. "So are you, princess."

She doesn't say anything to this and lets him hug her as waves of guilt wash over her.

They hold each other for a while until Blair finally pulls away.

"Do you want to tell me about it?" Nathan asks, looking down at her.

"No, I can't. I wish I could, but I can't talk about this."

"I'm a good listener."

"I know you are." She meets his eyes, steady and calm.

His voice softens as he takes her hand. "Blair, I'm here for you. You can tell me anything."

She lets out her breath. "Not this."

"Why? What could be so bad?"

"I just can't talk to you about this."

He's still studying her with compassion, trying to understand, when suddenly his whole demeanor changes. His jaw tightens. "Think I get it."

"Get what?"

"What has you all worked up." He lets go of her hand. "This is about him, isn't it?"

"Who?" Blair is baffled.

"The dipshit. That guy you're apparently still in love with."

Blair doesn't know what to say, though she knows what she wants to say. *Nathan, it's you! You're the dipshit!*

"Blair, I thought we had . . . something going here."

"We do."

"Then why are you still thinking about that guy?"

She shakes her head and sighs. "I'm not. This has nothing to do with him. It's just other stuff, stuff with my family." *What's one more lie? I'm already hip-deep in them anyway.*

"Oh." Nathan goes still with what appears to be embarrassment. "Guess I jumped to the wrong conclusion."

"That's all right."

"I have an idea that might help, though." He takes her hand again.

"You do?"

"Yeah, definitely." Leaning in close, he grins. "How about I make you some authentic Hungarian goulash?"

BLAIR KEEPS HER apron on and helps Nathan by chopping onions as he works with the beef. Some of the other ingredients appear to be bell peppers, potatoes, carrots, tomatoes, paprika, and lard.

"Lard?" she asks. "Do Hungarians have a lot of clogged arteries?"

Nathan smirks. "Don't know, but it's the way Judit and Bandi showed me how to make goulash. You won't care once you taste how good it is."

The onions are making her eyes water, and she keeps wiping her cheeks with the back of her hand. Nathan turned on Tori's iPod, still in its docking bay, so Heart's "What About Love" is playing on the stereo as they cook.

"My sister should have been a teenager in the '80s," he muses, cutting the beef into small cubes on the wood board.

All three of the dogs are hanging out in the kitchen, watching them, hoping for scraps.

"I know." Blair laughs with agreement. "I've always thought she would have fit in perfectly." Tori loves vibrant-colored clothes, big hair, and of course all those '80s bands.

Nathan eyes the dogs then finally feeds each of them some cubed beef, which they gobble up in two seconds.

"Sucker," she says. "Now those dogs will never leave you alone."

He glances down at Eddie, Duff, and Tommy Lee. "Look at those faces, though."

Blair smiles down at the dogs. They're watching Nathan's every movement with soulful eyes. Each one of them was a hard-luck case from an animal shelter, and it makes Blair happy to see them all so well-cared for.

"They're hard to resist," she agrees.

"So, how's your OCD doing anyway?" he asks. "Other than today."

She sighs. "It's been fine. Better than fine, actually." It occurs to her that her OCD has improved lately.

"No more checking toaster cords or front door locks?" he teases. "Lining up fridge items?"

"Just a little bit." Blair thinks about how she's been rechecking locks lately, but it's mostly because of that Chase guy who's been calling Tori. She wonders if she should mention it to Nathan. Tori won't like it, but Blair decides to anyway.

"There's this weird thing happening lately with some guy calling Tori."

Nathan looks up from giving the dogs more beef. "What do you mean?"

So Blair tells him about Tori dating Chase and how he won't leave her alone. "He calls Tori every day wanting to see her again."

Nathan listens with concern. "What does Tori say?"

"She says he's young and harmless and thinks he'll fade away like the others."

"My sister is too damn nice sometimes." He frowns and shakes his head.

"I know. I'm not trying to alarm you, but I just thought I should tell someone."

"Yeah, I'm glad you told me. I'll talk to her. Maybe I need to have a conversation with this guy."

Nathan takes the onions she chopped and adds them to the lard already melted in the pot, lets them brown before adding the garlic and beef.

They chop the rest of the vegetables and Blair asks Nathan if he wants a beer.

"Sure."

She takes her apron off and grabs two bottles, uncaps them, and hands one over. Then she leans back against the counter to sip her beer and admire Nathan's perfect backside as he continues to cook. She realizes there's something about him that both excites and calms her at the same time.

When everything is finally set up and simmering in the big pot, he turns around. "That should do it for now."

"How long does it have to simmer?"

"Couple hours."

"Really? That's a while."

"It is." He steps closer.

"Do you want to play Scrabble? Or how about a nice game of Old Maid?"

He smirks. "Think I have a better idea how we can pass the time."

"You do?" Her eyes go wide as she feigns innocence.

He puts his hand on her hips and pulls her in. "Where did that apron go? Thought you looked real cute in it."

Her breath catches.

"Turning me on, babe."

Blair laughs with surprise. "It was?"

He nods then bends his head to kiss her. She opens her mouth to his, lets their tongues stroke each other as her arms tighten around his neck, and the kiss goes from sweet to dirty very fast.

"Damn, you taste good," he murmurs, his hand gripping her ass. "Feel good, too."

She leans closer and bites his lip. He growls with approval and they kiss some more, but then Blair notices something. "Um, I think we have an audience." She motions downward. All three dogs—Eddie, Duff, and Tommy Lee—are staring up at them with rapt attention. Tongues lolling.

Nathan looks down and grins. "Guess these boys like to watch."

"Yes, that's what troubles me."

He laughs. "Sorry, guys."

Nathan takes her hand and they leave the kitchen, with him stopping by the entryway to pick up his leather backpack. When they get to her room, he closes the door.

"Poor doggies," Blair says, getting onto the bed. "I think we disappointed them."

"Probably." He drops his backpack next to the nightstand then climbs on the bed beside her. "Don't care, though, because nothing is getting in the way of you and me right now."

And then without another word, he reaches for her. They kiss with frantic passion, neither of them bothering to contain themselves. Nathan is on top of her and Blair can barely think straight as everything about him fills her senses—his taste, smell, the weight of his body. All so amazing.

God.

She knows he's been holding out waiting for her, but it's a wonder she's held out this long, too. It doesn't take but a few minutes before they've stripped each other naked, and Nathan is reaching down into his backpack for the box of condoms. He tears one open, slides it on, their frantic sexual energy still filling the room. Blair can't remember if she's ever wanted it like this before.

And then he's on top of her again, pushing inside, and they're both groaning with pleasure.

It's so good.

She's half out of her mind when she notices Nathan watching her face. He bends down to kiss her as she grabs his back, but then he pulls away abruptly. His lips part as he starts shaking his head. She's confused at first, but when he clutches her ass and starts groaning again she understands.

He's already coming.

"Shit," he mutters, still breathing hard. "Can't believe this."

"It's okay," she gulps, trying to catch her breath, too. She puts her hand on his jaw. "It happens."

Nathan rolls off her onto his back, still trying to breathe. "Sorry, babe, I was just really turned on." He looks over at her. "Been thinking about you a lot."

"I understand."

"Fuck." He snorts. "I even jerked off earlier, not that it did any good. Christ, you probably think I'm lousy in bed again now."

"Pardon?" Blair is taken aback. "Why would you say that?"

"Because it's what you told me."

"I don't know what you're talking about." She sits up halfway onto her elbows. "I never said anything like that."

He nods, chuckling. "You sure did. After you drank all those margaritas, you told me I was the worst lover you ever had."

"*What?* There's no way I would have said something like that!"

"Guess you don't remember."

Blair frowns and tries to think back to that night. *Was I really that rude?* She thought she remembered all the embarrassing stuff, but apparently there's more.

"Is it true?" Nathan asks. "Was I really the worst you ever had?"

"No."

"Then why did you say it?"

"I don't know. I had too many margaritas."

"For some people, tequila is like truth serum."

Apparently, I'm one of them.

"Be honest," he says earnestly. "I can take it."

"Okay." Blair lets out a long sigh. "Yes. You were the worst I ever had."

Nathan nods. "Now, don't try and candy-coat it to spare my feelings. Just be blunt."

She grabs a pillow and hits him with it.

He laughs, so she hits him with it again.

"I hope you're happy," she says. "Forcing me to tell you that."

He takes the pillow from her and tosses it aside. Grabs her, pulling her in close, then rolls on top of her again.

"Seriously, babe, just stab me in the heart next time. Be less painful."

"Maybe I will!"

He laughs some more, but then his laughter dies off and he goes quiet. "How about now?" he wants to know.

"What do you mean?"

"Am I still the worst lover you ever had?"

She looks into his green eyes, sees them flicker with humor, but there's something else, too. Vulnerability. Blair decides to be honest. *I can give him this much truth.*

"No, you aren't the worst I've ever had." She puts her hand to his jaw, then pulls his head closer to whisper, "You're the best."

Nathan's expression goes heated. She can see he likes this, can feel he likes it, too, as his hard-on presses against her thigh.

"Third time is going to be a charm," he says. "I just know it."

Blair is confused at first, but then she gets it and can't help giggling. "I have faith in you."

"Glad to hear that, princess."

And then he shows her just how well-deserved that faith is.

Chapter Twenty-One

Daily List

1. Be grateful.

2. Savor every moment.

3. Watch your dreams come true.

"LET'S JUST STAY naked all day," Nathan murmurs as Blair gets up to put her clothes on again. "Or better yet, you could wear that little apron and nothing else."

Blair laughs. "Maybe I'll bake you a cake sometime with that little apron on and nothing else."

"Mmm, sounds good."

Blair searches around through the covers for her shirt. She finally finds it on the floor along with her jeans and underwear. "Shouldn't we go check on the goulash?"

"Yeah, but I still think we should stay naked. We'd be like nudists." He gets up from the bed and puts his T-shirt on, reaches for his boxers. "No one would see us, except the dogs, and they'd never say anything."

"Please, those dogs are such blabbermouths. They'll tell everyone they know we were running around naked."

He chuckles. "You're just saying that to get out of it."

"No, I'm not." She slips into her jeans. "And, come on, do you really want Eddie, Duff, and Tommy Lee sniffing and licking your balls every two seconds?"

A strangled noise comes from the bed and when Blair turns, Nathan has collapsed onto it, shaking with laughter. "Damn . . . babe," is all he manages to say before he bursts into another laughing fit.

She laughs, too. "You know they would."

When they check on the goulash, it still isn't ready, even though the delicious aroma is drifting through the house.

"The smell is making me hungry," Blair admits.

"Yeah, me, too." Nathan stirs the pot then turns the heat down. "Needs more time, though."

Grabbing a couple of beers, along with some chips and a blanket, they head to the back deck where it's not quite sunset. Tori has a hammock in her backyard she puts up every year when the weather warms, and Nathan decides that's where they should hang out.

The lawn is cool against Blair's toes as she walks over to it, carrying her beer and the blanket she nabbed from the couch.

Nathan gets in first, and then helps Blair climb in so she's lying half on him and half next to him. They don't really need the blanket, so he tucks it behind his head like a pillow.

"This is nice and cozy," she says, as Nathan hands her beer back to her, the hammock rocking a little. "Plus, I like watching the sunset."

"Reminds me of you." He puts his hand up to the back of her head.

"Me?"

He nods. "Your hair."

"You really do like redheads, don't you?"

"There's one I especially like."

They smile at each other, and Blair's heart swells with joy. She realizes this is the happiest she's ever been in her entire life.

Without knowing it, Nathan has made all my dreams come true.

After a while, Blair hands him her beer and he puts both bottles along with the potato chips on the ground.

She scoots up a little, slides her fingers to the back of his neck, and leans over to put her mouth near his. "Nathan," she says softly, still enjoying the sound of his name. She kisses him on the lips first, then his cheeks, nose, and chin. Kisses him all over. Can feel him smiling the whole time.

Finally, Blair looks into his face. His eyes are closed, so she admires him. Runs her finger over his handsome features, tracing all the contours. Over his brow, forehead, and down his nose. Traces lightly over the bump where he broke it as a kid.

"Do you still remember how this happened?" she asks, curious.

"How what happened?"

"When you broke your nose. You fell off your bike when you were a kid?"

"Yeah." He nods. "That's right."

"How well do you remember it?"

Nathan shifts position, so he's lying more on his back and she's on her side looking at his profile, her arm draped across his chest. "I remember it real well."

"What happened?"

He glances at her then gazes up at the sky. "I was riding my bike on the street, going too fast, not paying attention. The bike skidded against the curb and I lost control. Fell off and hit my face right on the cement."

"How old were you?"

"Nine."

Blair shakes her head. "Was there a lot of blood?"

He nods. "Yeah, hurt like a sonofabitch, too. My mom had to take me to the ER, where they set it, but it healed with a bump. Told us later we could have a plastic surgeon fix it, but I didn't want to."

"Why not?"

He shrugs. "Just didn't."

They're both quiet after this while Blair studies the hawkish profile from his once-broken nose.

Nathan closes his eyes. "No." He lets out his breath. "That's not what really happened."

"What do you mean?"

He turns, so he's looking into her eyes. "I've been telling that same story for so many years. Truth is one of my mom's drunk boyfriends threw a full bottle of beer at me and hit me in the face."

"*What?*" Blair goes completely still.

"Broke my nose."

"Oh, my God," she whispers.

Nathan doesn't say anything more as Blair stares at him in shock.

"And you were only nine?"

"That's right."

She can barely breathe. "He could have killed you!"

"Yeah, lucky he didn't, huh?"

"I'm so sorry." She puts her hand to his cheek. "I don't even know what to say." Blair can barely wrap her mind around how terrible it is.

"Not much to say."

"Baby, you didn't deserve that. You know that, right?"

"I know." He licks his lips. "My mom made up that bike story on the way to the ER, and it's the same one I've been using all this time."

"That's so horrible." Blair's eyes fill with tears and she wishes she could do something.

Nathan is still watching her. "Never told the truth to anyone before."

"I'm glad you told me."

He nods, puts his thumb up to her cheek and wipes some of her tears away. "That's not even the worst part."

"How can that not be the worst part?"

"The worst part is nothing happened."

"What do you mean?"

"To *him*—Curtis, my mom's boyfriend." He shakes his head. "Didn't expect her to call the cops, but I expected her to throw him out. Instead, he lived with us for another year. We all just pretended the bike story was true."

Blair's mouth opens, but no words come out. And to think she's always liked his mom. She knew Lori had problems and was attracted to asshole men, but never realized it was this bad.

"Imagine it," he says. "Had to spend every holiday with that fucker. Christmas, my birthday . . ." He trails off. "I hated him."

"But why would she do that?" Blair is dumbfounded.

"Don't know . . ." He closes his eyes tight, pinching the bridge of his nose with his thumb and forefinger. "Guess she loved him more than *me*."

"Baby . . ." Blair shifts position and wraps her arms around Nathan, hugging him tight. He hugs her back and she can hear his heartbeat through his chest, his breath shaking. She wishes she could erase the pain.

Eventually, he draws back, wiping his eyes. "Kept that secret for years." He looks down at her with a wry smile. "See, I am a good liar after all."

She puts her hand to his jaw.

Nathan lets out his breath. "Irony is he eventually left *her*. Not the other way around."

"Lori does love you," Blair says. "I think she's just really messed-up."

"Yeah."

Something occurs to Blair. "What about your Uncle Lance? Did he know what happened?"

Nathan shakes his head, pressing his lips together. "No, he didn't know. My mom made me promise not to tell him."

"And you kept that promise?"

"I was a kid. And she's my mom, so yeah, I kept it." He looks at her. "Wanted to tell him, though. I hate secrets."

"What would your uncle have done?"

His face grows serious. "He would have beat the shit out of Curtis. Maybe even killed him."

Blair nods.

He picks up her hand, brings it to his mouth and kisses her palm. "It was probably best I didn't tell him. Didn't want the one person who really cared about me going to prison, you know?"

Blair watches him, but doesn't say anything more. Thinks about what a heavy burden that must have been for a child. Wishes she could do some damage to Curtis herself. Lori, too.

And then it dawns on her.

"Oh, my God, that's why you never had the bump fixed, isn't it?"

Nathan eyes flash to hers.

"You wanted her to have to see it every day, to remind her of what happened."

He's still holding her hand, and he clutches it tight. There's a storm of emotion behind his eyes, but then Blair watches them go calm and steady. "That's right."

WHEN THE GOULASH is done, they dish out a couple of big bowls for themselves and take it outside to eat on the back deck. The sun has gone down, and Blair lights two of Tori's IKEA lanterns.

It's a peaceful spring night, and the air almost tastes like summer.

Nathan can't seem to pull his eyes from her, so they're constantly gazing at each other. Blair discovers it's a relief to finally be able to look at him as much as she wants.

At least I don't have to hide that anymore.

"This is delicious," she says, devouring her bowl of goulash. "They taught you well. I'd say they almost turned you into a Hungarian."

Nathan laughs. "That's what they used to say, '*Egy magyar embert csinálok belőled.*' He grins. "A Hungarian man made it."

"Do you speak Hungarian, too?"

"I picked up a little."

"What other languages did you 'pick up'?"

"Learned some Thai and a little Marathi when I was in Mumbai."

"Really? That's impressive."

"Guess so." He shrugs, stirring his food. "Turns out I have kind of an ear for languages."

As they eat, Eddie, Duff, and Tommy Lee are sitting nearby, patiently watching. One of the cats, Joan, is also outside, but she doesn't seem interested in their food and wanders off into the yard to hunt for her own evening snack.

After finishing their bowls, Blair gets up and goes to put them in the kitchen sink with the dogs trailing behind her. They're following her every move with such anticipation that Blair finally decides, w*hat the heck,* and gives them each a little bowl of goulash.

"I decided to give the dogs some goulash," she tells Nathan when she goes back outside.

He's gazing up at the night sky, deep in thought, but turns to her with a grin tugging at his mouth. "Not sure if that was such a good idea, babe."

"Why not?"

"Goulash dog farts? Don't even want to know what those are going to smell like."

Blair's eyes go wide. "I didn't even think about that!"

He chuckles. "Probably have to fumigate the whole house."

"We'll just open all the windows. It'll be fine."

"If you say so."

She walks over to where he's sitting on one of the steps leading into Tori's yard.

He reaches up for her hand and pulls her down to sit close beside him, their legs touching. "So, what about you, princess?" He keeps her hand, intertwining their fingers. "Any dark skeletons in your childhood closet?"

Blair sighs. The truth is she had a great childhood. She always felt safe and loved, and she knows what a gift her parents gave her. Oddly, the only skeleton—if you could call it that—was her unrequited love for *him*. Her obsession nearly eclipsed everything in her life—at least during high school and into her twenties, all the way up until they got married. "No," she says. "I had a wonderful childhood."

He nods. "I can imagine. A beautiful princess living in a fairytale castle."

"I wouldn't go that far."

"Mom some kind of corporate hotshot, dad is a . . ." Nathan looks at her in confusion. "What does your dad do again?"

"He's a CFO."

"That's right. And two younger brothers to do your bidding."

She scoffs. "Hardly. It's more like they were there to annoy me. And I didn't live in a fairytale castle." But then she feels bad because she realizes, compared to the house he and Tori grew up in, it *was* a castle. "I'm not really a princess, either."

He tugs on her hand. "Stop talking and let me finish my story."

"Okay, go ahead."

"The beautiful princess has long, flowing red hair and pretty hazel eyes. She's kind of a crazy perfectionist, but at the same time, no one can deny the castle is clean and cozy."

Blair snorts with laughter.

"She has a little dog named Scooter and a white cat named Fluffy who adore her and follow her everywhere."

"Sorry to interject, Mr. Storyteller Man, but our dog's name was Gypsy and our *black* cat was Shadow."

"Scooter and Fluffy," he says pointedly, "sleep at the foot of the princess's pink canopy bed every night."

Blair looks at him in amazement. "How did you know I had a pink canopy bed?"

He smirks. "Because you're a princess."

"Hmm, I'm not sure what I think of this story."

"The beautiful princess has a beautiful life, with lots of friends and family who shower her with love every day."

She meets his eyes, but doesn't say anything.

He brings up her hand and kisses it. "I'm happy you had that, babe. Real glad for you."

Blair watches him, her heart in her throat. "Isn't there a prince in this story somewhere?"

"I'm getting to that part. Don't be so impatient."

She can't help her smile, notices the cat Joan has come over to them, and reaches down to pet her.

"One day, the princess meets a charming prince. He's not perfect, but he's a decent man and he falls deeply in love with the beautiful princess . . ."

Nathan goes quiet and when she looks at him, he's gazing at her in a way she's never seen before. His laser focus turned on, but softer.

"Do they get married and live happily ever after?"

"Course."

"Because I like a happy ending."

He's still gazing at her. "Don't know if you've figured it out yet, Blair."

"Figured what out?"

He continues to hold her hand, his eyes dazzling as jewels even under the night sky. "I've fallen for you."

Her breath catches as she stares at him. "What do you mean?" Her heart is pounding. There's a choir of angels ready to sing, but they're waiting to be sure. "When you say you've fallen for me."

Nathan grins a little. "It means I've fallen in love with you." He brings her hand to his mouth then turns to meet her gaze, his expression serious. "I love you, Blair."

She blinks. Then blinks again. Her mouth is open, but she can't manage any sound. There's a riot of emotion surging through her. Excitement, joy, and mostly amazement.

He's watching her. "Can see you're stunned. Do you have any kind of feelings for me at all?"

Blair closes her eyes. The angels are singing now and there's a parade, too, with streamers and a marching band.

"I do," she manages to say. She gazes at him with all the love she's held back for years. "I have feelings for you."

"Yeah?" Nathan smiles. "Because I can't stop thinking about you. You've changed my life."

"I have?"

He nods. "The way you are. I love being with you. No games. Straight-up about everything. It's a revelation for me." He licks his lips. "Never been with a woman I could trust like this."

She takes in his words. "Is that right?" she murmurs. The choir of angels is still singing, but they're giving each other nervous looks now.

"I know you had your heart broken not long ago," he goes on. "But do you think you could ever give *me* a chance?"

"Nathan, I don't think you understand. I'm already in love with you."

"Babe, it's okay. You don't have to say that."

"But it's true."

He's still smiling, and she can tell he doesn't believe her.

How ironic is this?

"I've been thinking about something else, too," he says. "And maybe it's a crazy idea, but what do you say we try and make things work between us? Give it a real shot?"

Blair closes her eyes again and lets out her breath. She's waited for this moment her whole life, dreamed about it, prayed for it, and now that it's finally here, she wants to revel in it.

But then something occurs to her.

I'm still locked in a box.

She can't tell him the true depths of her feelings, how she's been in love with him for years, not after all that stuff he just said about no games and being straight-up, about how much he trusts her. He'd never understand the way she's kept all these secrets, not to mention what she did to him.

I don't care. I want him. He never has to know the rest of it.

"I'd like that." She opens her eyes.

"You would?"

Blair studies his handsome face and knows this man is it for her. This is her prince. End of story. "And I'm not just saying 'I love you' because you did," she tells him fiercely. "I really *love* you."

His eyes widen with surprise. "You do?"

"Yes, I do." She puts her hand to his cheek and whispers, "You're the only one."

There's a glimmer of confusion on his face, but then it's gone, replaced with an incredulous joy, so beautiful to see. He grins. "Babe, I didn't know it was happening to you, too. You never said a word."

"I know."

Nathan's voice goes low and warm. "Sounds like we finally do have something to celebrate."

ROAD TOOK ANOTHER swig of whiskey.

"No more, okay?" Blair gently pulled the bottle from his hand and put

it on her nightstand. His tolerance for alcohol seemed remarkably high, but he'd drunk almost a full bottle of Jack Daniels, and she didn't want him to pass out on her.

"Sure." His eyes were on her body again, stroking her breasts. "Whatever you say, princess."

She climbed on the bed and he followed her, and it wasn't long before they were kissing.

Blair hugged him to her, and she loved the feel of his skin. The taste of his mouth. His incredible scent. Everything. Even with Road drinking, she could tell they had sexual chemistry, and she wasn't surprised at all. She always knew they would.

"Lie on your back," she whispered in his ear. "I want to go down on you."

Road grinned. "Words every man loves to hear."

He didn't do it, though, and instead kissed her some more before sitting up partway on his elbow. She'd been admiring him earlier, but now it seemed like he wanted to admire her.

She watched his eyes wander over her naked body. "Look at you," he said softly. "So elegant and pretty, and all mine tonight."

Blair's breath caught.

Road's hand traveled over her breasts, down her stomach, then lower to her inner thigh. He stared at her there for a few seconds, before slipping his hand between them.

Her eyes fell shut when he touched her, his fingers gentle. Stroking. She gasped as he slid them inside her.

When she opened her eyes, Road was studying her face. Lips parted. Blair couldn't resist pulling him down to her again. Moaning as she kissed him, her love and desire a current too strong to contain. A river overflowing its banks. His breath hitched as he brought up both hands to hold her head still, kissing her deeply. He tasted like whiskey, but something else, too. His own essence. The mystery of Road.

Finally, she pushed him onto his back and heard him chuckle a little. When she sat up and put her hand on his cock, he stopped chuckling. She heard his intake of breath.

He watched her, those amazing eyes, bleary with arousal and intoxication, as she lowered her mouth onto him.

"Goddamn," he whispered. His hand immediately grabbing a handful of her hair.

She used her mouth on him for a while, before stopping purposefully to look up at him, enjoying his pleasure in an almost selfish way. Blair ran her hand over his muscular stomach, up to his chest. His eyes were half-lidded, his breath unsteady.

I'll never forget this, she thought. Never.

"Come up," he said, pulling on her shoulders. "Best stop before things end too soon."

She laid on top of him as he stroked her body. His fingers trailing down to her ass, eyeing her with desire. "Think I have a condom," he said, his voice husky. "Should I get it?"

Blair could feel his hard-on pushing against her stomach. She closed her eyes, enjoying the feel of it, knowing he was hard for her. She didn't want a piece of rubber between them. She didn't want anything between them. Nothing. They had to be skin to skin. She wanted the whole experience.

It has to be pure Road.

She swallowed. And then Blair said the four words that would haunt her forever.

"I'm on the pill," she lied.

"You are?" His voice still husky, slightly slurred now, though she could hear the lust in it.

"Yes."

Without another word, he rolled them both over so she was on her back. The weight of him pressing her into the mattress. Road reached down, and she felt him right there, pushing at her center.

He wasn't rough, but he wasn't gentle either, thrusting into her. It didn't matter, though, because she wanted him any way she could have him. In fact, she was already grabbing his shoulders, gasping with pleasure.

Road started moving on top of her, breathing hard, as she closed her eyes and inhaled him. All the love and desire she had barreling through her. All the years of wanting him.

She'd fantasized about this so many times, it was hard to believe it was actually happening. The luxury of being intimate with Road.

Then suddenly, he was moving faster, groaning at the same time. Blair was confused.

No, it can't be.

He stopped moving, his weight heavy and still on top of her.

Yes, it was.

Road rolled off her onto his back, still breathing hard. "Nice . . ." he muttered. He muttered something else, too, but she couldn't tell what it was.

And then without further preamble, he snorted once and fell asleep.

Chapter Twenty-Two

How To Live Your Dream

1. Don't question your good fortune.
2. Spend as much time as possible with the man you love.
3. Try to relax.

EDGE OF ZEN hits number five on the list for *The New York Times* best sellers. It also hits the *USA Today* list for the first time and is in the top ten on Amazon.

Nathan stares at his computer screen in disbelief as Fiona paces the living room floor, talking rapidly into her phone.

"Perfect!" He hears her say, before walking over to him. "I managed to book you on a Seattle morning talk show."

Nathan pulls his eyes from the screen, still recovering from the shock of seeing his book ranked so high. "You want me to go on television?"

"Of course." She's scrolling through her phone. "We have to work the 'Seattle homeboy' angle as much as possible."

"When is this supposed to happen?"

"Tomorrow morning. We got lucky and they had a cancellation. Isn't that fantastic?"

"*Tomorrow?*" His mouth opens. "Are you fucking kidding me?"

She laughs at his expression. "Don't worry, you'll be fine. Just talk about *Edge of Zen*. And don't say anything embarrassing! I told them you had media training to help convince them to give us the spot."

"Christ," he mutters. "What the hell is media training?"

Fiona stares at her phone and sips the latte she somehow manages to have delivered every morning. "I'm calling my contact in Portland right now.

We'll hit the whole West Coast. Plus, I have some fabulous ads set to run next week in a few of the major papers. We need more A-list blogger support, too."

Road nods. "I could call in a few favors." He's always been happy to support other bloggers, and figures some of them would be willing to help him now.

"I'm going to call my contact at *Publisher's Weekly* and get the buzz. We should start looking at book signings, but mainly more ads and TV."

"*More* television?" Nathan lets out his breath. "I'm not so sure about all this, Fiona."

"Oh, my *God!*" She stares at him in exasperation. "Do you want your book at number one or not? Do you?"

"Course."

"Then man up!"

He glares at her for a few seconds, but then can't help himself and starts chuckling. "This is some crazy shit."

Fiona gets a wicked grin. "I know, but don't you love it?"

GOING TO WORK at the garage winds up being a whole other thing. The guys there hassle him nonstop about going on TV tomorrow.

"Jesus Christ, can't tell you assholes anything," Nathan mutters, closing the hood on a Volkswagen that came in with a substantial oil leak. "Should have kept my mouth shut."

"We're just jealous," Brody says with a grin. "Next thing we know, you'll be a movie star, and people will be asking for your autograph."

"He sure is pretty enough to be a movie star," one of the other mechanics, Chavez, teases. "All that long, blond hair."

"Let's see if you still think I'm pretty after I knock a few teeth out of your head," Nathan growls.

"Hey, bring it on, Goldilocks."

"Don't tempt me. It's been a while since I've given anybody a good ass-kicking."

Brody laughs. "Now, ladies, let's try and keep things civil. And besides," he turns to Chavez, "I can't have my pretty cousin here going on TV with swollen and bruised knuckles from punching your skull in."

At least the jokes keep his nerves at bay. By the time Nathan heads over to Tori's in the Honda, he's already edgy again. Knows he'll feel better once he's around Blair, though.

I'll be dammed if it wasn't a miracle to discover she's in love with me.

A woman like that? He knows he doesn't deserve her, knows she's too good for him, but he's accepting this gift life has brought him anyway.

She still hasn't agreed to move back home, though. He keeps trying to convince her, but for some reason she seems determined to put him off longer, keeps saying the timing isn't right yet.

Unfortunately, when he gets to Tori's, Blair isn't there yet. He takes a quick shower and after getting dressed, hears voices in the living room, discovers his sister and Blair, both of them chirping with excitement like two little birds.

"It's so wonderful!" Tori grins when she sees him. "Fiona just called. Why didn't you say anything?"

Blair goes over to hug him. "Congratulations!" He closes his eyes at the feel of her body pressed into his, enjoying it.

"Thanks," he murmurs. He inhales the clean scent of her hair, enjoying that, too. She pulls back, but he doesn't want to let her go, and only does so reluctantly.

"Fiona said you're going to be on TV tomorrow, promoting your book."

He lets out his breath. "Yeah, not sure how I got talked into that one."

Blair watches his face then reaches up to put her hand on his cheek. "You'll be great. Just be yourself."

He nods, feeling unsure again. Nervous. It's not hard to imagine the whole thing turning into a disaster. "Brody and Kiera invited us out tonight to watch some live music. If you're interested," he tells her.

"That sounds like fun. I'm going to go clean up first and get all this powdered sugar off me."

Nathan hangs out with Tori while he waits for Blair. They go over some of the new pages she added to his blog. It's crazy, but he's been managing his whole enterprise from Brody's office these days, his laptop set up next to the garage's main computer. Brody finally hired someone permanent, though, so it looks like his mechanic days are over. For a while, anyway.

Downtown, they meet Brody and his girlfriend, Kiera, at the same club they went out to last time. Unsurprisingly, it still reeks of alcohol and stale sweat. The band is good, though, and so is the company, but in truth, he's regretting going out at all. Wishes he hadn't mentioned it to Blair. Probably selfish, but he doesn't feel like sharing her with anyone.

They're sitting at a table having drinks. Kiera and Blair are discussing Kiki's upcoming wedding in great detail, the way women always discuss weddings, and he can hear Blair describing the cake she's making.

"That sounds incredible," Kiera says. "I can't wait to see it. I've heard your cakes are amazing."

"Thank you." Blair smiles.

Brody is talking to him about the new mechanic he just hired, how he hopes the guy has enough experience, though Nathan is only half-listening since he can't take his eyes off Blair.

She looks both sexy and elegant sitting there. Her hair long just the way he likes it—those wild, cinnamon curls bringing to mind the way it feels in his hands, or better yet the way it brushes against his face when she's moving on top of him.

Damn.

He picks up his beer and takes a long swallow.

Blair's wearing a dress that's blue with little white flowers. He likes that, too. Demure enough to be classy and short enough to show off her legs. Has to admit he's mostly eyeing the back zipper, taking note of the latch on top, making sure he's figured out the fastest way to get it off her later.

He sure as hell hopes Fiona isn't going to be around tonight. She mentioned she might be staying at Sachi's.

Blair turns to Brody and asks if he saw the email she sent him recently about new tire rims for Isadora.

"Yeah, I saw it," Brody says. "Think they'd look slick on her, too. What do you think, Road?"

"Sure, I suppose." He's still watching Blair, admiring her skin now, imagining the ways he's going to slide his hands all over her.

"You don't sound convinced," Brody says.

Nathan clears his throat and tries to bring himself into this conversation. "New rims would be all right, though have to admit, I'm more interested in getting Isadora painted red again."

"What?" Blair's eyes widen. "I hope you're kidding."

"No, I'm not kidding. That car's supposed to be red, not green."

She frowns at this, holds his gaze for a few seconds before turning away clearly unhappy. "I guess she's *your* car, right? So, I have nothing to say about it," she mutters.

Brody is eyeing them both with raised brows and looks over at Kiera, who gives a half-smile, but neither of them seems to know what to say, either.

Finally, Nathan licks his lips, motioning with his head at Blair. "Hey, do you know how Isadora got her name?"

Blair is still turned away, but this gets her attention. "No, I don't think I've ever heard."

"Kind of a tragic love story, really."

"It is?"

Nathan leans forward in his chair. "Isadora was this girl Uncle Lance was sweet on in high school."

"Isadora was a real person?"

"Yeah, her family was well off, and they weren't too happy about my uncle and Isadora dating, so they had to keep it a secret. The Mustang was her car, parents gave it to her as a gift on her sixteenth birthday." Nathan grins. "And apparently, Uncle Lance and Isadora spent a lot of quality time in that car."

They both smile as their eyes meet.

"Despite her family's disapproval," he continues, "Lance and Isadora fell in love and made plans to get married after high school, but it never happened."

"Why not?"

He lets out his breath. "Because her parents discovered their plans and talked Isadora out of marrying him. She broke it off and gave my uncle the Mustang as a parting gift, said she didn't want it anymore. He found out later she was marrying some other dude." Nathan shakes his head. "Before the wedding, though, Isadora realized the huge mistake she'd made and called it off, tried to find Uncle Lance, but by then it was too late."

"Too late how?"

"He already left town. Took the Mustang and just drove. Wound up in Florida for a while, then California. Isadora tried to find him, but he didn't want to be found." Nathan picks up his bottle. "Uncle Lance never got married. Said Isadora was the only woman he ever loved, and that's why he named the car after her." He takes a swallow from his beer.

Blair is silent, taking this in. "That doesn't explain why it has to be red." Her eyes flash to his with understanding though. "Did Isadora have red hair?"

"She sure did, babe."

Brody leans forward. "Didn't Uncle Lance finally meet up with Isadora again years later? Thought he did, and it turns out she never got married, either."

Nathan nods "Yeah, that's right. She still loved him, too, but he said he just couldn't trust her again."

Kiera sighs. "That is sad. It would be hard to love someone and have them betray you though."

"It's a terrible thing," Blair says quietly. There's an odd expression on her face and when she meets Nathan's eyes for a second, hers are troubled.

"You all right?" he asks.

"I'm fine." Blair smiles and her eyes almost clear. "I've just never heard that story about Isadora before."

NATHAN AND BLAIR decide to leave before the second band comes on. Kiera tries to convince them to stay, but Brody leans back in his chair and doesn't say a word. His cousin's been grinning at him half the night.

"Can't believe I was worried about Blair, when you're the one I should be worrying over." Brody laughs after the women go to the restroom. "Dude, you look ready to go caveman and throw her over your shoulder."

"Don't know what you're talking about."

"Yeah, sure you don't." He shakes his head. "Damn, I haven't seen you this bad off since Gwen."

"Whatever." Nathan picks up his beer, takes a long draw.

"So, what's happening? Has Blair moved back in?"

"No, not yet."

Brody considers this. "Don't worry, she'll come around. Her type just likes to be sure."

"Suppose so."

By the time Nathan gets Blair home, he knows Brody was right about one thing. He was ready to go caveman. Thank God Fiona wasn't there because as soon as they get inside, he can barely control himself.

"Be dammed if I can't stop thinking about you," he breathes, pushing her back up against the door, his hands on her ass, his cock so hard he's ready to burst. "Guess I'm the one having obsessive thoughts now."

Blair laughs, but it turns to a moan when he covers her mouth with his. Feels her arms wind tight around his neck, holding him to her. She moans again, and it's just one more thing about her that's been fanning the flames.

Every time he touches her.

She's all in.

It surprises him for some reason, like he expects her to hold back, give less, but she never does. And it's only making him want her more.

Nathan lets his hands slide up her body, enjoying the feel of her sweet curves. They're both breathing hard, and he's trying to keep it together. Pace himself. He reaches for the zipper on the back of her dress, remembers the latch on top, smiling as he pictures the trail of clothes they're going to leave scattered across the floor.

But then there's a mewing sound and something rubs against his ankles.

Blair pulls away from his mouth and looks down with delight. "Mr. Maurice!"

Nathan looks down, too, though it isn't delight he's feeling.

From one guy to another, give me a break here, cat.

"I haven't seen him all week," she says.

He watches Blair's pretty face as she smiles down at the cat. "Could see him every day if you wanted to."

"Yes, that's true, isn't it?" she murmurs.

Nathan lets out his breath, the breath he's been holding since he told her he loved her. "Could see *me* every day, too."

Blair's looks up at him. She doesn't reply, but he watches the way her eyes go soft, changing color, pulling at him, drawing him in so deep he knows he could get lost and never find his way out. *But maybe I don't need to find my way out*. They gaze at each other, and he wonders if for the first time in his life, he's finally found someone real. Someone who feels like home.

She puts her hand up to his cheek, stroking his jaw. He gives a wry grin. "Not that I'm as important as Mr. Maurice or anything."

"Of course not." Blair smiles, but then her smiles goes soft, too. "Okay," she whispers.

"Okay, what?"

"I'll move back in."

"You will?"

"Yes."

"Good. Let's go get your stuff."

"When?"

He snorts. "Right the hell now."

Blair laughs.

"You think I'm kidding, but I'm not." He puts his mouth to her neck, inhales her clean scent as he closes his eyes, letting relief wash through him. *Thank God*. "Need to make one pit stop first before we get your stuff, though," he tells her in a low voice.

"Where to?" She's playing with his hair, her fingers brush it behind his ear.

"Red Willow Valley. Still need to conduct further research for my book. *Lots* more," he adds.

Blair rolls her eyes. "I think we need anoth—aaah!" she squeals suddenly when he surprises her by reaching down to scoop her into his arms. "What are you doing?"

"Gathering the subject materials I need." He strides with her in his arms toward the bedroom. "Occurs to me now this is the real book I should be discussing on TV tomorrow anyway."

"Oh, my God." She squeals again, grabbing his neck. "Don't you dare!"

"*Journey to Red Willow Valley* would sure get people's attention once I explain what it is. Fiona will probably have a shit fit or," he chuckles with dry humor, "maybe she'll appreciate it."

"I will murder you in your sleep if you do such a thing." Blair laughs. "Just so you know."

"Babe, you're the one who said I'd make a million dollars. Don't you remember?"

When he gets to the bed, he climbs onto it with his knees and puts her down, so she's under him. Those legs of hers immediately wrap around the back of his thighs. She's breathless, and he can tell it's not just from laughing.

"Or maybe I should write a book on the delights of forbidden fruit," he murmurs.

"You keep saying that . . . but I was never forbidden to you."

"Course you were." He kisses her lips softly. "My little sister's best friend, plus your whole upper-crust family. There would have been a shit storm if I'd laid a finger on you."

Blair rolls her eyes. "Give me a break, you didn't even know I was alive."

"Trust me, babe, I knew you were alive. Hard to ignore since you were at our house all the time."

She goes still, and he can see his response has surprised her. "You always acted like I was invisible."

"It's the way things were back then."

"Do you remember that day we talked about *The Razor's Edge*?"

He nods. "Yeah."

"We were at the library downtown."

"I remember. Never met anybody who liked that book as much as I did."

Blair quieted, and her eyes became troubled like they were earlier. It's as if she wants to tell him something.

"What is it? Tell me," he insists.

Those hazel eyes roam his face and he wants to banish whatever is worrying her. "I want you to know I love you," she says. "Always remember that, okay?"

He puts his thumb on her brow, strokes the delicate arch, trying to figure out what could be the problem. "I love you, too."

Nathan wonders if maybe this whole thing has been too soon for her. Having her heart broken by that guy, the dipshit, is probably still lingering. And then he thinks of what happened between them years ago, knows it bothered her how he left, and hopes that isn't part of it.

"I won't hurt you, Blair. I promise."

"I know." She smiles. "You're a good man."

SWEAT COOLS ON his chest as Blair rides him sweet and slow. Like warm honey. Like the taste of sunshine at midnight.

Knows she enjoys being on top, and it suits her, too. Her long hair sweeping over his face and shoulders as she moves with focused heat, gasping a little each time she comes down onto him.

Nathan's hands travel over her body, her skin soft and smooth. He's so aware of her, of every breath, amazed at the way she fills his senses. No empty spaces left. Just Blair. Her fragrance rich and clean, the musk of it enveloping him.

This is all that matters. Right here in front of me. Beautiful and simple.

Her gasps change to something shaky as she increases the pace. He knows she's close, reaching for it.

"That's right, babe," he whispers. "Take what's yours."

Finally she cries out, long and loud as she gives in to ecstasy. When their eyes meet, even in the dark bedroom, he sees the way she looks at him. Unlike anything he's ever experienced. A brilliant light hitting him square in the chest. Leaves him wrecked and dazed every time.

When she lies down on him, Nathan closes his eyes, smoothing his hands over her back. He decides there aren't words invented yet for pleasure this ripe.

"That's my favorite part," he tells her, his voice low as it vibrates through the room.

Blair laughs against his chest. "You say that every time."

"Because it's true."

She rises off him and smiles. Runs her hands over his chest, tracing the letters in Sanskrit. He starts thrusting into her a little again, his hips moving of their own volition.

They do this for a while, lazily enjoying each other. Both of them have come twice, so there's no sense of urgency.

"Let's go from behind," he suggests, caressing her hips. "Haven't done that with you yet."

Blair hesitates, her eyes flash to his. "I don't know. I've never really enjoyed that."

"Babe, I'll stop right away if you don't like it."

She nods and lifts up, goes onto her knees. And there's something about it, Blair offering herself to him like this that speaks to his most basic self as a man. A primitive sorcery heats his blood.

He doesn't enter her right away, but slides his hands over her hips and ass. His fingertips trail down her spine, followed by his mouth. Tastes her skin—so sweet. He wraps his arm around her waist, her body firm yet pliant beneath him.

Can hear her unsteady breath. Her arousal. Wonders why Blair never enjoyed this before, but doesn't like to think of another man with her, especially someone doing something she didn't enjoy.

He caresses her all over as her hips move, her back arching. Be lying if he didn't admit he enjoyed seeing her this way. Hot and needy.

"Do you trust me, babe?" he asks, a fresh animal want growing in him.

"Yes," she says.

He pushes into her slow, resisting the urge to thrust hard and deep. Blair gasps, lifting and pushing her hips toward him, making it impossible to go either slow or shallow.

"You okay?" he asks, his voice guttural to his own ears. His body screams at him to keep moving, but he stops anyway.

Her arms stretch before her, grasping the sheets. "Nathan," she breathes. "Don't stop . . ."

His mouth opens as he pulls in a lungful of air, awash with lust and love. Groans.

And then he's deep within her. So deep, he wonders at all the places he's touching, certain her heart has to be one of them.

Chapter Twenty-Three

Daily List

1. Watch your man look hot on live television.
2. Live your bliss.
3. Stop worrying so much.

"IS ANYONE MANNING the front?" Blair asks, looking around their bakery's backroom as everyone crowds into the small space to watch Nathan on television.

"I'm keeping an eye on it," Carlos says. "The morning rush has died off, so we're good."

"There he is!" Natalie points to the screen.

"That's Blair's man?" Zoe, one of their bakers, leans in close. "Not what I expected, but he's hot."

Blair doesn't say anything, just watches as Nathan walks out and takes a seat in the chair next to the show's host. He looks great. Hot, like Zoe said. Jeans and a light blue Henley, not his usual red and black sneakers, but a dark pair Blair doesn't recognize. His hair's parted off-center and looks blonder on camera. She listens as they introduce him as 'Road Church, bestselling author, travel blogger, and Seattle native.'

"Welcome to Seattle Morning Edition," the pretty brunette host says, smiling at Nathan, and Blair feels a twinge of jealousy.

He nods, leans forward a little. "Thank you for having me. It's good to be here."

The brunette smiles again as she asks him about the success of *Edge of Zen,* then asks how it feels to be back in Seattle after traveling the world for the past five years.

Nathan seems relaxed, not in the least bit nervous as he talks. He cracks a joke about how when he started traveling, one of the biggest surprises was seeing people use umbrellas.

"I may come from Seattle, but I've never owned an umbrella in my life."

"That's so true!" The pretty brunette laughs with bubbly delight. "Nobody here uses umbrellas!"

Answering each question, Nathan is witty and engaging, and the host seems legitimately taken with him, though her flirtatious laughter is starting to get on Blair's nerves.

He's obviously in great spirits, really in the zone, and Blair can't help thinking back to last night and this morning, to how amazing things were between them.

They barely slept at all. Though, instead of feeling tired, there's a delicious energy humming through her. Every time she closes her eyes, she sees Nathan. Beautiful Nathan. The way he looked last night and this morning. Gazing at her with bliss, his eyes clearer and greener than she's ever seen them.

I can't believe it's me he was looking at with that expression.

Blair finally went down on him this morning, could tell he was surprised when she moved between his thighs, took him into her mouth. He watched her with rapt attention the whole time, breath harsh and unsteady, trembling with pleasure near the end. Blair felt guilty enjoying his strong response so much.

"I'm sorry I waited so long to do that," she told him quietly afterward, embarrassed for not doing it sooner. In some misguided way, she'd been trying to keep a small part of herself separate, a futile attempt to spare herself pain when this ends.

But maybe this won't end.

The thought has been coming to her more and more lately. That maybe she won't have to give him up. *Maybe he'll stay in love with me.*

"Figured you weren't ready, is all," he said afterward, and then grinned. "Glad that's changed."

She scooted up next to him, put her head on his chest, her fingers tracing the Sanskrit above his heart.

All those years she spent trying to imagine how good it would be between them. *Turns out, it's far better than anything I could have imagined.*

Which makes the strange unease that's settled over her lately all the more mysterious.

I need to relax and enjoy this.

Blair can't seem to shake the sense of foreboding, though.

A couple of times recently, she even thought of confessing everything to Nathan. Just take her chances. Be brave. *If he really loves me, wouldn't he stay?*

But then fear sinks in. Panic. What if he doesn't stay? And even worse, what if the truth hurts him? Because it will, and that's the last thing she wants.

She's been telling herself this foreboding is just her anxiety. She's just having her usual compulsive thoughts. Tries to remind herself there's no way Nathan will ever find out the truth.

And yet, the unease persists.

Hearing that story about Isadora last night didn't help matters. It hit way too close to home. Lance punishing the real Isadora their whole lives for one awful mistake.

"He's doing a great job, especially for his first time." Natalie looks over at her. "I'll bet he gets people interested in his book. Anthony's been interviewed on live television and he told me it's nerve-racking."

"Thanks, I'll tell him you said that." Blair watches as they wrap up the interview and go to commercial.

"How is everything between you two?"

"Incredible."

Natalie smiles. "I had a feeling things might work out. Especially after our girls' night. He seemed very . . . eager to be with you."

"I agreed to move back home finally."

"Really? I'm glad." Natalie grins. "Of course, I have to ask, does he pass the Bandito Test?"

Blair doesn't even have to think about it. "With flying colors."

EXCEPT BLAIR DOESN'T move back in right away.

"Babysitting?" Nathan stares at her, incredulous, from across the table of the infamous Mexican restaurant where she drank too many margaritas. "You've got to be kidding."

"No, I'm not."

"Can't believe this."

Blair picks up her Diet Coke. No margaritas this time. She doesn't want to get close to anything even resembling truth serum. "Tori called, and I promised to watch the boys while she volunteers at an animal shelter during the evenings next week, starting Wednesday."

"Those aren't boys," Nathan points out the obvious. "They're just dogs."

"She doesn't want to leave them alone. I can still stay with you until then. I'm just not bringing my stuff back yet."

He shakes his head and lets out a frustrated breath. "Swear to God, my sister . . ." He rolls his eyes, but doesn't finish his sentence.

"It's only a little longer. And besides, you're flying to San Francisco anyway." Fiona has another morning show interview lined up for Nathan next week.

"I want you all moved in when I get back."

"Okay, though you and Fiona need to make sure everything is cleaned up first."

"No worries, babe. Already got that covered." He digs into his macho burrito with enthusiasm.

She watches him eat. This is the fourth time they've had Mexican food in a week. It's clear Nathan could eat Mexican food for breakfast, lunch, and dinner. With a bowl of cereal for dessert.

"What do you mean 'covered'?" she asks. "How?"

He chews his food, nodding. "I've hired a cleaning crew to come in. Do the whole place."

Her brows go up. Her first thought is to wonder whether any cleaning crew could possibly meet her exacting standards. Although, her standards have certainly slipped.

"Planning to give Fiona half the bill when they're done," he says, chuckling. "Can't wait to see her reaction."

"Do you think she'll pay it?"

"Going to threaten her with telling Sachi if she doesn't."

Blair laughs now, too. "That should be fun. Have those two finally worked out their problems?"

"Yeah, looks that way," he says, picking up his glass of water. "Haven't told you the latest, though. Fiona told me this morning she's planning to move to Seattle—God help us."

"Seriously?" Blair dips a tortilla chip into her refried beans. "I guess she finally decided to make the sacrifice for love. I take it there's no more weeping?"

"Nope. In fact, she's going to be gone again tonight. We'll have the place all to ourselves." He gives her a long, meaningful look.

"*Fine.*" Blair pretends to act put upon. "I'll come over, but only because you're a famous TV star now."

His television interview earlier went so well that emails and texts poured in afterward. Nothing but positive viewer response. Apparently, his blog numbers went up, as did his sales on Amazon. Fiona already has him scheduled to go to Portland later this week for a show and then the one in San Francisco next week.

"Just doing whatever it takes to get laid," he says then laughs when Blair kicks him under the table.

"My parents are having a party this Saturday. It's an annual BBQ they have to kick off the summer." She picks up her Diet Coke again and tries to act nonchalant. "Do you want to come?"

Nathan stops chewing. "To your parents' house?"

She nods.

Their eyes meet across the table.

"What do they know about us?"

Us. A frisson of joy runs through her. "I haven't told them much," she says, being honest. "My mom knows we've been spending time together, and I told her about what's been happening with your book."

Nathan takes this in. "Guess it was inevitable I'd have to deal with them, huh?"

"They don't hate you."

He smirks. "Now who's a lousy liar?"

"I just mean they aren't stuck in the past. And they admire what you've accomplished." This much is true, or sort of true. Her parents both respect it when someone works hard and does well.

He doesn't say anything more, just goes back to eating his food. She knows he doesn't want to go on Saturday, but if they're going to be together, he's right. Her parents are an inevitability.

Nathan winds up spending two days in Portland. His interview went even better than the one in Seattle, and Blair leaves directly after work on Friday to pick him up from the airport. As it turns out, Sachi is there to pick up Fiona, too.

"I've heard so much about you!" Blair says. "It's great to meet you."

Sachi laughs. "It's nice to meet you, too."

"I'm really glad you and Fiona have worked things out."

Blair can't resist studying Sachi a little, and can see Nathan was right—Sachi is not what she expected. For starters, while she's attractive, she's nowhere near as beautiful as Fiona. She has short, dark hair and doesn't wear any makeup—her jeans and T-shirt are definitely non-designer.

Sachi has a great smile, though, and Blair senses an underlying toughness. Plus, she seems down to earth and unlikely to put up with any nonsense. She imagines it's good for Fiona to be with someone who can help keep her grounded.

When Blair and Nathan arrive at her condo, the cleaning crew has come and gone.

"I *guess* it's okay," she says, looking around. All the take-out boxes have been thrown away and most of the mess is picked up, though Fiona's suitcases are still there. Apparently, she plans to pick them up this weekend, so that's a relief. Everything appears to be vacuumed and tidied. Blair can smell the remnants of some kind of lemon-scented cleaning solvent. She doesn't bother to open her cabinets or fridge, can only imagine what a mess they are. Everything out of order and misaligned. In the past, she wouldn't have been able to resist the urge to fix them right away.

So maybe I'm making progress.

Nathan tosses his bag on the floor then flops down on the couch. Mr. Maurice immediately jumps onto his chest. "Hey, pal," he says, petting him as the cat purrs loudly.

"Looks like someone missed you." Blair stands next to the couch, watching the two of them.

Nathan's green eyes flash up to hers with a playful gleam. "Anybody else miss me?"

"I suppose." She tries to give him a haughty look, but is so glad to see him she can't pull it off even as a joke.

"Come here." Nathan pushes the cat aside and reaches for her hand so Blair can take Mr. Maurice's place.

She lies on top of him, soothed by the steady beat of his heart. Blair sighs with happiness. His hand is stroking her back and eventually she lifts her head to face him. "Just so you know, I missed you way more than Mr. Maurice."

"Sorry, babe, doubt that's possible. You've seen how much this cat loves me, right?"

She scoffs. "Please, that's just a boy crush." She points at herself. "This is the real thing."

"Is it?" His eyes roam her face.

"Yes, it is." She reaches up to stroke his jaw covered with blond stubble. "It's the real thing."

"I missed you, too," he acknowledges, then lowers his voice, his hand sliding down to her ass. "Missed all of you. Can't wait to taste some of that cinnamon snatch."

Blair stills for a moment before gawking at him. "*What* did you just call it?"

Nathan chuckles. "Too dirty for you?"

"You can't say . . . that!" she sputters, pushing on his chest. "Ever!"

He laughs. "Okay, how about petting the illustrious red beaver?"

"No!"

"Going to bronze beaver town?"

She sits up partway, looking around for a weapon of some kind. "Where are you getting these from?"

"Fire bush canal?"

Blair grabs a couch pillow. "I'm going to murder you with this pillow just to shut you up!"

He's laughing so hard now he's having difficulty catching his breath. "Wait," he holds up his hand to fend off the pillow. "I've got it! How about this—my favorite red lunch box."

Blair breaks down and laughs now, too. "Please, stop." She groans. "I can't believe I'm saying this, but let's just stick with Red Willow Valley."

"Yeah." Nathan chuckles some more then lets out a deep sigh. "You're right, that's still the best of the bunch."

"The bunch?"

He nods. "Thought them all up on the plane ride home."

"I don't believe it." Blair rolls her eyes. "*This* is how you spend your time?"

"Hey, I was sitting next to Fiona. Had to listen to her plot my entire career—hell, my whole life. Could only take so much before I tuned her out." He grins and takes her hand, intertwining their fingers. "Needed something real pleasant to think about, like," he gives her an earnest look, "your crimson curlies."

"Oh, my God," Blair groans, and laughs some more. "That's definitely the *worst* of the bunch."

THEY WAKE UP the next morning to dark clouds in the sky. It's Saturday, the day of her parents' BBQ, and Blair took the day off. She's letting Ginger and Carlos handle the wedding cake deliveries. It's not easy, but she's trying to be less of a control freak. After all, delegating is part of being the boss. The truth is she's never taken a single vacation since they opened La Dolce Vita.

"What if it rains?" Nathan wants to know. "Will they cancel their party?"

They're still lying in bed, his warm body wrapped behind her as they study the gray sky through her bedroom window. Blair should feel cozy and relaxed, especially after the wonderful night they had, but unfortunately, her sense of unease has returned.

Maybe it's just those dark clouds.

"No, they won't cancel. They'll just move the party indoors." She rolls over in bed so she's facing him. "You don't have to go if you don't want to. I'll understand."

They study each other. Nathan's face is so handsome and familiar in the morning light. Love surges through her.

"I want to go," he tells her firmly. "Need to clear the air. Let them see what I'm made of."

Blair nods. "Okay."

They spend the rest of the morning futzing around, each doing their own thing. Nathan is mostly holed up in front of his computer working on his blog, while Blair looks over the sketches for Kiki's cake—the wedding coming up in only a couple of weeks.

She tries to shake her disquiet, wonders if it's related to bringing Nathan to her parents' house, but can't imagine why. Yes, they were unhappy with what happened years ago, but her parents wouldn't be rude to him now. Plus, her mother has decided to hire Fiona, and is apparently impressed enough with the humorist Fiona introduced her to that there's talk of a book in the works.

By the time they're ready to leave, Blair's unease is so bad she considers canceling, but knows she can't. Not only are her parents expecting her, but she suspects Nathan would think she was canceling because of him.

They take Isadora, stopping at La Dolce Vita on the way so she can pick up the cakes she set aside yesterday for the party. Nathan helps her carry them to the car, and after some thought, Blair decides to strap two of them in the backseat, while she holds two more balanced on her lap.

"That's a lot of cake, babe."

"My mom asked me to bring them. I was supposed to bring cupcakes, too, but we sold out before I could put any aside."

She tied a coral scarf in her hair before they left, and Nathan slips his hand to the back of her neck at one of the stoplights. "You look real nice, princess. Like the scarf. Sexy."

"Thank you." She smiles.

He's still watching her, and even when the light turns, seems reluctant to turn back to the road.

The sun has come out and though it's turned into a warm day, they keep the convertible top up as they drive. Nathan's never been to her parents' house, which seems weird now that she thinks about it. She married him, and yet no one ever thought to invite him to the house?

Including me?

There are already quite a few cars parked in her parents' circular driveway, and Blair instructs Nathan to just park wherever he can. Her parents live in an upper middle class neighborhood, the houses all large and well-maintained.

She can see the way Nathan looks around, his laser focus turned on as he helps her carry the cakes inside. Blair tries to see her parents' house from his point of view and realizes it probably does look like she was a princess living in a fairytale castle.

Their eyes meet for a few seconds. She's not sure what to do with the grim determination she finds behind his.

Blair has him follow her around to the backyard. The party's already in full swing, and she sees the buffet tables lined up near the house with food, so she heads in that direction.

"Blair." Her dad is coming out one of the French doors which lead into the house.

"Hey, Dad. I come bearing sweets."

"Your mother will be relieved. She's already worried we're going to run out of food." He laughs, motioning at the long table loaded up with everything from salad to seafood. "Though I don't see how that's possible."

Blair laughs, too, notices an open spot near the desserts her mom must have left for the cakes. She's ready to say something about Nathan, but her dad's already noticed him.

"We haven't seen you in a while, Road," her dad says, his tone serious. "Though, I understand you go by Nathan now?"

"Yeah, that's right."

The two men eye each other, the tension palpable. Blair starts to panic, but then her dad puts his hand out, and Nathan shifts the cake boxes to one arm, so they can shake.

The tension is lessened, though not entirely gone. Blair decides to change the subject and asks if her brothers have arrived yet.

"Yes, they're both here," her dad says, though his eyes are still on Nathan, the two of them locked into some sort of staring contest now.

"Did they bring anyone or anything? I heard Ian has a new girlfriend," Blair asks with growing alarm, trying to stop whatever's happening here between her dad and Nathan.

Finally, her dad breaks eye contact and turns to her. "No, Ian came alone. Ashley is sporting an engagement ring, though."

"Really? Well, that's exciting news." Blair puts a false lilt in her voice. Marriage is the last thing she wants to talk about right now. "I guess I should get these cakes set up. Could you help me, Nathan?"

Her father gives him one last look then leaves. Blair doesn't know what to say or do. When she glances at Nathan, his expression is stony. Despite the sunny day, a sense of dread has settled over her like black smoke, thick enough to choke on. She can only hope things get better for the rest of the party.

And surprisingly, they do.

Blair can hardly believe it, but things don't get worse. At first they do, with more staring contests between her dad and Nathan, and between her brothers and Nathan, too. At one point, the tension gets so high, Blair even suggests they leave, but Nathan isn't having any of it.

"No, we're staying," he says resolutely, his laser-focused eyes surveying the backyard. "Not done here yet."

"Are you sure?"

"Positive."

As time passes, though, she notices a shift. It starts with Scott talking to Nathan. Just a few words, by the food table, but apparently it's enough because the staring contests go away, and the tension starts to ease. Then not long afterward, she sees Ian talking to Nathan, as well.

Blair tried to stay by Nathan's side, but she keeps getting pulled away. She's worried he's uncomfortable, but when she apologizes, he only shakes his head.

"Don't worry about me, babe. I'm good."

Eventually, she sees him talking to her dad and goes over to join them. They're discussing his travel blog. Nathan's explaining some of the plans he has to develop it more in the future.

"I've taken a look at it," her dad says, surprising her—and judging by the look on Nathan's face, surprising him, too. "I think you're right about selling products, expanding that element. You've got great potential for growth there." Her dad starts talking about market share and competition, and Blair is too much in shock to really pay attention.

She notices Nathan is listening carefully, though.

"I haven't read your book yet, but I know my wife has, and she said it's terrific," her dad continues. "Make sure you leverage that, because it'll give your site that much more visibility."

Blair blinks. Her mom read *Edge of Zen*? She's never said a word! Blair was just talking to her a short while ago. Her mom even mentioned seeing Nathan on that local morning show, but never told her she'd read his book.

And that's when it dawns on Blair.

Things are going well. Better than well. Things are fantastic.

So, why do I still feel uneasy?

As she's reflecting on this, her brother Ian jogs over. "Hey, Nathan, we're setting up a game of touch football. You in?"

"Sure. It's been a while, but I'm in." He looks over at Blair. "Babe, by chance do you have a rubber band I could use to pull my hair back?"

"I think so."

Blair gets a black hair band from the house and brings it out to Nathan, who by now is over on the other side of the yard with both her brothers and a bunch of friends and neighbors.

"Thanks, princess," he says, taking the band from her.

Blair watches as he pulls his chin-length blond hair into a 'man bun.' It should look silly but, of course, it doesn't. Nathan's guy-glamor instincts are infallible. Instead, he looks ten thousand shades of hot.

Oh, my God.

Blair swallows. She can't pull her eyes away and decides he's definitely wearing a man bun in the bedroom tonight. *Oh, heck yeah.* She watches him jog over to join the other guys. Someone makes a crack about his hair, but he just smiles.

The men are picking teams, with Nathan being sized up by everyone. He was a good football player in high school, and she imagines he's still good. Ian, who's always been naturally competitive, seems to be of the same mindset and immediately chooses Nathan for his team.

Blair goes off to the sidelines to stand next to Ashley, who's been flashing her engagement ring around all day. *You'd think she was the first woman in the world to get engaged.*

And then it hits Blair—*I'm jealous. Jealous of Ashley*—who could believe it? Blair's never had an engagement, though. Never had a real wedding or marriage. Her only pregnancy ended in miscarriage. *I paid for that one night's mistake in full, with interest.*

"Wow," Ashley says to her. "Your boyfriend is like super cute."

"Thanks." And she realizes Scott never told Ashley the story behind her and Nathan.

"Maybe you guys will get married, too!" Ashley squeals with delight. "Just like Scottie and me!" She starts waving her left hand around aimlessly again to show off the ring.

Blair smiles, finding it hard to not be glad for someone this happy. "Maybe we will."

NATHAN IS SURPRISED how well the day is going. Figured he'd come here, take the temperature of things, show them he's not out to screw Blair over, and then leave if it got too hot. Luckily, that hasn't been the case.

Lot of posturing at first, of course, but he expected that from the men. After what happened years ago, he knew her dad and brothers had to take his measure. Also knew he had to take theirs. Make things crystal clear all around. He's dealt with plenty worse, though, so that was no problem.

The only person in Blair's family he hasn't dealt with yet is her mom, so he's not surprised when Cherise comes over to where he's sitting in a lawn chair. He's relaxing with a beer, taking a breather after playing touch football. Blair is over by the desserts, talking to someone she went to college with.

"I wanted to thank you again for your input about Fiona," Cherise tells him, sitting in the chair next to him Blair vacated. "I've decided to work with her and so far, I'm very pleased."

"Glad to hear it. Like I said before, Fiona is something of a character, but she's very good at what she does. Doubt my book would be doing as well without her help."

"Yes, I'm certain you're right."

Cherise takes a sip from her glass of wine.

Nathan studies her a little. She has the same hair color as Blair, though there are pieces of silver sprinkled throughout. It doesn't look bad, and he figures Blair's will eventually look the same. Cherise's eyes are brown not hazel, though, and she doesn't have the same elegant bone structure as Blair. Cherise's features are more blunt-edged, but he has to admit she's still an attractive woman.

The silence between them stretches, and Nathan suspects she has something on her mind. Something to say about him and Blair, but decides to wait her out.

It doesn't take long for her to get to the real reason she came over to talk to him.

Cherise studies her wine for a few seconds and then looks up at him. "It appears you and my daughter have mended fences and are romantically involved again."

He nods. "That's true."

"Are you two planning to stay married then?"

"Guess you could say we're exploring things." His eyes go to Blair across the lawn, to where she's laughing with her friend. He considers telling Cherise how he and Blair are in love, but decides against it. Figures if Blair hasn't told her mom yet, there must be a reason.

"I see." Cherise is silent, taking this in. "And are you planning to leave without a word to anyone again?"

Nathan's jaw clenches, and he stares at Cherise, remembering all too clearly the way she treated him years ago. Always meddling.

"I don't want to see my daughter get hurt again," she says. "So that's why I'm asking."

He lets out his breath, understands her instinct to protect. "Didn't know at the time that Blair was hurt by my leaving, but no, I'm not planning on it."

"And are you being more careful this time? About other things?"

"Excuse me?"

"About using protection?" Cherise pauses. "I realize you're both adults, and that I may be crossing a line here, but I think it's worth asking."

Nathan snorts in amazement. "You sure as hell *are* crossing a line!"

"You two were reckless last time," her brown eyes drill into his, "and I don't want to see that happen again."

His face goes warm as his temper flares, though he manages to rein it back in. "Not that it's any of your business, but we were never reckless. Blair was on the pill. We just had lousy luck, is all."

"Please, don't lie to me, Nathan. We both know that isn't true."

"The hell it's not true."

Cherise shakes her head. "You think I don't know my own daughter's medical history? Blair has never been on the pill."

"Guess you don't know her medical history as well as you think then."

"I know it very well. Blair's not allowed to go on the pill because we have a family history of blood clots on my side."

"What?" Nathan stares at her, trying to make sense of this. "Don't know anything about that, but I do know she was on the pill back then because she told me so."

Cherise studies him and looks troubled. "I see." She nods. "Maybe I'm wrong about this after all."

"You *are* wrong. Guess Blair doesn't tell you everything."

"Apparently not."

Chapter Twenty-Four

How To Watch Your Dreams Die

1. Close your eyes.
2. Hold your breath.
3. Decide.

AFTER SUNSET, THE party starts to thin out, though there are still neighbors who stay and some other friends of Blair's parents. Ian leaves, but Scott and Ashley are still around, sitting off by themselves. Blair is amazed how great the day has gone.

See, I had nothing to worry about.

Her whole sense of foreboding was obviously her usual obsessiveness and nothing more. Oddly, she still feels a twinge of something, but brushes it aside.

"Shall I give you a tour of the house?" she asks Nathan, both of them standing alone in the kitchen where Blair is helping to clean up.

"Sure." He glances around, then pulls her in by the waist. "What I'd really like to see most, princess, is your bedroom."

"Is that right?"

He puts his mouth to her ear. "Might have to make use of that pink canopy bed."

Blair laughs softly. "I hate to disappoint you, but that pink canopy bed has been gone for years."

Nathan sighs. "Dammit, there goes that fantasy." But then he grins. "How about you show me your bedroom anyway?"

"It's become a guest bedroom now." She takes his hand. "But come on, I'll still show you."

They leave just as she hears voices from people entering the kitchen. She leads Nathan through the dining room, then the great room, feels him taking it all in as they finally reach the stairs.

"I'm curious about something," he says as they start to head upstairs. "Why did you and Tori hang out at our house so much?"

"What do you mean?"

"When you could hang out here instead? Why come to our house?"

Because you were there, she almost says. Blair remembers how she always pushed to stay at Tori's instead of here, anything to be under the same roof with him.

Blair turns to look at Nathan, his green eyes focused on her. Come to think of it, his laser focus has been turned on all day.

"We hung out here, too. We stayed in both places."

He snorts. "Not the way I remember it."

"Here it is," she says when they arrive, opening the white paneled door. "My former teenage bedroom."

They enter the place where she once spent hours lying on her bed, spinning her girlish dreams about him.

If he only knew.

Looking around the room, there's a bit of sadness in her heart that she can't share this with him, the way she once spent hours thinking about him. She suspects, if circumstances were different, he'd enjoy hearing about it.

She watches the way Nathan takes in the layout. The guest bedroom is nicely decorated in a nautical theme with various shades of blue and white. A big double bed is centered against the wall where her pink canopy once stood. Striped blue curtains hang over the alcove window.

Nathan walks over to the window to look outside. It faces the south side of the yard. The corner of her mom's art studio is just visible, and behind that, it's mostly wooded.

She goes to stand next to him, studies his profile as he studies the view. "Is that a tree house?" he asks, motioning at a structure near the edge of the woods.

"It is. My brothers and I built it with my dad."

He nods.

Standing there, Nathan seems so remote, so separate and removed from all this. She thinks about how he grew up without a father, how awful that must have been. Blair always knew he didn't have one, but this is the first time she really gets it. How it must have been terrible. He had his uncle, obviously, but that's not the same as having your dad.

She reaches down and takes his hand, squeezes it, wishing she could fix everything. Every lousy thing that ever happened to him as a kid. She starts to pull him close, to kiss him, but doesn't get the chance.

"Your mom said something really weird to me today." He's still studying the view out her window. "Probably nothing, but I got to ask you anyway." He turns to look at her. "Do you have a family history of blood clots?"

"What?"

"Your mom told me you have a history of blood clots and aren't supposed to go on the pill."

Blair goes still. "That's weird."

"I know, but it's what she told me."

"Actually," she tries to breathe, but is finding it difficult suddenly, "there's a history of blood clots on my mom's side."

Nathan nods. "She told me you're not supposed to take the pill. That true?"

Blair doesn't respond right away. And that's when it dawns on her.

This is it.

It's happening right now.

All her unease, her foreboding so thick, ready to choke her, it wasn't at all about how her parents might reject Nathan.

"Your mom said you've never been on the pill," he continues. "Told her that wasn't true, but she seemed so sure of herself."

Blair looks into his eyes, remembering back to the very first time she ever looked into them. How everything changed for her that day. Everything.

She knows there are two paths. The one she's on now, living in the shadows, living with lies and half-truths. *But with this path, I have Nathan. He's mine. And that's no small thing.*

Or the path of honesty. The truth. The honest path will bring her into the light, but in all likelihood, she'll lose Nathan forever. *No! I can't let that happen. The truth will only hurt him.*

"Why do you think she told me that?" he asks. She sees the trust on his face, hears it in his voice, still believing in her, assumes it's her mother who's wrong.

Blair gulps for air. Knows her decision. Her heart pounds so loud she can hear it, like the gallop of an approaching monster.

"My mom told you that because it's true." *I owe him this much.* Blair's head swims at all she's giving up. The love of her life. Her prince. The only one.

He looks at her with confusion, his trust still solid and whole. "Don't understand what you're saying, babe."

"I've never been on the pill." She gazes into his beautiful green eyes. "I lied to you."

Nathan stares at her.

"I wanted to tell you the truth sooner, but I didn't know how. And," she lets out a shaky breath, "I didn't want to hurt you."

She sees his mind working, sorting through it all. "You lied about being on the pill that night?"

"Yes."

His eyes roam her face. "Why would you do that?"

"It's hard to explain." Her mind searches desperately for some way out of this, to save things.

"Try," he insists.

And she can see his trust isn't solid and whole anymore. There's a crack—a tiny one, but it's spreading.

"Were you trying to get pregnant for some reason?" he asks. "But why? That makes no sense."

"No, that's not it."

"Then what?"

Blair understands now how the way she took advantage of him that night was indecent. For all her love, she wronged him in an ugly way, and she's ashamed for it.

"I wanted you," she finally admits. "I wanted *all* of you."

Nathan goes to sit on the bed. "Help me out here, Blair. I'm trying to understand, but none of this makes sense."

"I love you," she says.

He nods, wary. "I know."

"No, you *don't* know."

"Course I do."

She takes a deep breath then lets it out, lets it spill. The floodgates open. "I've loved you since the moment I first saw you, Nathan. The very first time Tori brought me to your house and I saw you there in the yard playing Frisbee." She smiles at him. "You blew my mind."

"The first time you saw me? But that was years ago. We were still teenagers."

"I know. And I've been in love with you every single day since then. Crazy in love with you."

"What?" Nathan blinks. "You serious?"

"I am." Blair is shaking all over, her breath erratic. There's a strange exhilaration coursing through her.

"You've been in love with me all these years? How come you never said anything?"

"Because I was too afraid. I didn't know how you'd react. And years ago, I never told you because I knew you didn't have any feelings for me."

"What about the dipshit, though? Obviously you loved him, too."

"My God, Nathan." She gives a humorless laugh. "It's you I was talking about."

"Me?"

"Yes, you. You're the guy I loved who didn't love me back."

He's quiet, taking this in. "All this time you let me think there's some other guy, when it's *me? I'm* the fucking dipshit?"

He gets off the bed now, starts pacing the room. "Were you trying to trick me into marrying you? That why you lied about being on the pill?"

"No." And in this, Blair knows she's telling the truth. That was the last thing on her mind. Strange as it sounds, she was so obsessively focused in the moment, pregnancy never even occurred to her.

"Then what? Why the hell did you lie?"

Blair licks her lips. "Because I wanted you, okay? I wanted the intimacy. I'd been in love with you for so long. I thought that was my only chance to be with you in every way."

Nathan stops pacing and stares at her, breathing hard. "Jesus Christ, is that really what you call love?" She realizes the crack in his trust is spreading fast. "I don't even know who you are. Thought I did," and she sees the hurt in his eyes, "thought I *knew* you, Blair. Thought I'd finally found someone real I could hold on to."

"You still can." She tries to go to him, but he moves away from her. "I'm so sorry," she says. "I made a mistake that night, a terrible mistake. I wish I could take it back."

Nathan shakes his head. "I changed my whole life because of that mistake."

"I know."

"You don't know shit!" He points to his chest. "Should I tell you what this Sanskrit means?"

He's wearing a short-sleeved T-shirt, but Blair has traced the lines of that tattoo over his heart so many times, she has it memorized.

"Got it right after I went to India. After you lost the baby."

She looks at his chest then flashes to his face. "I don't . . . understand."

"It says 'angel.'"

Blair opens her mouth. Stunned. It's like being struck—the blow nearly physical. She puts her hand against the wall to steady herself. "I didn't think you cared I lost the baby."

"I cared." His voice vibrates through the room. "I married you. You think I would have done that if I didn't care?"

"You never said anything to me." She thinks back to how he looked right after he found out about the miscarriage. His face grim, but unreadable, finally realizing now she's been misinterpreting his expression all these years. It turns out he was suffering.

"Didn't know I had to spell it out for you. Not that kind of loss."

Her throat grows so tight she can barely speak. "I suffered too."

"Yeah," he says, "I know you did."

She looks over at him, and when their eyes meet, an understanding passes between them.

He's still staring at her. "After the way I was raised, you think I don't take that shit seriously? That I'd allow any child of mine to live in this world unprotected and fatherless?"

"I just never knew it mattered so much to you." Her hand is still against the wall, trying to ground herself somehow.

"Then you don't know me."

Blair almost laughs at the irony of this. She studied him for years, obsessively cataloging every detail. But he's right. *I didn't know him.*

I do now.

"Thought you were different than anyone I'd ever been with," he says, his voice ragged. "That you changed my life, that I finally found someone I could really trust. But turns out you're worse than all of them."

Blair gazes out the window. The same window she looked through a thousand times, lovesick and dreaming of him. Pain slices through her. Almost from a distance she understands the real pain is still waiting for her. Wonders how she'll survive it. *It will either cure me or kill me.*

"Guess I'm not such a good girl after all," she whispers.

When she turns back to Nathan, she sees something in his eyes, something horrible. His trust is no longer cracked. It's shattered.

IT'S LATE, WELL after midnight, when her mom finds her curled up in the guest bedroom. Blair doesn't move or say anything, just lies there hugging herself. Her mom sits down near the edge of the bed, both of them silent.

"I did something terrible," Blair finally admits, her voice quiet. "Something I'm ashamed of."

Her mom's hand goes out to touch her hair, strokes it the way she used to when Blair was small. "I take it this involves Nathan."

Blair nods.

"You love him, don't you?"

"For a very long time."

"I see."

They're both silent again. Blair thinks of how this all took place in her old bedroom. The walls of this room infused with her hopes and dreams. Now this is the room where all her hopes and dreams died.

"Sometimes," her mom speaks, breaking the silence. "It's good when the truth comes out, even if it's painful."

Blair doesn't say anything.

"You don't want to build your life on lies, honey."

"I know."

Her mom gets up and fixes the bed for her so she can sleep in it. Removes the pillow shams, then pulls the duvet back. Helps her climb under the covers as if she were a child again.

"Do you want to borrow some pajamas to sleep in?" her mom asks.

"No, this is okay. I'll just sleep in my shirt and underwear."

"Okay."

After her mom leaves, Blair lies in the dark for a long time, listening to the familiar sounds of her old room. The occasional creak and groan of the walls and floorboards. Wonders where Nathan is right now and if he went back to the condo.

Maybe I should have gone after him.

But then realizes she doesn't even have a car, since he would have left with Isadora.

Blair tries to close her eyes and let sleep come. It doesn't work, though. Every time, all she sees is Nathan's face, that terrible expression. *The way I hurt him.*

The next morning, her mom gives her a ride back and drops her off. Neither of them talk about Nathan or what happened and for that, she's grateful. Blair hasn't cried yet. Instead, she feels this peculiar numbness all over, as if her body's been dipped in ice water.

Right away, Blair can tell he isn't there. She walks through her condo room by room anyway. She notices Fiona's suitcases are still there, stacked in the corner of her living room, though there's no sign of Fiona, either. When she gets to the office, she discovers the air mattress was slept on. Blankets and pillows tossed around.

So he did come back here.

The office furniture he bought is still there, but his computers are both gone. And when she looks through the desk drawers, they're all empty. He kept clothes in the office closet and those are gone, too.

She searches around for Mr. Maurice, but doesn't see him anywhere. For a moment, she considers the possibility Nathan might have taken her cat with him, but then finds him hiding under her bed.

"There you are."

Mr. Maurice comes out and lets her pet him as Blair tries to decide whether she should call Nathan again. She's already tried three times this morning, but he's not answering.

Finally, exhausted, she collapses onto her bed, and that's when she notices it. His smoky scent. On the pillows, the duvet, everywhere.

God.

She sticks her face in the sheets, breathes in his smell. The hint of autumn leaves burning. Blair shivers, like a fever coming on, the worst one ever. Her heart aches, the pain so deep it spreads through her whole body. She closes her eyes and the tears flow.

BLAIR SLEEPS A lot. Cries a lot. Doesn't have to be back at work until Tuesday, so she has two full days to sink further into this tarry blackness.

No one calls, so she figures no one knows yet. Blair doesn't call anyone either, not even Tori, since she doesn't want to put Tori in the middle. Wonders where Nathan went, if he'll leave Seattle again now. She stopped trying to call him after the fifteenth time when she realized she was only calling so she could hear his voicemail say, "This is Nathan. Not available right now, call you back when I get a chance."

I'm pitiful.

Mr. Maurice stays by her side, though his golden eyes are more accusing than sympathetic. *Where is he?* He wants to know. *How could you let him go?*

She doesn't bathe, or load the dishwasher, or lift a finger to clean a single thing. Orders take-out Chinese food and leaves the empty containers sitting on the counter just like Fiona does. When she opens her cabinets and fridge, everything is out of alignment. A total mess.

Just like my life.

She thinks about her normal compulsive behavior and it all seems silly now. Who cares if the toaster is plugged in all night? If there's a spoon mixed in with the forks?

None of that matters. Oddly, this heartbreak has given her perspective in a way she's never had before.

Her only obsession now is with how she can make things right between her and Nathan. Round and round, she replays what happened years ago. *I can't change the past, though.*

On Tuesday, Blair does something she's never done in the entire time they've owned La Dolce Vita. She calls in sick.

"Are you all right?" Natalie wants to know. "You sound awful."

"Nathan and I broke up. It's over."

"You broke up? I thought everything was going so well. He even passed the Bandito Test!"

"Yes, well . . . that's all changed."

Natalie tries to talk, but Blair tells her, "I have to go."

After hanging up, she lies on the couch and tries to sleep some more, but can't manage it. Instead, she turns on the TV. Flips channels. Stops when she sees *The Razor's Edge*—her favorite version with Bill Murray. Despite being panned by critics, Blair always thought Bill Murray did a great job as Larry Darrell.

She watches Larry and Isabel, a box of tissues beside her, crying. In the end, Isabel doesn't get Larry, but of course she doesn't deserve him, either.

Is that my fate? Do I not deserve Nathan?

Unfortunately, she knows the answer.

As Blair blows her nose, contemplating whether she should eat another bowl of cereal from the endless supply crowding her cabinets, her intercom buzzes. Hearing a woman's voice, it takes her a moment to realize Natalie is downstairs.

"You didn't have to come over," Blair says, letting her inside.

"Of course, I did." Natalie looks around the condo and takes in the mess, but doesn't say anything. "I wanted to make sure you're okay."

"I'm fine."

Natalie frowns. Her blonde hair is pulled back into a ponytail and Blair notices she's thickening around the waist a little, obviously starting to show from her pregnancy.

"You don't look fine." Natalie's eyes roam over her. "In fact, you look terrible."

They go in the living room to sit on the couch, and Blair shoves the blankets she was using aside. She started sleeping out here after the first night. Nathan's scent in her bed is too torturous. She could wash the sheets, but as perverse as it sounds, she doesn't want to lose his scent, either.

"Can I get you anything?" Blair asks. "I think I could pull together a glass of water. There's plenty of cereal."

"I just want to know what on earth happened."

Blair shakes her head, tries to smile, but can't. "I did something bad." And then she tells Natalie the whole story. Her deepest, darkest secret finally revealed.

"So, as you can see, I'm truly depraved," Blair says, once she's finished explaining it all.

"Give me a break. I agree, what you did was wrong, but you didn't get pregnant all by yourself."

Blair thinks about those words. "It wouldn't have happened if I hadn't lied. The whole marriage—all of it. I sometimes wonder if that's why I miscarried." Her throat tightens. "Like a punishment, you know?"

Natalie shakes her head, reaches over and takes Blair's hand. "Those things just happen sometimes. You can't blame yourself. Don't go there."

"Yeah," Blair says softly, trying to stop herself from crying again.

"He shouldn't punish you, either," Natalie says, frowning. "None of us are perfect. And if he really loves you, hopefully he'll realize that."

Before leaving to go back to work, Natalie turns to her in the doorway. "Lindsay and I love you, and we're only going to let you feel sorry for yourself so long. It's not good to wallow, and as you know, I speak from experience."

After she's gone, Blair gets another bowl of cereal and sits in front of the television again. Mr. Maurice, who was outside on the deck, comes in and gives her a disdainful glare before going over to his food dish.

"I don't care what you say," she mutters to the cat. "I love him just as much as you do."

By early evening, Blair falls asleep on the couch and her dreams are disjointed and strange. Dreams about Nathan, but then about a witch flying on a broomstick.

Ding Dong. Ding Dong.

The witch cackles, and her cackle sounds familiar. But what's that noise?

Ding Dong. Ding Dong.

Finally, Blair wakes up sweaty, kicking the blanket aside, and realizes that noise is her doorbell. When she answers it, she's surprised to discover Fiona and Sachi.

"What's wrong with you?" Fiona studies her from head to toe. "Have you no shame? You look *horrible*."

"It's nice to see you, too," Blair says.

"We're sorry to barge in on you unannounced like this," Sachi says, "but Fiona wanted to pick up her suitcases."

"Sure, of course." Blair motions behind her. "They're stacked over there in the corner."

By now, Fiona has pushed past her into the living room where she's gaping at the mess. "Look at this place! Nathan *forced* me to pay half the cost of a cleaning crew, and they haven't even been here yet."

Blair goes over and flops back down on the couch. "They've been here. They cleaned and left a few days ago."

"*What?*" Fiona shrieks. "I'm demanding my money back! Where did Nathan even find these people? They must be the worse cleaners on Earth. I could do better than *this!*"

"It's not them. They did a good job." Blair sighs. "I created this mess."

"*You?*" This stops Fiona cold. She doesn't speak or move for a full two seconds, then immediately goes over to sit in the living room chair. "Talk to me."

"Don't you know what's happened?" Blair asks. "Nathan hasn't told you?"

Sachi comes over and takes a seat on the opposite side of the couch as Blair.

"Told me what?" Fiona's blue eyes are rapt on Blair.

"We broke up." Blair swallows. "We're not together anymore."

"Nathan's moved out?" Fiona wants to know.

Blair nods. "His desk is still here, but everything else is gone."

"What happened?"

Blair fidgets with the blanket on the couch. "It's a long story."

"I like long stories." Fiona motions toward Sachi. "We both do."

And so, against her better judgment, Blair tells them what happened between her and Nathan years ago. Ironically, after living with this deep dark secret for so long, she's now blabbing it to everybody.

Including complete strangers.

She glances over at Sachi, who appears to be listening with sympathy, though Blair can only imagine what Sachi really thinks of her.

"My *God*, I'm gone for one week and this is what happens? See," Fiona looks over at Sachi, "I told you something was wrong. Nathan sounded so strange on the phone."

"So you've talked to him recently?" Blair asks.

Fiona nods. "Yes, but he never mentioned a word about this. Nothing! I could tell something was wrong, though."

"Do you know where he's staying?" Blair asks.

"No. Have you spoken to Tori? She might know."

Blair feels a pang of guilt. "I haven't talked to anybody, but I would have heard from Tori if he went there."

"This is not good at all." Fiona appears to be contemplating things. "We have to *fix* this."

Blair leans her head back on the couch and sighs. "I don't see how that's possible."

After they leave, Sachi struggling with Fiona's heavy Louis Vuitton suitcases, Blair thinks about how her condo used to be this peaceful sanctuary. Everything tidy and perfect. *But maybe too perfect.* She thinks back to how she resented Nathan's intrusion in the beginning, resented those globs of toothpaste in the sink, crumbs on the kitchen counter, the way he forced himself into her life, but now that's all changed.

She'd give anything to have him back.

NATHAN STARES OUT the airplane window, watching the clouds and wishing he were somewhere else—anywhere. He's already told Fiona he'll do this last talk show in San Francisco and then he's done. No more talk shows, no more book signings, no more anything. Of course, she balked, but he didn't care.

Just can't deal with this shit right now.

Fiona crosses her legs, sighing loudly as she studies her phone. "It just so happens, I know the entire story with you and Blair." She looks up at him over her reading glasses. "In case you're interested."

Nathan doesn't respond, hoping if he ignores her she'll shut up.

"Sachi and I went by to pick up my luggage, and Blair told us *everything*."

"When was this?"

"Yesterday."

He goes back to looking out the window. Should probably get his computer out, but doesn't feel like it. Hasn't felt like doing much lately.

Fiona lets out a dramatic sigh. "I admit, I was surprised by what she told me."

"Look, I don't want to talk about Blair."

"I don't blame you. Not at all, especially after what happened. If I were you, I wouldn't want to talk about her, either!"

Nathan nods, still gazing out the window. Even someone as self-involved as Fiona can understand how what Blair did was unforgivable. "It cut deep," he admits. "I'll say that much."

Unfortunately, he still can't stop thinking about Blair. As much as he tries, she's on his mind day and night. Constantly. And what's more, his emotions are all over the map. Keep going back and forth between hurt, anger, and betrayal. Can't settle on which one to feel the most.

"Blair's been torturing herself over this whole thing. Seriously," Fiona tells him, shifting around to get more comfortable in her seat. "She's torturing herself over something that's clearly *your* fault!"

Nathan's whips his head around from the window. "*My* fault?" he stares at her, incredulous. "How the hell do you figure that?"

She shrugs. "It's obvious, isn't it? You had a condom and didn't use it."

Nathan's brows go up with surprise. So Blair really *did* tell Fiona the whole story.

"She lied about being on the pill. Or did she conveniently leave that part out? Christ," he mutters. "Can't believe I'm even discussing this with you."

Fiona laughs. "She *lied* about the pill? Are you kidding me?"

"No, I'm not."

"Oh, my fucking *God*! Did Blair *force* you to have sex with her at gunpoint?"

"Keep your voice down." He glances around the plane, certain every person within earshot is enjoying this conversation.

"Well, *did* she? Because then I'd say it was her fault."

"Course not."

"And apparently you've never heard of something called 'safe sex'? Because it sounds to me like you decided to skip protection all on your own."

Nathan presses his lips together, and his eyes flash back to the window. In truth, this is where it all starts to fall apart for him a bit, too. Clearly neither of them were thinking along those lines that night. He knows why Blair lied about the pill, but he wasn't exactly eager to wear a rubber himself. Pretty sure he was relieved about not having to wear one.

He snorts. "None of this changes the fact that she's been lying to me. Christ, I married her and changed my whole life because of a lie."

"My *God*, you're an idiot!" She gawks at him. "I can't even believe how much."

"Fuck off, Fiona."

"In fact, is there a stronger word I can use than idiot? Because that's what I need right now. You're a writer, so surely you must know some?"

"Fuck. Off. How about those two words?"

She smirks. "You disappoint me, Nathan."

"Good."

"YOU SHOULD SEE how messy Blair's condo is," Fiona tells him, the two of them standing backstage at the television show in San Francisco, where Nathan's waiting to go on the air. A makeup artist just put some kind of powder on his face, and he can only hope he doesn't look ridiculous.

"What are you talking about? Place was spotless last time I saw it."

"Not anymore. Apparently, Blair has let it go."

"She has?" He's been trying not to listen to all of Fiona's incessant chatter about Blair, but finds he can't help himself. "How messy is it?"

Fiona snorts. "Worse than when I lived there."

"That's impossible."

There's no way Blair would let things get that out of control. In truth, he misses Blair's tidy ways. How relaxing he found that about her. Sure, it could get out of hand when she was in a state, upset about something, but overall he appreciated it.

Staying with Brody has been the opposite, too much like what he grew up with—chaos. Granted, Brody is a guy and not married, but Jesus Christ, his refrigerator looks like it hasn't been cleaned out since the nineties. He's actually worried about getting food poisoning for real.

"Her condo is basically a pigsty," Fiona tells him. "And she doesn't look any better herself, either. My *God*, she's so pale. Ghostly. She needs to pull it together and at least put on some makeup." Fiona puts a hand on her hip. "Even with a broken heart, I had my *standards!*"

Nathan's always thought Blair looked pretty without makeup, and obviously thinks her pale skin is beautiful. He frowns, though. Doesn't like a single thing he's hearing.

A broken heart. So Blair's heart is broken?

What about my heart?

Truth is he's been having a rough time of it. Hasn't slept in days. Feels like shit. Can't stop thinking about everything that happened between them.

How could she have lied for so long? Kept a secret like that? He hates secrets. Claims she loved him for years, but what kind of love is that? The kind where you trick someone into getting you pregnant and marrying you?

What do I care if Blair's heart is broken? She deserves it.

After what she did to me.

I trusted her completely. First time I ever trusted a woman like that.

Turns out she's been lying to me all along and right to my face. And to think I actually felt guilty all these years for sleeping with her and getting her pregnant.

Reflecting over what Fiona just told him, though, he has to admit he's concerned. *Blair letting her place go? Living with a mess?* Doesn't sound like her at all. Hard to even imagine her okay with that.

And then there's the other thing that's been on his mind. When he closes his eyes, he sees the same thing every time. The two of them together that night in Isadora. Blair on top, him moving inside her, so good, watching her, and it's what happened next that won't leave him alone. The way she looked at him when she came.

Never seen anything like it before in my life.

It's been torturing him. That expression on her face. He's seen it when they were together since then, too, but that first time, there was something about it.

Like it's the key to unlocking everything.

Chapter Twenty-Five

Daily List

1. Don't clean anything.
2. Who cares about the mess?
3. No one's perfect, especially you.

BLAIR GOES OVER to Tori's after work the next day to babysit the boys, finally telling her what happened.

"I can't believe you didn't call me!" Tori grabs Blair, hugging her. "Why didn't you let me know? I would have come over."

"I don't want to put you in the middle of this. I'm worried if Nathan finds out you knew the truth all along, he'll be angry with you."

Tori scoffs. "Are you kidding? I don't care if my brother finds out I knew. It wasn't my secret to tell."

"I suppose."

"I'm surprised he hasn't called me, though. He must be staying with Brody. If he were at my mom's, she would have said something."

Blair sits on the couch, where the boys are all gathering around her, tails wagging. She thinks back to how she fed them goulash that night with Nathan. *That wonderful night.* It turned out he was right about those deadly farts, though. They didn't start until the next morning, but they lasted all day and were so toxic that even Tori agreed the dogs needed to stay outside in the yard until the stench left, and they could all breathe again.

"You look terrible," Tori says, sitting next to her. "Did you go to work today?"

"I had to. I can't call in sick two days in a row." Natalie had coddled her all day, everybody at the bakery being super nice. Though, Blair still had to go hide in the bathroom to cry.

"I'm going to call off volunteering tonight." Tori grabs her phone off the coffee table. "I'm not leaving you alone."

"I'll be fine."

"No, and ugh." Tori rolls her eyes. "Not again. I thought I was done with him."

"What is it? Don't tell me it's Chase."

Tori nods. "I haven't heard from him in a while."

"I told Nathan about him harassing you." Blair goes quiet as she thinks back to that night again. *The night he said he loved me*. Her eyes sting with tears and she closes them.

Tori scrolls through her phone messages. "I told him Chase lost interest." She lets out a breath. "Guess I was wrong."

"Maybe you should call the police and let them handle it."

"No, he's just a young guy who's full of himself. I don't think he's used to women telling him no, so he thinks I'm playing hard to get. I'll have Road talk to him. It'll be fine."

She spends the rest of the evening at Tori's, the two of them watching chick flicks and eating junk food. Blair cries and tells Tori about the whole scene that happened at her parents' house in her old bedroom.

"My brother really is a dipshit." Tori shakes her head, handing her tissues. "Like he's so perfect."

"It's all my fault, though." Blair tells her about the Sanskrit over Nathan's heart. "I had no idea it mattered so much to him. I always thought he was secretly relieved about what happened. Turns out I was completely wrong."

Tori eyes fill with sympathy. "Yes, you were wrong, but I think it's time you both put it behind you. You've suffered enough."

KIKI'S WEDDING IS on a Saturday. Blair stays late Friday at La Dolce Vita and bakes the three tiers for the chocolate cake then assembles it early the next morning. It's an elaborate cake with more than fifty sugar-art flowers. Ginger and Carlos help her deliver it to the reception, which is being held in a mansion north of Seattle. There is an assortment of cupcakes, too, with more sugar flowers.

Afterward, she rushes back home to get ready for the wedding, barely arriving on time before the ceremony. Kiera and Brody are sitting about halfway down the crowded church and wave her over.

"Hey, you're late. We worried you weren't going to make it," Kiera says to Blair as they scoot over to let her in.

"I was just setting up the cake. It took a while." Blair nods hello to Brody, who gives her a nervous grin.

There's a very attractive woman sitting next to Brody who she's never seen before. She's about Blair's age with long, brown hair highlighted gold in the front. The woman stares at her with narrow brown eyes, and Blair gives her a brief smile, though the woman doesn't smile back.

Voices come from the rear of the church and then the groom, Austin, along with all the groomsmen make their way to the front getting ready for the ceremony.

Nathan is one of them. Blair spots him immediately and she can't pull her eyes away. A mixture of pleasure and pain rushes through her at the sight of him. She hasn't seen him since the night at her parents' house. He's wearing a dark suit, crisp white shirt, blue tie, and as she imagined, he looks devastatingly handsome in a suit. His blond hair contrasts perfectly with the dark fabric.

It's been two weeks and she misses him. Misses every single thing about him. Even the things that used to annoy her.

The men line up, waiting with Austin in front. One of the other groomsmen is talking to Nathan, and as Nathan bends his head slightly, listening, his eyes scan the church.

Blair's heart stops when they find her. Time is suspended as they stare at each other. Her mouth opens, and there's a flicker of something intense on Nathan's face, but then his expression turns to stone.

He looks away.

Blair blinks, feels her throat go tight and tries to pull herself together. She thinks about the video Fiona sent her the day after his interview in San Francisco.

It was horrible.

The complete opposite of how he was during his interview here and in Portland. Totally wooden, barely answered the interviewer's questions, and making it painfully clear he didn't want to be there. Fiona was furious afterward.

Blair only felt guiltier.

The irony is that *Edge of Zen* is still riding high. It hit number three on *The New York Times* best sellers last week and is doing well everywhere. Though apparently, Nathan has gone into hiding, according to Fiona. All Tori could confirm was that he's been staying with Brody.

Organ music flows through the church, and everyone turns and watches as each bridesmaid makes her way down the aisle. When it's Tori's turn, she looks pretty carrying a bouquet of pink flowers, her hair shiny and long, flowing down her back. Marla comes next, looking deeply tan, wearing her usual superior smirk. Finally, the familiar opening to Wagner's "Bridal Chorus" begins and the bride is there, too, smiling nervously at everyone. She's being walked down the aisle by Lori and a man she assumes is Kiki's dad, though Blair has never seen him before. Blair hasn't seen much of Kiki as an adult, but still feels an obligation toward her since she was around her quite a bit when they were growing up. She remembers babysitting her with Tori lots of times.

The church is mostly quiet as everyone watches the ceremony. Oddly, Blair can sense the woman sitting next to Brody staring at her. Finally, Blair looks at her, but the woman turns her head away.

Blair wonders who she could be. She doesn't recognize her as any family member. Considers maybe she's with Austin's family, but why would she be sitting with Brody and Kiera?

As Blair's trying to figure this out, the woman glances at her again and while her look isn't exactly hostile, it's not friendly, either.

Blair scans what she's wearing—a tight red dress, four-inch strappy heels, chandelier earrings. She's gorgeous, but her clothes are more appropriate for a night club than a wedding.

Who is she?

After the ceremony, everyone goes out front to blow bubbles at the bride and groom who get into a white stretch limousine. There's no sign of Nathan anywhere and that woman is gone, but Kiera comes over to ask Blair if she needs a ride to the reception.

"Thanks, but I drove here myself."

"Okay, just thought I'd ask. Brody and I are going to head over now."

Blair nods and is ready to go, but then decides to ask Kiera about that woman. "Who was that sitting next to Brody during the ceremony? I didn't recognize her."

Kiera gets a pained expression on her face. "She's with Nathan."

"What?"

"Yeah," Kiera says, pushing back some of her blonde curls from where the wind is blowing them around. "She's from Spain, arrived a few days ago. I just met her this morning."

Blair swallows, sick to her stomach.

"She's staying at a hotel downtown." Kiera puts her hand on Blair's arm. "Are you okay? I know you and Nathan broke up. I'm so sorry. I don't even understand what happened."

"I'm okay. I can't talk about it right now."

Kiera nods with sympathy. "All right. I'll see you at the reception."

Blair watches Kiera go over to Brody then heads out to her own car—the Honda. Once inside, Blair sits there. Doesn't move. Can barely breathe.

So that's Sonia.

Nathan must have asked her to fly out. *That was fast*. Apparently, he couldn't wait to get back together with her.

Blair closes her eyes to fight off tears. Tells herself it doesn't matter, which obviously isn't true, but she doesn't know what else to do. More than anything, she wishes she could just go home. Get in bed. Sleep until her heart doesn't hurt anymore.

Instead, she starts the car and drives toward the reception. She doesn't have much choice. Her cake is there, and she's expected to be there, too.

The party is already going full swing when she arrives, which isn't a big surprise. If Nathan's family is good at one thing, it's partying. Austin's family seems to be the same, so between the two of them, there's a lot of alcohol flowing.

Her cake is along the back wall and she goes over to inspect it. They haven't cut it yet, and it's still holding up well.

"The cake looks amazing!" Kiki says, coming up to give her a hug. "Everybody's been raving about it. Thank you so much!"

"You're welcome." Blair smiles.

They talk about the ceremony a little bit and how Kiki and Austin are planning to drive down the Oregon coast for their honeymoon.

There's some commotion on stage and it looks like the band is setting up, so Kiki leaves to speak with them.

Blair grabs a glass of wine and searches around for Tori, wishing she could just leave. Finally, she sees Tori with her mom, who Blair discovers is already drunk and talking loudly.

"I think you need to have a seat, Mom," Tori is saying to her, holding her mom's arm.

"I'm fine. Let go of me! It's that jackass's fault. What kind of asshole walks out on his woman the day of her daughter's wedding?"

"Hi, Lori," Blair says, coming up to them. "Everything okay?" She's dealt with Lori drunk before and knows the best thing is to keep an even voice, pretend everything is normal.

"That dirtbag, Garth, ran out on me this morning!" Lori says, even louder than before.

Blair isn't quite sure what to say. *Good riddance* comes to mind. Instead, she puts a sympathetic expression on her face.

"I'm just trying to get my mom to have a seat, relax a little bit." Tori smiles at Blair apologetically. It's a smile Blair has seen Tori wear a million times in regards to her mom.

"That's a good idea," Blair says. "Why don't we all go sit down?"

"Need another drink," Lori grumbles.

Blair studies her. Lori's eyes are bloodshot. There's pink lipstick smeared over the lines of her mouth with some of it on her teeth. Her blonde hair is pulled into an elaborate French twist. The blue cocktail dress she's wearing is tight and shows off a fair amount of overly tan, wrinkled cleavage. Despite all this, Lori still has a certain sex appeal.

Somehow, they manage to convince her to sit down, mostly by telling her they'll get her another whiskey sour. One of Lori's friends comes over, which becomes a good distraction.

"Thanks," Tori says to Blair. "Garth chose a great day to leave."

"Can't say I'm sorry to hear he's gone, though."

Tori sighs. "Me, either."

Blair's eyes search the room. As always, without effort, she spots Nathan. To her surprise, he's looking directly at her, and her heart skips a beat. Their eyes stay on each other for a long moment, but then he turns away. He's standing near the wedding cake, talking to a couple of people. Sonia is there beside him, and she now sees what she missed in the church earlier. Sonia is clearly Skank Factor X.

Tori notices where Blair's focused. "That's Sonia, the Spanish girlfriend. Apparently, she arrived a few days ago. Road brought her over to my mom's yesterday."

Blair lets out her breath. "What's she like?"

"You don't want to know." Tori pauses then shakes her head. "Horrible."

Instead of feeling jealous like she used to, Blair discovers she feels sad for Nathan. *He deserves better, even if it's with someone else and not me.*

The band starts playing a cover of The Romantics "What I Like About You" and Tori reaches over to grab her hand. "Come on, I love this song." She pulls Blair up from the chair. "Let's dance."

Blair resists at first, but then gives in. Figures why not. She goes out and dances with Tori. By the third song, a couple of young guys, friends of Austin's, come over and ask each of them to dance. Tori and Blair both say yes, and Blair almost has fun. The guy who asked her is named Jacob. He's a lot younger than she is, but cute. Tall with dark hair, and a good-humored face. He has a hip-hop style of dancing that keeps making Blair laugh.

"God, we're robbing the cradle here," Tori whispers in her ear at one point.

Blair shrugs. "Who cares?"

She still notices Nathan occasionally. Off to the side, he doesn't dance and mostly just stands there with a stony expression. Sonia is talking to Brody and Kiera, using elaborate hand gestures.

Eventually, she and Tori stop dancing and tell the two guys they're going to take a restroom break. The guys want to meet up later, but she and Tori only commit to a 'maybe.'

"Let me go find my mom first and check on her," Tori says. "I'll meet you in the bathroom."

"Okay." Blair grabs her purse and heads toward the restroom. The band is playing Def Leppard's "Pour Some Sugar On Me", though the sound is muffled as she walks down the hall away from the main room.

After peeing, Blair goes to wash her hands at the sink and winds up standing right next to Marla putting on lipstick.

"Nice ceremony," Blair says to her, being polite.

"Mmm," is all Marla says, studying herself in the mirror. Queen of her own skank universe.

Blair smiles to herself. The bathroom door opens and she glances at it, expecting Tori, but instead Sonia comes inside. Sonia's eyes search the large bathroom, and as soon as she spots Blair, heads straight over.

Marla is still standing there, and Blair watches with interest as the two women notice each other, wondering what will happen. *The clash of the skanks! Will there be a rift in the space time continuum? Will lightning bolts shoot from their eyes and fingertips?*

A battle to the death!

Blair is disappointed when all the women do is glare at each other and swap bitchy looks.

Come on, that's all? Seriously? Heck, I can do better than that.

If only Fiona were here, Blair muses. She could teach these amateurs a thing or two.

After Marla leaves, Sonia changes her focus. "You are Blair?" she asks, moving closer, enveloping her in a cloud of astringent perfume.

"Yes." Blair grabs some paper towels to dry her hands, wondering what Sonia could possibly want.

Sonia rakes her brown eyes over Blair from head to toe. Blair recognizes the way she's doing it. *Classic Skank Factor X behavior. Apparently, it's the same all over the world. Who knew?*

"What is this difficulty you are having with Nathan and me?" Sonia wants to know. She pronounces his name 'Naytun.'

"Difficulty?"

"You are jealous of us? Yes?"

Blair puts the paper towels in the trash. Sighs. "I don't know what you're talking about."

"Nathan is trying to get the divorce, but you will not give it to him. Why?"

"He wants to divorce me?"

"Yes." Sonia gives her a superior smile. "You have not seen him for many years. It is finished."

"I don't know what he's told you, but Nathan has never asked me for a divorce."

"But that is why he came back to Seattle!"

Blair goes still as this piece of news takes her by surprise. *Is this really true?*

"He came back to get the divorce from you, so we could be together. We love each other." Sonia looks at herself in the mirror and starts fluffing her hair out. "Do not make this so big a problem."

She stares at Sonia. This had never occurred to Blair before. Obviously, she never wanted a divorce, but it makes sense Nathan would have come back eventually wanting one. *He never said a word, though.*

BLAIR GOES BACK out to the reception, still in a daze, wondering if there's any truth in what Sonia told her. She doesn't see Tori and decides to go outside and get some fresh air instead.

There are a few people out back, most of them smoking, so Blair walks around to the other side of the building.

To her surprise, she discovers Nathan. He's standing alone, leaning against the wall as he drinks a beer and looks out at the mansion's manicured grounds.

He doesn't see her yet and Blair stops, unsure of what to do. She doesn't want him to think she followed him out here.

Just as she decides to leave and go back, he notices her.

Blair takes a deep breath and walks over to him. *Might as well.* Up close and in the light of the late afternoon, she can see he looks tired, though his grim expression isn't helping matters.

"Enjoying the party?" he says.

"I guess."

He nods and takes a drink from his beer. "Could see that."

She stands next to him, leaning back against the wall herself, wondering what he's talking about.

"Who's that guy you were dancing with?" he asks.

She glances at him to see if he's joking, but it doesn't look like it. "Some friend of Austin's."

They're both quiet and suddenly there's so much Blair wishes she could say, everything that's in her heart, but then it occurs to her. *I've already said it all. He knows everything. Knows I've loved him for years, and this is where it got me.*

"So, that's the famous Sonia from Spain." There's a bitter note in Blair's voice she doesn't intend. She wonders if she should ask him if it's true what Sonia told her, but then she's not even sure if she wants to know.

Nathan takes another swig of beer but doesn't reply, just stares out at the landscaped grounds. "How's Mr. Maurice doing?" he asks.

"Not good."

She feels him turning to look at her so she meets his gaze. Golden-green.

Her breath catches. She'd almost forgotten that dazzling color. Her whole life awash in gray since he left.

"What's wrong with Mr. Maurice?" he wants to know.

"He misses you."

Nathan reflects on this. "That so?"

"He blames me for everything. And he's right, of course, it is my fault."

Looking down, Nathan studies the bottle in his hand.

"But mostly Mr. Maurice sits around all day, glaring at me. Wishing I were you, I think."

Nathan chuckles softly. "Yeah, he gets an attitude sometimes."

"I should probably just give him to you. He prefers you, anyway."

They're both quiet again as the sounds from the party drift out to them.

"Fiona told me your place is a mess." He glances at her. "That true?"

Blair bites her lip. Thinks about her condo and the chaos she can't deal with. It's all too much. Overwhelming. Suddenly, she doesn't want Nathan to know this about her, though, how he's brought her to her knees. *I don't want to be an object of anybody's pity, least of all his.*

"It's fine. I don't know why Fiona would have said that."

He nods. "Don't know why, either."

Blair stares down at her crystal Jimmy Choos, and Nathan follows her eyes.

"Been taking selfies of your feet again?"

"Maybe a couple," she admits. Blair turns to him. "Did you really come back to Seattle to get a divorce from me," she tries to hide the quiver in her voice, "so you could marry Sonia?" *Apparently, I do want to know.*

"What?" He frowns, but she sees something in his eyes and realizes Sonia wasn't lying.

Apparently, Nathan has his secrets, too.

Someone comes around the corner. It's Sonia, of course. Skank Factor X always has impeccable timing.

"Nathan!" she says in her heavily accented English. "Why are you out here?" She gives Blair a once-over then dismissively looks back to him. "Tori is looking for you. There is a problem with your mother."

"There is?" Nathan pulls away from the wall.

"You must come now. Tori asked me to find you."

The three of them head back inside. The band is playing Loverboy's "Turn Me Loose", a song Blair has always liked, and judging by how many people are dancing, she isn't the only one.

Unfortunately, it doesn't take long to discover the problem with his mom.

She's out on the dance floor, very drunk, bumping into people and latching onto every guy she sees. People have stopped dancing around her and are watching the spectacle instead.

Tori is there, along with some of her cousins, except Lori is pushing them away.

"Jesus Christ," Nathan mutters.

"Get your fucking hands off me!" Lori shoves at Brody, who's trying to help.

Tori looks around, her face turning to relief when she spots Nathan.

"We need to get out of here," Tori says to him, talking loudly over the music. "She's wasted."

"Mom." Nathan goes over to Lori, tries to take her arm. "Come on, let's go sit down."

"I'm not done dancing!" she yells, swaying on her high-heeled sandals.

Blair is amazed she can even walk in them considering her state, but then she's seen Lori drunk so many times and knows she always manages to stay upright.

"That bastard left me!" Lori yells. "He can rot in hell while I dance!"

Tori is looking around in frustration, but then Nathan steps in closer to Lori. He puts his hand on her hip, his other hand out to his side. "It's okay. Dance with me, Mom."

Lori blinks, looks up at Nathan.

He grins. "Come on."

She takes his hand and the two of them start dancing together. Mother and son. The music is fast and loud, but they're dancing a slow two-step.

Blair watches the way Nathan dances with her, moving her away from the crowd. People have stopped staring and started dancing themselves again.

Finally, he gets her to one of the outer tables. By now, Lori is crying. "You understand, don't you, Road? Don't you?"

"Sure, course." He nods.

"We need to get her out of here," Tori says. "Like right now. I'm going to take her home."

Kiki joins them, observing her mom's drunkenness with annoyance. "You and Nathan can't leave! The photographer just arrived, so we're taking photos with the wedding party in a few minutes."

"Well, we can't leave her here like this, either," Tori says.

"I'll take her home." Blair steps forward.

"No," Nathan says. "I'll do it."

"You can't!" Kiki's eyes are wide with distress. "These are my wedding photos." She throws her mother an angry look. "God, she ruins everything!"

"I can take her," Blair says again. "It's not a problem."

"This is a family issue," Nathan says heatedly. "No offense, Blair."

"Are you *kidding?* You can't miss the photographer!" Kiki's voice takes on a note of hysteria.

Tori, who's standing next to Nathan, puts her hand on his arm. "Let Blair take her home. She's dealt with Mom like this before."

"She has?" Nathan's eyes flash over to Blair. "Since when?"

"Since you've been living out of the country for the past five years. Blair has helped me with Mom a lot."

"I see." Nathan goes quiet, seems to be processing this bit of news. He glances over at Sonia, sitting on the edge of the table, studying her phone and looking bored with the whole situation.

Tori goes over to their mom. "Blair is going to take you home now. Is that okay?

"All right." Lori looks up at Blair and smiles. "That'd be fine, hon."

"Come on, I'll help you get her to the car," Nathan says.

And with that, the two of them help walk Lori out to the parking lot.

"My car is just over there." Blair points toward her Honda.

But as soon as Lori sees Isadora in the opposite direction, she makes a beeline for it, dragging them both with her. "I want to ride in my big brother's car," Lori insists. "Lance always looked out for me and my kids."

He gives Blair a wry look. "Guess you'll be driving Isadora. That okay? I can pick her up from you later."

"Sure, that's fine."

Nathan helps get Lori into the passenger seat. She drops her purse on the ground and when Blair hands it to her, Lori smiles up at her with bloodshot eyes. "Thanks, hon. You're a sweet girl, always thought so. And I know how much you love my boy."

Blair's brows go up and she feels Nathan stiffen beside her, his hand on the open car door.

Lori cackles in her drunken way. "You think I never noticed it all those years? The way you look at him? Seen it a thousand times."

Nobody says anything for a few seconds, and then finally Blair gives Lori a helpless smile. "You're right, it's true."

"Of course it's true!"

Blair turns to Nathan. There's a strange expression on his face, one she's never seen before. He doesn't say anything, though, just appears deep in thought.

"Now, where's my damn cigarettes!" Lori says, rifling through her purse.

"You can't smoke in Isadora!" Blair says, and hears Nathan chuckling.

"Here," he says, handing Blair the Mustang's keys. "I'll come by later to bring you your car."

She gives him the keys to her Honda then climbs into Isadora's driver's seat. Sighs a little as she looks around the interior of the car, taking in the faint scent of warm leather seats. *I've missed you.* Just before she leaves, Nathan motions for her to roll the window down.

"What is it?" she asks.

He studies her for a long moment. “Thank you for doing this.” Lori starts going on about how Lance never had a problem with her smoking in his car. “She’s lying,” Nathan says softly. “My uncle never let anyone smoke in Isadora.”

Blair snorts. “Don’t worry, I’ll throw those cigarettes out the window before I let her light one up.”

Nathan chuckles. “You do that, babe.”

Chapter Twenty-Six

How To Fight Like A Princess

1. Discover that you're stronger than you think.
2. Use surprise to your advantage.
3. Never be afraid to kick some ass.

A FEW DAYS later, and Nathan still hasn't come by to trade cars. Not that Blair is complaining. In fact, driving Isadora has been helping her mental state so much that she finally started cleaning up her condo.

"Do you mind if I come by sometime next week and pick up the rest of my stuff?" Blair asks Tori over the phone. "I still have some clothes and a few other things at your house."

"Sure, that's fine."

"How's everything with your mom?"

"Much better, though she's still upset about Garth. Thank you again for taking her home from the wedding. You saved the day."

"I wouldn't go that far." Blair thought Nathan saved the day by getting Lori off the dance floor and calming her down.

All Blair did was take Lori back to the house, make her some tea, and tuck her into bed. Lori's hollering and swearing at the wedding reception must have gotten it out of her system, because she was downright docile with Blair. She made more comments to Blair about Nathan. "Was glad when he married you," Lori told her, drifting off to sleep. "Always thought you'd be good for him."

"Have you seen Nathan?" Blair asks Tori. "He still hasn't brought back my car."

"I haven't talked to him since the wedding. Fiona called me, though, trying to get a hold of him. His book has reached number two on *The New York Times* best seller's list."

"You're kidding? That's amazing."

"He's probably dealing with Sonia," Tori says with a sigh. "You should have seen her the rest of the night at the reception. All she talked about was herself, her family, and having my brother move to Madrid."

Blair's stomach drops. "Is that what he's planning to do?"

"I don't know. He never said anything either way. He was really quiet, now that I think about it."

They hang up and Blair gets back to cleaning, enjoying the way her place is starting to look tidy again. Though, she isn't lining up boxes or worrying about the exact location of every item. In the same way telling Nathan the truth finally freed her from secrets, she realizes it's also helped free her from obsessing about things that don't matter.

I'm the one seeing the big picture now.

Blair knows she'll never be completely over her OCD, that it's a part of her and always will be, but realizes she's at least gained some perspective on it. The same with her perfectionism. For the first time in her life, she can finally see past it.

People are what matter and none of us are perfect, no matter how hard we try.

She realizes something else, too. As hard as it's been since Nathan left, she's glad the truth came out. She loves him and wishes they could be together, but her mom was right. You can't build a life based on lies.

BY FRIDAY THE next week, Blair's condo is back in order, and she decides to swing by Tori's house after work and pick up the rest of her stuff.

There was no answer when she called, but she figures Tori might still be at the vet's office, since her hours there vary from week to week. Luckily, Blair still has her key.

Eddie, Duff, and Tommy Lee greet her at the door when she arrives, crowding around her legs, tails wagging.

"Hey, boys," Blair reaches down to pet them. They follow her to her bedroom where she goes through the drawers, pulling clothes out to stuff into the bag she brought along.

She remembers some of her clothes are hanging in the laundry room and goes to get them. On the way there, the boys are all crowded by the sliding door in the kitchen, so she lets them out into the backyard to run around.

After packing all her things, Blair checks the time and sees it's almost six o'clock, so she decides to wait for Tori. Figures she should be home soon.

As she's emptying the dishwasher, she hears a knock at the front door and puts the plate she's holding down to go check who it is.

Blair discovers it's some guy. Medium height with longish brown hair, wearing jeans and a black T-shirt. His expression changes from expectant to annoyed when he sees her.

"Who are you?" he asks.

Right away, Blair doesn't like his tone. "May I help you with something?" She wishes now she hadn't let the dogs out into the backyard—or even answered the door, for that matter.

"Where's Tori?" he wants to know. "She told me to meet her here."

Blair is surprised, since she has no idea who this guy is. "Sorry, I don't know anything about that. Tori's not here right now, but you could wait in your car for her."

She starts to shut the door, but he puts his hand out to hold it open. "I'm not waiting in my car. Why should I?"

"Stop it." Blair pulls on the door, getting annoyed. "Look, she's not here. How about if you take a seat on the porch, and I'll call her."

To her astonishment, he pushes past her, comes right into the house and starts yelling, "Tori! Are you in here?"

"Hey, you need to leave right now!"

He turns toward her. "Look, we're dating. She's been playing hard to get, but I could tell it was just an act. So, where is she?"

And that's when it dawns on Blair. *This must be Chase.* With growing panic, she realizes if he won't leave, the safest thing for her is to get out of the house. He looks harmless, but she has no idea what he's capable of.

The front door is still wide open, and she starts backing toward it.

Chase is watching her, though, moving closer. "Is she still playing games with me? She's not out with some other guy, is she?"

"What?" Blair tries to steady her breath. "No, of course not. In fact, I remember her mentioning you now."

"You do?"

"Yes, you're Chase, right?"

This seems to calm him a little. "So, she told you about me?"

"She did."

"What did she tell you?"

"Um . . . she just said you were dating."

Chase starts looking around the room. "So, where is she? She said she'd be here."

"She's running late, that's all."

He studies her, and what's weird is Blair can see why Tori went out with him. Chase is handsome. Kind of young, but definitely handsome. She's guessing Tori is right, and he doesn't hear the word 'no' a lot when it comes to women.

"Why didn't she call me if she's going to be late?" he asks.

"I think she's having trouble with her phone."

He shakes his head. "That sounds like a lie. Why are you lying to me?"

"I'm not." Blair takes another step away from him. Every time she does, though, he steps closer. "Look, I think you should leave now. You're making me uncomfortable."

He chuckles and seems to find this amusing. "I am?"

Blair turns toward the door and that's when Chase grabs her wrist.

"Hey, where are you going?" he says. "I'm not done talking to you yet."

Blair tries to pull her arm away. "Let go of me!"

"I don't think so. We're not finished here."

He won't release her and as she tries to pull away again, a wave of panic floods through her, immediately followed by a wave of anger.

"I said, let *go*!" Using a defensive move she learned in boxing class, she immediately twists her wrist out of his grip.

Chase seems surprised by this, though not as surprised as when she steps in and knees him in the groin as hard as she can.

His eyes open wide as he yelps with pain, bending over to clutch himself. Blair is running on automatic pilot now, and before he can straighten himself, she grabs his head and brings her knee up again, slamming him in the face with it.

"Stop it . . . what the hell?" He tries to grab her, but Blair is faster. Panting with adrenaline, she manages to kick him in the groin again using her shin. Finally, he moans and falls to the floor.

By now, Blair hears shouting and when she turns, she discovers Nathan and Brody running up the front porch, with Tori right behind them.

Chase is lying on the floor. "You crazy bitch," he gasps, as he holds his hands between his legs, tears streaming down his face. "What did you do that for? I was just trying to talk to you."

"Jesus Christ, are you okay?" Nathan says to Blair. Eyes wide, roaming over her.

She nods, shaking a little as she tries to catch her breath. "I'm okay."

"What happened?" Nathan is still looking at her.

"That's Chase." She motions toward the floor. "The guy who keeps calling Tori. I told him she wasn't here. He pushed his way into the house then grabbed me."

Nathan's jaw clenches hearing this. He glares down at Chase.

"I guess he came early," Tori says, her face ashen. "Blair, I had no idea you were going to be here. I would have warned you!"

"So, you actually *were* meeting him?" Blair asks. "Because that's what he told me."

Nathan continues to glare at Chase. "Brody and I came over to have a chat with him."

Blair's never seen Nathan so furious. His face is mottled red, and he looks ready to kill someone. He strides over to Chase, who's managed to scoot himself against the wall, and squats down in front of him.

"Listen to me, you worthless piece of shit, and listen good. You *ever* come here again, it won't be my wife kicking your sorry ass, it'll be *me*, got it?" Nathan lowers his voice dangerously soft. "And trust me, you won't be holding your nuts, crying like a pussy. You'll be in the hospital, wishing you were *dead*."

Chase doesn't say anything, just blinks a few times.

"You hear me?"

He nods.

"Good."

Nathan's eyes cut over to Brody, who's slowly shaking his head, jaw tight. "Motherfucker," Brody mutters.

"Think it's time we have that chat," Nathan says.

Brody nods, and some kind of silent message passes between them.

Nathan stands. "We're walking you to your car, asshole," he tells Chase. "Get up."

They all watch as Chase struggles to his feet. He limps along, glances at Blair again, and takes a wide berth around her. The three men go out the front door, with Brody and Nathan flanking Chase. "Is that really your wife?" she hears him ask Nathan as they walk toward the driveway. "Dude, she's crazy. I was only trying to talk to her!"

Once they're out the door, Tori immediately hugs Blair. "I'm so sorry, it's all my fault!"

"No, it's not." Blair hugs her back. "Don't even say such a ridiculous thing."

"Are you really okay?"

"I'm fine. Seriously." Now that her adrenaline is wearing off, Blair is amazed at the way she handled herself. "That boxing class really came in handy. I should start going again."

"I think I'll join you," Tori agrees. "That was impressive. Do you want anything? Water, or a shot of whiskey maybe?"

"Water sounds good."

They both go into the kitchen where Tori pours Blair a glass of ice water, hands it to her. "Did you hear what my brother called you? He said you were his *wife*!"

Blair drinks from her glass. She noticed it, too.

"What's going on between you guys?" Tori asks.

"I don't know. I haven't seen him since the wedding reception."

Tori suddenly sees the dogs all crowded by the sliding door and goes over to let them inside. They immediately scramble over to Blair, sensing something amiss.

She bends over to pet them, still holding her glass. "Hey, boys. I should have kept you in the house with me."

Eventually, Nathan and Brody come back inside, making their way into the kitchen. Both of their faces unreadable.

"What happened? Everything okay?" Tori asks.

"Everything's good. Turns out he's just a young idiot, but we set him straight." Nathan comes over and stands next to Blair. "How are you, babe?"

"I'm fine."

"You sure?"

"I'm all right." She smiles at him.

He puts his hand up and tucks a stray hair behind her ear. "Okay, just checking."

"Do you think we should call the police?" Blair asks.

"No," Tori, Brody, and Nathan all say at once.

"There's no need to get the cops involved," Nathan tells her. "Just be a big hassle, and trust me, that pissant won't be coming around again."

Blair nods. She knows this is how they always handle things, and isn't surprised.

"Especially not after that ass-kicking you just gave him," Brody says, grinning. "Think he was more afraid of you than us. Asshole was limping all the way to his car."

"Had trouble sitting down, too," Nathan chuckles. "Plus, I think you might have given him a black eye, princess."

"Pretty sure his great-grandkids felt that double kick to the nuts."

"If he's even able to have any!"

Both men are chuckling quite a bit now. Apparently, getting your ass kicked by a woman is cause for hilarity.

"Remind me never to piss you off, Blair," Brody says, wiping his eyes. "Seriously."

"Yeah, me, too." Nathan grins.

TORI TELLS THEM she needs to head over to Kiki and Austin's place to check on their parrot while they're away on their honeymoon. "I should check on Mom, too."

"I can stay the night here, if you want," Nathan tells her. "If you're feeling nervous."

"Okay, maybe just for tonight," Tori agrees.

"Should I get my car back?" Blair asks him. "The Honda?"

"Sure, it's at Brody's. We can drive Isadora over and get it."

They all leave together. Brody is in his truck and waves good-bye, apparently heading over to Kiera's.

Tori is in her minivan, while Nathan and Blair take Isadora.

"Damn, that was some crazy shit, babe," he says once they're driving. "I'm glad you're okay."

"What did you do to Chase?"

Nathan's face changes as his hand tightens on the wheel. "Let's just say we explained things."

Blair watches his profile as he drives. "Did you guys beat him up?"

"What?" He glances at her with surprise, then starts to chuckle. "Hell no, you took care of that for us. We just talked to him, made it clear if he tries to call or come around again there'll be consequences—that he's messed with the wrong people."

"Do you think he'll stay away?"

"Yeah, I do. The guy was mostly just confused. We had a talk about women and boundaries. Don't think he'll be bothering anyone again, to be honest."

Blair takes this in, and it occurs to her that Chase didn't really try to fight back with her at all. "Gosh." She licks her lips. "You know what? I think I might have beat him up by accident."

"What do you mean 'by accident'?"

"I kind of panicked when he grabbed my arm. He never even fought back."

Nathan's expression goes serious. "Screw that, he got what he deserved. He had no right to lay a hand on you. And trust me, he's dammed lucky he didn't fight back because then he'd be dealing with *me*."

Blair doesn't say anything more. She can't help wondering if she went overboard, but then decides Nathan is right. Chase had no business forcing his way into the house and grabbing her.

Brody doesn't live far, so it only takes them about ten minutes to get there. She glances around. His house is a medium-size rambler on a quiet street. While the house is in decent shape, the front lawn is overgrown and could stand to be mowed and weeded. She sees her silver Honda parked in the driveway.

"The keys are in the house," Nathan tells her. "Why don't you come inside? I have something I need to talk to you about anyway."

Blair follows him up the front walkway. There's a ceramic pot with flowers by the door that she suspects is Kiera's doing.

The inside is pretty much what she expects from a bachelor like Brody. The living room has a couple of leather sofas and is dominated by a huge flat-screen television. The place is basically a mess with junk mail, clothes, and various tools scattered everywhere. There's a case of motor oil that's been turned into a side table.

She continues to follow Nathan. "Been staying in the guest bedroom until I find my own place," he tells her.

They go inside a bedroom and right away, she sees his familiar leather backpack on the floor next to a double bed and his computer on the nightstand. The room smells musty, but also like some kind laundry soap.

"What did you want to talk to me about?" Blair asks.

To her surprise, Nathan pulls her in close. His arms go around her, and she's immediately surrounded by his smoky scent. So good, she can't stop herself from inhaling him.

God.

Blair hugs him, gives in to how amazing he feels. Her heart sings like it always does when she's near him. *I've missed him so much.* Tears fill her eyes, and she realizes maybe she's not okay. Between fighting off some guy, and now having Nathan this close, it's a little overwhelming.

"Hey, what's going on?" he asks, looking at her with concern.

"That was kind of scary and weird earlier," she admits.

"Course it was." He puts his thumb up and wipes the tears from her cheek. "That's understandable."

"I've never fought someone like that before." She rolls her eyes and tries to smile. "Even if he didn't really fight back."

He nods. "Scared me, too. Not Chase, but that he might have hurt you. Don't know what I'd do if something happened to you, Blair."

They gaze at each other, and Blair can see he means it, though it confuses her. "Why are you saying this?"

"Because it's true."

"I haven't heard from you in weeks. I thought it was over between us."

He takes a deep breath and lets it out. "I was pissed. Hurt, too, when you told me what you did. Just needed time to process it."

"Apparently, you needed another woman to help you process it."

"What?" Nathan's brows go up. "You kidding me with this?"

"No, I'm not."

"Sonia."

"Of course, who else would I be talking about?" *Your Spanish hoochie mama.* Blair steps away from him. "Is it true what she told me? That you came back to Seattle to get a divorce and marry her?"

Nathan licks his lips, meets her eyes. "Not exactly."

"God, you're still a terrible liar." She shakes her head in amazement. "How could you not have told me that?"

"It's true I came back thinking I should get a divorce, but not because of

Sonia, though," he says quickly. "Mostly just to tie up loose ends, but then something happened to change my mind."

"What?"

He gives her a wry grin. "You did, babe. *You* happened."

"Why is Sonia here then?"

"She's gone. Left right after the wedding."

Blair blinks. "She did?"

"Look, she came here on her own. I had nothing to do with it. Never invited her, she just showed up."

"All the way from Spain?"

"No, from LA. She's been visiting her aunt. I told her not to come, but she saw me on that talk show in San Francisco and flew up."

Blair considers this. Sonia did seem pushy, but then most Skank Factor X's were pushy.

Nathan sits on the bed. "Come here."

She walks over, and he reaches for her hand. Her pulse jumps. Even this bit of contact with him pulls her right back into the undertow. She tries to resist it.

"Did you sleep with her?" Blair wants to know.

"Jesus, course not. Can't even remember what I ever saw in her."

Blair looks down to where he's still holding her hand. He tugs on her arm, pulls her closer.

She gives in finally and sits on his lap, rests her head against his shoulder. Neither of them says anything for a long moment.

"I've missed you, Blair," he says quietly. "You have no idea how much."

She closes her eyes.

"It's been terrible," he admits. "Should have called you sooner, but I was being stubborn." He lets out a deep sigh. "Things that happened between us that night when you got pregnant, it wasn't your fault. I'm accountable, too."

Blair lifts her head to look at him. "Thank you for that."

"It's the truth."

"Earlier with Chase, you called me your wife. Why did you say that?"

He meets her gaze. "Because that's the truth, too."

Blair takes this in, allows his words to fill her soul. "Do you know why Isadora means so much to me?"

"No." He studies her. "Why does she?"

She looks down to where he's holding her hand. "After everything happened years ago and you left for India, I felt so lost, like I was being punished for the lie. And I thought you abandoned Isadora just like you abandoned me, so I decided to fix her. She needed a lot of work, and I didn't know anything about cars." She smiles at him. "But I learned, and as Isadora was restored, so was I."

"Babe." Nathan studies her with compassion, tightens his fingers.

"And do you know why I painted her green?"

He shakes his head.

"I spent months picking out the color. Looking at endless paint chips. Just about drove Brody batty with them all. She's green because I was trying to match her to your eyes."

Nathan stares at her.

"I didn't even realize it until you came back. After all these years, I thought I was over you, but I was wrong. The truth is I'll never be over you."

Blair pulls away from him and gets up. She walks over to the window, looks out into Brody's backyard. Surprisingly, there's a vegetable garden out there.

"I love you," she says, turning to face him. "Not like a princess living in a fairy tale, though. The way I love you is gritty and real. It's strong, too. Deep. But it has nothing to do with fairy tales."

Nathan gets up and comes to her.

"I just think you should know what you're getting into with me," she tells him. "Because I don't live in an ivory tower. I'm not perfect. And I make mistakes."

"I like gritty and real." He puts his hand up to hold her head still for him. "Always have."

And then his mouth is on hers, kissing her with passion. Not soft. No fairytale kisses, but a kiss filled with desire and wanting. Blair moans. She can't help it, just wraps her arms around him and holds him tight.

Still kissing, they make their way over to the bed, falling onto it. Joy fills her heart along with a relief so strong, she's dizzy with it. She thought she'd never get to be with him again. Making love with Nathan like this, free from all secrets and lies, is a revelation for Blair. So pure and good.

I finally deserve him.

Afterwards, lying on his chest, Nathan caresses her back. "You were wrong about one thing," he says. "May not be like a fairy tale for you, but it is for me."

"What do you mean?" She shifts position, so she can see his face.

"Kept thinking about something when we were apart," he murmurs. "Trying to figure it out, like finding the right key to a lock. About the way you looked at me that first time we were together in Isadora and I was inside you. Do you remember that?"

"Of course, I do."

Nathan closes his eyes for a long moment, appears to be struggling for composure. "Finally figured it out, too."

She reaches up to touch his face.

"Didn't know what it was because no one's ever looked at me like that before," he says, meeting her gaze. "Not ever."

"Nathan," she whispers.

"It's love." He takes a shaky breath and smiles at her. "You gave me that, Blair."

BY NEXT WEEK, all hell breaks loose. Nathan's book, *Edge of Zen*, has hit number one on *The New York Times* best seller's list. His blog is getting a crazy amount of activity, and his assistant James has been forwarding an avalanche of email. Fiona is also calling him every day, frantic, trying to schedule a media blitz. He's even gotten messages from filmmakers interested in buying the rights.

"What else is there to do, though?" Nathan asks, with his usual calm demeanor. "It's already at number one."

"Everything!" Fiona shrieks.

"Don't think so. I've got plans this week."

"*Plans?* What plans?"

"Important ones," he says. "Though, maybe you can help out."

He tells her his idea.

"Oh, my *God*, I love it! And I can't wait to read about it in your next book."

After talking to Fiona, he calls Tori then finally Natalie. Discovers both of them are on board and happy to help.

Good.

BLAIR SWIPES HER forehead with the back of her hand, then steps back for a second to study her work. She's building a classic two-tiered cake for a bride whose wedding colors are white and silver gray. Pure elegance.

It's coming along, Blair decides. *In fact, it's not bad.* Since she's been trying to be less hard on herself, 'not bad' is basically code for 'excellent.'

"Hey, babe."

Blair turns and is surprised to see Nathan standing in the doorway. He's leaning against the frame with his arms crossed, and she wonders how long he's been standing there watching her. He doesn't usually come into the bakery.

"What are you doing here?" she asks.

He uncrosses his arms and comes closer, motions his head at her. "Take off your apron."

"Why?"

"Just do it."

Blair doesn't move, though, wondering what he's up to. She notices Natalie now, and Ginger, too, both of them peeking around the corner. "What's going on?"

Nathan rolls his eyes and chuckles as he comes closer.

"Actually," she tells him. "I'm work—aaah!"

Before she knows it, Nathan has picked her up by the waist and thrown her over his shoulder. "Oh, my God!" she shrieks. "What are you doing?"

He doesn't reply, and her whole world is upside-down as he strides with her tossed over his shoulder out through the bakery's back door.

She hears everybody in the bakery whooping and hollering.

"Nathan!" She's laughing now, can see Isadora parked in back, and it's obviously where he's taking her. "Put me down!"

Once they're next to the Mustang, he bends low enough so she can slide off his shoulder, landing on her feet.

"Are you crazy?" She pushes the loose hair from her now-wrecked ponytail out of her face.

"Been thinking about that test of yours," he says, standing close, caging her in against the side door of the car.

"You mean the Bandito Test?"

He nods. "That's the one."

"What about it?" Blair glances behind Nathan and sees the whole bakery staff is standing by the back door now watching them. With surprise, she sees Tori is there now, too.

"I finally understand where I fit in."

"What do you mean?"

He lets out his breath. "I'm not the first guy who bails on you. I'm not the second one who saves you, either. I'm neither of those two."

"Who are you then?"

"Babe, haven't you figured it out yet?" He gives her an outlaw's grin. "I'm the damn bandito."

Blair laughs. *How could I not have seen this all along?*

"And just so you know," he says, his voice low and dangerous in her ear, "this is a kidnapping."

She reaches up and hugs him tight. "Where are you taking me?"

"Guess you'll find out. Your bags and passport are packed away in the trunk."

"Are you serious?"

He nods and motions over his shoulder. "I had some help with this kidnapping."

Blair waves to everyone. They all laugh, waving back. "Have fun!" Tori yells.

"And make sure that bandito treats you right!" Natalie calls out.

After they're in the car and driving, Nathan tells her he has to make a stop. He takes her to Gasworks Park, the same place where they were together in Isadora that rainy night. He even parks in the exact same location as last time.

"I'm not having sex with you in Isadora in broad daylight," Blair informs him. "Bandito or not."

He chuckles and tries to look earnest. "Damn, babe, you really know how to kill a dream."

Blair rolls her eyes.

"Have something for you," he says. "I never gave you a wedding gift, but hope this will do."

Blair watches as Nathan reaches into the glove box for an envelope and hands it to her.

"What is it?" She pulls out a folded piece of paper and when she sees what it is, her breath catches.

It's Isadora's title.

A new one. And where it says 'owner,' she still sees Nathan Church, but right beside it, she sees another name. Blair Thomas Church.

"Now we both own Isadora. I know you haven't taken my name, but I'm hoping you will."

Blair closes her eyes as joy washes over her. She looks at him. "Thank you."

He nods, then glances around the parking lot with narrow eyes, a smile tugging on his mouth. "I don't think the daylight is *that* broad."

She laughs. "Broad enough. So, where are we going now?"

"Home."

Her brows go up. "Really?"

Nathan takes her hand and intertwines their fingers. "Babe, I've been traveling so long, searching the world for something. A place. Never knew whether it existed or not."

She meets his eyes. Dazzling green. The color she fell in love with the first time she ever saw him.

"But I've found it in you," he says. "It's home. You're home to me, wherever I am."

Blair leans in, kisses him softly.

They're both quiet, gazing at each other.

"Please, tell me we're not really going home," she says.

Nathan chuckles. "Course not, we're flying to Mexico."

"Mexico?"

He grins. "Yeah, land of the banditos."

Epilogue

How To Live With A Travel Blogger

1. Be ready for any new adventure.

2. Understand passion as a way of life.

3. Enjoy the ride.

"YOU KNOW WE'RE doing everything backwards," Blair says.

She's lying on the beach under an umbrella, with sunblock that has a SPF rating of one zillion. As a redhead, she doesn't take chances with the sun.

Nathan's lying beside her, studying his phone, getting restless. They've been here in Mexico's Yucatán Peninsula for almost two weeks, and she knows the signs. He's planning their next adventure. So far, they've snorkeled with tropical fish, slammed tequila with local villagers, sampled the most delicious coffee she's ever tasted, hiked through lush jungles, and climbed a Mayan pyramid.

In truth, they've also seen quite a bit of the inside of their hotel room.

"We're having our honeymoon before the wedding," she says.

He chuckles. "Babe, you're married to a travel blogger. Trust me, our lives are going to be one long honeymoon."

She smiles, but doesn't say anything more. Just watches him, admiring his profile. His skin has been turning golden-brown since they've been here. When he glances at her, the whites of his eyes glow and the green is as clear as the Caribbean waters only a short distance away.

They've decided to get married again—a real ceremony, with family and friends to celebrate. She's already planning her wedding colors and the cake she wants.

Although, in the end, all she really wants is Nathan.

Blair thinks about *The Razor's Edge*, about Isabel and Larry, and how Isabel never got to have Larry as her own. She's grateful that isn't her fate, too.

I get to live the life she didn't.

Blair turns back to reading her Kindle. It's Nathan's new book. He finished it and loaded a draft of it for her to read.

It's incredible, which isn't a surprise. What's a surprise is that she's in it. Woven into the storyline is their story, the way they fell in love. *So amazing.*

Though she nearly choked on her margarita when she saw the title he gave it—*Journey to Red Willow Valley.*

"You're not seriously calling it that!"

"Course I am." His expression goes lazy. "What's wrong with it?"

"Nothing. It's brilliant, actually."

"Knew you'd agree. In fact, I've already started work on another book. This one's titled *Exploring the Land of Forbidden Fruit.*" He leans closer, lowers his voice. "I'm going to need a lot of research for this one, princess. Probably take me years to finish. You up to the task?"

She sighs with happiness. "I'll do my best."

The End

A Note from the Author

Thank you so much for reading *Return of the Jerk* and spending time with Blair and Nathan. I loved writing their story.

If you'd like to read more of my books, the first in the series Year of Living Blonde (Natalie and Anthony's story) is available on Amazon. The next book Some Like it Hotter (Lindsay and Giovanni) should be available spring 2016. Sweet Tori also gets her own book (her hero is a cop, of course!) I don't have a title yet, but my plan is for a release during the second half of 2016.

To hear about all my new releases and various giveaways please sign up for my mailing list at *www.andreasimonne.com*.

Lastly, if you enjoyed this book and have time would you consider writing a review? It's one of the best ways to help get the word out to other readers about my books. I sincerely appreciate it.

Thank you again for reading!

~ Andrea :)

Books by Andrea Simonne

Sweet Life in Seattle

Year of Living Blonde, Book 1

Return of the Jerk, Book 2

Some Like it Hotter, Book 3 (Coming 2016)

Book 4 (Tori's book, still untitled—Coming 2016)

~~The~~ Object of My Addiction

Other

Fire Down Below

Acknowledgements

I FEEL INCREDIBLY lucky to have such amazing support. My first reader and sister-friend Erika Preston read the earliest draft of *Return of the Jerk* and as always her suggestions helped make this story the best it could be. Thank you, Erika. You rock! (Fiona thanks you too and you know she doesn't tolerate anything less than the best!) I'm very thankful to Hot Tree Editing, especially my Editor Kristin Scearce, who did a wonderful job catching errors and helped make this book such a smooth read. I also want to thank all the betas from Hot Tree for their kind words, helpful input, and for their support on Goodreads before the book's release. My friend Susan Gideon proofread the final manuscript and as always did a fantastic job. Thank you so much Susan. I know I keep saying you're amazing, but that's because it's true! I'm also thankful to Christine Borgford at Perfectly Publishable who did the beautiful interior formatting & design for my last book and now the fantastic job on this one too. Writing can get lonely, but I'm lucky to have the awesome and talented Plot Princesses—Amy Rench, Haley Burke, and Tami Raymen—thank you ladies for your encouragement, inspiration, and for all those meetings that turn into laugh sessions. *Köszönöm* to my dad, who was kind enough to help me with the Hungarian translation I needed for Nathan. Lastly, I want to thank my wonderful husband, John, for always supporting my dreams. Baby, you are the best! John was also nice enough to come up with most of the alternative names for 'Red Willow Valley.' I was only looking for one or two ideas, but he came up with so many and they were so funny, I had to use them all. I mean, only a guy's brain could have come up with something like 'my favorite red lunchbox.' Seriously!

About the Author

ANDREA SIMONNE GREW up as an army brat and discovered she had a talent for creating personas at each new school. The most memorable was a surfer chick named "Ace" who never touched a surf board in her life, but had an impressive collection of puka shell necklaces. Eventually she turned her imagination towards writing. Andrea still enjoys creating personas, though these days they occupy her books. She's an Amazon bestseller in romantic comedy and the author of the series Sweet Life in Seattle. She currently makes her home in the Pacific Northwest with her husband and two sons.

Some of the places you can find her are:
Website: *www.andreasimonne.com*
Email: *authorsimonne@gmail.com*
Twitter
Facebook
Goodreads
Amazon

Made in the USA
Coppell, TX
28 August 2020